Praise for The White Lie

"*The White Lie* is a story of decline, of a crumbling hierarchy taking desperate measures to save face (and the bloodline and the silver) before the hordes sweep them away. Yet, more than that, it is an account of the unreliability of personal history ... The strength of this immersive story is that it does not require neat revelations. *The White Lie* is a page-turner. It is also, finally, very moving ..."

Francine Stock, *Guardian*

"There's an echo of Virginia Woolf, especially *To the Lighthouse*, that lifts Gillies' work above the average family drama. The fact that she also keeps a tight hold of the gossipy strands of her story is a great credit to her powers, as well as her ability to keep her readers guessing the truth to the end. This is an unusual, unsettling, often lovely story that plumbs the depths of what family means."

Lesley McDowell, *The Scotsman*

"Gillies handles her large cast and clashing versions of events with a precision that makes reading this imaginative novel a fascinating process of discovery. ****"

Metro

"Gillies writes magnificently on everything she touches, be it family secrets, Highland light, or the nature of memory."

Sunday Times

"The prose is elegant and beautiful, and Gillies has a skill for creating both character and a sense of place; Peattie is so vividly described that I had no trouble imagining the crumbling interior or the sun-baked loch. I couldn't put *The White Lie* down."

For Books' Sake

"Gilles excels both at describing the landscape and at delineating those subcutaneous secrets and shared assumptions that bind families together."

Literary Review

The

WHITE LIE

ANDREA GILLIES

First published in 2012 by
Short Books, 3A Exmouth House, Pine Street, EC1R 0JH

10 9 8 7 6 5 4 3 2 1

This paperback edition published in 2012

A CIP catalogue record for this book is available from the British Library.

ISBN: 978-1-78072-090-6

Printed and bound by CPI Group (UK) Ltd, Croydon, CR0 4YY

Cover design: Leo Nickolls

To my mother June Gillies
with love

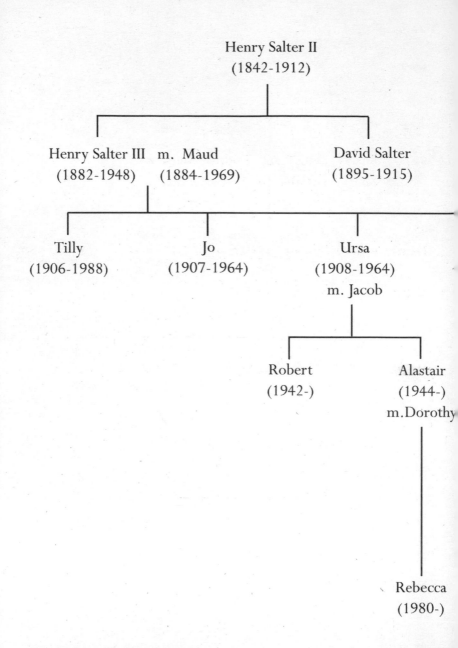

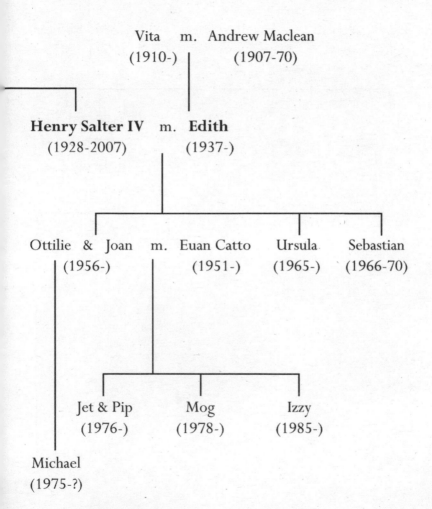

Vita   m.   Andrew Maclean
(1910-)   (1907-70)

Henry Salter IV m. **Edith**
(1928-2007)   (1937-)

Ottilie & Joan   m.   Euan Catto   Ursula   Sebastian
(1956-)   (1951-)   (1965-)   (1966-70)

Jet & Pip   Mog   Izzy
(1976-)   (1978-)   (1985-)

Michael
(1975-?)

white lie *n.* – a trivial and well-intentioned untruth, designed to spare someone's feelings

Chapter 1

2008

My name is Michael Salter, and I am dead; dead, that much I know for sure. All the rest of it – all of that I can only speculate about. I've had a lot of time to wonder about it: what I'm doing here and what it means, though thinking takes me round in circles, like Pooh Bear hunting the heffalump in the snow and realising he's been following his own footprints.

My mother Ottilie was here earlier, in the wood, talking to me about misapprehensions and about guilt. She comes at least once a week and always on Sundays, from her cottage out at the coast, and she comes alone. Lately she's been here almost every day and I've begun to act like somebody in hospital, alert at visiting hour for signs. I was watching as she came along the path this afternoon, a procession of one, slow-moving and stately in black. She came first to my memorial stone.

"Michael." She spoke as if I were close by. "Today's the day. We think today will be the day."

I can't remember seeing my mother ever wearing black before, but it's the 14th anniversary of my disappearance here and ... the truth is this hasn't been any ordinary anniversary. She was unusually restless, walking along the beach, up and down, pausing at the furthest corners of the shore and struggling at moments with the depth of the grit.

"It won't be long now," she said, looking out over the water which stretches almost to the horizon; a vast bowl of it, many fathoms deep. The domesticated green summits we see around us here are in reality only the tops of submerged mountains: that's what my grandfather used to say to me, when I was a child. They say in the village that the loch has moods, that when the wind blows it isn't only the waves that rise and surge; that when it's a dark, dark brown it's at its most dangerous; that when the surface becomes a mirror it will reflect your profoundest wants back at you. It's been viscous as mercury today, resembling something poured and inert, as if a silver skin has cooled on it.

Are you a ghost if nobody sees you, or are you something else? Ghost or not, I seem to have taken up residence in the grounds of the house where I was born, in the small wood planted here beside the loch in 1916. Not that I remember the moment exactly of arriving. Like the journey down the birth canal, some recollections are spared us. Too many, in fact. Memory reaches back, pausing at birthdays, Christmas mornings, the big conversations, key moments when we look into the eyes of our mother and know her in a new way; all the things that make impact on our little souls: the first bicycle, the first nightmarish week at the high school, the first proper kiss, the first cigarette and throwing up afterwards. I'm trying to get back to the earliest thing. I remember playing in the gardens at about the age of four, running along the sides of high topiary hedges. But for weeks and months that I know I was alive, there's nothing, worse than nothing; indistinct traces left behind of something that's gone.

My mother sat herself down, sitting up straight-backed in her usual way, in a dress that reached almost to her ankle, a black scarf twisted into use as a hair-band, her fringe flattened over her eyebrows. She rubbed gently at her shins and said, "Arthritis, apparently. I'm beginning to be old." Her thick and wavy hair, glorious once, a pinkish-gold colour, strawberry blonde, is filling with nylon-like grey. When she was young she wore it very long, flying behind her like a cape, but it's shorter now, and worn up, fixed by what look like chopsticks. At 52 she's beautiful still, or at least I think so, despite the creases around her eyes and the sad marionette lines around her mouth, but she's aged visibly since this time last year, when a gathering to celebrate a birthday was interrupted by startling news, news of me that certain of them had kept to themselves. I'm going to tell you about that, about my grandmother Edith's party and what happened afterwards. There have been sad conse-quences, introducing a new era. Not that catastrophe is anything new. The family has had more than an average share of disasters, of premature deaths, one generation after another, such that people refer quite routinely to the power of the Salter curse.

We've been going through a phase in which my mother is angry with me, though her visits take a circular shape, starting and ending with kindness. "You were such an idiot," she said to me today. "How could a clever person be so stupid? Why, Michael, *why* did you put yourself in that position?"

Her left hand wiped long tears from her cheeks, the movement rapid, like someone hoping to keep their crying unnoticed. With her right hand she lifted and dropped handfuls of shingle, pausing to inspect each palmful as it fell, looking at crumbs of grey-green granite, white quartz and orange sandstone. She has a labourer's hands, square with big flat nails on the ends of workmanlike fingers, residual paint lingering in the creases, her skin rough and red from cleaning and turpentine.

The sky was low and lilac-brown this afternoon, the sunlight streaming in fat columns from gaps in the cloud cover, like street lamps, pulsing its energy down. When Ottilie turned to face my way it was as if she looked right at me, though really she was looking back towards the house. Only the uppermost part of it is visible from here, through the trees, above and beyond the lime walk – a glimpse of turret, of crenellation, of the complex slate geometries of a swooping roofline: some French influence got mixed in with the Scots Baronial. It reminds me of an illustration from a book of fairy tales that I had once, a book that had been my mother's.

Peattie doesn't have that same Sleeping Beauty's castle look of being enshrouded in vegetation, though the gardens are thick with weed, the rhododendrons feral, the trees untamed, and in every direction elderflower and thorn have woven their grid.

The history of the Salters is coming to an end, and if it's hard to be definite about the attributing of malaise, there isn't any doubt that the beginnings reach back to 1970 and the loss of another boy, Ottilie's little brother, my child-uncle Sebastian. I've seen it, the death of Sebastian, although it happened before I was born. I've grown used to them now, these cinematic visitations, but I'll admit that they were deeply disconcerting at first. They started one day out of the blue: I began to have (to see) memories that are not mine, that couldn't be, because they pre-date me; they're seen from the vantage point of someone who wasn't there, as if the estate has its own record, soaked in deep and only just beginning to show itself. Perhaps it's merely a kind of evaporation, a process without a point, though it's hard to make a case for that: these are particular things and out of date order.

My aunt Ursula's arrival in the drawing room on the day I disappeared: that's an event I've seen more than once. Alan's and Ursula's account of my death, Alan's original version. In Alan's old passport he'd written under "occupation" handyman-gardener, and then he'd added *entrepreneur*. He doesn't live at Peattie any more, but really Alan was only ever the handyman-gardener's son, a man without official status, semi-permanently temporary.

⌇

The first sign of trouble was a noise. It was the wrong noise – wrong, at least, for someone who had spent so many years using the same doors. It could only be to do with panic, that Ursula seemed to have forgotten how it was that they worked, the entrance doors leading in from the terrace, pulling rather than pushing, yanking at them, at their heavy double oak, their panels carved with flowers and with thistles. They're hung doors, and she sent them rocking and echoing in their housing, before remembering to push.

When Ursula went running into the drawing room that afternoon she had angry red marks at the top of each arm, marks I inflicted, already purpling into finger-shaped bruises. So that helped with the defence, obviously, the private defence provided to the drawing-room court. They couldn't have gone on all these years, as they have, protecting her with quite such conviction, had they not been so sure that she was provoked. She makes an unlikely murderer in any case, Ursula the gardener, the vegetarian, the knitter; Ursula who if she isn't gardening or knitting is likely to spend the day in bed in marabou feathers, opera on the record player, engrossed in wholesome reading that's selected and vetted on her behalf.

She went charging in at quite a lick, across the hall and through the picture gallery. It wasn't only her swift light footsteps that registered, the squeaking of the plimsolls she wears, white plimsolls child-sized on bare feet, but also a high-pitched disjointed noise, an interrupted murmuring wail that kept time with the footfalls and exaggerated them. Hearing her coming, the family looked mildly alarmed around the eyes and in a certain stiffening of limbs, though these reactions were manifested in the usual guarded way. It was instinctive with them all, not making too much of a grazed knee or a poacher seen on the hill or any of the other things that might and do upset Ursula. If people didn't take their well-practised calming approach, upsets could swiftly become disproportionate. Her older sisters, the twins, of which my mother is one, were at this time 38 to Ursula's 29, and had spent pretty much all of their lives being careful about Ursula, being loyal, being sensitive to her *peculiarities*, objecting to anyone else's use of the word peculiarities, attesting good-humouredly to her being a one-off. Careful and loyal and tired.

Ursula burst into the room, her long brown hair flying. Edith went immediately to her, grasped her, holding her tight to her chest, saying, "What an earth is it?" and Ursula cried harder, extricating herself, her body convulsing with sobs. Her dress was pale blue, sleeveless, with shiny floral embroidery at the neckline, a dress that had belonged to one of the great aunts. Ursula won't wear new clothes. There was a tidemark at the thigh-line of the dress, and crinkling of the fabric reaching down to the hem.

"She's waded through water, she's been in the loch!" Ottilie exclaimed, and everyone was equally amazed because nothing could have been more unlikely. A faint loch aroma emanated. Ursula's skin was its customary near-white, though mild stripes of sunburn tracked the principal bones of her arms, and sweat had beaded pink along her hairline. The weather that June was almost freakish for the north, weather so hot that everything looked different, the landscape transformed, remade in new colours. Every window was open but it was just as stuffy in the room as before, a soup of thick and exhausted air.

Edith continued asking her youngest daughter what was wrong. Sometimes what's needed is that you repeat a question in different ways, trying out different intonations. Edith pushed her own head back on her neck, chin recessed into her throat, to look properly at Ursula's face, to signal to her that she was being scrutinised and that things were expected to come of this, but Ursula distanced herself, stepping back and shaking her head. Now my mother's twin came forward, Joan, looking (characteristically) as if she'd take charge, then thinking better of it and folding her arms against intervention. She moved back again, saying, "Oh for god's sake, get a grip."

Edith looked towards her husband, face perplexed. Henry, preoccupied with financial problems and believing this still to be something trivial, took a few extra moments to put down his letter.

"Michael!" Ursula shouted, and then again, and it was like an appeal, like she was calling after me still, and I was near at hand. She directed her calls towards the windows, as if I were waiting just outside and might hear. Now she went into distress mode, arms tight across her waist, grasping her own elbows as if holding tight to them mattered, stepping forward and sideways, back and sideways again, her eyes cast down. Henry got to his feet. Ottilie got onto her feet, her toast falling to the floor, its upturned buttered quarters pathetically domestic, out of place in any kind of crisis. She put one hand to her mouth, saying, "No, no, no, no," beginning to grieve even before the news was told. Now Ursula was squatting, her dress ridden up, holding tight to her knees, her nails indenting fiercely into her skin. "I've killed him, I've killed him," she said, and there was something about the tone that sounded vaguely surprised and as if pleading for contradiction.

Ottilie half fell and half sat on the floor, going down hard, jarring her back, her face registering the pain of the landing. She bent forward and clasped her hands over the top of her skull, demanding that Ursula explain – "What do you mean, what do you mean you've killed him, what do you mean?"

Henry went to Ursula, to the Chinese rug that has half the fringe missing, taking hold of her arms and pulling her gently up to stand. He had Ursula by both wrists and was saying, "Calm, calm; breathe, calm," his quasi-military authority to the fore. He opened her arms wide and closed them again as if they were bellows, a technique that had been used before with success. "Breathe" he said again, elongating the word. Ursula began to calm. "Look at me." Henry took her face in his hands and insisted on eye contact. "Where is Michael? Where is he?"

Ursula said that I was drowned, and that she hadn't meant it: they had to understand, please, that it hadn't been meant. She sagged again onto her haunches, and Henry was forced to let go of her. He took a step backwards. Those who hadn't been on their feet were on their feet now. Cups and tea plates had fallen in slow motion onto upholstery and onto the floorboards, splintering china into shards, a general exodus already in progress even as the china fell. They gathered up Ottilie, who was staring wide-eyed and unblinking, who went passively along as if sleepwalking, steered from the door. They went along the picture gallery and into the hall, Ottilie reacting as if blindfolded and having to be directed, only just dodging pedestal tables, into the gloom of the rear passage and towards the back stairs. The servants' entrance (as was) is the closest exit to the loch. Joan's husband Euan was first out, emerging at speed into the yard and almost cannoning into Alan, who was coming in. Euan, immensely tall, lanky, cool-skinned and cool-eyed, couldn't have presented a greater contrast to Alan, who was overheating and blowing hard. He's plump, has a tendency to blush, has a tendency to sweat, and his blonde hair is almost white.

"I'm sorry," he panted. "Can't run like she does." Bending over and breathless, like an athlete after a sprint. "And I was ill. I'm sorry." When he lifted his head there was dried vomit crusted around his mouth. His nose and left cheek were bruised and swollen.

"Alan," Euan said, with a gesture that could have been solidarity, putting a hand on his shoulder, those long bony fingers, but in truth pushing him gently back and out of the way. Alan turned to watch as Euan ran across the yard and disappeared onto the lane. As Alan swivelled, his pink face screwed up against the glare, moisture gathering on his brow and upper lip, Joan appeared from the stairway, calling after Euan and ignored.

"Alan," Joan said, as if introductorily, before abridging the thought into two words. "A crisis." She was business-like in a trouser suit and silk shirt, trim and blonde and smartly dressed; she and Euan had just returned from Glasgow, from a university open day, and she'd wanted to be impressive among the other mothers.

"Wait. Alan, what happened to your face?"

"I was there; I saw it all."

"But what happened to your face?"

"I swam into the boat."

"Come with us," Joan told him, and then, "But hang on. Wait a moment for my father."

Alan put his hands one to each side of his head. "I was there; I saw it all."

Now Henry approached, guiding Ottilie from behind, and then coming around to stand in front of her. "Alan," he said. "You saw Michael, Ursula and Michael. Alan, you're injured."

"It's okay. Looks worse than it is. I swam into the boat."

"Alan, tell us. Tell us if it is. What it was."

"Ursula has told you, then," Alan said, his voice full of regret. He left it to others to say what it was that Ursula told: later, that would seem significant. And now there she was, stepping out into the yard with Edith, holding hands tightly, out from the stairs and through the door into the light. Despite being close to five o'clock the day remained dazzling and golden, thick with yellow dust.

"I killed him and I can never get him back," Ursula said. "That's what Alan told me and it's true."

"You waded in – he was in trouble and you waded in a little way and couldn't go further. Was that how it was?" Edith was desperate for it to be so.

"I killed him," Ursula told her, calm and solemn.

"I'm so sorry, Mrs Salter," Alan said.

"We must get down there," Edith announced, and then, "Alan – what happened to your face?"

Alan touched his cheek with his fingertips. "I swam into the boat."

"We must get down there, and quickly."

"It's too late; he's gone," Ursula told them, almost irritably.

"It's too late; he's gone," Alan confirmed. "I spent half an hour looking." They'd remark on this later, that interpretation ran fluidly in his account: he followed only where Ursula led. But he looked like a man who'd had a great upset, even if only circumstantially. His left leg, his left shoe, were juddering nervously against the gravel.

"I'm sorry," he said. "I'm having a panic attack. It'll pass in a minute."

They watched as he did a little circuit of that area of the yard, hands casual on his hips, miming again that same runner's habit, though this was the look of a competitor in the moments before the race began, fingers hooked onto hip bones and shaking his legs out one at a time.

"But how did she?" Edith extended her hands palms-up in that biblical way that she has, and was looking at Ursula, who was walking away towards the loch path. "It doesn't make any sense. Are you absolutely sure? Are you sure?"

Ursula turned briefly to face them, walking backwards for a few paces. "The oar. I hit him with the oar across the head."

"Oh no, Jesus, no!" Henry pointed his head skyward, his words a shout.

"I told you, I told you," Joan said, "but nobody listens."

"Though that wasn't the first thing," Alan interrupted them, returning to the group. Ottilie remained in a trance, her eyes unseeing, and Alan put his fingers to her elbow, squeezing and stroking briefly down her forearm. There was something unmistakably proprietorial in the gesture. He cleared his throat. "The first thing. She pushed him with it and he lost his balance."

"She pushed him," Joan repeated. "And?"

"That was the first thing. And that was fine. He fell out of the boat. That was fine. They were fighting and he went out."

"The boat. What was she doing in the *boat*?"

"It was when he tried to climb back in. When he tried to climb back in, she ..." He trailed off, bending again. "I'm sorry. I'm really sorry. I can't believe it either and I'm ill."

"And I can't believe there isn't any *hope*," Edith said, her voice breaking on that last almost unsayable word. "Come on! Come on – we mustn't waste any more time."

Henry was already astride the old motorbike, a heavy black monster, tar-black, that survives from his father's day and that he used on the hill tracks. Alan got on behind him, by invitation that turned to insistence, and went off holding on lightly to Henry's waist.

Edith turned to Joan. "Where are the children? The children. We must tell them before someone else does. Where are they?" Her eyes swam in and out of focus and she put the heel of her hand to her forehead as if containing her racing thoughts physically.

"Mum," Joan said. "Mum. Are you listening? Only Mog is here. You know that. The others are all off around the village. We'll get messages out after."

Edith met her gaze. She looked as if she was going to speak and then didn't. She let her fingers trail down over her nose and mouth and chin.

Joan said, "She's still upstairs. She's up with Granny."

Edith's attention snapped back into the present. She turned and hurried back up the stairs, hearing as she approached the great hall her mother's shrill cries; seeing, as she approached the great hall, Vita standing remonstrating with Mog, Vita in orange and Mog in red, vivid against the black and white tiles of the floor and all the sombre wood colours. They stood in a rectangle of light created by one of two tall windows, and Mog was pleading with Vita to stay put, to return to the drawing room. Edith stepped in, telling her mother abruptly that Mog was right, that negotiating stairs and the walk to the loch were too much for her, and then she returned to the yard, her face wet, turning her head as she appeared and shouting back up the stairway, "No! Please! Stay put, stay there." Her hand went to her forehead. "That's all we can do; we can't physically restrain her." She spoke more quietly now, into the house, to someone unseen, and after a moment Mog emerged, blinking in the light, her mouth pulling down hard, Mog trying in vain to correct it. Without saying anything further, Edith took the bicycle that was left by the entrance and cycled away, wobbling and weaving. Joan and Mog followed down the lane on foot, each overtaking Ursula, who brought up the rear at a sedate and hopeless pace, her eyes three-quarters shut, talking rapidly to no one, gathering and then releasing the fabric of the skirt of her dress.

~

At the lochside there was a hastily discussed and amended plan of action, one that only Ottilie was oblivious to. Ottilie went down to the end of the jetty and strained herself towards the water, shouting my name again and again. "As if he's a lost dog," Joan said to Edith, Edith not responding. Euan ran back towards Ursula, who just at this moment had stepped onto the beach, demanding angrily to know where it was, the spot in question, approximately, approximately would have to do. Ursula ignored him, swerving around him, and so he turned to Alan, who was heaving the rowing boat from the shore. Edith and Joan decided they'd join Alan in there, wading into the shallows and boarding with his help, his steadying hand. As the boat floated free and Alan climbed aboard, Euan shouted after him for his opinion about location, about where they should be looking. Alan found it hard to say, and it was genuinely hard to say, on such a great expanse of water, where it was that the boat was sited earlier that afternoon. Their urgency, their cooperative urgency, was a touching thing to see. They acted as if there was something that could be done, as if even now I might be dragged up and out, coughing up water and alive after all.

Henry set out along the jetty, my mother turning to register his presence before facing the water again.

"People survive longer in cold water," she said as he came to stand beside her, her voice unrecognisable. "Don't they? Dad. Please. They survive longer in water this cold."

"Ottilie." His tone wasn't promising.

"I read something though. About breathing shutting down. Breathing shutting down. Please."

Euan had his shirt off over his head, had stepped out

of his trousers and was wading stoically, unflinchingly out in his boxers, before executing a strong forward dive. He gasped as he surfaced, treading water, because, yes, as it happens it was as cold as the grave. He went forward again, arcing his arms forward one after the other, swimming the crawl towards the spot that Alan suggested, that was Alan's best guess.

"If anyone can find him, Alan will," Edith said.

"My husband isn't completely pointless, Mother" Joan told her. A beat fell. "Though I agree he is mostly pointless."

Euan was beginning to make exploratory dives, dipping and resurfacing and diving again. Alan was out of the boat and doing the same, the two of them like feeding birds. Already the voices came at them, wanting news. "Anything? Anything at all? Not a sign? Nothing? Try further along." It's hundreds of feet deep and dark as a moonless night down there.

Joan took the opportunity of their being alone to say to Edith that when he saw what was happening, Alan should have come straight to the house. "Half an hour, he wasted half an hour trying to do it all himself and be the hero. The hero all over again."

Edith was brusque. "He did the right thing, Joan. He might have saved him." Sebastian's name was in the air unspoken.

❧

Later, a week or so after this, Alan surprised them all by going into the loch and coming up with one of my shoes, a brown leather boat shoe soaked almost black. He had found it on a rocky outcrop under the surface and this had sparked a new search much closer to shore. The fact that Alan found it would be thought to be important later, when the questions began in earnest. Later, you see, there wouldn't be certainty, but only deeper and greater doubt. Certainty has only come recently. At the time there was nothing systematic about the thing; it was and remained essentially amateurish. This might shock you, but the fact is that the police weren't involved in the aftermath of my disappearance, and not just not then, at the beginning, on the day. Not at all; not ever. The family could always have played the suicide card they held up their sleeves in readiness, if the authorities had come sniffing round, but it wasn't something they felt complacent about, not with the risk of a head wound revealing itself. Dragging the lake, in any case unfeasible, was quite impossible in these circumstances. This is something Henry had to be blunt about when dealing with my mother.

Alan surprised them all with his tact. There was no way of assuming him locked into the secret, but nonetheless Alan was meticulous in supporting the Salter version of events in the village. Henry tried to have a conversation with him at the beginning, a conversation about consistency, but Alan interrupted him in his full euphemistic flow, lifting his hand up as if it were a pledge and saying that if anyone asked, he would tell them – *of course* – that Michael left home, left a note, and that his current whereabouts remained unknown. All these assertions were, after all, true.

"The rumours are a disgrace." He said this almost as an afterthought, half out of the door.

"Rumours? What rumours are there?"

"That his car was left on the beach because Michael never left the loch. That Michael killed himself."

"Nothing about ... anyone else?"

"No. No, no. There's no implication –"

"I see. Well, thank you, Alan."

Some people have an aura about them, an unfortunate editorial addition to the facts of their physical selves, and Alan was one of these people: probably still is. At the time I disappeared he'd already taken on the doughy, shadowed-eyed look of a man who has lost faith in the idea of life, who senses that life has no great plan for him and finds consolations where he can. He'd adopted a daily uniform of formal black trousers, just a little too short, showing white socks in the gap between hem and shoe, and loudly patterned zipped sweaters that were stiff with acrylic. When he left here last year in disgrace, by then mostly bald, he'd grown out his monkish tonsure of hair so that it could be brushed across from one ear. At the time I was born things were different. At that time he was handsome in his sturdy soldier-boy way, unfashionable but well presented, a lover of well-pressed slacks and short-sleeved shirts finished with a knife crease down the upper arm, strong-chinned and even-featured, if rather hard-looking, his face usually closed on its outward side, with who knows what doors and windows on the inward-facing wall, but in middle age he'd become desperately unkempt.

"Well, what do you expect?" Henry would say, when the subject arose. "Two men living in that small house together."

꩜

Henry went along the shoreline, past Mog, who was walking briskly up and down, her hands held in front of her, massaging one with the other in turn. He went along to see Ursula, who was sitting at the edge of the wood, at the base of a tree, knees clasped tightly, but she wouldn't speak, wouldn't look at him. He knew these silences and knew that they end only when Ursula is ready, so he abandoned the attempt and returned to Ottilie on the jetty. They stood watching as the rescue effort became openly disheartened.

"No, no chance," I heard Henry say.

"But he'd float, wouldn't he?" Ottilie asked him. "He'd

float if he were drowned, wouldn't he? He wouldn't sink, would he? Or he wouldn't sink far, would he?"

Henry believed in honesty, always said so. It's what he was known for, his straight talking, that is if you could get him to talk at all. Ordinarily he was a man who didn't say much unless there was a practical need, and it had been like that since Sebastian died. Edith has always maintained that Henry was optimistic once, a happy, uncomplicated soul who found contentment in ordinary daily busyness and recuperated in good spirits afterwards, glad to spend time with his family. When I was born Sebastian had been dead five years, which was longer than he'd lived, and it wasn't any longer easy to engage Henry, but if you could engage him, he was disarmingly straight. Disasters did this to people, he said. He never pretended to a child that there's a Santa or a Tooth Fairy or (out of Edith's earshot, at least) that there was anything special about the Baby Jesus beyond being a man with a good heart, about whom many myths sprang up in his lifetime and then even more so afterwards, as is the way with celebrity. He wouldn't lie to Ottilie. She knew that. That's why she was asking.

"He might be ... suspended at a certain depth," he said to her, apparently unemotively, looking out at the two men, who were diving and surfacing and yelling at each other to move along a bit. Alan said that judging by the view of the wood they were 50 feet out, maybe, but it was so hard to say; it was almost impossible to say.

"It isn't just about the distance from the beach," Euan told him. "The location needs plotting in three dimensions."

"Whatever you say, professor," Alan sniped.

Ignoring this, Euan said Ursula should be with the women in the boat, shouting this ineffectually towards the shore. Then he was gone again, getting into his dive by surging firstly up, his breath held, his ribs obvious and wet, his boxers soaked against his hips, before plunging down, his long pale legs beating at the water as he tried to get more vertical and deeper.

"It depends on how long," Henry was saying.

"But people are found floating in rivers, in the sea," Ottilie countered.

"They have air trapped in their clothes. Or are carried along by the current, the tide. Or if not, if they sink, they tend to ... they tend to bob up again, at a certain point, at the point when ..." He stopped mid-sentence. Not even Henry could bear to tell my mother that my body would have to rot a little, made buoyant by decompositional gas.

"Carried along," she said.

"But in a loch this cold he might never resurface," he told her.

"What do you mean?"

"In water this cold, it's extremely cold: you understand that, don't you? It's ice cold down there in the deeps. The truth is that he won't be found."

"What do you mean? No. No, Dad. No, Dad. What are you saying?"

"I'm sorry. But you want to know. You want to know, don't you? The unvarnished truth of it?"

"No. I want to know something different. Take me back to the start of this and I would give anyone's life. Yours, Dad. Even yours."

"I'm so very sorry."

"Nobody's sorry enough."

Nothing further was said for a while. What Henry was thinking, I'd bet, is that this would be a good thing, a saving grace, my non-reappearance. Ghastly, tragic, terrible, too terrible to comprehend fully, a terrible day it had turned out to be, but at least I wouldn't reappear. That would be the arrived-at family perspective, the grown-on family orthodoxy. They didn't want me resurfacing, found bloated on the surface by a fisherman: the only thing

18

that lay on the other side of that eventuality was a more concrete disaster, a living human disaster, one that was unnavigable. Henry was reassured that I was unlikely to be found, and was too ashamed to admit it. Ashamed the whole rest of his life.

They spent another hour and ten minutes at the loch. Everyone knew it was hopeless and that there was little point, but nobody could bear to leave, to turn their backs on me, until Edith said that she must go and see Vita and that they should go back to the house, perhaps returning later. That *perhaps* was the mechanism for permission. Once they'd gone, they weren't going to return – other than for the private visits, three, four times daily at first, and then less and less often as the weeks passed, their resolve leaking into duty, duty turning into resignation. They came often at first, scanning the water, something nobody talked about but everybody did, individually and without mentioning it, waiting for the possibility of my showing as an object limp and buffeted, something foul and changed. Once human, now a repellent human debris.

What is it we learn as we grow older in the world? Nothing, it seems to me, besides what it is that love means. My mother loved me, but in a language I didn't understand. Things were obvious to her that I couldn't even guess at. My grandparents loved me in a way that was sincere and useless. Mog loved me in a way that left me anxious for her: her love was like another way of being lost. Everybody else loved me only after I'd gone.

Chapter 2

It's time to begin to tell you about the events of 12 months ago. We're going there now. The lilac-brown clouds and the sodium yellow light are gone. It's tepid and overcast weather, but with a brighter sky promised, a classic Scottish summer day. This isn't how it began but it will serve as a place to begin, with a conversation here in the wood between Ottilie and Joan, about the appropriateness of grandeur and its cost. This could have been an argument arising from one of many points of conflict that had dogged their lives together, but in this case was pegged specifically to Edith's 70th birthday and the arrangements for the coming weekend.

They had come here for privacy, far from Edith's ears; the finer details of the celebration had been kept from her. Joan had elected herself head of the event committee, and had delegated widely. She had demanded Ottilie come to the wood to look at the list. Each of the sisters was leaning on a different tree, each with her arms folded. Negotiations weren't going well.

"Why is it that you ascribe value only to things that are expensive?" Ottilie asked Joan.

The reply was obvious. "Why is it you're so determined to be cheap?"

"It's not about you," Ottilie told her sister.

Joan batted straight back. "It isn't about you, either."

Ottilie served a new ball. "What they want is simplicity. Simplicity and their old friends."

"They'll love every minute of it," Joan volleyed.

"You don't understand," Ottilie said, her tone changing. "This is about grief. Grief that's still fresh. Celebrations are in bad taste. It ought to be low key. It has to be low key."

"It's you who doesn't understand," Joan said. "What we need, what they need more than anything, is to draw a line. A party is symbolic. Enough time has elapsed."

"That's not for you to say." Ottilie's voice was shaking, and so were her hands.

"We need to get on and look at the list," Joan said without looking at her sister. They began perfunctorily to go through it, agreeing and disagreeing, each of them embarrassed by the way things had almost developed, the conversation they'd very nearly had.

Joan said she'd taken note of objections and would consider, but now she must get on because there were a hundred things to see to. They walked towards the house together, side by side and as far apart as possible, continuing the debate. Their voices grew louder. Abruptly, Ottilie turned away from Joan – who in so very many ways is her unidentical twin – and came back, gesticulating and far from pleased.

I know her even at great distances by her outline, by the way her arms swing through the step as her body moves forward, by the determined way she holds her head. She stopped to look at the verge, picking one seedhead and then another, storing her treasures away in her pockets. She's constantly on the lookout for things to take back to the studio, is madly prolific; her canvasses and boards are six deep at the cottage, an overflow of things she's not ready to sell. Many more are stored at Peattie, in dusty and unloved rooms.

She stands in front of things, looking at them as if they're already drawn, as if her eyes are scanning and drawing and the thing's already on the etching plate. Etchings are her preference, at the moment, though her first success was a series of vast smudgy boardroom oils, cream on white, pictures that paid for a home of her own. The gallery owners come to her there, surprised, or (very occasionally) charmed by the state of the place, and girding their loins. She's not going to do more work in the old style if she doesn't feel like it. She's not going to let work go that isn't right or isn't finished. Sometimes things sent to Peattie are retrieved and reworked, and sometimes they go back again afterwards: the process can take years.

In repose and in walking alone, her face sets into something that could be misinterpreted as sternness. She can be intimidating, my mother. She does classroom visits and frightens children; she's had a long-term association with the primary school in the village, and she was here with the graduating class the year they saw the great uncle. I'm not the ghost of Sanctuary Wood, you see. It isn't me that people see here, or say they have seen, but Great Uncle David. He's a famous ghost, mentioned in the guide books. Ottilie brought boards and a roll of lining paper to the school trip, unfolding a wooden ruler with brass hinges, marking and creasing the paper roll before tearing it efficiently into sections. She gave the pupils pieces of charcoal and asked them to draw trees. She can't talk to children as if they're children, never has been able to, and this has been a fertile source of family reproach. She wanted them to stop thinking they knew a tree and really look at it, she said. Some of the school children saw too much, more than they were bargaining for, though it was Ottilie's opinion that the ghost-seers were deluded, were wanting to see something, had willed themselves to, had undergone a domesticated sort of group hysteria. She's better with older children, teenagers, who go to her by invitation to work on their portfolios for applying to art college.

"Don't assume too much, don't rush to judgment," she'll say to them, her eyes showing their green ice under the grey, fierce but meaning, always, to be kinder; set on her path of inculcating into people the value of *making*. The fierceness comes from meeting resistance. "That may look like a nothing to you," she said to a man overheard at an exhibition, "but a barnacle-covered shell was the starting point and what happened in between was art, no matter what you think of it. Art is doing."

So, Joan went off in a huff, and Ottilie returned to the wood alone. She had one of Joan's clipboards, a brown clipboard with a bulldog clip, a pink sheet of paper fixed to it, and she threw it down hard on the great uncle's tomb. She took her hair down and put it up again, something she does when she needs to think or to delay her reactions, something self-calming. Drawing closer, I could smell her chamomile shampoo, her violet scent, face cream, the scent of inhabited fabrics. The handwriting on the pink sheet was Joan's, a list written in her usual jagged calligraphy: *Fairy lights, but only the white ones, 50 strings. 20 of the large-bulb strings (children's, the coloured ones). Storm lanterns furnished with pillar candles. Jam jars and tea-lights and wire.* Underneath, added in pencil and underlined, it said *Linen napkins.* Napkins were the start of the day's controversy. Paper ones made more sense to my mother.

Ottilie pursed up her mouth in a way that I remember from childhood, in the same way that Edith does, and it twitched with words she couldn't or wouldn't articulate, her hands smoothing and re-smoothing her skirt. Ordinarily my mother wears Victorian colours, deep green and inky velvets and toffee and claret shades of brocade; these, or men's blue overalls, bought at the chandlery and stiff with paint. But on this particular day she was head to toe in stone-coloured linen with a matching thin coat of

23

the same shin length, its pockets bulbous with finds, and creased up at the waist and around the back from sitting. Perhaps the forecast had been for sunshine.

It's good to have something to think about, to see this cinema of the past, and better still when it overlays the night. It's lonely in the wood in the dark; it can be hard to be alone. Great Uncle David, who died in the First World War and whose body lies just a few feet away from me here, he would be company at least. He's not my great uncle, strictly speaking, but my mother's, though everybody calls him "great uncle", all the same. He seems to be another kind of ghost, the kind that's an apparition, appearing in scenes from his life and not really present in the present. He's seen muttering nonsense to himself, his uniform thick with mud and dried blood and the smell terrible. Sometimes people say that he looks so three-dimensional that they have gone to him, thinking him the survivor of a car crash or air accident or suchlike, but trying to get closer is like approaching a rainbow, with predictable results. The children from the village school reported seeing him sitting crying on a tree stump, his hat in his hands, no boots on and his feet grey. The great uncle, dead at 20, is the one that inspired the planting of the wood, his corpse having been moved at the direction of the family under special licence from his Flanders field. Ursula sees him, or so Ursula says, but I'm dead and I don't, which is part irritating and part relief. There have been no reunions. I'm not sure I'd want community, anyway. All that small talk. All that means-of-death oneupmanship.

Though I don't see David Salter myself, I see people seeing him; I see them getting spooked and running. The last episode was only a few days ago: an academic, the wrong side of 50, his stomach convex over the belt of his jeans, who spent a methodical, peaceful afternoon here, noting down in more than one of his colour-coded notebooks, drinking coffee from his flask, slow and thoughtful in drinking it, practising an absent-minded style of eating his sandwich. He was taking a photograph when it happened. He jumped backwards like he'd been shot, dropping his camera bag and recovering it, not taking his eyes off the tomb, feeling for the strap at a snatch. He could turn on some speed for a guy with a pot belly.

A sudden intimate noise, feet heard crunching over last autumn's remnant leaves and tinder twigs, announced that Joan had returned.

"You're wrong about my being a control freak," she said without preamble, rolling up the sleeves of her sweater. She's fair-skinned and bony; she still has the stretched-drum stomach of her teenage self, still boyishly flat as if she'd never been pregnant. Her jeans were tight and her boots high and pointed; she isn't shy about promoting the distinction from her soft and rounded sister. Approval rests on the side of the visible clavicle. Great rows of worked gilt bangles clattered on her wrist.

Ottilie stared at her. "Is that all you came back for?"

"It's not fair. You know it isn't. Somebody – somebody – for god's sake, just one person, has to be the one who gets things done."

"Fine," Ottilie told her. "Linen napkins it is. Linen napkins and a champagne toast. You win." She could have left it at that, and looked for a few moments as if she would. But no. "You've got everything screwed down so tight, Joan. The last detail. It'll all be perfect in the details, perfect and lifeless. Nothing control-freakish there. Now go, will you. You're interrupting."

Joan looked around theatrically, left to right and then behind her. "Interrupting what?"

"Sanctuary Wood. Sanctuary. From your prattling, among other things."

"You have been a liar your whole life," Joan said, as if it were a known fact, a word like "overweight". Ottilie remained expressionless. It wasn't the first time she'd heard it. "Just admit it. You come here to talk to Michael."

"Michael's not here, Joan."

"I know that," Joan said, "but I don't believe you do."

"Don't do this. Don't. You know you'll hate yourself later."

"Why do you want him to be dead?"

"Because he is dead. We all know that he's dead and why." Ottilie closed her eyes. "Tell me why you want him not to be. Is it because that's worse for me?"

Joan took a step backwards, felt the tomb cold and heavy behind her, and reached her hands back to rest against its decorated marble lip. Great Uncle David lay there, not once but twice: once within the marble box and a second time in the carved marble effigy.

The wood was planted and titled for the place where David fell. I don't know what it was called before, that wartime wood. Something Flemish, no doubt; something else: the south wood maybe, the squirrel wood, the wood with no name. It became known as Sanctuary Wood in 1914 (to English-speaking soldiers, anyway), when it was a safety zone, a place of unlikely peace, where it was possible to step out of the war as if off the stage, to be out of character there for a spell and rest. Men who'd been separated from their units gathered within its boundaries, safe beneath its canopy, until they could be reunited with them, well behind the lines. But by 1915 the wood had moved into the dead centre of the war and there were terrible losses. Where once there was sanctuary now there was carnage. Huge numbers of his battalion were killed there, and David too, among splintered trees and scorched and blood-stained earth.

"The worst of it is that he was killed by his own men," Henry said to me once. Henry was forthcoming if you happened to touch on something that interested him, something at one remove from autobiography. "David and the men he was with had got beyond their own lines," he told me. "They had stormed and taken three German trenches, but the rear gunners didn't know this and continued firing on them. Anyone in those trenches was a sitting duck, because the Germans had abandoned their posts further up and other allies had taken this higher ground. The German trenches were only designed to be defended towards the Allied positions. They were open at the back and defenceless."

"This was in France."

"Belgium, actually. The cemetery is just a few miles from Ypres, in the north-western corner. It was also called Hill 62. Hardly a hill, but they called all the ridges Hill something. The number was the height above sea level."

"Have you been there?"

"I have."

"What's it like?"

"It's a wood. Quite ordinary. Green and mature again, other than for the occasional relic dead tree. Woods regenerate, you know. That's the thing; it all grows back and you'd never know. The day I was there it was very quiet, other than for the birds. It was a spring morning and very bright. The birdsong was intense; it was almost unseemly. But it has all these great vast craters in it where the bombs fell. There are tunnels, and a labyrinth of trenches, and lots of corrugated iron. It isn't very big, no bigger than our wood here. There's farmland all around, more woods across the fields, though it's only a couple of miles out of the town."

I couldn't help thinking how young Henry looked, when you succeeded in enthusing him. Though he always looked much younger than his age. Even at 79, last year when he died, he was possessed of the same good proportions of his prime. He had the classic Salter features, the faintly Asiatic eyes and the narrow mouth, the lower lip deeper than the upper and with a determined set to it. His military-short, pink-blonde hair, faded but not greyed, retained its youthful crinkle, lying obediently cropped to his head and radically side-parted. A fondness for khakis and zips and many-pocketed utility clothes added to the military effect. Henry was never tweedy. Towards the end of his life he developed a passion for expensive, supposedly technologically advanced trainers.

I get visitors – non-family visitors – coming here to the wood, especially in the summer. Of course they're really David's visitors. Whole coachloads of foreigners wander in and out – the path to the loch is a public right of way – dressed as foreigners on coach holidays in Scotland do, in many precautionary layers. Then there are the tomb hunters, the war nerds and art historians, who come ready for the north in hi-tech fabrics, in jackets made up of goose-down duvet layers and boots bought for the occasion, as if they'd have to scrabble up a crag and wade through knee-high heather to get here, instead of, anti-climactically, walking a few minutes along a signposted and only mildly rutted lane. I enjoy the moment when first they catch sight of the tomb through the trees: that first glimpse, the intake of breath, the exclamation, the efficient Anglo-Saxon curse. The great uncle's grave is celebrated, almost a cult. It's said to emanate its own supernatural glow, and it's true that there's a moment at dusk after a sunny day when it seems like the marble holds onto the light a little longer than ought to be possible. They sell postcards of the phenomenon at the village post office and stores.

Joan levered herself up to sit on the tomb, and sat there, looking sharper-featured than ever and lighter-haired: a conventional blonde.

"I was thinking about giving Mum her presents during the party. Get the cake piped in, raise our glasses to her."

"Don't ever mention Michael's name to me again," Ottilie told her.

It's a big, solid thing, the great uncle's tomb. It sits on a complicated plinth, on bands of faux-gothic ornamentation, and David's effigy lies on top, like the 1916 equivalent of the cathedral resting place of a medieval knight, the willows rising around him in slim columns, their poles knitting together into a roof. David was interred here on a freezing autumn morning, with pomp and ceremony, with a quartet rented for the day, with roses and poetry and sombre family dogs assembled seated in black collars. I had nothing like that. My ceremony in the wood here – for there was a ceremony of sorts, at my mother's insistence, despite the lack of a body to bury – was characterised by a kind of bewilderment. Nobody knew quite what to say or how to achieve the right tone, and so an atmosphere that could have been pious was, instead, marked by an absence of clarity. Ottilie had provided memorials: a round marble disc was set into the floor of the wood, and a marble standing stone, about two and a half feet high and carved with an angel on one side, was installed beside it. The angel looks down on the disc, its face downcast and even its wings worn at a defeated angle. Seeking anonymity, the status of garden statuary, the stones are assumed to be a secondary testament to a hero's passing, a modern honouring of the family soldier, an assumption that suits everyone. The mourners spent much of the time bickering about the siting of these objects, before wrestling the angel into place, ineptly from a rusting green wheelbarrow.

≈

"Do you really think he's here?" Joan asked my mother, her tone seeking to make amends.

"I'm warning you," Ottilie said. "Go back to your lists. Things you have a hope of understanding."

Joan took her Filofax diary out of her bag in a way that suggested great offence. She took a pen and began to write, flicking between pages and frowning with a concentration that might have been faked. Ottilie walked away, deeper into the wood, and got her sketchbook out.

The comparison with the medieval knight goes only so far. David's effigy isn't remotely heraldic. He isn't portrayed as if sleeping in stone-carved chain mail, as if he might at any moment open his eyes and raise himself onto his elbows, blinking heavy-lidded, looking down his long marble nose. Instead of all that, the great uncle is dead, plainly dead and broken, and he emerges from the lid of the tomb only at points. His forehead and cap are clear of the stone, and his face with its unseeing stare, his eyes featureless white rounds. The tips of his shoulders are shown, the top of his breastbone, his lower arms. Veins in the marble feed down into dead hands. His belly, groin and thighs are engulfed, though the boyish rounds of his knees, his lower legs, his ankles and feet are visible. His brother was determined about this: that David should be shown to be a dead man, shown killed in the Flemish mud.

The family intended that people should want to be here to socialise with him. There's a table of teak slats – dulled now to a flat mouse grey – where tourist picnics take place, and seats fashioned from the stumpy remains of felled trees. There's a particular tree stump I used to lean against when I was a teenager, a lanky black-eyed boy, long-limbed and olive-skinned, solemn-looking and sitting for hours, the earth hard underneath me – you can still see the imprint left by my sitting there – with French and Russian novels and creased battered notebooks. They were nothing like as real to me, the people I lived with, as the people in those books.

Nothing explicit connects the marble disc and standing stone to me. Until recently, when the truth emerged, the family had kept the facts of my disappearance a secret for very nearly 14 years, and if that sounds preposterous, criminal, strange, I have to tell you that it wasn't really, at the time. It was easy. All it required was that nothing further be done, and doing nothing, shelving decision-making, is always easiest. As the days pass and become weeks, doing nothing gets easier and easier. There was no case, in any case. There was no proof, there was no consensus, there was no body, and (most crucially of all) there was no witness, other than Alan, who was keen to be part of the circle of trust. What, you think it's an unusual situation, a family manslaughter and then silence: the ease of doing nothing, the temptations of doing nothing, leading to nothing being done? It's a lot more common than you think. Consider the many missing persons, never heard from or seen again. Some of those disappearances must have been family events, hushed and camouflaged. Consider the many dead babies that turn up mummified in tea towels, in suitcases in attics; those that make it to the newspapers must be a fraction of those lost. At the time that I disappeared, secrecy was perfectly rational and best for everyone, almost everyone, and I can see how the reasoning went. Things could only have been made worse by disclosure. So, the memorial stones are non-committal, but I'm there if you know where to look. The disc of marble that was set into the floor of the wood is a camco, its decorated edging framing a man's profile. The edging marks my passing in a code of Ottilie's devising; my initials are hidden within it, and my dates, expressed in the arrangement of leaves, branches and berries. The profile within it could be that of a hundred men, the great uncle included, but in fact is mine, taken from a photograph.

Ottilie had been doing a drawing based on the contours of a raised bark pattern, twisted and raised as a skin disease. Now she left off her sketching and began to walk back towards her sister, stopping when she got within clear sight of her.

"I meant it when I said I wanted to be here alone."

"Fine." Joan dropped neatly off the tomb and lightly

31

onto the grass. She didn't look towards Ottilie. She put the top back on her pen with a firm click, and dropped the pen and the diary back into the bag.

"Linen," she said. "Not paper. Details matter."

"Not the wrong details. It's always the wrong details."

Joan left without replying, out of the wood and along the path.

Smelling strongly of violets and bathing and hair products and dry-cleaning and shoe leather and, now that she was closer, also of wine, Ottilie squatted low, balancing herself, bracing one arm against the angel, and put her other hand onto my profile, and spoke to me.

"I'm not sure I can stand another minute of that Joan," she said (*that Joan* is an in-joke), "and I'm beginning to wish I'd killed her when I had the chance."

She was referring back to an incident when the twins were 13 and a tandem hired at a seaside village very nearly went off a cliff. Ottilie wasn't even steering, she says, but got the blame nonetheless, as did the quality of the machine, the integrity of the bike hire shack and the council decision to leave the precipice unfenced, a diatribe concluding that the whole village was second-rate. It's the village where subsequently my mother bought a cottage. Would someone choose a house purely on the basis of its irritation value? In this case I'm afraid that they might.

In general black humour went unexercised at Peattie, when Henry was alive. Too many deaths had left the family afraid of irreverence. (More deaths than are quite right, than are quite explicable, they say in the village, where they tell eager tourists the details of the Salter curse). At Peattie, irony had been reclassified as bad taste, and Joan was its most enthusiastic sentry. This, of course, made it difficult for Ottilie to resist. Out of so many years of grieving, a dark sort of comedy had begun to emerge. Ottilie patted the stone angel softly as if she were behind me and it were my shoulder, and I was 12 years old again, being bullied at school, and she'd just told me that if it happened again I was to hit the bastards. "Punch them in the nose, Michael. And if I have to, I'll come in and do it myself."

She'd warned me often enough and so I knew the truth about people, that people were selfish, immoral, messed up, untrustworthy, and above all things, reliably stupid. That they'd exploit you, use and discard you; that all too often in life, even an apparently genuine friendship was introductory to this outcome. These are things I learned early: that we were *we* and they were otherwise. That we had to be vigilant. That we had to be aware. There were always going to be exceptions – she'd allow for exceptions – but it was important that I realised that I'd only ever be able to rely on myself. I don't know if it was a deliberate thing, this positioning, ensuring our exclusivity to one another, but that was the effect for a long time. Not that this made us inseparable – it didn't. We were each individually lonely and wary. We didn't spend a lot of time together, and we didn't talk all that much – there was one persistent barrier to that – but we were aware (I was aware) that the two of us were different from the rest, not least in having this characteristic, and in Ottilie's case, hard-earned world view. It wasn't even always spoken, but it was inculcated in me early, nonetheless, the real sense of our being a race apart, like the first two native Americans brought to the English court and misunderstood there. It adhered deeply, this idea. It took me a long time to make a proper friend, and that was with one of the cousins, and a girl.

Squatting had proven uncomfortable so Ottilie sat down, gathering up dried brown leaves beneath her to protect the linen from the earth.

"Will you make a special appearance and haunt her a

little?" she asked me. "Just for a couple of days, and only if you have an opening, obviously."

I could smell, now, in detail that separated out into its colours like a prism, the elements of the dark-red wine, its bruised fruit and spice and alcohol. I'm all faculties now, and my sense of smell is near canine. The loch is pungent as never in life. The beach has a personality, each pebble. Each of the trees in the wood is marked by its own bark-fibrous, leaf-sap, earth-and-root aroma, some floral and some herbal, some mushroomy and fungal, and each its own self. If I find myself in the formal gardens just after Euan's been up and down with the push mower, the smell of cut grass is like an assault and I have to withdraw. Each room in the house produces its own raw odours: the cryptish smells of damp stone and the chemical whiff of old paint, the fusty sharpness of rot, the gluey wet of bubbling wallpapers, the dust scent of wood floors, the dyed-cotton smells of worn velvet and corduroy, the human traces unlaundered in cushions and rugs, and the animal imprint superimposed on it all. I have to turn nauseated away from Henry's various dogs. It's odd and on occasion disturbing, being among the living. Sometimes, the scent of flesh offends me and I feel an involuntary repugnance, but at other times only empathy on behalf of them all, for their being tubes and pumps and chemistry. If the family could hear me, I'd tell them that life continues when the machinery has failed. Perhaps it's just as well they can't hear me, then. I'm not sure I could be convincing about the benefits. Nor could I bear to tell Edith that in death there is no reunion. I haven't seen Henry, Sebastian, the great aunts, Grandpa Andrew. There have been no touching scenes as we gather in the wood, greeting each other with wry smiles, finding ourselves sitting together on a wall like the ghosts in old films.

"Freak her out a little, would you?" Ottilie said. "Just enough for her to take to her bed with nervous fatigue a few days and let us have our shindig as casual as we like. A few supermarket bottles, the furniture pushed back, sausage rolls in the oven. Instead of being organised by clipboard woman. And in-vig-i-lated." She gave the word slow and special emphasis. "But no. That won't do. Instead it's meetings and lists and phone calls and endless fussing." She shook her head, her lips pressed together. "Where does it come from, this idea of things having to be correct, everything having to be *correct* all the time? It presses down on us, Michael. It must press down on her, mustn't it? I almost feel sorry for her."

Her hand was raised an inch or two above the cameo, now, and her fingers fluttered slightly, as if there were an energy coming off it, some static, some heat. She pushed gently through this forcefield every now and then, making momentary contact. I remembered, suddenly, being ill with the flu aged about 15, and these very hand movements, my mother approaching as I slept and her palm hovering over my hair.

Chapter 3

The day that I disappeared I knew from very early in the morning that it was going to be a big day in the history of the family, but not how big a day. Looking back to the hours preceding the bringing of the news, seeing everybody else behaving as if it's another mundane 24 hours in a heatwave, as if it's heat that's their enemy, is unfair to the others: their not knowing can make them look as if they are unimaginative, or worse, heartless.

I met my cousin Mog in the linen room at Peattie straight after breakfast, just as we'd arranged the day before. She was having trouble with her maths coursework. She was 16 and her mother still bought her clothes: that day, a brown cotton skirt that reached almost to her ankles, swishy with excess fabric panels, and flat brown sandals with bridle buckles. She was wearing a red t-shirt, straining across the softness of her belly, and had a brown cardigan tied looped around her neck. I sat beside her on the lowest shelf, and while I was looking at the textbook she untied the cardigan, fanning her face inefficiently with it, its empty arms flapping. Her brown hair, the Salter tight waves frizzing out over her shoulders, was tied back lightly in a red ribbon. She had spots on her chin, perspiration rings beneath her armpits. It was stultifyingly hot in there. When I'd come in I had opened the room's one high window, pushing it out to its furthest hole, but the air coming in was just as torpid as the rest.

Mog stood up and went to the lower shelf opposite, where school books had been dumped untidily over a blanket, and sorted through them, keeping her eye on me: I was looking at her attempts to answer the maths questions, and not bothering to mask my incredulity at the mess she'd made of them. We'd had this conversation before: basic principles weren't being applied. They smell so strongly in memory, these books, of old cupboards and the insides of satchels and remnants of lunch. They prompt a view of other pupils, previous users, their names listed and crossed out in black and blue on front pages in outmoded handwriting, and I have to concentrate on staying here and now. This is what happens: fresh narratives try to open, taking me off at tangents. I have to damp them down and resist; it takes effort.

Mog had an apple and a banana supplied by her mother, who'd forbidden non-fruit snacks. I ate the banana and fixed the peel as hair for the apple, balancing it over the top, using stickers from Mog's pencil case to give it a face. The apple-faced banana-haired monstrosity grins at me now in recognition, like a Halloween pumpkin, its sparkly hearts arranged like teeth. I came here to say goodbye and then didn't. "See you," I said, not knowing when it would be, not knowing it wouldn't be ever, aside from when she comes to the wood, only in that perverse one-sided manner. I said I had things to do, having shown Mog the method again and having satirised her muddle-headedness. I was unkind, sarcastic. I see that. It's easy to see that from here. I left the room and barely five minutes later she was stuck fast. "But it doesn't work, it doesn't work. Damn it all. I'll have to go and find him."

She packed up the books in the bag she always carried then, a maroon-coloured canvas bag that hooked across the body. Joan bought her these ugly things with a consistency that couldn't have been accidental. Mog had said she'd have to find me, but she didn't come and find me; she went home to the gatehouse and sprawled on her bed, returning to a pile of favourite childhood books that Joan had boxed ready for a jumble sale. Decluttering, Joan said, was the first step to serenity. Mog looked out from time to time at the parched garden, the sky, feeling the heat burning through the open window, telling herself she should be out there. She had lunch, alone, a crispbread with cheese and a tomato, and continued reading through the Malory Towers books, enjoying favourite old scenes; she must have had passages almost by heart. Finally the nagging idea that it was a waste to be in the shade when the sun was shining, a thought spoken in her mother's voice, sent her out to lie on the grass. She lay flat out in shorts and a bikini top, scorching her shoulders and the backs of her knees, until her head was woozy. When she came in again she drank some water, went and curled up on a sofa with the book and fell promptly asleep. It was training that woke her at ten to four, knowing she'd be expected at tea. Heading up the drive, she saw her parents' car parked in its usual spot: they must have arrived back late and gone straight in. Sure enough there was Pip, her 18-year-old brother, sitting on the steps that lead up to the terrace.

She waved at him, calling out her question as she went. "How was Glasgow?"

It was too hot to sit beside him on the stone tread in the full glare. Her head was still thumping its quiet background thump.

"Glasgowish. Mum and Dad bickered all the way home. I'm just coming in."

She ruffled his hair as she passed by and he ducked and veered to escape it. "Gerroff."

"Rarrr," she said. "Grumpy."

He followed her into the hall.

38

"How was it then?" she asked him.

"Alright."

"Details please."

"We talked all day. The motherator talked all day. I'm sick of talking about it."

"But could you spend four years there? Did you see the student houses?"

"Yeah yeah yeah."

"You don't have to go, you know."

He opened the drawing-room door. "I know. I'm still thinking."

Unusually, all the windows were open to their fullest extent. Earlier there had been a fuss about a starling, which blundered in and was scooped up and repatriated to the garden in a sheet. It wasn't just hot, this June day, but the hottest of a week of hot days, each ascending in temperature. The grasses were bleached and dried and the earth, baked iron hard, lay cracked in the fields, the hot air sitting over it custard yellow; we seemed to walk through the world as if through some thicker kind of atmosphere, some cataclysmic meteorological thickening, the air hindering our progress. When Mog went to the sideboard, a cherry-wood beast of a thing with many legs, and poured lemon squash into a glass from a jug, the ice cubes clinking, a stripe of sweat appeared on her back. She untied her hair and put it up again, bunching it into a knot on the top of her head from which ends sprayed in all directions, and held the drink against her forehead, rolling it across her skin. She has the typical Salter face: the short, neat nose, long upper lip, small mouth, pointed chin, slightly Asiatic-looking eyes. She picked up a flapjack and went and sat on the window seat, adjusting the ankle-skimming skirt to sit folded just above her knees. The seat's set within a squared-off bay, its three long cushions a dull turquoise that's faded and flattened and piped in black. The shutters are carved with ivy and thistle motifs, done by the same workshop that produced the decorated front doors, and gleam with a dull waxed honey-glow.

Long minutes passed while Mog ate her flapjack and cast an eye over one of her mother's décor magazines, pausing every now and then to fan herself with it, directing the warm fanned air towards closed eyes. The others were late in arriving, but then they came in all at once, bunched as if they'd just come out of the theatre, looking to each other and mid-conversation. Henry, Edith, Joan and Euan, Vita and her live-in companion Mrs Hammill. Pip arrived sluggishly in the rear.

"The financial sub-committee," Vita said in Mog's direction.

"But you're quite wrong," Joan was saying. "Hot drinks are the most cooling. That's how tea drinking in India got started."

"Have you seen Michael?" Mog said to nobody in particular. Nobody paid attention. "I'll go and check his room."

She got up to go, but on her way out noticed that Vita was struggling with the teapot – unable to free two hands at once from balancing herself at the table, unable to use the teapot one-handed. She saw too that Mrs Hammill hadn't noticed this, as she was standing talking to Joan. Mog went to help, and poured her own tea, and helped Vita to her seat, and didn't go to find me. If she had, the letter would have been discovered then, and not hours later. It was sitting in open view on the quilt.

The letter was addressed to my mother. News of its writing, its finding, spread quickly into and around the village, once I was gone. As far as the rest of the world knew I had run away to seek my fortune. That was the official story anyway, but small communities are rarely content to be told what to think. Certainly there was no lack of gossip in the shop. Jock, the village alcoholic (there are others, of course, but Jock's status is iconic) was of the opinion that I was eaten by the Peattie Loch Monster. Because yes, amusing as it may seem, Peattie has its own monster legend, just as persist at Ness and Morar.

Jock lives next door to the shop and sits on his wall most days, a low front wall, in all weathers, a half-drunk bottle of whisky at his feet, addressing remarks to those going in and out. If you're a Salter they're likely to be remarks about the loch. The loch's an obsession. His brother James drowned here in the 1970s, from a boat launched at the hotel pier a mile upwater. People assume a lake's a calm entity, a giant puddle, but only a few miles of land separate loch from ocean and this is a region of abruptly stormy weather. The day James was lost it was more abrupt than most, and storm-force winds funnelled down between the hills created high loch waves. Deaths on the lochs aren't that unusual in Scotland, and Peattie is fairly typical in its once-every-three-or-four-yearly cull of canoeists, fishermen and swimmers. The villagers describe the loch as *hungry* if there's been a long period without fatalities. A sighting of the monster, shown in old drawings as resembling a wider, fat-nosed crocodile, is said to be a harbinger of doom and death for the Salters, though this must be nonsense as they're drawings that precede our arrival in 1846. It's one of the myths the village likes to torture us with. Ursula claims to have seen the creature once when she was small and can't be persuaded that it was one of the seals or occasional whales that are said to stray this far inland, through underground tunnel access from the sea.

Nothing much was said at teatime usually, other than for desultory conversation, trivial, vital and tribal: the quiet clinking of teaspoons on china, plans for the day, remarks about how the garden was looking, shopping needing doing and the well-being of the dogs. The dogs were very much

Henry's, and were replaced as they died, breed for breed. I missed them very much when Ottilie and I moved out of Peattie, mourning the loss of the deerhounds particularly, great long-legged things that floated around the corridors, moving with a gliding trot, their iron-grey coats tufting stiffly up around shiny black eyes. They had an other-worldly look to them, as if their thoughts were elsewhere. This is what attracted me to them, their detachment, their foreignness in a drawing room, their dignified tolerance of drawing-room behaviour. The Jack Russells came too, fat-bellied, hairy-faced terriers, dogs with a teatime agenda, sitting as politely as they knew how beside chairs, tracking the progress of biscuits and cake as they were transported from tea plates to human mouths. Generally the dogs announced Henry's arrival, surging in first and finding their usual spots, but Crispin, favourite of the black Labradors, came in always at the rear, white-muzzled and stiffly. Today Crispin circled and then settled, exhaling hard, by Henry's chair, trying to keep awake and waiting for orders. The dogs were useful distractions at teatime. If conversation failed they became the natural focus for everyone's atten-tion. Often Mog would go and sit at Henry's feet, sitting by Crispin and picking at ticks and burrs, the old dog's breathing thickening into purring.

Teatime was a calendar that marked the passing of days into years, and also a much more subtle device, making it obvious to all in a hundred incremental ways how it was that people stood with one another, picking up differences from one day to the next. For another five minutes, today would be no different. Mog sat on the window seat, by one of the open windows, her shoes shed and one knee up, looking out at the gardens, the view shimmering in the heat, tapping a rhythm on the sill to some internal music. Henry was opening his mail with a letter knife; he always brought something to do. Vita and her friend Mrs Hammill were drinking tea and talking about books. Vita was reading Tolstoy; Mrs Hammill was putting the case for Georgette Heyer. Joan was reading the décor magazine, retrieved from Mog, and was jotting down phone numbers in her diary. Edith was talking to Euan about the repointing he said was urgent to the north-west corner, and what it might cost; Henry watching and noting over the top of his correspondence. Ottilie, who'd arrived late, was reading a book about Japan – she was supposed to be going to Tokyo later that week. Pip had excused himself after a cursory visit; he'd eaten six biscuits in a hurry and swigged two glasses of the lemon squash, and had gone off on his bike to see a friend. His twin hadn't turned up to tea, location unknown (smoking weed in his bedroom would be my guess). Their younger sister wasn't there either, gone to another nine-year-old's house with her collection of plastic horses in a pink zipped bag.

≈

The disaster has occurred. We needn't revisit its unfolding again. Ursula has come and delivered her news and Alan has intercepted the family in the yard, agreeing with her story, and we have been to the loch together. They were just as before, the progress of events and the things said. It's reassuring when history doesn't present variations; it feels as if memory is confirming itself as the facts, achieving a kind of objectivity. They have been to the loch and they have come back, on foot and on bike and in silence. Edith has provided her permission to abandon the vigil. They have given up on finding me. They have given up on hope. They have returned to the drawing room, encountering Mrs Welsh in the hall on the way in. She could see at once that something was amiss.

"Tell me all about it when I bring the tea," she said. Mrs Welsh is of the school of thought that one must have fresh tea in a crisis.

She came into the room with the trolley to find that broken crockery from earlier was being gathered and piled, with careful fingers, onto a tablecloth that had been laid on the floor. Exclaiming, she went off to get a dustpan and brush. She returned to find the whole family sitting looking as stunned as fish.

"I can see that there's something wrong, and I don't want to intrude, but if I can be of any assistance, you're only to say, you know that," she said. "I'll make more toast, will I?"

Nobody took on the question of toast directly.

"There's something we need to tell you," Joan said to her, just as Mog burst into the room with the letter.

This is when the explanation first was aired that I had left, had run away, had left a note, was gone and nobody knew where. Mrs Welsh tutted her response, half sympathetic and half unsurprised. (We'd never really got along. Mrs Welsh had been blunt about my needing to spend more time at home and less at Peattie; I'd been blunt in telling her she didn't know anything about it.) Toast was provided, toast that nobody ate and which Mog fed, when it had cooled and was pliable, folded in smaller triangles to waiting terriers. Nobody seemed to want to leave the drawing room, not even after my mother had been put to bed and the phone call had been made to the village surgery. Edith went upstairs with Ottilie and stayed with her.

When Mrs Welsh came back into the room to say she was going now and was there anything she could do for anyone first, she found the rest of them drinking whisky, three of Henry's bottles on the table and none of them particularly full. Vita was asleep in her chair in the window, still with a glass in her hand. They heard the bell, the Edwardian tinkle of bells at the door, a chord of high and low notes, one full of antique certainty. Mog at the window said that she could see the doctor's car. Dr Nixon had been called to deal with Ottilie's panic, her medical levels of panic, her not being able to breathe. The doctor's visit: that was my mother's chance to tell someone what and who, to raise the alarm, but she didn't take that chance, falling into line with Edith's explanation that Michael had left them, and a sedative was administered. Edith stayed at the bedside until Ottilie was sleeping. The rest huddled in chairs, not able to talk but finding comfort, or at least a sort of membership, in having gone through this big thing together.

At just after eight o'clock, when Mrs Welsh was safely out of the house and the doctor had gone, after they'd heard the final definitive closing of the double doors, and the car engine starting up: that was the signal, and everybody recognised it. A new sort of attentiveness arrived with Edith's return to the room, mutually and simultaneously among the slouched forms of whisky drinkers; people getting up and stretching, people looking to Henry in recognition that it was down to Henry to begin. Henry, too, recognised that it was time. He began to talk to Ursula about what had happened.

Ursula had been sitting, for all of this time, on the floor with her back to the window seat, her face giving nothing away. She'd moved exhausted out of distress and contrition and into recovery, all cried out, wiping her face with a white hand, turning and turning the hem of the blue dress in her fingers, and finally into quietness, sitting still, her face remote and her fidgeting having ceased.

"Ursula, I need to talk to you now, about what happened today," Henry said, going to the window seat and sitting on it. "Could you come and sit by me?" Ursula complied, all eyes in the room upon her.

Edith left her chair and went and sat on the floor beside the fireplace, resting her back against the wall. Unusually, Sirius, one of the deerhounds, shuffled towards her on his stomach and rested his big hairy head on her lap. Edith leaned forward with her head in her hands, as if she wanted to hear but not see Ursula as she spoke, Sirius looking up at her with a look that was unmistakably of concern.

"What happened? Tell me exactly what happened," Henry repeated.

"I hit him," Ursula said.

"You hit him. How did you hit him?"

"We were fighting. He was being annoying. I was annoyed. I didn't hate him. I loved him. But I lost my temper."

"You were sitting together in the boat, you say. Tell us exactly what happened next."

"No. We were on the jetty."

"You were on the jetty at first, but then you got into the boat, with Michael. You and Michael. In the boat together."

"He didn't love me. I realised that I hated him."

Edith looked at Ursula for a moment and returned her head into the cradle of her palms.

Henry said, "But I thought you were friends."

"Friends. No."

"Yes. You were good friends, you and Michael. We saw you often in the wood together, and in the garden. You had long talks. Of course you were friends."

"We had sex together," Ursula told him.

There was a silence. Then Joan said, "Oh sweet Jesus." Mrs Hammill rose and left the room without a word. Henry's cheeks were filling with a stinging red. Edith's fingertips were pushed tight against her eyebrows. Her breathing had quickened.

"Ursula. You slept with Michael?" Euan's voice. "But you are his aunt. He's 19, a boy."

Everybody else was looking at Mog. "I didn't know; he didn't tell me," she said. "I'm sorry."

They wouldn't blame her for this until later.

"And so he told you that your ... that it was finished?"

Henry's voice was unsteady. "You hit him because he told you that?"

"He was so angry," Ursula said.

"*He* was angry?"

She crossed her hands and patted tentatively at her upper arms, her expression pained. Euan went to her, lifting her hair in order to see better. Ursula squirmed out of his attempted closer look, reacting noisily to his hand making contact on her shoulder. Euan said that there were marks, red fingerprints and scratches.

Everybody looked now towards Alan, who was perched on the edge of a nursing chair that sits by the door, one that might give out at any moment. His face was moist and pink and his eyes alarmed.

"You saw this, Alan?" Henry prompted him.

"The boat was quite far out, as I said. But there was one hell of a commotion."

"You didn't see Michael attacking her?"

"I was in the wood, as I told you. My lunch break. I'd had a tiff with my dad."

"Yes, you said, about the tomatoes," Euan stepped in curtly. "About who was supposed to water them. But what were you doing in the wood?"

"I told you. It was my lunch break. I often go down there. It's hot. It's cooler by the water, and there's a breeze."

"You were spying on Michael and Ursula," Euan said, pointing.

Alan, I should tell you, had been cautioned by the police in the weeks preceding this for peeping through windows, through inadequately closed curtains, at night in the village. He would admit to being nosy, he'd said, but that was all.

"I was not," Alan insisted. "I was in the wood. I was at the grave. I was there on my bike. I was bothered about the fight with my dad. I didn't see them till I heard the commotion. I heard the carry-on. I went out there onto the beach.

47

The glare's bad but I see Ursula and Michael jostling each other in the boat and tipping it. They have the oar –"

"Both of them." Joan's voice.

"Both. They have it one at each end and it looks like they're playing, but there's shouting."

"You could hear what was being said?"

"I can hear but the words aren't right, it's just noise, I can't make it out."

"I see," Henry murmured. "I see."

"Michael loses his balance and goes over. Ursula jabs him hard with the oar and he's pushed back and over he goes."

"And?"

"He's swimming round the boat and she's yelling at him. She's got her back to me. He gets his arms onto the side of the boat and his head comes up over the edge; he looks up from the edge, holding onto the side, and he's saying something to her. And that's when it happens."

"Go on."

"She hits him hard across the head."

"She hits him hard."

"It's like a golf swing, wham, into the temple."

Edith cried out in grief.

"I'm sorry to be so graphic," Alan said. "I apologise."

"Go on," Henry told him.

"Michael doesn't make a sound. Nothing. His arms disappear off the boat and he's gone under." Alan opened his hands as if encompassing a ball. "And that's it, that's all."

Henry didn't speak at first. Nobody spoke. The clock on the mantlepiece was very noisy.

Henry was looking at Ursula, and Ursula was averting her eyes.

Finally he said "Why did you hit him?"

She didn't answer.

"Why was he so angry?"

She twisted and untwisted her hem.

"Tell us what happened. In your words. What happened, Ursula?"

Nothing.

"Ursula." More urgently now. "We need to understand."

"I told him."

"What did you tell him?"

"I told him the secret."

"What secret?"

She looked at her father as if he must be stupid. "It's a secret."

"You need to tell us what the secret was," Henry said, but Ursula was already shaking her head. "Ursula," Henry insisted, his voice remaining patient. "We need to know. This is important."

Ursula looked at Alan, and kept looking at him.

Alan said, "Would you rather I left the room, Mr Salter?"

"Stay, Alan. A little longer."

"It's just that my dad will be worried."

"Oh goodness." Edith spoke for the first time. "Of course you must go. Go and see him and then come straight back, would you?" She appeared composed but Edith is a coper, an apparent coper. Nobody was fooled.

Nothing was said until Alan had left the room and they heard the main door closing.

"He was going to push me in," Ursula said then, her voice high-pitched. The words had been pent up in her.

"Alan?"

"Michael. Michael was trying to push me in."

This I'm afraid is true. It was also the moment of forgiveness.

Edith beckoned to her, and she went and joined her mother on the floor, the vast fireplace looming over them, its brick interior dark as a mouth. Ursula put her head in the crook of Edith's arm, her knees balled up tight. Edith put a discreet hand up to the rest of them, one that requested quiet.

"Was it something to do with Alan, the secret?" She spoke to the top of her daughter's head.

"I can't," Ursula told her. Euan had given Edith another whisky and she gulped it now, wincing.

There's no way out of a promise, they knew that much. A promise isn't negotiable. Some things that Ursula was taught as a child have set fast in her character and this is one of those things.

"So you had an argument."

Ursula's words were muffled by Edith's lap. "We were shouting. The fish were scared. The birds flew out of the wood. It was hot. There wasn't enough air. Even the water was hot."

Ursula sat up, extricating herself, putting her fingertips to each eyebrow and hooking her thumbs under her chin.

"Tell us more about Michael," Edith said to her.

"He went down into the water so quietly, so quietly, just a ripple and – gone." She spoke through a tent of fingers. "And then there was nobody there." She sounded genuinely surprised. Her hands were lowered. "He was gone. He was already gone. I saw the bubbles coming up." She paused, looking as if she were seeing it again, her eyes flickering side to side. "I leaned and I was saying his name. But he wasn't there; I couldn't see him. He was already gone."

Euan interrupted her. "And what about Alan?"

"Alan."

"Alan came out to the boat, swimming."

"No," Ursula said firmly. "Alan dived in and looked for him, off the jetty, looking and looking, and then he brought him up."

"What?"

"Sebastian was dead."

"Ursula," Henry said. "Concentrate. We're not talking

about that. This afternoon. Ursula. In the boat with Michael. He fell overboard and then he tried to climb back in."

"He went in the water, and he just *sank*. Sank and gone."

"He didn't just sink," Joan said. "He came back, and he tried to get into the boat, and you hit him with the oar."

"He wasn't going to climb back in."

"What?"

"He had me by my ankle. He grabbed me hard on my leg and he was pulling. He was going to pull me in. You can't breathe in the water. You can't breathe. It will fill every space in you and stop your heart."

She began violently to shiver. Mog took a blanket from the folded pile in the corner, set in readiness there for more ordinary days when the fire can't seem to puncture the chill, and put it around her shoulders.

Ursula tucked her chin into the hem of the blanket, her nose and eyes all that was visible of her face.

"Tell us about Alan," Joan said.

"Alan tried. Alan tried his hardest. But it was too late."

"What happened then?"

"I ran home. But it was a long time after."

"Why did it take so long?"

"The oar. The other oar was in the water."

"You couldn't reach it?"

"I wouldn't reach. I don't go towards the water. Water will kill me. Sebastian … you know about my brother Sebastian."

"Indeed."

"The Salters are cursed. We were cursed by a witch in 1852."

Vita says she believes in the curse. Vita believes in evil as an entity, something conscious, something waiting for its moment. She says that really it was the witch who killed me, the supposedly "dark-skinned" woman who turned up in 1852, claiming the then Henry Salter was wicked and must pay. *Many of ye shall die by water and meet the devil in hereafter*. In the village they like to list the names of all those who've complied (with the first clause, at any rate), counting them off on their fingers.

After they'd talked and talked, to Ursula and to Alan, and there seemed nothing new to discover, the family went away and individually they considered what had happened. They had their real reactions to events alone in bedrooms and bathrooms and in corners of the garden. Then, when feelings had subsided enough into words, they began to talk among themselves, at first in family groups, in family discussions. Later, the things they believed (and more importantly, didn't believe) became controversial, contradictory, and the conversations shrank into twosomes, but for now there was talk among the group. The group established the words that could be said and the words that couldn't. Each person tried out the role through step and misstep that they would assume later in the drama, and in so doing the language of the disaster was established. It felt dangerous to leave the safety of that new culture, and encounter those not anointed into it. How could the forbidden thing not rise to the surface of its own volition, like a splinter out of a finger, rising of its own accord and speaking itself? It threatened to, even in the safety of the family circle. Something so momentous: how could it go on being contained and private? A way of dealing with it was to introduce, even at this very early stage, the possibility of doubt. In doubting, the big thing was fractured, split, spread. In doing so, the big thing was diminished.

~

It's another day. People are a little older and in different clothes. Mog's younger sister looks about 13, so it's about four years later. Edith and the cousins are in the kitchen,

buttering toast. It's the only thing that makes me something like hungry; terrible yearning resides in that smell.
Mog and Pip are back for the weekend from the city with
their city news. It's autumn, to judge by the scene outside;
brown leaves are circling and heaping against the trees,
and then unheaping, raked invisibly along the paths. Four
years later and they were still talking about it. Will they
ever stop talking about it?

"Okay then, well let's see it from Ursula's viewpoint if
we can for a moment," Edith said, in her sweet and reasonable way. "Ursula fell *violently* in love with her 19-year-old
nephew, and thought he was in love with her – no truly,
please don't smirk, Pip, that's genuinely what she thought.
She had an affair with him in secret, and –"

"We don't know that, Gran."

"We do, we do know that. Ursula doesn't tell lies. She
tells the truth always, too much of it sometimes."

"I know, I know, truth is her religion," Pip said, with
thinly veiled sarcasm.

"Had an affair with him in secret," Edith continued,
"and no doubt she was intense about it, and it wouldn't
surprise me if that was the real reason Michael decided to
go. On the day he was leaving he persuaded her to go out
in the boat with him. We'll never know how he managed it.
Perhaps he dangled the possibility that she could go away
with him."

"It's possible," Pip said, in a way that suggested it wasn't
at all likely.

"Ursula, made very upset, said something to Michael
that caused him to lose his temper, about which we can
only speculate as she's unlikely to tell us."

"That Alan is his father."

"Pip. We don't know that."

"Of course we do. Everybody knows. Everybody but
Michael."

"She told him a secret, and was attacked by him in the

rowing boat and feared she would fall into the water. He threatened to push her in. When she pushed back, he lost his balance."

Pip made his sceptical noise.

"He lost his balance," Edith repeated. "And then, when he got his forearms back over the side of the boat, what did he do then? Was he content to climb back in? No. He grabbed her by the leg and tried to pull her into the water. Do you have any idea, do you have *any idea*, what that would have meant to Ursula?"

"Of course."

"Well, I hope so. Michael used her fear against her. He used her terror and that was a deplorable thing to do. I'm not saying that injuring Michael was right –"

"Injuring?"

"It was the loch that did the rest, Pip. If it had happened on land, he would have been taken to casualty and that would have been that."

"We don't know that."

"We do. He was hit by someone in a panic, terrified, who found themselves in a life-and-death struggle. You weren't here Pip. You didn't see her. Terror is the right word. He went under. It was an accident."

"It was not an accident."

"I don't think Izzy should be here," Edith said. Mog's younger sister was staring open-mouthed.

"Izzy is fine," Pip told her. "Izzy is the blood-thirstiest of us all and has been entertaining us with her theories."

"Hitting him. That was wrong. But was Michael right? We all idolise Michael, beautiful Michael who's dead, but let's just remember what he did that day."

The one thing all acknowledge that Ursula could not do, under any circumstances, was follow me out of the boat. Nobody, not even Ottilie in her raging grief, could blame Ursula for her lifelong aquaphobia. Ursula, who has trouble with the idea of fiction, believes in the monster and

54

has always feared it. She thought, when it looked as if I would push her into the water (knowing that she couldn't swim), that drowning would be only the end of the ordeal. She thought that she would find the creature swimming beneath her, the rough shark skin of his nose skimming her kneebone, his pitiless liquid eye, his Triassic mouth opening onto a hundred knife-sharp teeth, her limbs torn off in front of her eyes.

Jock must take some of the blame for this. He'd see the child Ursula cycling up and going in to buy sweets, her bike parked by the wall her great-great-grandfather built. At that time Ursula was his particular target.

"Oh if it isn't Miss Salter, and will you be seeing the monster today? Are you aware that I count that monster as my particular friend? He's been speaking to me about you. Swimming silent in the dark and hungry. He's waiting for you; it's you he wants"

Jock would be waiting for her when she came out again, with her sherbet fountain and bottle of dandelion and burdock. "Don't go dipping a toe in the loch now, the beast is waiting for you." Laughing after her as she ran with her bike jingling, too afraid to stop and get on it, the pedals catching at her legs.

Chapter 4

In the evening Mog arrived from Edinburgh, summoned by Joan to help with the birthday party arrangements. Mog, too, had been the recipient of a pink sheet, some of its listed tasks marked with her initials. I don't often find myself at the gates to Peattie, but I was there, beside one of the stone pillars carved with wildcats and eagles, when she arrived in a taxi from the station. The sun had dipped below the cloud cover a half-hour before twilight, as often it does here, sinking below its grey hat, and so the end to the day was glorious; Mog emerged from the cab into soft violet light, ultra-violet, the kind that illuminates tennis balls and teeth and plunges everything else into sepia. She walked right past me, a rucksack on her back, past iron-work gates pushed permanently open, their feet enmeshed in weed, and went immediately left, through a gap in the rhododendron hedge, out of sight from the gatehouse, following the inner side of the wall and trailing one hand at intervals along it, the other outstretched to make fleeting contact with specimen pines, the old holly, the monkey puzzle, the birches. The pines soaring, pungently antiseptic and their bark coarse. The holly stunted and corkscrew twisted. Birch bark silky, peeling in silvery ribbons. The monkey puzzle holding its pairs of spiked arms up like an Indian god. When she emerged into the formal garden she chose the path that leads to a now-defunct fountain, a table of mossy lawn, and beyond that, the folly.

The folly is an octagonal room, encircled by eight Doric columns and crowned by a cupola that's been weathered into a streaky jade green. Inside, there's a saggy brown sofa, a mouse-chewed desk and plastic garden chairs stacked high, streaked by muddy rain; last autumn's brittle leaves still hugging the walls. Vita, at the drawing- room window with binoculars, spotted Mog sitting on the top step of the veranda. Vita had asked for the binoculars for her birthday; it would be a way of enlarging her society, she'd said, even if only in meeting new birds.

Vita's voice enunciated every slow syllable. "I'm standing at the window, Edith, and I can see Mog, sitting outside the folly."

"I thought she was coming tomorrow."

"Ah, she's going to the gatehouse now."

"So we'll see her tomorrow." Edith was reading a book, an American title, its typefaces and syntax satisfyingly unfamiliar – Pip orders them for her, off the internet – about talking to God and getting God to reply.

"Tomorrow? I think that's unlikely. When did any of Joan's children last spend a night at the gatehouse?"

Sure enough, Mog was with them a few minutes later.

"It's good that you're here," Vita told her. "This afternoon it was napkins and tonight it was candles. Ottilie thinks your mother is going to set fire to the house."

"Can we get you something to eat, Mog?" Edith's trying constantly to feed people.

Mog said she'd had something on the train.

I think about that train journey often, seeing it again in my mind's eye. The sweeping views across forest and upland; yellow light on orange hills and deep purple shade; birds rising startled slow motion from the woods, and sudden glimpses of hamlets, the country roads surfacing and submerging. We would go sometimes to Inverness together, Mog and I, on the rumbly local service. We'd drink takeaway coffee down by the river, and stand shamelessly long in bookshops reading. We'd sit on benches with tins of coke and compete to produce the best short description of the lives of strangers walking by us, people unaware they were being photographed in words and their souls stolen. These were good days, but best of all I loved the journey, my notebook and pen on the train table, travelling free of time, feeling it stretch and contract, watching possible lives flash past the window, revelling in the luxury of not having to be definite.

Henry came into the room. Henry was still with us, at the time of the party. Really, the story of the gathering and what precipitated out of it is Henry's and not mine.

"Good to see you," he said in Mog's direction, and then, not looking at Edith – in general he avoided looking at his wife – "I take it the rooms are ready."

"Of course." Edith, her voice patient and gentle as always, folded her hands in her lap. "They're always ready, Henry."

"So everything is organised for the weekend visitors?" he asked the window.

"Of course. Have you had the talk with Ursula?" Edith picked dog hair from her trouser legs.

"You don't need to ask. I said that I would and I have."

Edith opened her mouth and closed it again.

"It isn't Ursula who's the problem," Henry said. "I think you'll find. I'm afraid it's Ottilie who needs the confidential chat."

"I've spoken to her: I spoke to her about it at the beginning."

"Very good." Henry left the room.

Edith looked to Mog, her expression sorrowful. "Henry

seems to think that it's my fault, somehow. We were standing together, both standing in the kitchen, equally ignorant of what was coming, when Joan sprang her surprise. And he agreed to it. We agreed in just the same way, for the same reasons; I'd swear to that. So quite how I'm implicated, I'm not sure. Perhaps secretly he's convinced that I was in on it at the beginning with your mother, conniving with her to bring jollity into the house."

Mog clasped her arm momentarily around Edith's shoulder and touched their heads gently together. Really, that was the only response possible.

Vita got her cigarettes out and Edith began to protest.

"I'm so old and decrepit," Vita said. "And I'm tired today. Don't make me leave the room."

"You shouldn't, Mother. It's so bad for you."

"Edith, I'm 97 years old."

"96."

"I'm almost 97 years old, and past caring."

It was widely suspected that Vita smoked only to get some respite from Mrs Hammill, who had declared herself allergic to the fumes, citing weakness of chest. Stout, manicured and imperious, a sailing ship under full sail, her copious blue-grey hair worn in a smooth dome above her head, Mrs Hammill had taken root at Peattie before I was born. Already widowed herself, she was invited to help Vita through the aftermath of bereavement, and never went home, as indeed didn't Vita. A bedroom had been made out of the old music room, as Vita could no longer manage the stairs, and she shuffled along the corridor to the study each morning to have a cigarette and to look at the newspaper with Henry, the two of them dividing the pages up and then swapping. The daily paper was locked up in a drawer when Henry wasn't there.

Mog came down to the wood in the near-dark. It has a different atmosphere here at dusk. The loch looks like a hard grey jewel in green folds of moth-eaten velvet. First she went to the shore, bending and dipping one hand into the shallows, the water cold and silky, before raising and kissing her index finger: her eccentric way of saying hello to me. She came next to the tomb, running her other hand over the great uncle's cap in a practised swift motion, something the children of the family have always done, a kind of superstition. The loch kiss, the cap: these are two of her three rituals. The third is to come to my stone, to sit with her back irreligiously against the angel, as if blocking the angel from the conversation. Like my mother, she acts as if the cameo is my grave-marker and as if I were beneath it, listening.

"Hello, Michael," she said, in her usual sad way, speaking to me as if commiserating, as if I was the one who'd had bad news, though I suppose that was accurate enough. The wood is plagued by flies in summer, tiny winged black flies that bite, and they were persistent around her eyes. She reached down into a trouser pocket, adjusting her stance, pulled out a soft crushed pouch of cigarettes and lit one up. The evening college of midges was fumigated by a semicircular exhalation of smoke.

"Sometimes I think I can hear you talking to me, Michael," she said in a hoarse whisper. As if she didn't want David to hear.

It's probably my fault that Mog smokes. There were always cigarette papers and a tin of Old Holborn, pleasingly archaic, when I talked her through her maths work in the linen room at weekends. She'd roll her own, the thinnest possible, with barely five strands of tobacco, attempting smoke-aided slang expressions, a smoke-provoked shift in personality, one outside the scope of her mother's approval.

"When he was 19 we were close friends, as close as anyone, or so I thought," she used to say to people curious to know whether anything was ever heard again of the cousin who vanished. She's grieved over me in all the years since, I know that. I know how it's got in the way, this grief, of other things she should have done and also felt, and if I could I would help her disengage from it. She'd said to me sometimes, on sporadic visits in the months preceding, that she hadn't come to Peattie much, despite longing to, despite almost going to the station and almost catching a train every Friday after work, because she thought that weekends spent here weren't helping her settle, that settling was the hardest thing she could imagine doing. But now she'd given up on that attempted life.

"So, the plan is to stay on, live here for a year, help Edith and Henry manage things, work in the village. A year off and then we'll see." She paused. "There's something else you need to know. Johnnie and I have parted. That's the other news. Don't say I told you so. Though I can tell that you're thinking it." I was. "Edinburgh's too small to live there being nervous always of seeing someone you dread seeing." So he was the reason she was back. "I read somewhere that it's normal to get over-attached to the first man you sleep with."

I've heard Mog described as plain, though plain is unfair. She has lovely eyes, long lashes, and her sweetness is obvious in her face, but she dresses like one of the great aunts, in twinsets, in tweed skirts tight over her rounded stomach, in dowdy warm stockings, in sensible and unlovely shoes. Lately she'd taken to wearing jeans and sturdy laced boots; they looked wrong, look forced, as if imposed on someone from the wrong generation for denim.

She'd written in her notebook in the train. She has a daily journal habit, like I used to, rewriting the day into something that makes narrative sense and feeds back meaning into it. She's said to me that her notebook's the only way of saying what she's thinking, that there's nobody else who wants to hear it.

If I'm to be permanent, and failure follows me there, failing might make me hate Peattie and I couldn't bear that.

There seemed to be a better than average chance of this. The mind clenches, braced against pessimism, but facts had to be faced and this was one of them. She'd learned things about herself lately. Edinburgh had become tainted with a thin film of defeatism. By the end she could see it everywhere: in the flat, in her job, coating the trees in the square, accompanying her on the route round the shops at lunchtime, visiting and revisiting the duffel coats at Marks & Spencer, her mood marked by a despairing sort of compulsive disinterest.

"There's so much I have to tell you," she said, "but talking to thin air feels more idiotic than usual." And then she was gone, walking and then running back up the path to the house.

It's Joan's fault that the Salter-Catto children have names that proved ideal for school bullying. She it was who decided that white-skinned, dark-haired James should be Jet, that Peter, the fair-haired smaller twin, should be Pip, and that Mary, who at three referred to herself as Mary Salty-Cat, should be Mog. Only Elizabeth retitled herself, finding the pronunciation impossible. Nobody would ever think to tease the remarkably beautiful, straight-talking Izzy about anything: the combination of beauty and bluntness is always silencing of hecklers. Jet coped fine, though it helped that he was always tall. Mog and Pip did less well with the bullies, especially poor Pip, who's smallest of the Salter men and as an adolescent had a punch like a sock puppet. Izzy from the first was happy with her name. The rest of them found resistance to be futile. Wherever they went, Joan had been there first, and had indoctrinated schools, friends, parents of friends, doctors. It was Euan who picked the christening names, thinking he was getting his own way, Joan agreeing before marriage that Catto traditions would take precedence in this one instance, as so little of Catto was to be otherwise on offer and in evidence at tradition-soaked Peattie, where Euan and Joan, when they lived at the gatehouse, were ostensible guardians of the whole Salter world.

~

Ursula was standing at the back door, brushing a spaniel and singing "*You Are My Sunshine*" to a tune of her own devising.

"What are you doing out here?" she asked as Mog approached from behind her. "I thought you hated the dark. I heard you running."

"I like running."

"You were afraid." Ursula turned and grinned. "Mummy says you're back, you're going to live here."

"For a while."

"What do you do there? I've forgotten. I know you've told me before."

"In Edinburgh? I worked on a newspaper."

"That's right. I saw it. At the airport. But Mummy wouldn't let me buy it. That was annoying. But I'm not going to fight with her. Not outside." She returned to brushing. "Anyway. Pip says your newspaper is terrible."

"It's not great, I admit."

"We get our news from the radiogram, if we want news, but we don't usually, because it's all sadness and lies. Pip says that's what politics means."

"Does he. Right."

"It's important to try to be happy."

"Yes."

"People are much happier without the news."

"Probably."

"No, it's a certainty. That's our family philosophy, Mummy says. When we're at Peattie."

"I know."

"You corrected the spelling. At the newspaper, didn't you?"

"I corrected the spelling, shortened the articles, wrote the headings."

"I'd love that. What made you give it up and come back here? What are you going to do here? There's nothing here. Nothing."

"I'm going to work at the hotel for a while. I needed a change. The city is very busy and crowded; too many cars, too many people."

"Was it because you didn't want to live with Pip any more, now Angelica's there?"

"Not really, no. It was nice, living with them."

Ursula stared at her. She dropped the brush. "Why do you talk to me like that?"

"Like what?"

"*It was nice, living with them.*" She impersonated Mog's low and steady voice, identical to Edith's. "*The city is very busy and crowded.* Like I'm stupid and backward."

"I'm sorry. I don't think that at all."

"I have a high IQ, you know. It was tested and I'm a member of MENSA. Do you know what that means? It means I'm cleverer than all of you."

❧

Edith and Henry were waiting for Mog in the drawing room. It's a large room and was lovely once, when its blue and gilt wallpaper, its composite tropical birds chirping silently from their paper bower, set the tone for beautiful imported furnishings, their gleaming wood surfaces and lavish silks. The best of these were sold off in the winter that the plumbing failed, and the ensuing vacuum drew replacements seemingly arbitrarily from other rooms, so that now it's a cheerful mish-mash in which garnet red and linden green and powder blue upholsteries clash free-spiritedly with Turkish rugs. Things are heavily worn, their wear and sag serving to unite them beneath a suspended fine dust that seems never to land, and through which the light pumps gauzily. This time last year, before the renovations began, the pitch pine window surrounds were beginning to ridge and split with water ingress. In the corner furthest from the fire, a ragged brown ring on the ceiling and drooping plaster malformations marked the site of the worst of that old winter leakage.

"There's something we need to speak to you about," Henry said. His brow wrinkled up in the way that it did – corrugating softly – when he was about to deliver a prepared statement. Though it looked now as if the announcement had died in his mouth.

"It's about the visitors," Edith said. "Your grandfather felt – "

"Don't speak for what I feel," Henry said, quietly. "We haven't spoken of this for a long time," he continued, glancing towards Mog, "so I thought I should have a word with you. I've been having the same word with everyone concerned." He came to a halt.

"Yes?" Mog said. "A word about?"

Henry clasped his hands together. "Edith. Please."

Edith's face was shadowed visibly with pity. She'd inched forward on her chair and was straining herself towards Henry, her hands open. "Shall I?" she asked him.

"Go ahead."

Edith turned to face Mog. Edith's square-jawed, with wide pronounced cheekbones and chin-length iron-grey hair parted in the middle, hair that sits firm in its shape as a sort of thatch. She has her father's mildly roman nose, its pronounced nostrils, and deep-set eyes that are an unusual grey-green. Today she was dressed in her usual uniform: baggy cotton trousers, white plimsolls, an artist's-style long canvas smock and long open cardigan (blue today; it's only the colours that change), and multiple ropes of pebble necklaces in amber and red.

"It's a small thing, really," she began.

"How can you call it a small thing?" Henry interjected.

"I've never been good with words," Edith said. "Your grandfather reads far too much into them."

"Precision's important: say what you mean," Henry told her.

"We simply – we need to remind you of something, and that's all it is. It's nothing terrible." She closed her eyes and turned to Henry. "Yes, Henry. I know. It's terrible. It *is* terrible. I'm sorry."

"What on earth is going on?" Mog went and sat on the arm of Edith's chair.

"It's about the visitors," Henry said. "We need to remind you that they don't know that Michael is … that is, they don't know that we and they might have different ideas about what happened to Michael."

"I see," Mog said. "I do see."

"I'd appreciate it very much if you could talk to your brothers and sister, before the weekend."

"Of course I will," Mog told him.

Walking to the shop the following morning on an errand for Edith, it was evident that Mog was thinking ahead to what Mrs Pym might ask and how she might reply, rehearsing under her breath as she went. Mrs Pym didn't like Mog but that wouldn't stop her probing; rather the reverse. Even the rhetorical question was dangerous.

How are you, Miss Salter?

Bloody but unbowed, Mrs Pym, thanks.

Well, obviously anything but that would do. She mustn't say that. The village is an entity, a cooperatively multi-celled creature, with ears and a mouth and a brain of sorts. Every appearance, every statement, is added by the bee mind to the hive. Bloody, she says. Unbowed. What's she going on about now?

"Miss Salter," Mrs Pym said. "And how are you?" As if Mog were an unpleasant item found at the back of the fridge. That kind of tone.

"Fine, thanks. Well, not really. Generally okay. Fine. Fine-ish."

Mrs Pym let her eyes linger a meaningful extra few seconds before responding.

"Righto then." Frank lack of interest on her face. Worse than that, a hint of something satirical. Fiddling with the buttons on her housecoat.

Alfred Pym came out from the storeroom when Mog had gone. He's a small man, a grey man, a man pared back to the eye, to the place where he's still living, a dark-pooled intelligence. He said, apparently sincerely, "I expect she was bringing our invitation to the ball."

Mog had told Johnnie all about the Pyms, on the way north for his first visit in the spring. She was unhappy then, already, but her unhappiness was taking the form – a last, humiliating phase – of trying at length and in vain to please him; worse, offering Peattie as a kind of collateral, reminding him of all she brings with her. She introduced Alf to Johnnie when they went in to get a newspaper, earning a nod but no spoken response. The morning queue for papers and milk and flat, floury rolls proceeds in silence if Alf's manning the till. Regulars might get a nod; favourites get their change put into their hand with a monotonous "cheerio". Mog's is put on the counter for her to pick up, under a flattened hand. He's already serving the person behind as she struggles to pick up the coins.

Joan isn't popular in the village either, though her mother is. When Edith lived here she made an effort to ask the right questions, and remembered the answers for next time. It all went onto Edith's mental roladex, where it settled into complex but seemingly effortless cross-referencing: birthdays, doctors, anniversaries, pregnancies, who's at university and who's in Iraq. It turned out that this news management was vital.

"Mrs Salter's a real lady," Mrs Pym has been heard to comment, emphasising the "real" as if it were known that there are different sorts. "Not like that Joan."

Mog had been sent to the village to get ham. Henry and Edith ate ham daily, in sandwiches for winter lunch and at suppertime in summer, with fresh-cut salad and garden potatoes buttered with mint. Henry was a traditional eater. His eyes boggled when he described the seafood pasta Euan presented to him when Edith was in hospital. Garlic. Things with tentacles and suckers. Edith would live happily on toast and soup and pieces of cheese eaten standing up at the kitchen worktop, trying to minimise eating, collapsing it into something merely necessary. She's beginning to learn to cook, now she lives with Ottilie, but in the old days her efforts were famously terrible. Blackened sausages pink in the middle (or worse, proving still to be frozen), chicken reduced to the texture of a woven textile. Guests were prompted to take to the kitchen themselves, or would ask, as innocently as possible, if Edith could make her famous broth. The broth was placed furthest west on the edible-inedible axis.

Mog came back in the afternoon to the wood, and sat on the tomb for almost two hours, her face blank, intent seemingly on some hidden blankness, busy with it behind an impregnable door, before moving herself to the stump, realigning herself with the faint grooves that day after day of sitting there, my sitting there, had established. She didn't say anything to me, nor read, nor write, and when the tea bell rang I went with her to the house. Going into the drawing room, I braced myself for the sensory onslaught. There was a lot to stay neutral about: 160 years of Salters and their dogs, their whiskies and fires, their teatimes and all the hidden residues of things talked about. It was another chilly, breezy summer's day, and the fireplace had logs laid across its vast slatted grate, the biggest of these a substantial chunk of tree, a piece of aromatic chestnut, black and charred with a soft lick of blue and orange stroking across it. The mantelpiece is a grand and beautifully carved thing, despite being chipped and cracked; Ursula, the year that Sebastian died, went through a period of throwing the hearth tools at it. Even on warm days it can be cold indoors: Peattie has that knack that some big houses do of insulating itself somehow against the natural warming of sunlight, and most summers the hearth is never left to go cold.

Henry, characteristically, was handling the teapot as if it were his first experience of tea pouring, making vaguely exploratory noises, sniffing at the milk in the jug. His whole life, he affected a tactical continuous ignorance of how domestic life manifested itself in the detail of things. Edith sat beside Vita on a worn velvet sofa, one that was beginning to show patches of its hessian backing. Ordinarily Vita sat in her own chair, an ugly but vital piece of kit with a tilting mechanism that allows for easier mounting and dismounting. It's one of the collection of seats that inhabit the rectangular bay of the window. She doesn't live at Peattie now, but the chair remains. Vita liked to sit as close to the window as she could and look out, like a dog waiting for its people to get home. When it was sunny the glass-magnified warmth was soporific, and Vita's snoring, done at a full chair-tilt, her little feet pointed up and mouth fallen open, was often a part of the teatime experience.

Ursula wasn't at tea that day, because Ottilie was there. Ottilie and Ursula hadn't spoken to one another since my disappearance. *Disappearance* continues to be the word used. The word *murder* has never been spoken in Edith's presence, not the word murder nor the word manslaughter. Edith is the wellspring of all family vocabulary, its dictionary, its thesaurus, its well-fount of abstract nouns. The 13 years between my disappearance and Edith's party were years of accommodation of the unthinkable, of acclimatisation to an emergency form of morality among the Salters, though it hadn't to be the morality of proximity. Ursula lived here, in one of the cottages in the grounds, and Ottilie lived at the coast, so the two of them came into each other's orbit only rarely and accidentally. Officially there was a policy – Ottilie's policy – of no contact. No gifts or cards change hands on birthdays or at Christmas, which was organised as a day of two halves, each mirroring the other, with two roasted geese, two puddings; these were occasions that involved a chair left empty. No one remarked on this. It was normal. It was their normality. In case of inadvertently coming within range of one another, Ursula had a facility for melting away. She's light-footed and fast, small and narrow: at 43, the size and build of a pubertal child.

Afterwards, Vita and Mog found themselves together in the drawing room. In old age, Edith's mother has shrunk to about four feet and ten inches high, straining to be upright despite the curve of her upper spine. With her round black eyes, a habit she has of cocking her head while listening, her bony nose thrust forward by time and her once elegant hands curled with arthritis, there's something truly bird-like about Vita. She's almost bald now, with a few dead wisps of hair, yellowish white: something she likes to illustrate by whisking off her wig in company, dewigging with a flourish and showing all eleven remaining teeth. She looks like a mummy in the British Museum. Though usually she's presentable in the immaculate black bob, a copy of the hairstyle of her youth. Her mother was Italian and she was the instigator of the olive complexion and near-black hair in the Salters, which skipped two generations and popped up again in Mog, and in me.

Edith brought fresh coffee in and then withdrew, as if withdrawing had been pre-arranged: instant coffee in old mugs that Joan grew exercised about and Edith wouldn't throw away.

"There are lovely porcelain ones at the back of the cupboard, Mother," Joan said, "which you never use because you only use and then wash and reuse the horrible ones at the front. I'm switching them around for you."

Edith's reaction to this kind of thing was always puzzlement. "But it doesn't matter, does it, Joan? Why does it matter?"

Vita had gestured with her cane that she wanted to talk, directing Mog towards the easy chairs positioned by the fire. Various dogs wandered in and helped themselves to the sofas, rising up on front legs and heaving themselves into position, settling with blissful sighs and grunts. Nobody bothered to move them off when Edith wasn't there.

"Now, about this Johnnie fellow," Vita began. "You are free of him?"

"Yes."

"Free so that he regards you as free."

"I'm free, but I can't speak for him, Vita."

"Why would you want to entertain even the notion of such a person?"

"It's hard to say."

Vita looked thoughtful.

"What is it that you are looking for in a husband?"

"A husband!"

"You're almost 30 years old."

"Yes, but – "

71

"Husband. So. What are you looking for?"

"Love; friendship," Mog offered uncertainly.

"Friendship's far more important. Marry your very best available friend. Someone plain-looking and grateful." She pondered a moment. "We'll need to search in our own circle. Not that we have much of a circle now. Don't you meet any young men here? I suppose not. It's not like it was. There doesn't seem to be any society now."

Mog looked as if she was about to speak, but didn't take it further. Vita knew as well as anyone that Peattie was as isolated from the world as it wished to be. Thickets of intangible social bramble and rose had surrounded the house for very many years.

"When Edith was young ... and even in your mother's day. Parties and boating and tennis and croquet. House parties all summer, which were of course entirely about sex."

"Surely not."

"Oh yes, oh my, yes. The late 20s. The early 30s. I'm not a Victorian, you know, despite appearing ancient. We post-war girls – post-Great War I mean – were highly progressive. We thought ourselves terribly daring and modern. Course, it was really only in the upper classes. The peasantry I'm not sure about; they've always been rather slyly liberated. But the middle class are a terribly conventional bunch."

"You can't say peasantry, Vita."

"I will probably die tonight in my sleep, so I can say what I please." Vita was enjoying herself now. "I hear there are some rather personable young men coming to this event. Sons and grandsons of friends and neighbours. People we haven't seen for so very long. Young men, too, some of them. I trust you'll make best use of the opportunity."

Mog looked doubtful and Vita pressed on. "It's such a pity that none of you children went to university. That's the place to catch husbands now, I'm told."

"Apparently."

"Your sister could have gone to Oxford."

"She didn't want to. She just wanted them to offer. To prove something to Dad."

"I do see that. But if she had gone, imagine all the delicious young men she would have brought home at the weekends, trailing after her unrequited. You could have had some of her cast-offs."

Mog made an indeterminate noise.

"Christian Grant," Vita said suddenly. "He's coming, you know. With his father."

Christian's kind horse face loomed up. His bearded chin and tombstone smile.

"So I hear."

"He's more your mother's age, but that's not necessarily a bad thing. I believe you had dinner once."

"We had dinner once. Not to be repeated."

"Terrible thing, poor Henrietta. Terribly sad. But he can't mourn for ever." Was that a wink? "It's vital not to choose too handsome a man," Vita continued. "He must above all have reverence for you, his wife, and be attentive to your desires and preferences. In my younger day, I was rather renowned for my good sense in the guidance of marriageable young girls."

"Yes. I've heard about that."

"And I devised a six-point test that I feel moved to share with you now."

"Thank you."

"Point one. Temperature. He should be sensitive to your comfort. Such as at an evening party. Have your shawl in a convenient location that prompts him to offer it to you."

"I expect this also applies to cardigans."

"Point two. The morning test. Engineer an early meeting, for hiking or suchlike at your own suggestion. Is he tolerant about the effort required?"

"Right."

"Point three." Vita faltered and then rallied. "Point three. Illness. How he treats you when you are under the wardrobe."

"The weather, you mean."

"The weather. What did I say?"

"The wardrobe."

"Good Lord. Under the wardrobe. Well. How he treats you when you are under the weather. The weak in body are highly attuned to a fake."

"Okay."

"All one can hope for is to hook up with a likely man. There are no certainties. If a potential husband satisfies on all six points, for the full period of the engagement, at least in my own experience I have found him to be sound."

"What's point four?"

"I don't know. Oh. Yes. Point four: Is he charming to the plainer and duller among your friends and family? Can he resist the temptation to satirise them in private company?"

"That's a good one."

"Five. I'm astonished that I can remember this. Imaginative gift giving. Very important. A man with a good heart knows the taste of his wife and goes to lengths to show his love."

"Right."

Vita's fingernails were pale blue and there were prominent blue veins in her hands, through which life pulsed hesitantly.

"Six. He must be a man of action and of the arts. A man who returns from the office and drinks and watches television may be a man to have for Christmas but is not a man to have for life."

"All good advice."

Vita reached into the faded carpet bag that she always carried with her and produced her notebook, which was leather covered, saddle brown, and finished with a leather tie.

"Would you be a darling and write them down for me? I rather fear that I have them in mind for the last time."

Mog found a pen on the mantel and began to write, noticing that the book was almost full, had only a few blank pages remaining, and that the rest, as she flicked forward from the middle, was closely written in a tidy black script.

"What about your Johnnie? How would he fare?"

"In the test you mean? Badly. Let's see. He's never been interested in the whereabouts of my cardigan. He's not a man who talks in the mornings unless he has to, and at any rate is at the office by eight. He's violently allergic to other people's illness and won't go into a hospital. Johnnie considers illness a character flaw. He gets points for charm, not that that counts for much; self-interest, alas. He doesn't give presents and hates to receive them."

"He sounds utterly appalling."

"Yes."

"He must have been divine in bed."

Chapter 5

Peattie House, the morning after I disappeared, presumed dead, was a deathly quiet house. It had a fresh kind of quiet about it, some new kind. It wasn't unlike a morning I remember when I was ten, my last winter resident at Peattie, when we woke to find that two feet of snow had fallen in the night and muffled the world of usual noises. The heat continued, the suffocating oven-like heat, falling in heat-blizzards into heat-drifts. People waded through the days. It was hot even at dawn, the pink sky giving way to deep and unblemished blueness, a promise that began to be ominous. The nights were brief, dipping into darkness, though Henry was to say later that this one, the one after I'd gone, passed with extraordinary slowness, each minute making its presence felt. He was at the loch to see the sun rise. Ottilie remained in my room all that day – my old Peattie room – where she had insisted on spending the night, insisting at just after 2am that Edith must leave, insisting on being alone, still woozy from the tranquiliser but insistent on this much. Edith returned to the drawing room to say that Ottilie wanted solitude, though it wasn't solitude that she wanted but communion; the freedom to be with the dead unhindered.

Edith was afraid, at 2am, that first night. She feared that Ottilie would kill herself, that that's what she meant by saying that she wanted to be with Michael. Edith had said to her through the closed door that God would forgive her whatever she was about to do; that God had physical experience of despair and of loss, that His experience of seeing Jesus die had made him human … and then she had apologised. She said that God would forgive, but she didn't think that she, Edith, would be able to. And she had apologised again.

"Is it my suicide you're talking about, Mother, or is it Michael's?" Ottilie had said, equally quietly, each of their faces pressed to the wood. "I'm going to bed now. I'm not going to kill myself. I'm going to take a pill and go to sleep and in the morning it isn't going to be true."

"Ottilie. Please."

"I'm not joking. It isn't going to be true. I'm not even exaggerating. I want you all to prepare for it and abide by it. No one is ever to say to me that my son is dead. He's missing and that is all."

She said this, though it was precisely the opposite of what she believed.

At 2.15 Edith returned to the drawing room and spoke to Mog and to Pip, to Vita and to Euan, none of whom knew where Henry had gone. She went to the bedroom and found that Henry wasn't there, or in his study, or anywhere in the house that she could think to look. Eventually she found him in the garden, standing in a glasshouse holding a bottle of malt close to his chest with both hands. He wouldn't go back inside with her. Henry's way of being drunk is unlike other people's. Some grow voluble, recklessly so. In alcohol, Edith says, Henry finds a more profound silence. In excess of alcohol she says that he finds something that's akin to

prayer. What Edith calls prayer, that's a therapeutic sort of self-hosted conversation, I think: one held in a deeper place in the brain than is usual, giving hidden parts of the self permission to speak.

Henry didn't respond to Edith's urgings to come inside, or to Euan's when Euan was sent to fetch him. Instead Henry went back to the loch and spent the night on the jetty, first of all sitting at its end with his legs hanging over the side, and then curled dozing in a foetal huddle, having hurled the empty bottle into the water. Henry had warned that nobody must follow him to the wood, that he would take it badly if he was pursued. He'd said this quite matter-of-factly to Euan as he left the glasshouse, and Euan had passed the message on. There didn't seem to be anything further that could be done, other than checking covertly on him, approaching at intervals out of sight from over the field. Euan and Edith took turns to do this in the night. The Salter-Cattos returned to the gatehouse, and Joan gathered her children around her on the sofa and hugged them untidily and spoke in a way in which nobody had heard her speak before, nor has encountered since, about the overriding importance of love.

"It was sincerely meant, I suppose," Pip conceded, talking recently to Mog about that evening, "but it occurred to me even then that really it was just another opportunity for dissing Ottilie."

Nobody got to bed until it was light, and Henry not at all. He woke on the jetty chilled and stiff-limbed and went into the house to get something to eat, scavenging for biscuits and finding a slice of pork pie left over from lunch the day before. The sight of the pie made him sob. It was pre-disaster, an innocent pie, a pie ignorant of the immediate future. An untidy, hastily cut mark had been left in it by another man, another Henry, and he had begun already to grieve for him. When he'd recovered his composure sufficiently he returned to the loch with another bottle. He was severely drunk and blundering along half blinded. It came to him that he could walk off the end of the jetty and die in a blur of uncaring, finding drowning a detached kind of end to things, fitting and in a perverse way almost funny. He could imagine laughing and gurgling his way into the deeps; he could feel the first tickle of hysteria even as he considered it. But when it came to it he didn't have the courage.

Nobody appeared for breakfast. Mrs Welsh, down in the village buying the morning groceries, told the Pyms and interested eavesdroppers that Michael had run away and that it was being taken very hard. People came together in the late afternoon, when hunger pangs could no longer be dismissed. Even then, the moral scruple that eating and drinking were too banal to admit to and failures of tact had to be overcome.

"I'm sorry but I have to eat something," Pip had said at last, apologies seeming necessary, opening the sliced bread packet and plugging in the toaster. He'd toasted the whole loaf, others' hunger being awakened by the smell. Then the freezer had been consulted for a second loaf, and they had begun to relish the group activity, to feel bolstered by it, by this joint experience of grief mediated by buttered bread. A second loaf was found and toasted, four pieces at a time, each slice eased away frozen from its neighbour, stiff and icy, before being inserted into the slot. The buttered toast was cut and plated and passed along the table where the family were gathered knee to knee. All but Ottilie and Ursula were there. Ottilie was sleeping, the doctor having been called out a second time, and Ursula was back at the cottage, at work on her knitting machine. Edith had been to her and found her quiet and calm and coping, insisting she was fine and needed to be left to think. The rest of the family sat together around the kitchen table, not discussing the situation. Toast was eaten and nothing relevant was said. It didn't need to be said. Toast said it for them. They didn't meet again that day.

The following morning, shock thawed and poured forth like meltwater. Many of the subsequent responses were raw and misdirected. Joan was angry with Alan, and Euan was peevish with Joan, and Pip was angry with everybody. Edith was angry with herself, and Mog was angry with me. Henry wasn't much seen. Henry chose absence. It was on the second day that Ottilie appeared, in a long dress with deep pockets, her hands thrust into them, her feet bare, her face blood-less, hair loose and breath terrible. She was given coffee with sugar, and professed not to be hungry, her hand shaking on the handle of the cup. It was ensured that somebody remained with her at all times, shadowing her as she wandered from hall to drawing room, from library to kitchen, in and out of Vita's sitting room, taking Vita's offered hand each time in passing, and up and down the stairs to my bedroom. She didn't want to make eye contact or to talk, but ate all the food delivered to her, and drank all the wine that Euan offered. Eventually, having attempted communication many times through the course of the day, the family left her alone and let her wander. After eating a bowl of Edith's broth, at just after seven in the evening, she retreated into my room and locked the door, saying that she was taking another pill and that she needed to sleep. That's when the discussions in the drawing room began in earnest.

Ursula was brought from the cottage, but it didn't do any good. She had come into the house in the afternoon, it turned out, and had stood in the hall, stock-still, watching Ottilie as she ascended the stairs, making slow progress and supporting herself on the bannister. Ottilie had sensed her there and had turned, and their eyes had met. Ursula stepped forward, urging her to stop and listen, but Ottilie had behaved as if she couldn't hear. She'd turned away and continued upward.

Ursula was brought and was silent. She ignored requests to go over things and pleas made no difference. The door had closed. Those around her saw this occur as a physical event: the closing of Ursula's mind against disaster. It resembled the lion face of dementia, the mask that she adopted, or which adopted her. It wasn't just that she didn't speak when spoken to, but that her eyes and mouth ceased to be indicators, the wiring disconnected to the place in her brain where the catastrophe had been walled in. All they could do was wait until she was ready.

"What are we going to do about Ursula?" Edith asked Henry in the early morning of day three, noting from the bedside clock that it wasn't yet 6am. She'd slept fitfully at best, disturbed by visions that took recent memory and elaborated it obscenely and violently. She had opened her eyes from sleep to see Henry sitting a few feet away, dressed and shaved, sitting on the dressing-table stool, neat in his usual khaki, though his feet were bare. He was folding and refolding an invitation to a neighbour's grandchild's christening, which had been slotted part-way into the mirror frame, where all such invitations were lodged before being declined, inevitably and with regret. Nobody expected the Salters to say yes to such things; they never did. The stiff card yielded only reluctantly to quartering and eighthing and refused point blank to be sixteenthed, at which point in the process it was opened and resmoothed on the dressing- table surface before the process began again.

Edith hauled herself up into a sitting position in bed, arranging the pillows vertically behind her. She was wearing a lemon-yellow bed jacket, which she'd worn crumpled in the night and sweltered in.

"What are we going to do about Ursula?" Such were Edith's first thoughts. "When will there be an end to it?"

"There won't," Henry said to the invitation. "There won't be an end to it."

"I'm worried she's not going to come back."

"Come back where?" He went to the window. "She's out there," he said. "Ursula. She's in the garden cutting flowers."

Edith came to stand beside him just as Henry turned, brushing past her, his eyes averted, leaving the room without saying anything further.

She imagined he'd gone down to her, but when Edith went into the garden there was only Ursula. The heat was growing stronger, and though it was so early it occurred to Edith as she crossed the gravel into the flower garden that she ought to have been wearing a hat. She shrugged off and then picked up the slippers, pointed leather slippers that Ottilie had brought back from North Africa. The grass was cool, softly spiky, the day already yellow and ripe.

Ursula, too, was out in her nightdress – a Victorian linen shift that fell to her ankle and was decorated with ruffles around the bodice. Her hair was fanned out over her shoulders, falling to her waist in its usual dull and tangled way: it seems never to reflect the light but to absorb it like dark matter. She was singing one of her songs, one of those that sound like folk songs and that she makes up as she's singing them. She didn't notice Edith approaching until Edith was almost upon her. Ursula was barefoot, her childish feet vividly pink at their edges, vividly pink-toed. She was standing in a still-dewy patch of lawn, in the cool and damp of the shadow cast by a vast escallonia bush. She had a pair of kitchen scissors and was snipping at holly-hocks, at yellow rudbeckia, at the stems of blue-grey allium globes, and gathering an armful of a plant that produced many tiny white flowers, the effect like a cloud. All of these went into the rush-woven trug that lay at her feet.

To Edith's surprise, Ursula turned to her smiling, an apparently uncompromised smile, eyes and mouth together.

"It's the most beautiful morning there ever was," she said. "So much beauty that it's almost painful, do you know what I mean? There isn't enough that can signify, that can be crammed in, that will feel like enough. Do you know what I mean?" Her smile continued beatific and untroubled.

Edith said nothing.

"I want to run and jump. Doesn't it make you want to run and jump? But first I've got flowers for you, for your room. When I'm finished, anyway. You've interrupted the surprise."

"Thank you," Edith said uncertainly.

"The thing is not to waste a day worrying about things that can't be changed. That's right, isn't it? That's what you said to me once, remember? When I was so sad about Sebastian."

She dropped the scissors into the trug, onto its neat pile of stalks and blooms, and came at her mother and hugged her hard. "I love you so much."

"And I you."

"And I know it seems wrong in a way, to be happy – because of Michael – but I can't help it, I'm happy. It's better to be happy than not happy. The day is so, so glorious and it's good to be alive. I think it might be a sort of survivor's euphoria. It could have been me. It wasn't me. And the day is a day God gave me. I think we should try to make it a good day if we can. Have a picnic? Shall we have a picnic in the meadow?"

"Ursula."

"We can't do that. I can see that. Sensitivity. I know. I haven't forgotten."

Abruptly she grasped at her belly with both arms, her face momentarily stricken. "I don't know why I said that, about the picnic."

"It's just that today is about Ottilie," Edith said to her softly. "Ottilie is in the house, in bed, still on the pills to calm her down, and sleeping. We can't go having any picnics."

Ursula handed the basket to her mother. "Here. I'll go home. I'll stay at home today. You can telephone me when Ottilie has gone. Though I have to talk to her first. I need to talk to her; will you tell her?"

"She doesn't want to see you, I'm afraid."

"But I have something very important to say."

"I'm sorry. But you're not going to be able to do that. Not for a while. Not until Ottilie is ready."

"She won't see me."

"No. Not yet. She may change her mind, though. I'll tell you when it comes."

"She thinks it's my fault."

"Ursula –"

"It wasn't my fault. He would have killed me. He was trying to kill me, pulling me into the water."

"I know."

"And the fact that it was the oar. I've thought about this, the last two days, over it and over it. And this is the truth: the fact that it was the oar – that's irrelevant. That was nothing to do with me. If it had been a book in my hand, I would have hit him with the book. It was what was there. You must see that. You must see."

"Yes. But Michael is dead."

"That was what killed him, getting hold of my leg. You do understand that. Does everybody understand? I need to talk to them. All of them. Ottilie needs to be there. Tell her. Tell her."

"Ottilie won't come."

"All the rest of them, then. That was what killed him, getting hold of my leg and pulling. Wanting me to go into the water. Wanting me to die."

"I'm sure he didn't."

"Wanting me to die."

"I realise that it seemed that way."

"It was suicide. They realise that, don't they? You realise that, don't you?"

"Ursula."

"No. I mean it. I mean it. It isn't a lie. It isn't even a stretch from the true thing."

"It wasn't suicide, sweetheart. It wasn't."

"It was. I swear to you and promise on my life. He did it to get me to hit him. He wanted me to hit him. He said to me. He wanted to die."

"He said – why would he say that?"

"When I told him. He said that he wanted to die. He said it was too much. He said his life was over. He said that he was going somewhere but now he'd have to go somewhere else. I thought at first that he meant that he wasn't going to Yorkshire, that he was going to Somerset."

"Somerset?"

"Yes. He was going to Yorkshire, to work in the forest there. But then he said that he needed a new family. He was trying to hurt my feelings. He was going to Alastair and Robert."

"I can't bear it."

"But I was wrong. It wasn't about Yorkshire and Somerset."

"I can't bear it."

"He meant that he wanted to die, that he was going to kill himself."

"But that doesn't mean –"

"For ever he said. Never ever to return ever."

"You're interpreting. Don't interpret."

"I'm not interpreting. I'm remembering."

"Sometimes it's the same thing."

"I'm not adding. I'm not elaborating."

"It's facts that we need. Interpretation isn't going to get us anywhere."

"He grabbed me, and he pulled. He wanted me to do it. He knew I wouldn't have a choice. I was standing with the oar, and I was angry. Why would Michael come and pull my leg and try to pull me into the loch? When I had the big wooden oar in my hands?"

Edith said nothing, though she looked as if her mind was busy.

"You see. You do see. He came back to the boat. He could have swum away. Alan was on the shore. He could have swum to Alan and talked to him about me and they would have decided what to do. He didn't. He swam to the boat and he pulled himself up and he took hold of my leg so tight – so tightly – look."

She hitched up her nightdress slightly and offered her right leg, Edith gasping at the sight of it, the yellow and purple hand-print faintly visible just below the knee, wrapped there like marbled paper. Ursula has always bruised easily.

"Why didn't you tell us this?"

"It's fine, it's just sore. It's okay." Ursula let her night-dress return to full length. "But you see. That's what Michael decided. And I didn't hit him hard enough to kill him. Nothing like. He raised his hand at the last second and his arm was bashed more than his head."

"Why haven't you said this before, about the arm? Why hasn't Alan?"

"Alan saw. It was Alan who saw. Michael was thrown off the boat, let go of the boat and sank. There was pain on his face. I'm sorry about his wrist. It might be broken and I'm sorry. He made a decision. He was knocked underneath and it was him who decided not to come up again."

Edith sank down onto the grass.

"I find it hard to believe," she said, though not in an accusing way.

"I can see that," Ursula said.

"That Michael would want that. That he would choose. Why a 19-year-old boy, so vigorous, so beautiful; I don't see. Not even that. Not even the secret, the father. It's not enough. It makes no sense to me." She glanced at Ursula. "It was about the father, wasn't it?"

Ursula joined her seated on the grass and said nothing. Edith looked up and saw Henry watching from the bedroom window. She raised her hand to him but he didn't react, just stared down as before.

"Michael's happy now, in heaven," Ursula said, putting her hand over her mother's.

"I wish I believed in heaven like you do," Edith told her.

"Don't say that. Don't. God is listening to you," Ursula said. "It's too dangerous to lie. It's the truth that matters. Being sorry is the main thing."

"Tell me about the secret," Edith said, and then, seeing Ursula's face, "I know, I know you shouldn't but this is an emergency and I need to know. An emergency's different."

Ursula looked blankly back.

"Not the secret itself. But I need some clue. You can give me a clue. I need that, Ursula. It's about his father, isn't it?"

Ursula closed her eyes. Something she still does when she wants the situation to go away.

"Can't you just. Ursula, please. I'm so. So." Edith began to cry, quite suddenly, and Ursula crawled to her on all fours and nestled, her head resting on her mother's leg, a signal that she wanted her hair played with. Edith patted her head softly as she sobbed.

"I'm so sorry, I'm so so sorry," Ursula told her, and then, "Don't cry, Mummy. Don't cry. It's too lovely a day. Look at the day. It's all over. It's over. Michael chose and he's gone and it's over. Michael's in heaven with God and he doesn't want to see you crying over him."

"I wish I was so sure."

"If we know there is heaven, how can we be sad about death?" Ursula asked her. "After a little while of being sad – that's normal. But then, think about it: heaven! Remember? That's what you said to me, after Sebastian died."

"Yes."

"I remember it, every word."

"I know you do."

Something about Edith's tone made Ursula stare at her. "You weren't lying to me, were you?"

"Of course not," Edith said. "I told you. I will never lie to you."

"Yes."

"I told you when Sebastian died. We will always tell the truth to one another, no matter what."

Ursula raised herself and crawled away, and, remaining on all fours, splayed her fingers supportively on the grass, looking intently down at it. "So detailed a little world," she said. "How far do you think the suffering goes?"

Edith put her hands over her eyes.

"Can't we all just decide to be happy?" Ursula picked a daisy and lay down flat on her back and twirled it in her fingers, looking at the sun shining through and around it. "Those of us who can choose."

"Michael's dead," Edith said. "You have to allow for people to be sad. And for people to be angry. They're going to be angry."

"They're going to be angry with the wrong person, though. The time to cry about Michael was before he died."

"Ursula, really."

"I mean it. Ottilie had the power in the question. It wasn't me that had the power. I told him something she should have told him a long time ago, when asking and asking was making him so unhappy and ill. Ottilie: she's the one you need to talk to. It's her secret and I have no right to share it."

"You shared it with Michael."

"I shouldn't have. But otherwise, he would never have known. Nobody ever thought he should know and that was a worse wrong thing."

"You told him about Alan. Alan, wasn't it? The secret. Alan Dixon." Edith spoke the name with care, watching for a reaction. None was evident. Ursula began making a daisy chain.

"It was wrong but I was angry," she said to the chain, bringing her face close and squinting as she tried to get one

88

small hairy stalk into a slit in another. "It was right but at the wrong time. I thought he'd be glad. I thought he'd rush off and find him and it would all be alright in the end. What I thought was that it was only the lie that was stopping it being alright."

She looked at Edith, then returned to the chain. "I can see what's going to happen now."

"What's going to happen?"

"Me, I'll be the one blamed. Ottilie, she'll be the one sanctified. Me, I'll be the one demonised. Ottilie will be St Ottilie of the Cross."

"Ursula, that's cruel of you. Resist the urge to be cruel."

"It's what happens when people are beautiful."

"Nonsense."

"I can see what's going to happen now," she said again, and then, scarcely letting a beat fall, "Are you really going to leave him down there?"

They were interrupted by Henry, who was striding towards them out of the yellow glare and across the sun-faded grass, past sun-faded shrubs, the greenish-grey stone of the flower garden wall rendered near colourless. Henry's feet remained unshod and unsocked. They were surprisingly youthful feet, almost shockingly youthful, as if from a different generation from his hands.

"Are you? Are you really going to leave him down there?" Ursula asked him, raising her hand to shield her eyes from the light. "Michael. In the loch. Isn't that a crime?"

Henry said, "Ursula, go to the cottage and dress, and then come back and see me in the study, please. Directly to the study." Then he turned and walked away.

～

The study is a lovely old room, positioned at the back of the hall. More or less untouched for over a hundred years, it retains its original tartan wallpaper and clashing plaid chairs, its leather globe on a stand, its 19th-century photographs of other Salters, busy upholding the empire. It's a big room, with sofas and seats, but dominated by the vast, heavy desk, which is made of thick oak, and the captain's chair that sits behind it. When Ursula got to the study an hour or so later, having taken her time dressing, sitting on her bed between items, she found that it wasn't just her father but a group of people that awaited her. They were looking towards Henry: Joan and Euan and Vita, turned away from her; Mog, red-eyed in a dowdy floral dress; Pip, shock-haired in torn jeans; Edith, in the same clothes as yesterday, but her usual clash of heavy beads missing.

Henry had his back to them. He was standing on a chair trying to force the upper half of the window sash down, saying that he couldn't recall ever opening it before and that it seemed to be painted shut, the words drying in his mouth as he spoke, making me think of something dead and dried to a husk on a beach. An ex-bird, eyeless. But it wasn't that. When he turned to them, his face was almost too painful to look at, the courage overlaying it only transparently.

Henry saw Ursula first. She was standing in the doorway: it was towards Ursula that Henry's torment and courage were directed.

"It's like a greenhouse in here," Ursula said. "Why don't we go outside?"

"Because we can't risk Ottilie seeing us," Joan told her, looking at Edith and widening her eyes.

"You should know that I've told them what you said to me earlier," Edith said to Ursula, her face and voice fervent, leaning forward and extending her hands. "I've just been telling them, so they know where you stand. And we all have sympathy for you."

There were murmurs that could have been dissent.

"Edith –" Henry began.

Edith raised her voice. "Anyone here who doesn't have sympathy for Ursula, please speak up now."

No one said anything but the space between them all was bisected again and again by silent eye-to-eye exchanges.

"Look," Edith said, getting to her feet. "This is painful. This is painful and in a way absurd. But decisions have to be made and they have to be made now, before anything is said or done that will ..." The sentence petered out. "This is how this is going to have to be. Henry and I have discussed it. Protecting Ursula is our priority. About the dead we can do nothing."

"Dad," Joan said in a warning voice.

"I don't want to talk to you now, Joan," Henry told her. "I'm too tired for arguments. There's nothing to discuss." She ignored him and began to speak. "Quiet!" he said. "I've told you already. Go away and think about it, and at three o'clock I want you back here, all of you, with your decision. And that's absolutely all I have to say for now."

Joan lingered as the rest filed out. Henry pre-empted her.

"I've told you. I'm not going to debate it individually with people. This has got to be a family decision. A family process of deciding."

"But you've already decided for us."

"That's what we need to talk about. At three."

"Just one point. I have a point to make that I want you to think about between now and then."

Henry looked at his watch. "Which is?"

"Murder will out."

"That's a terrible thing to say. You shock me. You appal me."

"I appal you?"

"I'm not going to discuss this now."

"But he'll be found. What do you think – that he'll stay neatly tucked away at the bottom of the loch, and we can

91

all pretend he isn't there and resume our lives? What kind of madness is this?"

"I'm not going to discuss it with you. But you're wrong about – if you think that the remains ..." His voice began to break.

"Dad. Please."

"I don't think even the police divers would find him. Not if they spent days. What you have to understand is that the water is too cold. It takes people and it doesn't give them back." He saw that her face was sceptical. "It's happened before, you know. Michael isn't the first."

"What do you mean?"

"In the loch. People have gone missing there."

"I know that, Dad. I've been here all my life."

"Not because of any moronic stories about monsters and evil spirits, but just because it's dangerous. You must know about James."

"Jock's brother."

Mog brought it up with Henry later, the story of Jock's brother on the loch.

"They never found him?"

"They looked and they looked. And there have been others. Over the years. You know there have. People get out of their depth, get cramp, whatever it is. They ignore the sign."

There's a danger sign planted in the beach.

"We ignore the sign all the time," Mog told him.

"There was another one when you were younger. Similar case. All over the papers. Someone older than you at your school. Swimming at night. A dare. You might remember."

"I don't remember."

"I think you were quite young."

Henry said to me once that Peattie is like a ravine full of water. Imagine falling, falling off the edge of the boat down and down into that ravine, the water incidental to your fall, proving merely to be a cushioned form of slow and smothering gravity.

~

At their three o'clock meeting in the study, the family had already arrived at a quiet, hopeless unanimity.

"You see – if there was any chance at all of their finding him ..." Henry didn't finish the thought.

"But that isn't really the reason," Edith clarified.

"Each of us must come to our own position," Henry said. "It's too much to ask of us that we think all alike. But we can agree on what it is we must do, and that's something different." Everyone was sent away again until seven.

"Hear me out," Joan said at the evening meeting. "What if we were to pick up the phone right now, and tell the police. I'm just thinking aloud. But we have to discuss it at least."

Euan cut her off. "Not possible."

"They'd put her in prison," Edith said.

"No, they wouldn't," Joan asserted. "Of course they wouldn't."

"You have a romantic idea of justice," Euan snapped at her.

"They'd put her in an institution." Edith's eyes swam with tears. "Is that what we want?"

"This is what we will do," Henry told them all. "We will consecrate the place where he was lost, in our own family way. We will regard it as a burial at sea. As if it were a burial at sea."

The idea of a ceremony was a lovely one, but nothing like it was put into action – not on the water, at least, because the practicalities came up against the problem of ensuring privacy, and the thing was dropped. The wood was a different matter. Memorial activities in Sanctuary

Wood would always be assumed to be to do with the great uncle.

"Dad," Joan said. She looked around at the others. "Is it just me? Dad, this is all quite bizarre. You're not thinking straight. You won't be able to make this work." Nobody else spoke. "How can we make them see?" she said, but nobody answered her. "What are we saying – that we're prepared to keep this quiet for the rest of our lives? It's too much, Dad. It's insane."

"This isn't a matter of debate," Henry said, blowing his nose. "This – the way we have explained it to you – this is our decision. This is what we are going to do. And I'm afraid that anyone who can't agree to honour our wishes had better find somewhere else to live."

"I need to talk to you," Joan persisted. "This isn't the end of this discussion."

"Yes Joan, it is" Henry told her.

Chapter 6

After she'd written Vita's six-point test for husbands in
the journal, Mog came to the wood, her feet on the
grit of the path making the only noise in the absolute stillness. She sat for a long time on the beach with a notebook
in her lap, not writing anything but the date.

Finally she spoke. "Here's the thing," she said to me.

Then nothing. Then, "All I want is a light heart. When
will it get light again? It's been so long. Ten of those years
I've spent living with Pip. A ridiculous length of time to be
temporary."

I waited. People talk differently to me than they do to
anyone else. They speak to me with unfiltered sincerity,
because really they think they're just talking aloud to
themselves. Sometimes I feel like a confessional priest, and
sometimes like God.

"Everything is shrouded in the same heaviness now,"
Mog went on. "I don't know how I managed it, when I
was young, when everything was so difficult at home; the
bickering, trying to outdo each other with their meanness.
But it seemed easy."

She scuffed at the soil, the old leaves, with her shoe.

"Lately, so heavy, Michael. So heavy, so weighed down. Like I'm physically carrying something around. So weighed down I can feel it against my ribs, pushing against the top of my stomach. You'll laugh at this: I thought I had a tumour. I went to the doctor. Had an ultrasound. Nothing there. Marked as a hysteric in the notes. Big red emphatic H."

"Hypochondriac," I said to her.

"I can't get free of it. Can't see how to get free of it. No longer believe it's possible to get free of it. I was sent to a psychotherapist. She was repellently sympathetic. Said the heaviness was a reservoir of tears. I should have asked to see her qualifications at that point. I'm too polite. That, I blame my parents for. I sat there for another 45 minutes, trying to come up with the answers she wanted, aware I was failing the test. I couldn't talk back to her in her own language. It turned out the session was almost all about her, reassuring herself of her own expertise."

She took some chocolate out of her bag and snapped off a line and ate it. "My mother wonders why I don't eat at the gatehouse. Simple: because chocolate has to be explained. Chocolate's noted and logged." She ate another line. "I don't know how I feel about leaving Edinburgh. I don't seem to feel anything. This is one of the problems, one of the other problems. Not feeling things. The psychotherapist said I had to start taking responsibility for making myself happy. I didn't go back. But I tried the homework: making an effort with Angelica's friends at the drinks party they had for her birthday. Impossible. Humiliating, actually. I was gregarious and rabbited on and asked questions and they couldn't have cared less."

Poor Mog.

"The problem is that I don't really like people. Not really. Not beyond the people here. I don't know why that is. But it means I'm on my own a lot. I spend a lot of time reading, now; you'd be amazed. Angelica wasn't impressed.

96

She thinks reading's something you do on holiday; certainly not something you do when the dishwasher hasn't been emptied. Turns out she's pretty much my mother's deputy and clone. My mother's thrilled about Angelica, and you can see it crossing his mind sometimes, crossing Pip's mind; dawning that this might not be a good sign." She laughed, making that characteristic noise afterwards, the long "hmmm" that's almost laughing, subsiding into a long note. "And I've realised something about people who read. People who read: it's not quietness. It's not passivity. They're having conversations with the writer, with the characters, are part living in that other situation. It's like a judgment on everyone they know, that they go there, into the quiet world looking for friendship. That's how it's been for me, at least. I said a lot more than that – to the therapist. Some of it was stuff of yours. I plagiarised a bit. Adolescent and simplistic, that's what she thought. It's the kind of thing we thought we knew when we were 19. Well, you were 19. I was younger. I've never found anybody else who talks to me the way we spoke to one another."

Most of our interactions with other people are rehearsed and cowardly. That's the kind of thing it says in the notebooks. It worries me, that Mog seems still to be living in the world of that thinking. I was very sure of myself then, reading philosophy and interested in the failings of language, the disconnect from thoughts, (I used the word *disconnect* a lot), the way we absorb the limitations of language into ourselves, tipping complex things into a crude vocabulary like pigs into sausages. It helped explain things to me, the life language delivers up to us. We'd stretch out together on the linen room shelf, Mog's head in the crook of my arm and the rain beating down. We lie to ourselves, thinking the embryo life we've had frozen and stored will stay viable until we're ready for it. It won't, and in any case we're never ready. It's perhaps the most frustrating thing of all: not being able to tell Mog that there's hope, that there's every kind of compensation imaginable in love, in partnership in life. It would take some explaining, how it is that I know that; what my life has been since I left Peattie. Ironic, isn't it, in the circumstances, that I'm the one who's moved on.

"Johnnie left a message on Pip's answerphone," Mog said, "the day before I came home. He said he was worried for me. If Johnnie says he's worried for you, you're in trouble. His being worried is a reprimand. He said that I was something hollowed out: that was the phrase he used, hollowed out. Pip and Angelica heard it first. So humiliating. That I wasn't really a person and that I needed help. The horrible thing was that I believed him. I did. It rang true to me. And then I had this weird thought. I thought, I'm like a piece of furniture that's had dust cloths laid over it, more and more of them until the edges and outlines are blurred. I don't know why I thought of that, of furniture and dustcloths. Peattie, I suppose, from way back, from when I was little. Seeing Edith closing up rooms. Johnnie said he wanted to have one conversation: just one last conversation, and that I owed him that much. I thought, *Well damn you to hell, I don't owe you anything*. After that, the truth is that I hid. There was actual literal hiding. I barely went out. I'll do almost anything to avoid confrontation. Even if I'm plainly in the right. Being in the right makes it worse. If I'm in the right I make sure to put myself in the wrong at the first opportunity. I tell you, Michael, it's just an absolute disaster, my trying to have relationships with anyone outside this wall."

❧

I knew about the depression. I saw her living in Edinburgh, just occasionally in fleeting visits, the window opening and closing. I saw her napping on Pip's sofa with a novel on her face. I saw Angelica come home from the office and rip the book away from her like a plaster from a scabby knee.

"Sleeping again; sleeping your life away," she'd said, proceeding into the kitchen and tutting over the sub-pristine state of things. Angelica thought she needed a kick up the jacksie. Pip defended her; she'd been unwell.

"Feeling sorry for herself, you mean," Angelica said. They were in the kitchen together while Mog dozed on. "You need to stop pandering to her. Stop going to the bookshop for her. Stop making her eggs on toast."

Later, sitting with Angelica watching the news while Pip was cooking up pasta, whizzing up pesto in the mixer, the smell like the meadow when it's just been cut, herbs mixed into the warm grass, Mog announced that she was leaving Edinburgh, that she'd decided against going back to the office on Monday after all. She said that she was going home. Angelica hadn't said anything, just left the room, still holding the TV remote. A few minutes later Pip had come in and crouched beside her.

"You're sure about this? We'll miss you."

"I'm sure about it." He got up to go. "Pip?"

"Yes?"

"How do you do it?"

"Do what?"

"This. All this. How do you keep going?"

"I don't understand you."

"It doesn't matter."

In fact she had been sure for months, since long before the break-up with Johnnie. The world – and Edinburgh was as little and as much *the world* as anywhere else – seemed opaque to her, seemed closed. At first she'd blamed it on youth, inexperience, newness: her mother had concurred with this. But nothing developed. Nothing changed. It was hard to get a job, she said, and then when you did it just went on and on: a life of working and then recovering from and anticipating work. Pip made work the centre not only of his life but also of his identity and seemed to be thriving. Was she missing something? A social life, Joan insisted, would make everything fall into place. Mog knew people, but knew, also, that she was never other than peripheral to these other people's lives; this was unsentimentally just the fact of the matter. No social circle drew itself around her and embraced her into itself, breaking hands to link with hers and admit her, and nor did it seem likely to. She went to the pub on Fridays with workmates. On Saturdays she went shopping – even if only for socks or toiletries, it got her out of the flat – and then to the cinema. She went to the Botanic Gardens in all weathers on Sundays and sometimes met people she knew there (awkwardly swapping dull news, as she put it), but sometimes she didn't, sitting alone on the café terrace, self-conscious among the chattering groups, watching small children frolic and shout on the lawn. That was her week. That, it seemed certain, would continue to be her week, until weeks ran unchecked into decades.

The irony was that Euan and Joan had encouraged her so much and so long to be a person of achievement, of *substance* – that was Euan's word. It had started early. "This year, now that you're 12, you need to be thinking hard about your future," her father had said. "If it's writing you want, you should be writing and not talking about being a writer. Talking's nothing and nowhere. Write. Get submitting. There's no reason why it shouldn't be you. I have pretty good contacts."

Joan had joined in, bright-eyed. "There's a girl of 14 who's just published a novel."

The Christmas presents Joan bought for her offspring tended to the practical. For Mog there were books in French, to help with her language difficulty, and clothes a size too small as an incentive. *I'm a project*, Mog confided to her diary, *and I'm not going terribly well.*

❧

When she went back to the house it was her mother she saw first.

"What on earth's wrong with you?" Joan asked her.

"Nothing. Everything's fine. Why?"

"You look like you're about to burst into tears."

"I'm fine. Just a bit of a headache."

"Well, take some pills and get back down here. I need a hand." She frowned at Mog as if reading faraway print on a sign. "Where have you been?"

"Just at the wood."

"Ah."

"Ah what?"

"Talking to Michael. Spilling out all your deeply under-privileged woes."

"I've never said I'm under-privileged. Where do you get that from?"

"Emotionally so, I imagine. You fit with the coming generation. Expect their parents to be their staff and to behave only as permitted, for their own well-being. There was a piece on the radio. Modern children think parents who are also humans with human vices are guilty of abuse."

"Right. That's me exactly. Spot on again. What do you need a hand with?"

"He isn't there, you know."

"Come again?"

"Michael. He isn't there."

"Okay."

"What is it with this family? Constantly wallowing. Terrible things happen to people. Boo hoo. Shocking and tragic. But there comes a point when grief becomes a sort of disorder."

"Just tell me what you want a hand with."

"You see. You see. Exactly. Exactly."

"I'm not wallowing. I'm trying to get on with things. Isn't that what you want? But you know, Mother, since you brought it up, you haven't ever seemed overly dynamic to me."

"My god, you have a lot to learn." Joan opened her handbag and took out her Filofax. "Sit down." She flicked through and sat opposite Mog at the kitchen table. "There's a ridiculous amount to do. If only people had made an effort, the party could have been tremendous. It could have been important to us. You children might have been invited back to things. But it's the same old problem. It's not appropriate to be happy, or to make an effort or to have things look nice. It's morally far preferable to have pony shit on the lawn and peacock droppings in the hall."

"What?"

"There used to be. After Seb died. It was emblematic, you see. Being not clean. My sister turning all Bohemian, which as we know is just another word for dirty. The place is going to rack and ruin. Mrs Welsh is worse than useless."

"That's unfair."

"She doesn't get into the corners, and nobody cares. Slut's lace under the tables."

"Slut's lace?"

"Dog hair and dust, gathered into hairy piles. Chairs on the point of collapse. Chipped paintwork. Nobody cares. Cobwebs on every window. The windows! What am I supposed to do about them, by Saturday? There are dead flies inside the glazing. I can't do it all on my own. I can't."

"It doesn't matter. It's one evening. People will drink and talk and not notice any of it. They're not going to be running their fingers along the mantelpieces."

"You're just as bad as Edith. The two of you. Don't think I haven't seen you. Having confidential chats."

"You're objecting to my talking to my grandmother."

"It's a discourtesy."

"What? What?"

"You know exactly what I mean."

"I've had enough of this." Mog left the room, Joan calling after her, "Oh that's right, that's the thing you always do: just run away from things instead of facing up to them."

~

Out of the frying pan and into the fire. Euan was in the drawing room, at the card table by the window, a pile of essays and a pen sitting in front of him. He was on the phone and had his back to her. She heard him say into his mobile, "I came over here to get away from her and lo and behold, she had done the same." Mog stood stock-still. If he concentrated on the changed configuration of shapes and colours reflected back by old glass, her father would realise she was standing at the door. She backed out of the room and returned down the corridor.

Edith was in the hall going through the mail, which lay unopened for days sometimes, accruing in the clay rack Ottilie had made for her mother at school, its ochre-yellow glaze dotted with acorns and oak leaves. Mog came up behind Edith on stockinged feet, and saw that what she held in her hand was a brochure for a residential home. It was dense and fat and glossy, saturated with design and ink and money. Young adults smiled out of the cover illustrations. Edith turned to find Mog standing behind her.

"Mog! What are you doing creeping about?"

"I didn't mean to intrude, sorry."

Edith and Mog both looked at the brochure, still in Edith's hand.

"It's because I'm thinking about Ursula."

"Ursula?"

"Henry and I are both getting old. We need to think about what happens to Ursula when we're gone. We can't

103

expect any of you children to take on her care. She doesn't need care. That's not the word. Her supervision. It wouldn't be fair."

"I think you might have trouble convincing Ursula to move."

"It's more for you children's sakes. I'll leave it in the office drawer with the wills."

"You are feeling alright?"

"Perfectly. But I've had a reminder lately, being so ill, that we're none of us immortal."

"I thought you believed we were."

"It's good to see you. It's been so long. I was beginning to think something was amiss. Putting us off and off."

"I wasn't well. Just a virus that wouldn't go away. And busy at work, and the weeks passed. I kept meaning to come and then it didn't happen."

Edith hugged her, lingering over it, running one hand over her hair and down her back, and rubbing at the place between her shoulder blades. "You don't have to explain. Just very glad to see you."

⁓

The last time Mog had been to Peattie was almost two months before. She'd volunteered to relinquish her bedroom at Pip's flat for a long weekend so that Joan could have it. Joan had been hinting for over a year that she'd love a weekend visit, and finally Angelica had invited her.

Euan and Joan are pleased unanimously with Pip. Pip they agree about. Jet they agree partly about, united in seeing that he's a disaster, though Euan considers him lost, has written him off and has told him so, flat calmly, without the opinion seeming to affect him at all, like dispensing with a car that hadn't been worth much to start with. Joan still thinks that Jet will change, that his revelation and ambition are on their way to him. All four of her children, she says, will turn out to be exceptional in some way or other, though one or two of them might mature late and take their time.

Even Joan had to concede that the Edinburgh visit hadn't been a great success. She didn't know enough people in town and Pip worked long hours at the bank. Angelica seemed to expect her to have things to do, her own friends to see, arrangements of her own. She had been surprised to get home to the flat in the evening and find Joan there, watching television. Her surprise had seemed exaggerated. She'd given the unmistakable impression that she'd really rather be alone.

Joan had picked up on this, and then Angelica saw that she had, and became immediately more solicitous. "I hope you've helped yourself to coffee, cake, lunch."

"No, but I've been fine," Joan told her, returning to the newspaper, feeling satisfied that she'd managed in some part to replicate Angelica's don't-fuss approach, her shrinking from elaboration, which Joan, quick to absorb and adapt, was fast making her own.

When Pip came home, his shirt sleeves turned up, bringing in a photocopier scent and the smell of fabric conditioner mixed with sweat, and had been into the kitchen to see Angelica, he'd come and sat by his mother bearing two gins, and had mentioned, with studied casualness, Joan's lack of initiative with the kettle.

"I don't like to poke about in other people's cupboards," Joan told him.

"Other people? I'm hardly that."

Pip saw at once that his mother's refusal to relax and treat the flat as a home from home was a punishment. She was punishing him for his being too busy to welcome her properly (though he had warned her of this on the phone beforehand), for not making more time to ensure she was happy.

They'd taken her to a drinks party in a flat across the road. Joan stood at the window of this other flat and pointed out her son's equally grand accommodation, just visible through the trees: there was a private garden, accessible only by key, in the centre of the square, which wasn't a square at all, in fact, but rounded – two handsome, semi-circular stone terraces known collectively as a circus. She'd taken up position at the window, intercepting others there. Going into the kitchen for another drink, she'd found three women standing together, work colleagues, their briefcases piled on a chair. They were kind enough to welcome her and agreed good-humouredly to change the subject from that of the bank and banking's travails. One of them was having an affair, it transpired. The lover and the husband were both there, in the other room.

"How long has this been going on?" Joan asked, fascinated.

"Two years."

"How do you manage it, keeping it secret?"

"Actually it's easy. I'm not having a problem with it."

"I have a secret," Joan told her. "One I've had to keep for over a decade. I'm finding it almost impossible. It gets worse as time passes, not better: be warned."

"Thanks, but I'll be fine," the woman said.

"You say that now."

"That's right. I do."

"So what kind of secret?" one of the other women asked.

"Well, you know, if I told you that …"

"Give us a hint."

"It's something that – how do I put this? – something that makes you sit up in bed in your sleep and open your eyes and fight to breathe."

"Bloody hell."

"You're a callgirl," the affair woman chipped in, gesturing with her drink and delighted. "No, wait, I've got it. You do those older woman sex chat lines."

Everybody had laughed, even Joan. Then she said, "Actually, that's not the secret. The secret is that I dislike my husband."

Pip came into her field of vision from the left. She could tell by his face that he'd heard. Angelica took her elbow and steered her away. They'd gone out of the room and out of the front door, straight down the stairs without pause, and into the car. Nobody spoke on the way to the Private View, and immediately they got there Joan was forcibly seated, shoulders pressed gently down, into the soft deep welcome of an armchair, placed there by Angelica and told not to move, a soda water with lemon slices put into her hand, a black coffee placed on the side table. She'd fallen asleep and had woken with her head thrown back against the wall, mouth ajar and a crick in her neck. The crush had diminished into a last lingering half-dozen, Pip and Angelica among them, coats over their arms, the dark sculpted voids of the exhibit rising behind.

On the final evening they went out to dinner, to a restaurant close to the castle, one in a sort of dungeon, with gothic accoutrements and many drippy candelabras. Another threesome awaited them there, and spotted them as they arrived. Hands waved from out of the gloom.

"Welcome, Salter party – over here!" an American voice rang out from within the throng and the hum, the polished silver glinting, the tablecloths starched and white. There was a seductive smell of hot bread and shellfish and beef, and Joan realised that she was starving. She'd missed lunch, having insisted to Pip that she wasn't hungry.

Their friends Siobhan and Jerry had brought Jerry's mother Amelia, a tall Boston widow with a severe short haircut and lipstick that was the darkest sort of red. Jerry and Pip worked together. Amelia was quite open about her dislike of Jerry's corporate life.

"I mean to say, a bank's the last thing we'd have wished on them, isn't it?" she'd said, turning confidentially towards Joan.

Amelia seemed to be treated with affectionate respect by her son, and yet she was constantly picking fault with him.

"God, you're so full of horseshit," she'd said, laughing roaringly.

"I believe it's genetic," Jerry parried back. He'd stretched out his hand and placed it over his mother's and she'd taken it in hers.

In the car on the way home, Pip had hoped aloud that Joan had liked Amelia.

"She's very nice, but she's one of those smothering mothers," Joan told him.

"I wouldn't say that. They're just very close since his father died."

"I found it creepy," Joan said. "All that touchy stuff, the hand holding."

≈

After dinner Mog went into the garden. The light was just beginning to fail. In summer, the long evenings bring with them an immensely gradual greying and softening. She went across the grass, the swallows dipping and swooping. The front lawn had grown long, the dandelions and buttercups shining their yellow lights, and the side lawn, cut more recently, was white with tiny daisies like stars. She went down the slope into the trees and, strolling, followed the inner perimeter of the wall, running her hand from time to time along its top surface, the stone rough with colonies of lichen and yellow fungus. She went past the back of the folly and over the stile, and stood leaning against the wall a little while. When she began to move again it was with a new purposefulness. She went to the end of the field, where the red cows under the cypresses stared and flicked their tails, over the second stile and into the garden, past the pond and onto the drive, crunching across the gravel, then up the steps to the terrace. Into the house, across the hall, down the back stairs and into the yard she went, past the greenhouses and onto the loch path.

There was a paperback in her jacket pocket, one of my books, taken from my room, a Rilke *Selected Letters* that I'd written all over, whose margins were almost obliterated by jottings, rubbings-out, question marks, exclamations. There's a lot of someone left residually in their annotations. The book had been rolled laterally and had to be rolled the other way to even it out. It was a cloudy evening and just beginning to get dark; it proved too dark to read, and so she stood looking out at the water.

"I don't seem to be able to stay away, Michael," she said aloud. "I don't know why I feel so compelled. It's like checking your inbox when you've sent an important email, waiting for the answer, checking and checking."

"He isn't ever going to reply, you know," a voice said, Ursula's voice, startling Mog, who dropped the book. She turned to see her aunt standing a few feet away. "Ursula, Jesus, where did you spring from?"

"Don't blaspheme. I've been here a while. I was sitting on the tomb when you got here. I was waiting to see if you'd notice me but it was obvious you weren't going to and I got bored."

"How are you?"

"I wish people wouldn't ask that question. They never really want to know the answer."

"I'll leave you to it." It's understood among the family that the person who gets to the wood first has precedence. Most of them prefer to be here alone.

"I don't subscribe to this idea, that Michael's listening to us, the old Michael," Ursula told her. "I think it's safe to talk."

"It's not that."

"There's a part of Michael that's here, but he's no longer a person. Conversations amongst ourselves don't have the same significance. Nor does being naked or weeing. I've asked about the toilet because it bothered me. Once people pass, these things look different to them."

"Pass?"

"Die. Once they die. You would say die, I imagine, but it's the wrong word. Dying means ending and people don't end. There's a part of Michael that's still here but it isn't the Michael you knew. It's the same for David, Great Uncle David, and Sebastian also."

"Sebastian's here?"

"Of course. In a sense. But not the same one. The consciousness has gone to heaven, cleaned of its nostalgia and its ties to us."

No, Ursula. I am here with you. Time passes here just as anywhere, and I see the seasons come and go in the fields; I'm there when the heating's turned off for summer and the rugs are hauled onto the lawn for beating; I see the Christmas trees being dragged in from the hill. I was only sorry that I couldn't produce by a special effort all the leaves cascading out of the willow trees, falling like holy confetti around the two of them. Consciousness is everything that remains of me here, and I'm confident this isn't heaven. If we can agree that death is what makes us human: the knowledge of it, the life that we live unaware of anticipating it – and I think that we must – then it follows that I continue to be human, because even now I'm afraid that it's coming.

Chapter 7

While Mog was talking to Ursula, Joan was sitting on her bed, the diary opened beside her, its pages full of ticks and question marks. She'd been engaged in refurbishing the house, again, and her bedroom had been the most recently decorated, done since Euan moved into the guest room. There was cream and grey painted furniture in here now, and the walls had been painted a pale coral pink, a colour she matched from silk underwear found in a trunk. The wall behind the bed was lined with old photographs, black-and-white images that she had hung in broad cream mounts and thin black frames. She'd begun doing similar groups on Peattie walls, selecting pictures from the shoeboxes stacked in the attics and hanging them in groups. When she had come across the box of pictures of me she had closed it again immediately, without burrowing beneath the top photograph, an instinctive rapid reclosing of the box as if it were disease-bearing. She'd gone off and found fresh sticky tape.

Now Joan went and sat at the dressing table, looking into her Venetian mirror, a vast and elaborate thing about which she and Euan had exercised their last substantial row: one that dealt simultaneously with his purchase of a beanbag for the sitting room, a particularly large one, its colours particularly adamantly chemical. She had claimed he had no taste. He had countered that it was no doubt the case, that all evidence supported the idea, but that notwithstanding, the seating she'd installed was all unbearably uncomfortable.

Euan put his head around the door and reminded her that they were due at the pub. When he was at home he spent most evenings with his public bar friends and Joan wasn't ordinarily invited, but another wife was coming tonight and Euan had offered Joan as a companion.

"So, are you coming or not?"

Joan didn't answer and Euan withdrew.

He wasn't often here during the week, but was showing willing in honour of Saturday's event. The truth was that he'd been summoned and had complied. He was commuting daily to work, a situation he'd already let it be known that he regretted. When weekends turned out this way, in childishness as he put it, he'd likely as not go back to his flat in town early. A Saturday departure was a bad sign, though pressure of work, essay marking piling up unmarked, was the usual attribution. They had bought the flat in town when the children were small and it was difficult, Euan said, to find the peace and stillness to hear himself think. He can teach literature classes with one eye shut, he says. Poetry's the real job, he says (he's had two collections published), and it just wasn't possible under those circumstances, with the pram in the hall. Joan asked what pram in the hall, and was chided for not picking up the reference.

"The enemy of promise," he'd said. And then again, with greater emphasis: "The *enemy*, of promise."

"Nice," she'd said.

"Why did I marry someone who doesn't read?" he'd asked the wall. "I should have married somebody who reads."

"I agree heartily," Joan told him. "I don't heartily agree, though, as that splits the infinitive. There you go. I know that, and am thus a better person."

When Euan had gone Joan went into the kitchen, to the cupboard in the corner to which she'd made access purposely difficult with a full-size bin. She had to take the bin out to get the door open, and turn the carousel shelving within, and ignore the warnings she'd taped there. She made and drank a vodka tonic, standing with one hand braced on the worktop, then made another and took it with her into the den, past the sewing machine and the ironing board, past the cork noticeboard, which was covered still in bright-headed pins with shreds of old school schedules attached to them. She brushed past an unused exercise bike and a dismantled piano keyboard, and reached into a flowerpot that acted as a bookend. Euan was supposed to have given up years ago but he smoked when she'd gone to bed, out of the sitting room's open window. She'd seen the ash there in the mornings and smelled it in the window creases.

What I've always liked best is the idea of smoking, just the idea: the view of myself that others may have to adjust to, adjusting my own internal view of myself in turn. The experience of smoking could only ever be inferior to the idea. The idea is saturated with associations – associations that lend us some moments in an old world. The idea gets past the ludicrous fact of setting fire to paper tubes of dried plants and inhaling the smoke. And though it's true that the Salter smoking and drinking to excess began in earnest about 14 years ago, it's also true that our history as a family is full of cigs and booze. Cigs and booze have been there at every fork in the road. One of Joan's recent framings, a picture she was staring at now, was a photograph taken at her and Ottilie's 21st birthday. It was an unusual coming-of-age party. Joan had been married three years and had year-old twin boys. Ottilie had a boy aged two and no husband. It wasn't the usual key-of-the-door event, by any means.

In the photograph Joan is sitting in the corner of the party marquee, on the floor with her legs crossed, toes pointing from a slinky blue dress, hair up in a bun, and she is talking to a handsome dark-haired boy (name forgotten), in full flow, and there's that same cigarette gesture, the one she's looking for now, hand held to the side during debate, her palm facing up. In that upward palm, the confident angle of that shoulder, is a whole atlas of the Joan that didn't quite come to pass.

～

When she got back from the loch, Mog went into the new kitchen. It's habit, calling it the new kitchen. It's no longer new; in fact, it wasn't new even when it was new. It's a clunky, ugly cream-and-brown affair, reclaimed from the Grants across the valley 20 years ago, when they were renovating. It was installed on the first floor in what was Henry's mother's private sitting room, when stairs were becoming too difficult for Vita and when the size, scale and gloom of the Victorian original downstairs, formidably authentic, was acknowledged, finally, as oppressive. Mog found Ottilie there, sitting at the table and drawing a striped yellow jug with white roses in it, having produced a box of oil pastels from her pocket. The jug in the sketch had colours it didn't really have, and light and shapes and shadows that were new. In this jug, she'd seen another.

They talked about tensions at the gatehouse. Mog, needing something to do, whisked chocolate powder into a pan of hot milk at the stove.

"Sorry to go on like this," she said, whisking harder.

"It's fine," Ottilie assured her. "Don't apologise, for heaven's sake."

"It's hard for us. You know. Because it's obvious they shouldn't be together. And I think they only stay together for our sakes." She paused. "And we wish that they wouldn't. I'd rather they didn't. But that's an impossible thing to say to them."

Ottilie said nothing, taking the offered mug of chocolate and sipping at it.

"They must have been happy once," Mog said to her. They looked at each other over the top of the mugs. "It's just that I don't remember it."

Joan got the wedding she wanted, at least in the material details. She got a restaurant to supply the canapés and Chinese duck, the near-translucent brandy snaps and the plump Perthshire raspberries with gooey meringues, delivered in ribbon-tied boxes. She cancelled Euan's surprise within ten minutes of its being revealed, the hire of a flower-bedecked horse and trap to take them away from the church, replacing it with a Daimler and uniformed driver.

"Discord even then."

"Your mother had a real battle with Euan's mother. Poor Joyce. Trying to chip in and being rebuffed. A lot of vetoing. No small cute nieces with silver horseshoes. No rice. It was all very tense for a while."

"A control freak even then."

"Joan did the flowers, too, you know. Found the grower, went there, gave her orders. They were terrified. Kept ringing us up, worried that the buds wouldn't be small enough."

"You helped with the church."

"Yes. Me and Ursula. Press-ganged."

Ottilie's face acquired that look that it gets when she finds herself unexpectedly having mentioned Ursula's name: her mind unsure where to go next, and her face unsure how to follow.

At Mog's suggestion they went out onto the terrace. They sat on the stone balustrade, their legs hanging over

115

a 15-foot drop, looking over the drive and into the night garden. Moths flitted about and a nightjar screamed.

"She was only nine, you know," Ottilie said. "Of course you know. You know that was when she started speaking again, at your mother's wedding."

This was radical, as departures from the norm go. Ottilie never mentioned Seb's death, had never before referred to the events of the evening of the wedding. Some sea change appeared to be in progress. It occurred to me suddenly, out of the blue, that Ottilie was squaring herself up to confession. Mog didn't say, though she was dying to, "Yes, and we all know why she started speaking that night, don't we: she had news to tell us all." She didn't say, though she was dying to, "Tell me, tell me now, about that night and about Alan: haven't there been enough years of secrecy?" She didn't, but her face said it all for her. Ottilie glanced over, recognising this, and if she was going to speak out, made a decision now to back down, her face signalling this and then her voice. "Poor Seb," she said instead.

"Poor Seb indeed," Mog agreed, faintly ridiculously.

He was never called Seb while alive. He's usually called Seb now he's dead. In a way it keeps the two separate. Perhaps abbreviation has helped denature the horror of it. It must be exhausting having to feel so much and so often. Shorthand must help. The word Sebastian is invested so completely with grief.

"You should have seen Ursula," Ottilie continued. "She was brilliant with the flowers. We'd turn round from fussing at the altar and see her, her nimble white fingers busy and totally absorbed, lacing cream roses into the pew ends, trailing ivy down with cream ribbons. It looked gorgeous. Joan was amazed. Hugged Ursula, even made her smile."

"Lovely." Poor Mog was now deep in confusion about the way this conversation was going.

"You know that your mother insisted on a preview of what everybody was to wear?" Ottilie said. "Joyce's floral two-piece was declared impossible. Joan took her shopping and got her into a bronze-coloured coat dress and matching feather-trimmed hat."

"You seem well," Mog said. "You look really well."

"I'm going to Madrid with the new work at the end of the summer," Ottilie told her. "There's excitement about the exhibition and I'm feeling quite ... purposeful. Still can't sleep, though." She made a self-deprecating face. "And the party should be fun. Strangely enough, I find myself looking forward to it." She let down and put up her hair. "I hear you're joining me on the lighting sub-committee. Shall we meet tomorrow after breakfast, at nine thirty? Here for coffee and the list, then do the tour?"

∿

The next morning was cold and damp, as it had rained all night. Mog and Ottilie met and allocated the buying and the putting-up of lights, as Joan demanded. Joan had gone to Edinburgh shopping and would be away all day, and so, daringly, in her absence, they made adjustments and additions to the list. When they'd finished, Mog retreated to the warmth of the linen room. Finally, belatedly, she was working her way through the piles of books I'd left in my room at Peattie, starting with the stuff I'd said was mandatory. I'd ranged them for her in a row along the length of the window sill, and they sat there still. When Alastair and Rebecca arrived, their airport hire car crunching slowly across the gravel, Mog was lying on the usual broad shelf, one padded out with old blankets, reading *David Copperfield*, an ancient edition bound in a tea-stained blue cloth. It's warm in the linen room when the heating is on, pumping ineffectually away; it has one of the few radiators that work properly and houses the boiler in a corner cupboard.

Mog wasn't really reading properly, and recognising this, kept turning back to the beginning of the chapter, trying and failing to make the sentences adhere. She'd confided in Ottilie that she was nervous about Rebecca's arrival, having to entertain Rebecca. She was hoping and praying that her second cousin wouldn't turn out to be one of those guests that's like a hungry baby bird on a branch, constantly wanting attention and unable to fend for itself. But here they were: the moment had come. Rebecca and Alastair had arrived and there wasn't any escaping this. She closed the book and went along the corridor, dawdling. Down the stairs one at a time, hearing Edith calling Henry's name. Into the hall, and out onto the terrace, where wide stone steps flare elegantly onto the drive.

Edith was standing by the car talking to the visitors, when Mog went down to be introduced. Henry arrived from the yard and he and Alastair greeted each other with a handshake, one that Alastair prolonged, placing his free hand on Henry's upper arm. Alastair was paunchy, had a veiny nose, was kind-faced, his white hair swept back. He had a close cropped pepper-and-salt beard that might have been unshaven stubble. The ice that had formed over more than 40 years of not talking had broken now between Henry and his nephew Alastair, in exclaiming how very alike Rebecca and Mog looked, except for their colouring. Rebecca's nut-brown hair and creamy skin were gifted by Alastair's mother.

They'd only been in the new kitchen a few minutes when Ursula came in. Edith had tried to steer the group towards the drawing room, but Alastair expressed a liking for sitting around a kitchen table, so here they were staying. Vita and Mrs Hammill had come in to join them, Vita warmly welcoming and Mrs H stand-offish. Ottilie was out at the cottage, in her studio, no doubt, with Mozart and Bach, and wouldn't return until tonight. Ursula, knowing this, was in the house to meet the visitors.

She came into the kitchen quietly, tiptoeing, wanting to surprise: creeping up on them as they were standing at the window having the view explained. It had a long history, this idea of fun, and it was usual in the family to indulge her, to pretend not to have noticed, to pretend to be caught out. Ursula's smile is slightly crooked and one side of her face is mildly less mobile than the other. She had a minor stroke a few years ago and the doctors wanted to probe further, but Ursula wouldn't allow it and Edith wouldn't intervene. Edith has always been adamant about not wanting anything purely diagnostic said or done. The shock of Sebastian's death, when he was four and she was five, a death she and her 14-year-old sisters were helpless witnesses to: that's considered sufficient to explain Ursula's oddness. The idea that it might be a condition, a matter merely of health, and might always have been, is one that Edith repelled, and people respected her wishes.

Alastair and Rebecca didn't know much about Ursula, when they arrived. They didn't know much about any of us, which is what made conversation so stilted. After so long a time there were big themes in the offing, but they seemed too big to embark on over marmite toast. The questions suggesting themselves were too heavy with significance. They seemed all to lead back to the rift, one that had prevented any but the stiffest and briefest of annual exchanges, hurried summings-up of the year added at the bottom of Christmas cards, summaries that in Alastair's case were scrawled in barely legible handwriting (illegibility, Edith had sometimes thought, that was making a point).

It was Edith who sent the cards at Christmas, the same card every year, showing the house sparkling in frost, thick snow over the gardens, trees starkly and two-dimensionally white. The cards didn't give much away, not until 1970, at least. There was news in the December of 1970 that Sebastian had died. I've seen Alastair at the moment of opening that card: the announcement falling out and onto the floor, its heavy linen weave denoting importance, its ominous black embossed edge. He was eating a mince pie at the time of its arrival, opening the mail while listening to carols, chiding the cat for patting at the tree decorations. He was distracted from all those things, came to a halt, mince pie in hand, reading and rereading the news that a four-year-old boy, his cousin Sebastian, had drowned in the loch in the summer. There was news but no scene setting, no real explanation. His first reaction was shouted – "No! No! For pity's sake, no!" – and his second reaction another sort of sorrow, one that took on the truth that his uncle had waited four months and left it to Edith to tell him about the disaster. Alastair had heard of my "running away" in just the same manner, and felt, I'm sure, that it'd be tactless to bring it up, that it shouldn't be mentioned unless the family mentioned it first. Over the years my status had morphed from *runaway* to *lost*; in every subsequent Christmas card, Edith had written "Michael's still missing" at the bottom of her message. Missing presumed dead, Alastair thought, after so long a period of silence; missing presumed heartless, Rebecca's side of the argument went. They'd talked about little else on the way up here, causing airline rows of a two-back and two-front radius to fall silent and listen, engrossed.

Alastair and Rebecca didn't know that Ursula is "eccentric", nor any of the other possible synonyms attaching to that, though they might have been guessing as much, right now, as Ursula stepped forward. She had her child's white hand outstretched, and was moving it smoothly up and down, saying, "Shake, please; be polite." She was wearing a pink cocktail dress that was layers of frills from the waist down, with a tiara, a yellow cardigan that had once been Henry's, and green wellingtons.

"That's quite an outfit. Amateur dramatics?" Alastair asked her.

"And you look very boring," Ursula told him, in her clipped, flat-toned way. She speaks very fast in general, but with longish pauses between pronouncements. Alastair, robustly conversational in his practised, businesslike manner, proceeded over tea and packet cake to quiz Ursula about her life, whether she married, where she lived now, what she did for a living, and was bemused by the style and content of her replies. It was Ursula who brought up the rift.

"Why haven't I met you before? We're cousins. We should know each other."

Alastair glanced at Henry. "Your father and I had a falling out. A long time ago, before you were born."

"But you didn't fall out with *me*."

"No, you're quite right. But we live hundreds of miles apart and I'm terrible at letter writing. And I'm a lot older than you. And you're a girl. That's also a factor obviously. I don't often talk to girls. Ask my daughter here."

All of this completely deadpan.

Ursula smiled crookedly. "Why did you drive off in the middle of the night?"

"Ursula, no," Henry said sharply.

"It's fine, Henry," Alastair said. "Ursula's right, we need to talk about it. We can't go on acting like it didn't happen. I owe you an apology."

"Not at all," Henry said. "Or rather, I owe you one equally."

Alastair turned to Ursula. "My brother Robert, he's a sensitive soul. A bit like you, I imagine."

"Oh dear: sensitive is nearly always a euphemism."

"Euphemism's a good word."

Ursula's mouth turned scornful. "I read a lot. I have a good vocabulary. I'm not *backward*."

"Of course not. And nor is Robert. He's the brightest man I've ever met. But he's sensitive too. He got very upset,

Robert, about our mother being buried here with her sister, and not at home with us. He decided he couldn't come up for the funeral. I didn't explain him to your father very well. It turned into an argument and it got out of hand. We were all upset. The truth is that though I was defending him so hotly, I was angry with my brother too."

"I'm named after her, after your mother."

"Yes. That was a lovely gesture."

"Not really: I was always going to be Ursula. There was already a Joan and an Ottilie."

Alastair smiled. "Quite right. Did you know that we called my mother Ursa rather than Ursula, and that Joan was always called Jo, and Ottilie always Tilly?"

"Tilly lived here, after her sisters died. I knew her. Didn't you know that about her?"

"Of course, of course she did."

"She was everybody's favourite. I loved her. I'm sure I would have loved Ursa and Jo too, if I'd known them."

"That's kind of you to say."

"I can be kind sometimes. Do you believe in the curse?"

"Ursula, no," Henry said again.

"I don't know what I think about the curse," Alastair said. "Life's full of mystery, isn't it? It might be a mistake to be dismissive of mystery." He turned to Henry. "I've been sitting all day and I'd love a walk in the gardens, if you've time to show me around."

Henry said he'd be delighted. They went off to do the tour, and Mog brought Rebecca to the loch.

They sat on the bench together at the edge of the wood. The bench has feet that are sunk deeply in shingle, and sits with its back to the great uncle. One of the willows planted around the great uncle's grave had colonised it a little, had extended one of its many sad long branches, supple and slender, with its many feathery leaves, over this bench, so Mog had to take it in hand and bend it behind the seat before they could use it. It had more determination and exerted more force than she was expecting.

"It isn't particularly warm for mid-June, I grant you," she said to Rebecca, seeing her wrap her thin jacket tighter around herself.

"I was warned. I have a sweater with me. Should have thought."

"We must be acclimatised. We used to go swimming in there on colder days than this and play on the beach soaked through afterwards. Me and Michael. But that was a long time ago."

"I'd like to know more about Michael, the mysterious Michael," Rebecca said.

Mog took her to the great uncle's tomb and answered the usual questions. Even the great uncle's effigy looked bored.

"And what's this, more commemorations for David?" Rebecca was standing beside the angel.

"For Michael," Mog told her. "For his being missing. Ottilie thought it would help."

"Did he look like Ottilie? I haven't seen a photograph."

"He was a real mixture. Very tall like Grandpa Andrew. That was Vita's husband's name. Olive-skinned like Vita."

"And like you."

"Ottilie's hands and mouth, and her way of walking. Tall, dark, clever, the works. Big nose. Lovely eyes, very brown. Long lashes. Deep voice. Funny when not being neurotic." I may have blushed, though *neurotic* smarted a bit.

"You'll have to show me a photograph."

"I don't have any. I didn't have a camera until after he'd gone. You'd have to ask Ottilie. She took hundreds. You won't see any at Peattie, though. You won't see pictures of Michael here."

"Why's that?"

"Because Henry had them taken down and put away."

"Angry with him."

"Grieving."

"So what was the trouble, what was it that made him go off?"

"You know how they say everybody has a story," Mog said to her. "Sometimes a trivial thing. Mine is not finding what Dad calls my vocation, so far, anyway, or even a job I can bear to do. Well, anyway. That's very dull news. Michael's story was his being fatherless. He was obsessed. Even from ten years old."

"How do you mean, obsessed?"

"With not knowing who he was."

"Who he was?"

"Michael. Didn't know who his father was. Ottilie wouldn't tell him."

"Oh god. That's horrible."

"You don't know about Ottilie getting pregnant, the whole scandal, then."

"No. I think I might have been protected from something so shocking."

"Well. Ottilie, my mother's twin, goes to a house party the weekend after my parents are married, while they're off in Italy on honeymoon, and sleeps with some boy. Some random boy she met there. She's 18 and one week old at the time. Exactly 18 and a week. I know that because my parents got married on my mother's 18th birthday."

"Also Ottilie's birthday, surely."

"Also Ottilie's birthday. But because my mother declared she wanted to marry on her 18th, that only her 18th would do, the party that Gran was planning had to be cancelled, and the family across the valley, the Grants, offered to host it there instead, feeling sorry for poor Ottilie, done out of her 18th birthday."

"I'm getting the feeling that Joan and Ottilie didn't get on."

"Rivalry. Bitter rivalry. Always."

"That was kind of mean of your mother, hogging the limelight."

"You're right. Mean is the right word. Well, anyway. Ottilie goes off to this party, sleeps with some boy, won't tell anybody who it was."

"But surely. Process of elimination."

"Fourteen boys. But don't think Henry didn't try. He went all over the county eliminating."

"Ouch."

"They didn't know she was pregnant until ages later. Four months gone, when she started to show. Was never sick or anything. Too scared to speak up."

"Blimey. And she never married?"

"No. No partners, boyfriends that we know of. Though Pip has a theory that she has lovers abroad, that that's what all the trips overseas are really about."

"Poor Ottilie."

"Michael was always fighting with his mother. Like they say, it's never about what it's about. It was always really about his father, not knowing. He was angry a lot of the time. Everybody was irritated. But now I think, well, why didn't you just tell him, Ottilie? If you'd just told him the name of the boy, the man. He could have tracked him down, confronted him, upset his wife, freaked out his half-siblings. Lots of upset, maybe, but then over. Over. The boil lanced. She wouldn't talk, though. He couldn't get her to talk about it."

Even in my very earliest memories it's clear that my mother didn't want to talk much about anything. Not unless it was about the work. She didn't mean just her own work, by that, but any kind of creativity. She was absolutely clear that a life without it – *the work* – was a waste. That was a cultural divide with other people; a cliff, a wall, quite often a hole. She had very few friends, few I knew about, anyway. But this was the point, I suppose, and it's something I've had time to think about, that the real romance of my mother's life is with herself, her experience of being alive, her journey: this ongoing dialogue she has with her own consciousness. It made the rest of us pretty much redundant. She approved of me, as a teenager, in so far as I was a voracious reader, always reading, would walk down the street with a book open, walking into things. And writing. I was always writing something. So I passed muster, as far as it went. We had something to talk about, but it wasn't a frequent conversation and of course it wasn't what I wanted to talk about.

Not that I was neglected; people use that word and they've got it totally arse about face, but there's no small talk with my mother, and even those who love her most would agree that she's benignly self-absorbed. Shining a positive light on her behaviour would involve words like drive, focus, concentration. She has admirable levels of these. Her first thought when she wakes is how quickly she can get coffee and get into her studio. Sometimes eating is neglected. Foraging was the norm when I was young, and so I learned from an early age to help myself to something to eat. Often it was as if my mother forgot I was there, that I lived there. I'd interrupt her and she'd be surprised to see me, genuinely so, as if my being there was unexpected.

Our confrontations were tediously repetitive, seemed often to repeat almost word for word.

"You know I don't talk about that, Michael."

"But why not?"

"I don't talk about it. It's private. It's a long time ago. It's irrelevant."

"Not to me."

"Yes. To you. It was a one-night stand. I've told you and told you. He didn't love you, Michael. He wasn't interested."

126

"But he's my father. Imagine not knowing Henry. Imagine Edith not believing you had a right to know who Henry was."

"A right! A right?"

"Yes. A right."

"I've told you. A hundred times. You don't have anything of his. He's made no impact, negligible impact on you. You're a Salter. You're a Maclean. You're Grandpa Andrew, you're me, you're Henry, you're Vita. He doesn't figure. He's irrelevant to both of us."

"Have I met him?"

"Michael!"

"Is he dead?"

"He might as well be."

When I was 17, 18, it was Mog I talked to about it. Later, at 19, there developed for a time an odd intimacy with Ursula, but at 17 and 18 Mog was the confidante. That was the period of barely ever speaking about it with my mother; two years that she thought were years of improvement, ceasefire, peace. She'd talk to me more about the work, thinking it was safe to talk because things wouldn't escalate. She thought I was listening and that we were getting on better. Edith would say to me as much: "I'm glad you and Ottilie are getting on better." So it was an unpleasant surprise to all when the question began to itch again. It itched and it wouldn't stop. The spring and summer weeks before I disappeared: that was the time of my most concerted and organised digging. I would do anything, embarrass anyone, create a scene anywhere. I had no sense of propriety, as Henry reminded me, though he slipped up one evening, telling me angrily that bad genes on my father's side were no doubt to blame for my being so lazy and feckless (both of which I admit to readily).

Mog and Rebecca were walking back to the house. "It wasn't just at home, either," Mog said. "He was constantly in trouble. Fighting. Arguing with teachers about homework, grades, fairness, school policies, a real pain in the arse. Then when he's 17 he decides he's not going to go to university, he's not going to sit his exams, he wants to work for the forestry commission, write, travel round the world – round countries that have forestry, anyway. Ottilie goes into a decline and Henry has *caniptions*. There's a lot of arguing. Michael gets worse at school. They send him to an educational psychologist. Michael argues with her as well. Then he's caught with drugs on him at school and expelled."

"Oh god."

"Quite. So he goes to the sixth-form college and lasts a week. Gets a series of low-paid jobs around here and doesn't last long in any of them. Starts spending more and more time at Peattie. And then ..."

Now is the moment to tell her about Ursula. It would be a relief to confide. "Then one day he leaves home. Not even a big fight, Ottilie says. Just the same kind of conversation they'd been having for years. But something snaps. Evidently. We don't know why. He packs a bag, drives away, leaves his car at the loch, goes off on foot. Leaves a note in his room here."

"In his room here?"

"Yes. They took a while to find it."

"So he still had a room from when he was 11?"

"We all have rooms here. It's a big house. It makes my grandmother happy. We can come and go. Stay any time. We help out while we're here. It's a good system."

"What did the note say?"

"Hardly anything. No real clues. The father. Unhappiness about Ottilie's attitude. His wanting to make a new life. That kind of thing."

"Can I see it?"

"I don't have it."

"Why did he leave his car at the lake?"

"Mystery. That's the mystery. Don't know. Decided he didn't want it, maybe. It was a present from Henry for his 18th. He'd had a row with Henry, too."

"About his father?"

"About his father, about his treatment by the family."

"What do you mean, treatment?"

"He never felt Henry treated him the same. Because he was illegitimate."

"Surely that was wrong, he was wrong."

"And he thought Henry knew."

"Who his father was."

"Yes."

"And since that, nothing."

"And since that, nothing," Mog agreed.

Chapter 8

On the fourth day after I disappeared, Joan invited Alan to tea. She said she needed clarification on a few things. She said to the family that she was going to have a conversation with Alan, at teatime, and that she'd welcome their being there. They were, of course, going to be there anyway. She was warning them against interfering, signalling that she was going to be running the show. Alan got there expecting tea with Joan but found himself in a situation rather more like an interview by a board of directors, with Joan chairing.

"It was good of you to come, Alan," she said, handing him a teacup. "I wanted to ask you a last few things. I hope that's alright."

"Of course," Alan said, "I'm happy to help in any way I can."

Joan consulted her notes. "You said that you lost your shoes in the loch. The day Michael disappeared. New trainers I think it was."

"That's right."

"That seems odd to me."

Joan was suspicious of Alan at this time, believing him more likely than her sister to be the killer. By the autumn she would come to a different conclusion, deciding that I was alive and Alan a liar and Ursula easily indoctrinated, though I think that most of the impetus of this change rested in exonerating her parents from their inaction: if there was no death then there was no need for guilt, after all, and licence was granted to concentrate on the liar and the person misled. For now, however, Joan was the suspicious inquisitor general. "Why still have your shoes on? You didn't remove them to go into the loch? You're saying you took your trousers off over your shoes and left your shoes on?"

"I took them off, took off my trousers, then I put them back on." Alan looked and sounded nervous.

"But why would you do that?" Joan asked him.

"I always swim in the loch in shoes. Don't you? Everyone does. The pebbles are sharp. I've never swum there barefoot. Never. Nobody does."

"Did you lose your shoes every time you swam there? Seems an expensive way to go swimming."

"Not usually. But that day, I was in a panic. I didn't tie them tight enough. That wasn't even it. The point is, I didn't untie and retie them. I shrugged them off, then forced my feet in again. I was in a hurry. You understand that. I'd seen Michael hit across the head, I'd seen him disappear into the loch. In fact, I was undressing even before she hit him. I didn't tie them tight, like I would usually. They came off."

"Even before she hit him? How do you mean?"

"I had a bad feeling. It came over me. A bad feeling."

He swam out there, he said, just in his underpants and his shoes and it was freezing cold. There was no sign of me. He dived and dived, and he couldn't see anything. There was no trace of me. Gone like a stone.

Joan interrupted the flow of the narrative. "Forgive me, but I have trouble with this part of the story."

"It's not a story." Alan's contempt was obvious. "It's just as I told you. No matter how many times you ask me

131

it will be the same. And this will be the last time. I should tell you that. I'm not going to talk about this again unless it's to somebody in uniform."

"Are you threatening us?" Joan's hostility was just as obvious.

Euan got hold of her arm. "I'm sorry, Alan. Joan isn't herself. This will be the last time we ask you, unless, as you say, we wish you to present your story to the police."

"My *story*?"

Alan's breathing had quickened into panting; the weather continued freakishly hot. He wiped his brow with one of his large white handkerchiefs, and folded it carefully up again. The implications of Euan's words weren't lost on him. Perhaps he was thinking, as I was, that Ursula's credulity could swing two ways. Perhaps all it would take would be for someone to take her aside, and say they saw Alan kill Michael. Furthermore, that they saw that *she* saw Alan kill Michael.

Joan was sceptical about his not being able to see me under the water. But I've been down there and I can tell you that there's nothing at all to be seen, there's nothing he could have seen, unless he went very deep into the dark and was lucky enough to blunder into me. It would have had to be that accidental. And it's likely he didn't go far down. You will have to take my word for this, but conditions beneath the surface, out there in the middle of the loch, are claustrophobic and also agoraphobic. A phobia paradox. There is a feeling of enclosure, visibility being so poor, and yet at the same time this fact whispers in your brain: that the water stretches underneath you for hundreds of feet, stretching dizzyingly away, first of tea-coloured brown like strong milkless tea (peaty, in fact), but then, but then blackness, the abyss deep and unknowable as a starless night. Though actually it's worse than that, is more like something grasping, a void that wants to clasp itself about you. It will pull you down and down in its embrace. Beyond a certain point there is the illusion of a gentle and constant suction, an uncompromising suction that will not let you rise. It's occurred to me that people who've survived near-drowning here have spoken only metaphorically about the creature.

Alan went over the story again. Ursula was hysterical in the boat, Ursula was raving, not making sense, not letting him board, not letting him give her the oar back that he found floating. He'd propped one end for her against the boat hull, holding onto the other, an offering. She swung at it with the remaining oar, knocking it back into the loch and yelling like a banshee. This was the point at which he began to feel dreadfully unwell. He swam away, fearing he was going to pass out, and went and sat on the shore, hearing her yelling subside and end. He sat on the shore, feeling too ill to move, lying back on the gravel, his knees up, looking up at the blue sky, wet and hot and beginning already to be clammy, his heart thumping unevenly, his chest hurting him, spasms contracting his heart like a belt drawn repeatedly tight, and feeling at the same time that somehow it had bruised. He lay back and expected to die and must have slept – actually he thought he might have lost consciousness – because then, the next thing he knew, he'd come round with a jolt. He didn't know how much later it was (his watch was waterlogged and useless), and Ursula was there, still sitting in the boat, sitting quietly and not moving. He felt very tired but otherwise normal. He swam back out to her, very slowly, anxious that the pains might return, and she let him board without a word, without a flicker of interest in him, and then he rowed her back to the beach.

"So. You had chest pain and you passed out, you think, on the shore," Euan said. "But then when you woke you felt well enough to swim, to climb into the rowing boat, to row Ursula back."

"I know it sounds unlikely, but it's what happened. The pain had gone off and I had to do something."

133

"I see."

"It was the chest pain that stopped me keeping looking for him. You understand that?"

"I understand that," Euan said, closing and opening his eyes in acceptance.

"I spent a good ten minutes diving and looking, even before I tried to board the boat. I want you to see that. And after ten minutes of looking …"

"Yes," Euan told him. "We do see."

"Please go on," Henry said.

He paints it well, the word picture. I see him, Alan on the shore, his arms to his chest, his groaning. I see him sleep. I see him waking, going out to Ursula again, swimming very slowly, barely more than floating, an assisted sort of floating, on his back for some of the time, a great pale starfish creature, blinking, just his arms moving and making slow progress. I see her letting him board, the oar that was floating going into the boat first, and then Alan landing like a big fish over the side, landing heavily like something thought extinct rising out of the deeps, over and onto the deck, and I see him seat himself opposite her.

I see Alan rowing Ursula back to the shore. I see Ursula becoming upset, now that she has to step from the boat.

"She was in a panic, you see, by the time we got back. She wanted to get here and get you. And there wasn't any choice except to get out of the boat."

"Why didn't you pull the boat onto the shore for her so that she wouldn't have to get wet?"

"I did. I did that. But I was very slow, I'm afraid. I felt unwell and shaky. I was worried I was going to have a heart attack. She couldn't wait. She got out into the shallows and tripped, immediately, and went down on her knees. She was very frightened."

"Right," Euan said. "And then."

"I watched her go. Coming up here. Crying, making a noise."

She looked like a little girl who'd hurt herself, running like a child does, her arms held out at her sides.

"I wanted to go after her but I was afraid. The pain was coming back. My chest muscles felt stretched."

"That was probably to do with the swimming, the effort and the cold."

"And then I went home. I went home first."

"That part I don't get," Joan chipped in. Euan rolled his eyes at Alan and Alan showed that he was aware of the compliment. "Why go to the cottage first?"

"I told you, I lost my shoes, I had to get new ones. I couldn't come up here without shoes."

"But this was an emergency," Joan persisted.

"He was dead, Mrs Catto." Alan swivelled to face her. "He was dead. That's not an emergency. I went across the field to the cottage and came straight here after that. I was out of breath, remember, when Mr Catto and I met, almost ran into each other, off the back stairs. I still had chest pain. I did my best, Mrs Catto, you know. I did my very best for Michael."

"I'm sure you did," Euan said, "and I know we don't sound it, but we are genuinely immensely grateful to you, Alan. We will be. Very grateful. But at the moment I'm afraid none of us is ourselves. We've had a terrible shock."

Alan was nodding.

I spent the night before I disappeared in my room at Peattie. I sat on the bed for a long time, trying to articulate the thing I was about to do, to justify it to myself, walking the arc of reasoning, hoping to find that when I made the thing definite in my head, rehearsing it already in the past tense, that there wasn't any immediate recoil, no plunging loss of conviction. I wanted a practised justification, one I could repeat to myself at low moments, but it didn't work: I failed to feel anything much at all. I failed utterly to have any real thoughts about it. It made no sense; I knew that. I knew even then that taking myself away was never going to satisfy me as a revenge, but I knew I'd do it anyway. I went to dinner and was monosyllabic, and looked as if I were deep in thought, when actually nothing was going on in my head whatsoever. I seemed preoccupied, Edith was to say later, though she'd been positive enough on the phone when Ottilie rang to check I was there. My mother told Edith she'd be at Peattie for tea the next day and hoped to see me, but not to tell me she was coming.

The morning of the day I disappeared I went out for an early loch swim, came back and ate a bacon sandwich and then retreated to my room. It was already so hot that my body had dried, my shorts had dried, on the walk back, shoeless over the gravel. Going into my room, everything looked and felt new; it was as if I'd already left and it had passed into history. My room at Peattie still bore the look, the deserted ossified look of a boy's, as if the boy had died aged 11, when we moved away. It still does. Nothing changes, other than the linens and the few things, books mostly, that I added to it later as a weekend visitor. Airfix kit aeroplanes hang by strings, drifting gently in the draught. The ceiling has a zodiac painted on it, in blue and gold. Boys' books and games, souvenirs, flags, are propped up on shelves. Great framed maps are lined up on the walls, antique maps that showed confidence in a partly charted and partly imagined world. These all are things Henry provided for me when I was a child.

I opened the window and sat by it, shoving the screaming reluctant sash upward. I pulled the desk over, scraping and bouncing it across the parquet floor, to sit by the window and write the letter to my mother. I couldn't find any paper at first. My pen proved low on ink. It all took longer than it should have, and so I got to the linen room ten minutes late, Mog frowning at me for my bad timekeeping. I didn't stay long. I helped her with the maths, not really in the mood for explaining, and fixed the banana skin hair on the apple head, my mind swimming with the things I'd said and not said in the letter. I told Mog that I had things to do. I went back and read the letter over, my hand poised over it, and sat for a while looking out in case anything else should occur to me, but nothing did. It was shocking, how brief the farewell seemed to be. I left the letter sitting on the bed and went down early to lunch. I was first down and didn't tarry. I packed a sandwich, folding it into a napkin, took a green apple from the blue glass bowl, and on my way out, shouted to Vita, who was making her way slowly to the drawing room with Mrs Hammill, that I was going now. That's what I said to her. "Going now." With, in retrospect, embarrassing fierceness. Not caring how she interpreted it. I didn't answer her query, her answer; I don't know what it was. Something was said and not acknowledged. Poor Vita I left staring after me, Mrs H saying something tart about manners and the young. Vita may have realised – though perhaps only later – that in a way it was her fault that I'd decided to go. Henry I didn't see. Edith I avoided because she's too intuitive about things like this. I didn't want to have to look into Edith's eyes. She'd have read me in an instant and all would have been revealed.

I took my car along the drive as if I were leaving, and then along the lane 200 yards, before turning back in along the loch road, past the cottages. George and Alan were in and around the greenhouses that lunchtime, seeing to tomato trusses and cucumbers and the competition flowers, and bickering. George had been made uncharacteristically short-tempered by the weather. Everything was overheating, the vegetables engorged with sunshine, the tomatoes drying and splitting on the plants. In gardening terms the heat wave was becoming a crisis. It didn't help that George was unwell – with prostate trouble as well as a bad back – but had insisted that Henry forego his planned temporary replacement, fearing the relief gardener would become permanent and displace him. George had told Henry that Alan would help and didn't want to be paid, that his son would be offended by money in this situation.

Alan said that he had an argument with his father, about the tomatoes. He didn't add that it had developed from a dispute about technique, multiplying exponentially, from skill into responsibility, from duty to honour, and thence, devastatingly, into notions of self-respect. Money was at the heart of it; George's having volunteered Alan to work unpaid. In any case, Alan's trip down to the loch wasn't really about the fight he'd had with his father. When he went down to the wood on his bike, Alan was intending to do a spot of fishing. When it's hot, the trout gather in the deep shady pools beneath the jetty. Some of the older villagers fish here, with Henry's blessing, but Alan's a poacher, selling his catch in quantity at the back doors of local hotels. He'd sold some the previous evening to the holidaymakers: the cottage adjoining the Dixons' place is let by the week in summer.

I sat on the jetty a long time. I sat at its end, my lower legs over the edge, leaning back hard on my hands, looking at the familiar view, the stretch of water enclosed in hills, a heat haze blurring the horizon. I see him now, this boy, this 19-year-old not-quite-man. His shirt's rolled up at the sleeves, and he has tanned arms, his skin taking and burnishing the sunlight. His hair's wavy, falling layered past the collar. His features – his nose too big, as Mog says – are set into contempt, and there's something resigned there, also. It's made a decision, that face. He's looking thoughtfully out at the water, not moving. He has fine hands, large and with long fingers that are tanned darker than his forearms. His nails are well shaped, pinker than his hands, and set deep into his fingers. It was a good body.

I didn't appreciate that. His shoulders are wide and strong – a swimmer's body. His legs are long in his jeans. Now he sits up straighter, bringing one leg up, resting his foot against the plank edge, which is worn gently away like a stone tread on a cathedral stair, leaning forward and grasping the shin, and his feet are bare in the boat shoes, a tanned and hairy ankle just visible.

I heard Ursula before I saw her, and only at the last minute. I heard only the last few pairs of footfalls as she ran barefoot up behind me and put her small white hands over my eyes. She asked me, sitting down beside me on the jetty, why the car was there, half on the beach, its doors and boot open. That last part was easy: it was because of the heat. I told her what I was about to do.

"Leaving? When are you coming home?"

"I'm not, Ursula. I'm not coming home."

"For a while. Are you going to work somewhere? Do the forestry job somewhere?"

"Yes. The forestry job, I hope. But down in England somewhere. Maybe Yorkshire. It's beautiful there."

"You've never been to Yorkshire, liar."

"Wrong. Twice with the climbing club."

"Oh." And then, "Can I come visit you on your hill, climb up to see you?"

"I'm afraid not; that won't be possible."

"When will you be home?"

"I'm not coming back. I'm going to make a home somewhere else and live there."

She was quiet, digesting this, and then she said, "You don't love me."

"Of course I love you." It was obvious even to me that this was a lie.

"You don't love me. I knew you didn't."

"I do love you. You're my friend."

"I want to be your wife."

"Don't be an idiot."

I'd offended her. "You're young and your heart is very small and tight," she told me.

I didn't say anything.

"And green and unripe."

I knew better than to take issue with her on any of this.

"Some things go rotten without ever ripening," she added.

I murmured something that could have been construed as assent.

"You need to be tested to understand love," she said, matter-of-factly. "You're untested."

I don't know where she gets this stuff. From the novels, none of them post-1970, that Edith acquires on her behalf, I can only presume, believing them harmless. Edith has faith in the essential goodness of the pre-1970 world.

"My father," I began, finding that I couldn't complete the sentence.

"But that was a negative," she said. "That wasn't anything. The past is a nothing until you make it a something, and you did, you wanted to. Why did you want to? I think there's something very destructive about you, Michael." Her chin was on my shoulder and she turned it to kiss my neck.

"You may never have anybody love you like I do, never again," she said.

"I hope I do," I told her, as soulfully as I could manage.

Something new had occurred to her. "What does your mother think? She's letting you go off to Yorkshire?"

"She hasn't been asked."

Ursula lay back on the jetty, her fingers laced across her eyes, and was quiet, and we sat in silence.

Ursula wasn't really familiar with the idea of children growing up and moving away. It wasn't something she'd had experience of, other than for Ottilie's flight to the coast, though that only took place at about the same age that Ursula was at now, so wasn't the usual sort of fledging. Perhaps she'd read something about it, that in the normal course of things children grow up and move away. It's possible. Everything she knew came from the family and from permitted books, and also from music. I don't know how it stands now, with the paid companion; Edith said that she'd leave this kind of thing to her judgment and didn't need consulting. They could reinvent Ursula's life between the two of them, she said. But certainly in the old days, although there were boxes and boxes of well-used LPs (and still are; Ursula's devoted to vinyl), first the television was removed and then the radio, so as to avoid talk programmes, which might have caused confusion and upset. This wasn't alarmist – they would, I'm afraid, have caused confusion and upset. Ursula thinks that every problem she hears of is a problem she's being called upon to solve. A broadcast made in her presence, in her hearing, is a message to her, an appeal. She never learned to carry the world's tragedies lightly and cast them off again, letting her own concerns obliterate them, as the rest of us do. She'd urge Edith and Henry to help, to go to the place of crisis, to sort out the problem, or to give all their things away, and then she'd worry about their absence and the ramifications of their needing to donate of themselves or their possessions, and the world's problems would inter-nalise into her own, the distress building and spreading. I know this because it's what used to happen, before the radiogram was set to one safe music station and then removed, and the televisions at Peattie were given away, and the daily newspaper was locked up in the office. The televisions were lost when Ursula was eight, when she was taken out of school. In that year of heightened emotion the news upset her, drama upset her, and moving pictures were abandoned. Fiction and non-fiction were indistinguishable to her and each equally threatening. Even now she talks about the characters in the novels she reads as if they're real, as if they have lives pre- and post-dating the narrative. She said to me once that she didn't think the books always ended the same way, but that might have been a joke. It's hard to tell what's playfulness and what's something else in Ursula's case.

"I'm going out in the boat," I said to her. That was the only thing I could come up with in order to shed Ursula and her judgments.

Her response astonished me. "Can I come with you?"

"You don't ever – I thought you didn't ..." I was taken aback.

"If I come out in the boat, I can change," she told me, her face deadly earnest.

"No, no," I said. "That's such a bad idea."

"Bad?"

"Well, look. Well, look, alright. If you're sure."

"I'm sure."

"You can come out in the boat," I told her. I had my own discreditable reasons for changing my mind. "Would you like to row?"

She shook her head, eyes shut. "I could never do that."

She got into the boat where it stood, beached high on the shore. She was so slight that her weight made very little difference to the effort involved in the launch. She gasped as the water took hold, as her seat lifted and slid into buoyancy and the oars began their work. She was wearing Great Aunt Tilly's pale blue dress, which had bluer embroidery, cornflowers, raised and silky on the bodice and around the scalloped hem. I would see her sitting there in the boat very many times in the days that followed: Ursula smiling at me from under her white hat, also one of Tilly's, a hat woven out of a kind of knitted white nylon straw, broad-brimmed and opaque, throwing open-weave shadows over her face.

I had a plan now. One I'd had to improvise. I'd done a stupid, reckless thing telling her that I was leaving. Unless I took Ursula with me in the boat there was nothing I could do to delay her running back to the house and raising the alarm, shouting out her news and bringing them all running down here. Finding that I'd already left, they might have given chase in the old car: an absurd, Buster-Keatonish scenario but also one that was possible. Here was a way out of the problem. Here's what I could do. I could get her out into the middle of the loch and I could leave her there. I could dive into the water, out of the boat, leaving her stranded there until Alan came for her. That way her news would be greatly delayed and I'd have plenty of time to make a head start. This would work. Alan was already on his way. I looked at my watch. We'd arranged to meet on the beach in 20 minutes and I needed to get on with this.

Had Ursula left the loch immediately, running off to tell my mother that I was leaving, she would in any case have found the drawing room deserted. It was too early yet for the afternoon assembly. Edith and Henry had been into town, each with their own mission; it had been so long since Henry had left the estate that he'd had first sight of the then eight-year-old one way road system. It was only blind luck that he didn't blunder in on the scene at the loch when he got back. Ordinarily he'd bring the dogs down to the beach for a swim when they'd been penned in for any time, but he was tired and hot from driving and shops, and took them out the other way, a shorter greener way, through the planted arch that leads towards the folly and pond, over the stile and into the pasture, walking along in the tree shade at the edge of the field while the dogs ran about sniffing and peeing.

Edith, who was finding the heatwave exhausting, was having a nap. Mog was in her room at the gatehouse. Joan and Euan were on their way back from Glasgow with Pip and Izzy. Jet was in his cottage, which had been granted to him, at 17, on the same terms of domestic half-independence as Ursula's; the minimum conditions he'd accept in order to stay in the vicinity of home. Jet was no longer speaking to his father, having, according to Euan, purposely sabotaged his future by doing zero work for his exams. Jet said he was asleep and didn't hear or see anything useful.

Which leaves Vita and Mrs Hammill. They were in the drawing room together. Mrs Hammill was doing puzzles from her crossword book, using the tortoiseshell-rimmed glasses that hang around her neck on a chain, fingering the back of her hairline, saying to Vita that she must make an appointment for another permanent wave. Vita, who has poor circulation and feels cold almost all of the time, was dozing by the window, enjoying a warming patch of sunlight, which fell in window-blocked rectangles that flowed like draped cloths over the furnishings and onto the floor. Because she had her chair on a three-quarter tilt, Vita saw no one come up the steps, though she did hear footsteps above her, she said, running across the ceiling and running back a few minutes later. Of course, as she pointed out at the time, her not seeing an approach from the front wasn't really significant anyway; it was just as possible Michael had come in the rear entrance. The doors weren't locked during the day. She didn't say anything to Mrs Hammill at the time, about the footsteps; Mrs Hammill was engrossed and didn't appear to have noticed. Pity, as she would have known the time and Vita had no idea, couldn't even guess at it. She didn't think anything of it, the footsteps creaking on the stairs and on the floor above, the sounds of doors being opened and closed. Children were always running about, in and out: Izzy and her friends from the village, other children here to play tennis, she said. Mog and Michael had been playing almost every day.

❧

Pressed for more details, Mog told Rebecca about the money and the picture: about my theft, on the day I disappeared, of two things, of £2000 from Henry, from a supposedly secret drawer in Henry's bureau, and of a watercolour of Sanctuary Wood that used to hang above it. These things I am assumed by strangers to have taken with me when I left. The brown-paper parcel with the £2000 in it has prompted several interesting questions. What was it doing there?

"Isn't it amazing how the opportunistic burglars of old folk are always finding great wads of cash in tea caddies and in sock drawers?" Christian Grant had said to Mog over their ill-starred dinner, having heard about the money and trying, unsuccessfully, to winkle more out of her. Christian, a widowed neighbour, was invited to ask Mog out by her mother, and Mog had only agreed because it was too embarrassing to refuse. It had been a stilted evening in a solemn restaurant, waiters outnumbering diners, cutlery noisy on china; there had been an inept kiss goodnight, Mog turning away and kissed on the ear. But he's right, it is amazing that Burglar Bill has such luck with the old folk, when the rest of us – bank-trusting, ATM-savvy, plastic-trained – might only be able to offer him some loose change in a plant pot behind the kettle amounting to £4.55.

Here's the family version: *Michael ran up the stairs unseen. He went along the corridor to his room, where regularly he spent the night and where he kept some of his things. He may have taken some personal effects; the drawers were left askew, suggesting haste and upset, though as nobody knows what was there it's hard to say what. He went into his grandparents' bedroom and took the watercolour from the wall. He opened the secret drawer of Henry's bureau, hidden inside what appears to be the moulding, and took a brown envelope containing £2000.*

Except it wasn't me. It was Alan Dixon.

Chapter 9

When she arrived at the high school Ottilie was told to wait in the corridor outside the rector's office. The rector: that's what they call headteachers round here. It was a cold and blustery day, and having been summoned to see him, she was on a recognisably war footing; at her most disarmingly anachronistic, wearing a long fitted dress in a green that flattered her colouring and a dark blue velvet cloak, her hair elaborately up. The rector came round the corner holding a bulging buff-coloured file, and seeing Ottilie waiting, and her armouring, he was thrown off his stride for a moment; thrown sideways, but only for a moment. Tall, crop-haired, flat across the hips and shoulders, long legs an undefined presence in his trousers, Mr Dunstane looked like an ex-policeman and that's what he was. He loped along with a swinging gait, big feet pointed slightly out, in his dark grey suit and school tie, his shoes and identity pin gleaming, and when he caught Ottilie's eye he glanced quickly away again. The proffered hand was cool and dry.

Mr Dunstane spent a few moments arranging his jacket around his chair, easing his trousers free at the knees before sitting. His fingers flicked through the file. One finger caressed his nose, up and down and along the line of the septum, up and down as he was reading. Then the file was closed. Now he was ready to look at Ottilie. He told my mother that I was to be asked to leave.

"What? Just like that? On what grounds?"

"I'm coming to that."

"Because of the Coterie?"

"That and other things."

"What harm does the Coterie do, can I ask?"

Mr Dunstane's brow furrowed. His nostrils flared. "The *Corrupt* Coterie," he said, by way of reply.

Ottilie couldn't keep from tutting. "It's just a reference," she said impatiently. "For heaven's sake."

"A reference?"

"It wasn't a name they dreamed up. Have you read the membership book? It was the name of a society at Oxford that a relative of his was involved in. It's a sort of homage."

"That's what worries me."

Anticipating this conversation, she had a copy of the book, skinny in its faded paper covers, really only a pamphlet, folded lengthwise in her hand, and she placed it on the table between them.

"You do know about the family connection?"

"David Salter. The soldier. Thank you, I have my own copy." He took it out of the back of the file and opened it at centre pages that were heavily marked in yellow highlighter.

"Articles of Faith. Item one. There is no god but pleasure." He looked at Ottilie as if expecting a reaction but didn't get one. "The Coterie have been introducing drugs in the school."

"Marijuana, you mean."

Mr Dunstane produced a small plastic bag, in a corner of which a variety of pills had clustered. He reached across to hold it up in front of Ottilie's face. "This, I believe, is not marijuana."

"Michael wouldn't –"

"Michael won't deny that these are his property."

"Where did you find them?"

"In the common room, behind the encyclopedias."

"How did you know they were there?"

"We were tipped off. I'm not prepared to say more than that at this time."

"And how do you know they are Michael's?"

"Information received. He hasn't denied that they are his property."

"What did he say? I presume this happened today."

"This morning. Michael and I had an interview and then Michael left the school."

"He's not here?"

"We imagined he'd gone home."

"He'll have gone to Peattie."

"Ah."

"What did he say at this interview?"

"He wouldn't speak to me."

"He hasn't said anything at all?"

"He said 'it makes no difference'. That was all."

"Will you go to the police?"

"No. Not if you take Michael out of sixth year by Friday." Mr Dunstane put his fingertips together, making a triangle of his hands, and looked intently at it. "I'm a great believer in facing facts, and the plain fact is that Michael doesn't want to be here. He's 18; he should be doing something that interests him. He has no interest in learning."

"I'd dispute that."

"His apathy is highly infectious."

"It's a Corrupt Coterie thing, that young men should look charmingly bored."

"He has been coming into school wearing make-up."

"Eyeliner, cravat, cigarette holder, black nail polish. Look at photographs of David Salter – I have one here and you'll see that –"

"Please." His hand came up. "Article two. Awake from the opium dream of the cosy life."

"He's quoting Edmund Gosse. Misquoting him."

"What would you say about this? I quote: the lower classes must learn once more to know their place."

"It's satire."

"Is it? Michael's set to inherit Glen of Peattie estate, I believe. I'm afraid that one of our teachers interprets these sorts of statements as harassment of the less privileged."

"That's idiotic."

"That's how she feels, and I have to tell you that she has some support here."

"It's been decided Michael won't inherit singly, as it happens. Peattie's to be divided up, in ownership I mean, not literally, between the grandchildren equally. Him and his cousins." Now she spoke more irritably: "You do know what it means, Peattie, don't you? It's a responsibility, it's a tie, it's a money pit. It's more of a burden than anything. It costs a fortune to maintain."

"And Michael knows this: that he won't inherit singly?"

"Of course."

"And how does he feel about it?"

"He isn't happy. That's my point. You ought to make allowance for that. He isn't as privileged as he thought."

Why did she tell him all this? I wish she hadn't. It would be all round the Rotary Club by Saturday.

"Miss Salter," he said, wearily. "It is *Miss* Salter, isn't it? The ethos of a school is very important, I think you'll agree. Its spirit. Its collective sense of purpose."

"Which is undermined by black nail polish and silly undergraduate humour?"

"Which is undermined by drugs."

"I need to talk to Michael," she told him, rising and leaving the room.

149

"Jet," she said to her driving mirror. "He will come forward and confess or I will have his guts for garters."

At Peattie, Edith counselled caution.

"Did you mention Jet's name to the school? As the likely party?"

"No. Has Jet been dealing in drugs, Mother? Has there been any hint from Joan?"

"Absolutely not. It isn't possible, Ottilie."

"Of course it's possible." She didn't mention that she knew Jet had been selling marijuana around the sixth form. The school knew that most of the sixth form had been smoking weed. It was smoked on such a scale that they didn't really have a choice but to ignore it: one expulsion would have led to mass expulsions, and inevitable media disgrace.

Now I came into the room.

"I'm leaving school anyway," I said, before Ottilie could speak. "I'd rather do the exams at the college. No point getting Jet booted out as well. Let me deal with him."

"The college is a terrible place," Edith piped up. "Do they even do Highers? I thought it was all welding and hairdressing there."

"You sound like Vita, Mother," Ottilie said. "Of course they do Highers. Not Latin, though. But we can get around that."

❧

We're moving on, to a day about 12 months later, to an afternoon in the study at Peattie. Edith and Henry were talking about what was to be done with me, the 19-year-old me. I was there also, but they were talking over my head. I was sitting and they were standing. There were other times in my life in which I was a ghost.

"And why was he sacked from the bookshop?" Henry was pacing, slapping a thin hardback volume against his thigh as he paced. It was Tilly's book once. Every time he slapped it, it released its sickroom smell.

"For reading," Edith admitted placidly.

"And the gallery job Ottilie got him? Tardiness. And the hotel position? Persistent scruffiness, despite being warned in writing. You can't serve tourists their cream tea in torn jeans. What's wrong with black trousers and a clean white shirt? Turning up late with his hair unbrushed and over his eyes."

"He's a teenager, Henry," Edith said. "And six feet two inches tall. He's grown like a beanstalk this year. He's tired a lot of the time. And he maintains that the denims were new."

"He keeps too-late hours," Henry told her. "A man can't expect to go to bed at two and rise for work at seven."

He caught sight of me now as if I'd just appeared. "You keep too-late hours, Michael. You have to grow up a bit. If you're not going to college you need to take work seriously. Your mother can't afford to keep you."

I didn't respond to this, although I could have, pointing out that Ottilie volunteered a sizable chunk of her earnings to estate maintenance. Henry opened the book and looked at it blindly, before throwing it on to the desk. "It's like you don't really have respect for the working week, Michael," he said. "Like it's beneath you."

"Of course it's beneath me," I said. "It's beneath everybody." I didn't make the speech that I wanted to, the one in which I'd point out that Henry didn't know much about the working week either, and was in no position to judge.

Looking back on these encounters, I'm not sure what kind of a human being I was then or whether I was adequate, even. I think I'm kinder now. Teenagers, boys especially, aren't renowned for their engagement with others, and especially not with those who have or assert authority. If they have fires, these boys, they're damped down in the presence of those people, or misdirected.

If they have vital sources of empathy, they might reveal them only obliquely or not at all. In many ways I was a typical teenager, though whether I was typical of myself, my hidden self, I couldn't say. There seemed too much that was inexpressible. A lot of the time damping down was overdone. I felt as if I were standing on the wall of a vast dam looking out at a great dry valley, aware of millions, trillions of tons of water at my back. You could have taken a photograph of it from the air, that vast wide dam, and spotted a tiny figure supporting it, his arms held wide, and that would have been me.

Embarking on anything amounting to a shared confidence, any admission of weakness or doubt, felt as if it would ease open a low door in the wall, that the door wouldn't hold, that the pressure would bow and break it and torrents would rain down. When I was young I loved that 1960s film *Jason and the Argonauts*, the one with all the stop-motion characters in it. We didn't have television at the cottage but Henry would alert me if it was on and we'd watch it together, sound turned low, on his secret bedroom TV. It was taken out of a locked cupboard, a small black-and-white set, and placed on the bureau top; the internal aerial took endless fiddling with to bring any picture out of snow and crackle. Talos, the giant bronze figure who in mythology had one vein running from head to toe, a vein that could be undone via a single brass nail in his ankle (Achilles-like, then, but with a much more obvious case of fundamentally bad design): Talos, I understood. Bad news about my father: it's possible that it would have undone me far worse than no news, so perhaps my mother's judgment was good. At least in the arena of ignorance there was also mystery, and mystery could talk itself into a romance. Dam walls; metal gods with fatal weaknesses: the metaphors mixed themselves in dreams. And of course, a key point, one you will already have noticed, is that I thought of myself, my situation, too much and too deeply.

Too much and too often. It was a fatal, unbreachable inwardness. Not that I think it was particularly unusual, to be that way. It's a condition common to teenage boys, I suspect; not that lack of rarity helps anybody. The circumstances were atypical, but not that weight of emotion, that pressing weight, and the contradictory (it seemed at the time) pressure to be self-contained, certain, strong, unemotive at all costs. Because that was manly. The example of the great uncle hung heavily over all of us.

I loved and hated my mother. This simultaneous reality seemed to be unique to me. It wasn't something I could talk even to Mog about, which was ironic because she would have generalised her own experience and told me that it was a state of affairs near universal in its ordinariness. There are certain subjects that can't be discussed: there are things that once entertained as possibilities set themselves into fact, though they are also just the sorts of things that retreat from factualness when re-examined. These are things that change our relationships, not least with ourselves. They're things that are true only in their own inconsistent, paradoxical way, and that dissolve when we grasp them; sometimes it's only by speaking the words that something becomes true. Trying to be definitive on questions of love and hatred didn't help. Hatred wasn't in any case even remotely the right word. If anyone spoke out against Ottilie, if they speak up against her now, I feel my blood rising to her defence.

I'm embarrassed to admit to this, but I'm afraid that all the clichés about insecure children testing parental boundaries applied illustratively to me. Could my mother find me intolerable to live with and still love me? Could she put up with constant questioning about my father and my rage, and still love me? Would the family – by which I meant Edith and Henry – take in their stride my distaste for school, for "getting on in life" via university and a profession, and be able to respect my intention to work in forestry, to earn little and live simply, and still love me? Looking back, there was something more than a little tedious in this, in the daily unrelenting task of living in and with this mind and travelling its daily circumlocutions. But these are among the memories that have persisted and survived. So much has been forgotten, so much lost. I wish often, in the wood in the night, that I could live my life over again in sequence, eidetically and a day at a time, and pencil in my footnotes. But memory won't allow for that. So much has been lost.

What do I remember from my very early life? As little as most people. Running along topiary hedges. The iconography of the house, a sequence of rooms that seemed gigantic to me as a small boy, each with its own mood and smell. I remember wearing a small stiff coat in light blue tweed, its dark velvet collar, the matching short trousers, and thick white tights that showed between knee and patent shoe. Why would anyone dress a modern child that way? It was done for Christmas, aping old traditions, for Henry's sake, no doubt. I remember being put into this uncomfortable clothing. Or maybe I don't remember it. Maybe what I'm remembering is what I imagine happened when I saw the photograph – as often I did as it was mounted in a dark wood frame on the wall of Henry's study for years. It showed me in the blue tweed, standing by a vast tree in the hall, its lights glinting behind me, the nose of a recumbent brown Labrador reaching up to sniff at my hand from beneath. It's one of the photographs Henry took down from the wall, moving silently and methodically around the house with a box. It's possible that I looked at it once and imagined what it must have been like to be three and dressed that way, and that the imagining has taken root as fact.

I'm sentimental about these early photographs. I have my own internal ones to add, especially of first days at school. There are images of a happy boy there. By six, though, the look had arrived: the look I'd have ever after.

At six my mother had begun to educate me. She wanted me to know that my father was worthless, and that it wasn't to be talked about other than for this key fact, one that prevented it being talked about. A single fact should be enough. In later years there was a little more elaboration. She wanted me to know how frequently and how casually men abuse women, that even a happy marriage abuses women in its pleasant dreadful way: that abuse of every kind was the norm from which she was determined I'd prove exceptional.

It was only when I'd gone that Edith noticed the look.

"He seems so angry in the photographs," she said to Henry, two weeks after my disappearance, the two of them together late at night in their bedroom. "Look at him, Henry." She began laying down successive images of me, one after another on the dressing table. "Look at him, Henry. Here, look at that defiance. Did you see that defiance? When he was – when he was with us?"

Henry didn't answer.

"I don't know why I haven't seen it before" Edith said. "Was it there before? It looks new. It's new to me."

Henry went over to his wardrobe and began rearranging sweaters, taking them out of the cupboard in a heap, flicking their empty arms into position before folding and restacking them.

"Henry."

"Yes," Henry said. "I think there was something psychological from the beginning."

"Psychological?"

"Some predisposition, I mean."

"Predisposition – to be sad?"

"I think we should have pressed Ottilie to get him seen and onto medication of some kind."

"You don't think that her refusal to talk about Alan was enough of a reason? In itself?"

"I'm tired, Edith. I need to go to bed and to read."

This was Henry's way of bringing her late-night attempts at discussion to a halt, a historic one with many citable precedents. Tiredness can only be contested by the unsympathetic, after all, and Edith is never going to be that. Wanting to read: that's a sacred desire.

When I was small and we lived at Peattie, I spent much of my time under the supervision of my grandmother. Henry was doing a little farming still at that time and wasn't to be seen in the house and gardens much, so it was predominantly a female household of middle-aged and elderly women, comprising not just Edith but also Vita, Great Aunt Tilly, Mrs Hammill. My mother was absent most hours of the day, at the art college or else working.

My cousins at the gatehouse weren't friends, in those early years. That only happened later, when we were teenagers and I came to the house alone. Chess with Jet, swimming with Mog, tennis with Pip and Mog: these were the beginnings of my intimacy with the Salter-Cattos, when I was 14. Before sport began to be a bridge, relations had remained formal and mutually suspicious. I was a serious child, sullen, given to sullen pronouncements, attempting serious reading beyond my age and scowling at interruptions. The gatehouse children kept their distance. Other boys were imported from the village for me to play with, when I lived at Peattie, but these experiments weren't often a success. It was clear that special and hypocritical effort was being made, and children can sense that. I'd watch from the window seat in my room, watching the car coming up the drive, the mother reassuring the boy in the passenger seat that he was going to have a fun time, and clear knowledge of exactly the opposite written all over the victim's face. I'd make an effort, at least for a half-hour or so, but then I could feel it failing, my interest in them, my determination to make the afternoon a success. Making an effort was almost worse. I asked about the fathers and how they made their money. I didn't know this was rude. Why should it be rude? I was trying to be interested in them. I was just trying to do what Edith recommended and look interested.

It's easy to point the finger at Ottilie, at the way she brought me up, at her remoteness, and I've been as guilty of this as anyone when it suited me. Generally, though, I'd speak up for her – to Joan and Euan, specifically, who were forever on our case once we'd left the estate, chipping away at what confidence remained. They weren't buying Ottilie's earnest pronouncements about hands-off parenting being best for children, about boredom leading to resourcefulness. The disdain was mutual. Ottilie was horrified by Joan's approach to motherhood, and told her so, that she disapproved of Joan's monitoring every hour of her children's development, her scheduling-in of activities that filled the evenings. Poor Mog had ballet on her schedule, which she loathed, and also piano and French and gymnastics. Ballet and gymnastics were torture for a heavy child. Ottilie said that Joan wasn't prepared to let her children be separate people with separate personalities and ideas. In turn, Joan made occasional threats about social workers.

But I might not have defended my mother energetically enough. There were times when I enjoyed Joan and Euan's claims that they felt sorry for me, though it became obvious over time that this didn't entail their attention or love. If I think of Peattie throughout my childhood and imagine how it would have been with no Joan and Euan in the gatehouse, having decommissioned them from the family, I'm afraid that it would have been vastly improved (though I'm not willing to let go of the cousins, who would've had to be painlessly orphaned). Joan and Euan were like two chemicals that when mixed together appear not to react very much – no explosions, no smoke – but who seep their poisons into the surroundings in a steady and deadly way. And of course, as is the way of these things, certainly for the deeply insecure, the harder a nut to crack their approval of me grew, the more I craved and yielded to it and offered up the sledgehammer.

From Joan there was constant advice to widen my social network.

"Don't you have friends you can go to tea with after school?"

"Not really."

"You'd be properly fed at least."

"It's fine."

"You could come to us, of course, but we're here and you're there. Not exactly handy. There must be someone nearby. Do you have friends at school who'd let you spend the weekend with them?"

"I come to Peattie at the weekends."

"Of course you do. At least you have Peattie."

From Euan there was the manifesto of single-minded hard work.

"You do a lot of reading at the cottage, I hear."

"That's right."

"Well, at least, not having a television, you get your school work done. Ours is on all the time."

I couldn't think of a reply to this.

"You're very able, and you apply yourself, and that impresses me, Michael."

"Thanks, Uncle Euan."

"I wish I could convince Joan to get rid of our TV. Pip's barely read a book he didn't have to since he was ten. Good for you – you'll go far."

Why does this outstandingly banal conversation stick in my head? I think they were the kindest words Euan ever spoke to me.

In the autumn Edith got the photographs out of the box again. Henry came into the bedroom late at night, as was now his habit, much later than had ever previously been usual. He'd begun staying up drinking, alone in his study with the dogs watching him. He wouldn't talk to anybody about it. He'd wait until he was sure Edith must be asleep before he came to their room, dreading the intimacy of conversations held in the dark. But on this particular night she was lying in wait patiently in her nightclothes, a rug wrapped around cold shoulders, sitting on her bed with the box. Henry came into the room and turned on his heel when he saw what awaited him. Edith pleaded for just one more conversation about the photographs, just one more and she promised there wouldn't be another. After this the box would be resealed and would go into the attic to be among the photographed dead.

"I know you're tired," she said. "I'm tired too. It's a relief, sleep. It takes us out of this. Reading takes us out of this. Drinking takes us out of this. This situation."

Henry considered her words, and then he said, "The thing is, Edith, that we don't think the situation is the same."

"Not that again."

"It's not an *again*. It's a *still*. I still feel it. I'll keep feeling it. And that's that."

"Henry," she said. "I admire you. I admire your hanging on to the hope that Michael's not dead. But Henry." Her hands turned palms upward. "I think it would be better for you if you didn't."

"You're saying to me that it would be better if he had drowned, Edith. Is that really what you're saying?"

"It would be better if you could let go of your anger. Thinking he's out there and doesn't care, hasn't loved us enough to spare us this. To take this burden from us.

Thinking there's a kind of evil in him."

Henry was looking intently at his shoes. Flexing his toes in his trainers.

"You have to face facts," Edith told him. "Face them, Henry. Ursula has never told a lie. Alan has his faults but there's no earthly reason why he'd claim Michael was dead if he wasn't. Alan, of all people. And look." She paused. "Here's the thing, Henry, that I want to say to you. Michael loved you. He loved you, Henry."

Henry was in tears. He took his handkerchief out of his pocket and pressed it folded to his eyes. His fingernails were bitten short.

"The trouble is," he said through his hands, "the trouble is that I'm sure Michael's alive."

"How? Why are you sure?"

Henry didn't answer.

"Henry. This is important. Look at me. Promise you'll answer this question honestly. Henry. Promise."

"I promise."

"Have you heard anything of Michael, since he disappeared? Something you're not telling me?"

"No."

"You promise."

"I promise."

Chapter 10

On the ninth day after I disappeared my mother was well enough to talk, or at least it was the first day that Edith found her willing to. Edith went out to the coast, driving very slowly in the lumbering old car (a vehicle they didn't have road tax or an MOT for, thinking it hardly worth the effort, it was used so seldom), not really wanting to arrive anywhere and with no expectations. She sat parked for quite a while, her face registering her internal battle, before she got out and went to the door. It wasn't just the events and politics of my disappearance that kept her coming here, day after day. She had something she wanted Ottilie to know, something she'd never talked about with anyone. She thought that Ottilie knew already. She thought it probable that Ottilie didn't know that Edith knew: at this point in the thinking the whole thing presented itself as a knot, knotted up with possibilities, and Edith was desperate for it to be unknotted. What she wanted was for the two of them, she and Ottilie, to admit to each other the truth, long-buried and long-mourned. This was her seventh day of visiting, and the previous six attempts had all ended in failure, in ducking out; she'd been too nervous to embark.

For a seaside house the cottage is surprisingly gloomy. It was built in the early 18th century, and its tiny windows were designed to keep the sea and the weather out. It's in an unshowy working village, with harbour walls of a thick grey stone, walls thick enough to promenade along the top of in fine weather, ascending from precarious, worn stone stairways. The cottages along the harbour-front are harled with gritty outer coatings and painted in sugar almond colours, and stand shoulder to shoulder against the wind. Creels are piled on the quayside, smelling powerfully of seaweed and stale water and foul crustacean panic, alongside coils of blue rope and oddments of orange twine. Outsized metal rings remain set into concrete for the tying-up of ships that no longer visit; the hobby yachts bob on their moorings among the few remaining fishing boats, though no one makes much of a living any more; a modest net of haddock's landed for the locals, and a box or two of lobsters take the overnight train. This is the community that my mother has made fiercely her own. She's seen often at the wilder stretches of coast, a few miles' drive away, taking photographs and sketching. Lately she's been working on big canvases that look like they are made up of patches of scratchings and doodles up close, but resolve themselves, once the viewer steps back, into almost life-size observations of sections of cliffside geology and botany, cross-hatched by rain.

Ottilie hadn't left the cottage for a week, other than to go out onto the road to get groceries when the mobile shop came round. She spent the days in the studio and the nights in my old room, in my unwashed sheets with my unwashed pyjamas bundled up as a pillow. Edith knocked on the main door and, getting no answer, went round to the rear of the house and was let into the studio without a word. It's a separate building, converted and extended from a shed: the conversion won an architectural award. Ottilie was immersed, had reimmersed herself there, in work and in ocean light. Charcoal in hand, she had already noted, guiltily, that sorrow seemed to have improved her line. Work was going surprisingly well.

This is the world after a bereavement, a self-bereavement, self-mourned. Days and nights continue their cold-hearted progress, undaunted by your loss, the numbers on the calendar and minutes on the clock continually in motion. In the days following my death the allium opened in their hundreds in the woods, in garlic-scented massed ranks. Nothing comes to a slow stop to accommodate grief. The world fails to tip its cap. The sun might shine, the morning after you're gone, and it's hard not to take offence at such blatant disregard. Dogs need feeding, and so do people, and washing piles up, and there's little point in forsaking clean socks. From that inevitable basis a kind of normality springs. Whether it should or not is moot. You could make a case for the need of greater ritual. You could make a case, in this instance, for some vital link having been missed out in the family's journey from catastrophe to stoicism; you could argue that it moved from catastrophe to stoicism all too smoothly.

Ottilie let it be known in various unspoken ways that she wasn't pleased to be interrupted.

"We have to talk about Michael," Edith said to her, following her in.

Ottilie's answer was immediate and forceful. "There's nothing to say though, is there? You don't want to talk about justice. All you're interested in is protecting Ursula." She scrutinised her mother's face. "You don't look well."

"I'm fine," Edith said. "Is that coffee hot?"

It was difficult to know how to proceed. Ottilie poured their coffee from the pot in silence, and they drank in silence, each looking in different directions, Edith out at the view, Ottilie towards her sketchbook on the table.

"Please don't think that I don't understand," Edith said at last, quietly to the dunes and the sea.

"Understanding isn't the point," Ottilie told her.

"No justice could be possible now, though, could it? Not now. We've passed out of the zone of justice; we're in the zone of disaster here, and all that can be done about a disaster is that people try to recover. That's how it is after an accident."

"It was no accident."

"After an accident blaming is natural; it's natural but futile, my darling. All we can do now is grieve. Not just for Michael, but also for Ursula. The way her life has changed."

"The way her life has changed?" Incredulously.

"Yes."

"You can't just let her go unpunished – that's monstrous," Ottilie said. She got up and poured her coffee down the sink. "What upsets me is that you never look at this from Michael's viewpoint. It isn't fair that he's thought to have run away and never got in touch again. Think for a moment how that makes me look. And please: come on. *Come on.* You're not thinking straight about the gravity of this."

"Accident," Edith murmured.

"It makes no sense to me that you of all people would deny your grandson a Christian burial, Mother."

While Edith and Ottilie were having this conversation, Henry was going methodically around the house with the box, removing all remaining photographs of me and photographs that included me, as if I were being disinherited: more and worse than that, as if I were being disborn. Edith was distressed by this, by getting home to find the box of photographs sitting by the study door, but said nothing. The one of me in the little blue coat sat on top of the pile.

❧

Edith said that she would leave Ottilie to it; she could see that she was busy.

164

"Please don't be huffy with me," Ottilie said. "I can't take it. I can't."

"I'm not being huffy. There was something I wanted to talk to you about but this isn't the time."

Ottilie didn't rise to the bait. "Okay," she said, opening the door. "Another time. And can you call me before you come again. It's very hard to take up the spirit of a drawing again once you've been interrupted."

"I'm sorry."

"Come at lunchtime next time."

As Edith went back to the road, she could hear Ottilie weeping, a loud and uninhibited weeping, desolate and unrestrained. Coincidentally it sounded as if she was saying *her* over and over: her-her-her-her. A-her, her, her her. Edith paused on the path listening; it looked for a few minutes as if she'd return to the studio, but she didn't return. She turned away. She said aloud to herself, "If it was me, I'd rather do that alone." She herself began to weep, then, and her journey home was one in which she had frequently to wipe her face and blow her nose, driving one-handed, fumbling for fresh tissues from a box on the passenger seat of the car.

"You'll have to tell her that you know," she said to herself several times.

Her eyes were puffy and her nose pink, and so, feeling that she couldn't go back into the house, Edith went into Peattie via the loch entrance, parked by the back door and went down the path to the wood. As she drew closer she could hear shouts, shouts interrupted by laughter, a high-spirited argument, and as the loch came into view she saw that kids from the village – four boys, about 14 years old – had helped themselves to the boat and were having a high old time. Three of them, that is, were having a high old time: a fourth was the unfortunate they were trying to throw into the loch, his pleas reverberating along the valley. They promised him that he was about to have an encounter with Michael Salter that he wouldn't forget. He'd been manoeuvred almost to loss of balance, his back braced and one leg raised ready to kick, hanging on tight to the edge of the boat with determined white hands. Edith hurried back down the path to the house. She had to tell somebody. Who could she tell? Not Henry. Who then? Joan was sitting in the kitchen looking at paint charts, and so it was Joan that she told.

"Oh god. What will we do?" Joan jumped up. "What will we do? We have to do something."

"It's got to the village," Edith said. "They know in the village. It must have been Alan."

"I'm going to find him and have this out," Joan said, leaving the room. Edith paced up and down the kitchen while she was away. Twenty five minutes felt like hours, but when Joan got back she looked more relaxed.

"It's alright," she said, as she came back in. "It's alright. I'm sure it wasn't Alan. He seemed as horrified as we are. But he had an explanation. Suicide. There's a suicide rumour."

Privately, Joan wasn't as sure as she made out that Alan hadn't started the rumour, but she wanted, above all else, to provide her mother with certainties.

❦

The first time that the family used the boat again was on the first anniversary of my disappearance.

Pip came home for the weekend from his new job in Edinburgh, full of carefully disguised enthusiasms for it, for the city, for work, for the shabby rental over a video hire shop that he shared with three law students. He knew that, diplomatically, it must always be said that it's hard to be away from home. Almost the same minute he arrived, he announced that he and Mog were going out on the loch, that they'd decided that it was time. Joan protested that it was too soon. Euan said that was nonsense and they could do what they liked, but they had better not be seen doing it.

"There isn't any aspect of this that's about searching," Pip argued. "It's the opposite of that. It's about resuming. Has it occurred to you that in the village they'll also be wondering why nobody uses the boat any more?"

"That's a good point," Joan said immediately.

Pip and Mog went down the loch path in silence. Together they hauled the boat from the shore, dragging furrows in the shingle, and they rowed out, still not having spoken, away at a diagonal towards the ruin that hugs the western side, a stumpy medieval relic, its walls weathered lower than man high. They rowed to the orange buoy, a fishing buoy, tied the boat off and stowed the oars. Though it was June, heavy sweaters were worn over shorts; there would be no repeat of the heatwave summer. They took two mildew-spotted cushions of faded cotton paisley out from under the tarpaulin that was stored folded at one end, adjusting them into pillows for their heads, and slouched down each at their own end of the boat, positioned just high enough to see each other's faces across the thwart, the boat's central raised plank.

At 19 Pip was slight, delicate-looking, and appalled to resemble his mother. By 25 he would become a different Pip entirely, having remade himself at the gym, and would return to Peattie wider across the shoulders, densely muscled in the upper arms, his neck and jawline bulked decisively away from their earlier femininity, in good tailoring in an open-top car, and would make them all, every last dismissive villager, eat flies open-mouthed. For now though, he was still mistaken with humiliating frequency for a girl.

They lay in silence for a while and then Pip said, "Do you think he's dead? I don't think Michael's dead."

Mog sat up straighter and looked out across the water. They were safely out of the death zone, having positioned themselves over at one side, a place in which it was just about possible to interact with the loch in the old way, free of associations and fears. She put a hand into the water, pushing it to and fro, feeling its weight and resistance, then raised it wet to her lips and kissed her fingers.

"What are you doing?"

Mog didn't respond.

"Where did the money go?" Pip asked her. "And where's the picture?"

"Into the boat with him."

"Crap," Pip said. "Crapissimo. Multo, multo turdo."

"Maybe Henry misplaced it, lent it out, left it at the framer's, sold it years ago and then forgot."

"Nope." Pip tapped his fingers against the boat interior, his hands above his head. There was safety in lying so low, at or under the waterline, the gunwales cupping around you. When we were young this was the ultimate venue for private talks: we'd drape the tarp across and make a cabin and take picnics that we'd eat lying almost flat, propped up just enough to avoid choking.

Mog twisted sideways to lean her forearms against the boat edge, for once unselfconscious about it, looking out with real curiosity across the water. They'd dream about it: each had confessed this to the other, about me in the loch: stumbling upon me washed up on the shore half-rotted, or encountering me while swimming, diving down and blundering into me, the thing I'd become. Mog had written about it in her journal. *Michael is down there somewhere, his flesh floating from his bones in long pale strands, waving gently like pondweed, his face obliterated. Even though Henry says not. What's that Eliot line? "Those are pearls that were his eyes." Though that always makes me think of a cooked trout on a plate.*

"He's alive then," she conceded. "He went off with the picture and the cash and left his clothes and his wallet in the car. Odd behaviour, but okay. I'll buy it. So where is he? Why hasn't he been in touch?"

"Ursula told him a secret. One so terrible that we can never be forgiven. But what could it be, this secret? Really? Other than the obvious, Alan's the father, so what? So terrible that we can never be forgiven?"

He spoke to the sky, which was low and uniformly cotton-woollish, the clouds having laid themselves out in regular soft pleats. He was rapping lightly, in repeating sequences; a steady, piano-like chord-making against the wood.

"You're saying that Ursula made it up. Ursula and Alan, both. That Michael survived: he left Ursula and swam across the loch and took Henry's cash and the painting from the car, but left his clothes and his wallet and his books. And then left Peattie on foot in dripping wet clothes." Pip began to answer but Mog's voice drowned him out. "And it's still not a good enough excuse for not phoning or writing. Not just an excuse; not a good enough *reason*. Michael wouldn't do that to us. I knew Michael. He wouldn't."

"But you didn't know him, did you? As it turned out."

"I knew enough."

"Look," Pip said. "It isn't just me, you know. Henry doesn't think he's dead either."

"Why does Henry think he's alive?"

"It's a trick he lets his brain play on him. I don't know. Maybe he knows something he's not telling. He grows – what's the word? – sheepish. He turns a bit sheepish and coy when I mention it."

"You mention it?"

"We don't talk about it often. But sometimes. On the phone. He's unexpectedly forthcoming and frank on the phone. He told me a story about a young man, old enough to have young children, who died in the mountains and wasn't recovered. True story. He was encased in ice. His son grew up and went into the mountains looking for him, and came upon him unexpectedly. He was perfectly preserved. The two of them looked almost identical, and his father was younger than he was."

"Imagine if that were true of Michael, in the deeps. Michael, suspended in the water and still 19."

"I know. The night after Henry told me the glacier story, I dreamed we found Michael, you and me, a long way in the future, that we had him retrieved once everyone else had died."

"Everyone else had died?"

"We were old and grey, and he was younger than your grandchildren."

"Mine? You didn't have grandchildren?"

"My son didn't live long enough. Curse got him. Don't you ever dream that the curse gets you? Course, I don't believe in it when I'm awake."

"I can't bear to think about it. Michael. Michael hit hard with the oar and drowning."

"Apparently I shout in my sleep. I see her face, Ursula's. The look on her face. You don't beat somebody about the head with a heavy wooden object by accident."

"Don't tell me you're sceptical. It's not a small thing, you know, her fear. She was frightened and struck out and hit harder than she meant to."

"Or she's a psycho. One we protect and are prepared to perjure ourselves for. Who might do it again."

Mog looked at him, eyebrows raised, and shook her head. "I don't think you've ever taken it seriously enough. Her aquaphobia. If that's the right word. Her water-terror."

"What do you mean 'not seriously enough'? I know what you know. I know she's terrified of water."

"I don't think you do, Pip. Did you hear about Shetland?"

"Gran told me. She flew up to Shetland to see the wool, to the farm where they spin her wool. Got upset on the plane."

"Upset is understating it somewhat. Went into one of her *things*. Not listening. Chanting. Freaked the other passengers out. The cabin crew hovering, offering solutions but insisting on her being seated and supervised, all the same. She was told not to look. And it was fine at first. She was placed on an aisle seat, given an eye mask; held Edith's hand. All going well. And then she decides she wants to see. Disaster."

"I don't understand why Gran thought she'd manage it."

"Ursula said she was sure. And she never goes anywhere. It was supposed to be a treat, a 30th-birthday treat."

"I see where this is going. Ursula thrown into a panic on the loch with Michael, not really responsible for her actions. Going into one of her 'things'. Not really herself. Not really responsible. But tell me this, Mary Salter-Catto. Who's responsible when nobody's responsible?"

"Don't start on the law speak."

"I'm not starting on the law speak."

"She won't get in the bath, you know. Ah, you didn't know that. I'm serious. Afraid of the bath. Even when it's just the shower running. Afraid of the feel of it on her skin. You know that Gran has to wash her hair for her? You've no idea how bad it is. She has to go to the cottage, twice a week, get Ursula into the shower, play music to cover the water noise, and even then sometimes she gets upset, gets out with her hair full of soap, and it has to be finished in the sink, Ursula sitting with her back to it, eyes tight shut and Gran singing."

"I don't think he's dead, Mog."

"But Ursula always tells the truth. Always."

"Yes, but don't you see? That applies just as earnestly to mistakes. Misapprehensions. Doesn't it? You're not lying if you believe utterly in what you say, and it proves untrue; you're just wrong. I think she welded two disasters together when she gave her account. The front half of it was Michael, the back half Sebastian, seeing Sebastian fall into the loch and disappear. Barely a ripple and then gone. That's the death of Sebastian. Mother says she used exactly the same words."

"So Ursula is mistaken. And Alan?"

"Is a liar."

"But why would she get the two events mixed up?"

"Perhaps she was encouraged to, by a 'friend' who talked to her as he rowed her back to shore."

"Oh, come off it."

"I'm not joking. I think he's capable of anything. I think he's a very dangerous man."

"On what evidence?"

"Well, I know this much for certain: Ursula would parrot whatever he told her. I've tried it, experimentally. I know this for sure. She'll repeat any old rubbish to Edith that you tell her, and insist that it's true."

"What did you say to her?"

"It was about aliens. It doesn't matter."

"Oh, Pip."

"It was important. It proved something."

"I suppose."

"Alan told his lie, this big lie, to somebody who takes absolutely everything at face value."

Mog put one hand to her breastbone and closed her eyes. Her fingers and her eyelids fluttered and her breathing pattern grew fast.

"What's the matter?"

"It's nothing. Just having a moment. Imagining it. All that going on while I was … while I was having the hard-hearted nerve to feel bored, half a mile away and not knowing. You in a car on the motorway listening to music. None of us even aware. His lungs filling with water. Don't you believe in the curse, sometimes, even when you're awake?"

"Mog, small children who can't swim die in pools and ponds every day."

"Yes."

"Sebastian. That was an ordinary event, I'm afraid to say. Shockingly ordinary and meaningless."

"Yes."

"And Michael. Ursula was his curse, Mog."

"That's horrible. You don't really think it was that callous. God and Moses."

"No way of knowing."

"That's the problem. What we'll never know and what's crucial to know is what she meant. It matters so much, what it was that she meant. How much malice there was, how much planning, how much understanding. That's what makes the difference, that judgment."

"Okay," Pip said, sliding sideways onto one hip, and then onto his knees, holding onto the edge and looking over. "Murder in the boat. We need to try this out. You can be Ursula."

Even before her name was out of his mouth, Pip had gone quietly over, was over the edge and gone, with an economical gymnastic ease. His head disappeared for a moment, but reappeared just as Mog lunged towards him. His hands came over the side first, clutching on, his fingers flattened and whitened. "Bloody freezing. Hurry up."

"Hurry up and what?"

"Oar. Take oar out of oarlock." His breath came in gasps. He waited while she fumbled with it. "More towards the middle; spread your hands. Like ice in here. Never swum this far out. Michael, holding on and looking up at you. Now, go to – no! Slowly! Jesus Christ."

"Only kidding." She had mimed rage, but Pip had time to duck the oar as it came at him. Mog had slowed its pace, and when it landed on the edge of the boat, rocked it only gently side to side. She looked nervously at the place where it struck as if waiting for water to spurt up or for the thing to break decisively in two and sink, pointing its ends upward, leaving the two of them looking as surprised as cartoon animals.

He had clambered back in. Mog was already looking under the tarpaulin. "Is there a rug in there? Thanks." Water streamed off him and his teeth were chattering.

"You're an idiot. We'd better get back. Are you sane enough to row?"

They hurried back to the house, Pip still wrapped in the grimy old boat blanket, purple rings around his eyes and his lips dark blue.

Chapter 11

The morning of the day before I vanished I went out early with my surfboard, but there was no swell at all, and the sea, unusually tropically blue, was an unprecedented flat calm. Day on day the heat had built and intensified until it was near sinister, the sky so faultlessly blue that it appeared two dimensional, a painted canvas heaven. There would be no surfing today. It seemed as if there would never be surfing again, as if there would never be rain; like weather had come to an end and in the sky there were only ever to be these vast open blue fields.

There being nothing remotely like a wave, I threw down my board and settled for swimming, ploughing up and down in the water. I took a lot of exercise at that time, exercising alone. It was important to be physically tired. If I was tired I could settle to work, to reading and thinking and writing. The sentence-making, paragraph-forming impulse was becoming systematic and diseased and I wrote and wrote compulsively in notebooks. I exercised alone and I worked alone, and each was in its own way a strategy. It broke my obsession into manageable parts. When I was swimming I thought about the father, and my mother's attitude to him and to me. When I was working I didn't have to. That was the respite. I knew that when exercising and work were done for the day, Mog would telephone at her usual time. We were close again, my friendship with Ursula having taken a bizarre turn. Often our phone calls started arbitrarily and ended the same way, taking up a point from earlier or from an earlier day without need of much of a preamble. I thought Mog was immensely generous, the kindest person I'd ever met. I didn't really cotton on that there was more to it than that, though Pip tried to warn me, jokingly, just how attached to me she had become.

My mother came out and sat on the bench, which sits sand-embedded in front of the studio's big rear window, only 20 feet or so from the edge of the cliff, among the marram grasses. The word cliff gives the wrong impression, as it's only a short scramble onto the beach. Footholds worked into the slope lead down to a bank of rough pink pebbles that in turn gives way to orange sand, a wide hard slick of it that resists footprints unless the tide's newly out. Ottilie was wearing a long, thin greyish-green dress; she brought a notebook and a cup of coffee and watched me. She was drawing me. She has hundreds of drawings of me that nobody has seen. I swam, and then I sat in the shallows a while, and swam again, and my mother watched me and drew. After a while she went back in and made us both a sandwich. She signalled to me that lunch was ready, holding up a plate with one hand and pointing at it with the other. I raised my arm in acknowledgment and came to her slowly up the shoreline, feeling the sun already burning off the sea water and hot on my head. I can feel that bench beneath me, even now, how rough and hard it was, the hot wood slats and the marram grass tickling; I can taste the warm curds of egg, the grain of the bread and the cold butter. There were dolphins out in the bay and we watched them sewing through the water, up and down. It was growing misty out there: a sea fret was building, the bane of hot weather on this part of the coast.

While we were eating, Ottilie asked me whether I'd thought any more about going back to the college and doing the exams. Disappointment flooded through me. This, then, was the real point of the sandwich. I told her that all I knew for certain was that going to university would be a waste of time, that it was a different kind of education I craved: a line of argument that had already prompted Henry to find me ungrateful. Escalating, the row moved sideways into the usual territory, broadening and then narrowing into the one usual thing, our own predictable imploding star.

This day, this memory of a day, was made again, conjured up with words. Mog had been telling Rebecca about it. Rebecca had been probing more on the question of my disappearance, and Mog was beginning to suffer the onset of a slow and deadly social panic, the effect of which was to make her voluble; certain of the things she swore she wouldn't say, she heard herself saying, rolling through the prohibition noisily as coins.

"Ottilie said once, during one of her low periods, that his conception was *a mistake,*" she told Rebecca. "His being a mistake was an idea – the idea – that Michael was drawn to more and more."

"A mistake – that's horrible."

"But Ottilie persisted in thinking that it could be talked about rationally between them. Trying to be honest and precise, she said that yes, a mistake, but a mistake only in so far as few people would want to get pregnant at 18 after a one-night stand. As you can imagine this wasn't the affirmation Michael was hoping for. So Ottilie told him that in retrospect it was serendipity, the happiest of accidents. It was too late to erase the word, though, and qualifying it was a disaster."

"So you don't know who the father was?"

"Everyone has their own theory. She got very drunk, apparently, and it's hard to believe but she'd never drunk alcohol before my parents' wedding. Different world, then. Got drunk on punch and was found at 2am more or less unconscious on a sofa."

When it became obvious that she was pregnant, Henry went across the country banging on doors late at night, bellowing his need for admission and for answers. Some of these families haven't spoken to the Salters since. Subsequently, Henry and Edith came up with what's referred to as the Family Version, which can be summed up as "Young girl introduced by some bounder to drink and seduced". The village story was and is slightly different: "Little slut was sleeping around."

We had a row, my mother and I, on the bench, under the interrogatory white light of the overhead sun. I said I'd had enough of it all, I couldn't go on, feeling disgust at the use of this language even as I was speaking, the cliché-ridden language of not being able to go on. I said it was time to think about a life of my own. This didn't alarm her unduly: it wasn't the first or third or 13th time that she'd heard it. The monologue deteriorated into wounding generalisations, as these things do, to all of which my mother gave her usual stoical responses. I stormed off into the house, slamming the door, and I watched her from the window as she returned to her sketchbook. There was an extraordinary light effect, out there in the bay. The sea fret was building and rolling, like some physical arrival, like an armada of ghost ships, the strong sunshine illuminating and piercing it. It was too individual an encounter to give up. She had reached already for the box of pastels.

I went to my room and dressed. Dark jeans, a thick brown belt, the one with the cowboy buckle, the favourite blue shirt, brown leather boat shoes. Forgive me if I fetishise a little. I like these words, the cotton feel of them, cool on my skin, the buttons. I packed a bag, took my wallet and passport and diary, and drove down to Peattie. As I left the cottage I had one last view of my mother. She stood up, upsetting cold coffee onto the sketch, got up onto the seating planks of the bench and waved after the car with one extended arm. My parting view of her was in a wing mirror.

~

Mog brought the conversation to a halt by asking if Rebecca had seen the painting of the great aunts, and having been assured that she hadn't, led the way down the stairs to the study. On the wall above Henry's desk, three painted women gazed serenely out of a dark brown frame. Three brown-haired heads, three ivory-skinned faces, sultana brown eyes, pomegranate-tinted mouths, their facial shadows judged skilfully in mauve and blue.

"Is that them?"

"Great Aunt Ursa and sisters. It was done in 1930. One of the few pictures that survived the round-up. The painter's quite well known now. They took a photograph of it for a book."

"Like you and me. Only better."

"He made the noses longer and their mouths wider. But they were all incredibly skinny; that's accurate."

Great Aunt Ursa is pictured in a mid-green suit with darker satin lapels. The neckline descends into a broad V, no cleavage discernible. Skinny is right. They were bony, tall, too tall to be matched easily at dances with men, and were famously undeferential to male opinion, but wore clothes well. Clothes hung unimpeded from their shoulders. Great Aunt Jo's in a dark-red dress, and Great Aunt Tilly's in aubergine purple. All three have collar-length bobbed hair waved tight across the top of the head from severe side partings. It's like three views of one woman.

"My mother and Ottilie were born on Tilly's birthday, on her 50th, and Tilly and Jo were both childless. It was a way of honouring them. Perpetuating them, I suppose.

They couldn't leave Ursa out, so Ursula turned up nine years later pre-named."

"Long gap. What if she'd been a boy?"

"Miscarriages. She'd have been Henry. Or should have been. Henry the fifth. But there was a boy. A year after her. Sebastian. You must know about Sebastian."

"Why wasn't he a Henry?"

"I'm told it was time for a change. It got shunted to a middle name. He died, though, Sebastian, aged four, in the loch."

"Dad told me … How on earth? He fell in? He was on his own?"

"His sisters were with him, and also a German au pair."

"Did anyone see what happened?"

"Yes, Mum and Ottilie saw. And Ursula. Ursula's never been the same. It was the au pair's fault. The au pair had got distracted. She was flirting with Alan Dixon."

"So what happened to him – to Sebastian?"

"He was throwing stones into the loch, off the end of the jetty, lobbing them in to see how far he could get them. He lost his balance. It was that simple and trivial. Lost his balance, toppled in. My mother went in after him and couldn't find him. Alan and the au pair were too busy arguing to notice; flirting had turned into a row. By the time Alan got there it was too late."

"It can't be deep there, surely."

"It's surprisingly deep, and dark, and very weedy. We don't swim anywhere near the jetty."

"How horrible. How truly dreadful."

"Ursula was completely traumatised. She didn't speak for years after."

"She didn't speak?"

"She didn't say a word."

They went together to Rebecca's room, which was Ursa's old bedroom, a forget-me-not blue room with dark furniture. When Edith lived here she maintained these family rooms, had them cleaned and the sheets refreshed as if perpetually we were expected for the weekend, and let us leave our things lying around undisturbed. When family members died, their rooms took on a sort of double identity, half shrine and half guest room; they were never decorated again or improved. Ursa's room had retained her chosen décor, its framed sewn things from her youth and childish accumulations. Silk scarves that were hers hung from the vanity mirror and jewellery of hers was clustered on the top of the chest of drawers as if it had just been put there. Some of her clothes remained in the wardrobe, pushed tightly to one side to allow Rebecca space to hang her own things. There were also towels and blankets put out, and a water jug by the bed, and books and a tin of biscuits, ready for the visitations of the living.

"I love this, being surrounded by my grandmother's things," Rebecca said. "It feels as if the past isn't really over."

Ursa's room was the scene of some drama one afternoon, during the winter before this. It was during the time that Edith was ill; it was her having been so very ill that prompted Joan to announce there'd be a party in the summer. The crisis had arrived unannounced one evening with back pain and breathlessness and had turned out to be an embolism, a clot that had travelled from a vein in her calf to her lung. Edith was in the hospital on a clot-busting drug. It was almost the end of January. After a mild, damp December, an un-christmassy Christmas, truly wintry weather had arrived with the new year; earth had stood hard as iron, water like a stone. But then in the third week, the thaw had come. Grey snow lay piled up and dirty at the sides of the roads. The trees dripped. Sleet fell soft and wet against the windows and sills, clogging the last glimmer of afternoon light, clogging the windscreen wipers as the family returned in the car from visiting. It had been a cheerful hour at Edith's bedside, despite the seriousness of her condition, but there was a price for false confidence: Joan and Ottilie had argued in the car afterwards and bad feeling followed them into the house. It was almost as cold inside as out, and so when Ottilie came into Ursa's room she was still wearing her military-looking overcoat and fake-fur hat, and the woolly green socks that had lined her wellingtons. She sat on the bed with a thump, her hands clasped firmly. One foot drummed against the carpet.

Mog and Pip came in, wearing the Norwegian patterned sweaters that Edith had given them for Christmas, Mog in her matching hat and Pip in his matching scarf. Pip turned on the bedside lamp and the twilight of the room became blue. Mog shut the door behind her with exaggerated care so that its catch barely clicked at all, and went and sat beside Ottilie.

"She'll be alright. They caught it in time. She'll be out in a few days. Gran's tough as old boots, you know that. Don't worry."

Joan came down the corridor outside, calling Ottilie's name, opening and closing other doors. Ottilie pulled her fur hat down further over her ears. Joan was stalled for a few minutes by finding Henry in my old room. They heard the door opening and her exclamation.

"Dad? What on earth are you doing in here?"

The door was closed on the two of them and things went quiet again. One of Ursa's scarves had fallen to the floor and for some reason Mog put it not on the chest but on the radiator, where Ursa's scent wafted stalely out of it.

"You won't really go to the police?" she asked Ottilie.

My mother got up and went to the window. She began to draw five-pointed stars in the condensation on the glass. "All I meant was that I'd tell them my theory that he committed suicide and that he's in there."

"That's not what you meant," Pip said.

"I want him found, Pip."

"Gran's going to be fine. She's on the drug and getting better."

"I want him," Ottilie said. "I want him back. I want to bury him. I want to visit his grave, his proper grave, and talk to him. I can't bear another year of him there in the loch, unloved and unretrieved."

"Not unloved, never that," Pip said, his voice wavering.

The door opened, making Mog jump. Joan came in and closed it behind her. "What are you doing in here?"

No one answered her.

Joan stayed by the door, leaning against it with her hands behind her back. Ottilie didn't acknowledge her. She had her eyes fixed on Pip.

"I've realised lately that I expected to lose him; I'd expected it for a long time."

"Ottilie," Joan said. "There's a reason why this is the thing we don't talk about. A good reason. It doesn't help. It just upsets people. It doesn't go anywhere new."

"Ottilie's talking," Pip said quietly.

"Well, I'm talking now," Joan told him. "And what I want to say, Ottilie, is that I hope you go in to Dad and apologise for that outburst. There wasn't any excuse."

"Shut up, Mother," Pip said.

"He's worried sick," Joan continued, "and the last thing he needs is you making threats about Ursula."

"I knew deep down there was a disaster coming," Ottilie said, sitting on the window seat. The condensation ran in drips from the star points. "I knew about his unhappiness. I should have done something. Stubborn *fucking* pride." I hadn't ever heard my mother use this word before. It was drawn out and emphasised, quietly and almost menacingly,

183

as if she'd just discovered its full weight and power. "I'd been visited by premonitions all that week. I woke in the middle of the night, three, four days before he died. Visited by premonitions. Waking with a start. Terrible engulfing dread. An awful doomy feeling, like the phone was going to ring and somebody was already dead."

"Oh, for pity's sake," Joan said.

"I'd go and look at him asleep," Ottilie continued. "I'd watch him sleeping, stroke the side of his face with my hand, tell him I loved him. Things I couldn't any longer do when he was awake. He'd disagree, you see. He'd want to talk definitions."

Joan tried to share a look with Mog, a complicit look, but Mog averted her eyes.

"I'm going home," Joan said, opening the door. "Ring me if there's news."

Shortly after this we heard the sound of Henry being ushered down the corridor to bed. Ottilie said she was tired and was turning in too.

Mog and Pip saw her to my room, where she'd said she wanted to sleep that night, and then they went down to the kitchen. Pip brewed up some coffee using the Italian beast of a machine they'd bought for Christmas for Edith and Henry. Mog pressed her cold fingers against the useless lukewarm kitchen radiator. Thin gold strands of tinsel drooped from the curtain rail.

"Ottilie thinks he killed himself," she said to Pip's back. "Suicide."

"Today she does."

"Today she does."

Pip looked round at her. "It varies, though, doesn't it? The certainties come and go. It's the same with all of us."

"What could be worse than your child killing itself? What a slap in the face. What a knife turned in the guts. There couldn't be any greater punishment, could there?"

"You take her too literally, Mog."

"It says 'you failed me', doesn't it? It's not a neutral act. There's accusation in it."

Pip put a cup of coffee on the table in front of her. "She's talking about going out to the wolf. Doesn't mean Ursula didn't do it."

"Ursula won't tell secrets; won't ever," Mog said, sipping. "Perhaps Michael's death is one. She's covering for him."

"What total crap you do talk sometimes." Pip sank into the chair opposite. "That's the thing, though. Ursula. She's the wolf."

Someone passed by the kitchen door, and went off down the corridor. Pip lowered his voice. "Suicide makes no sense. Why kill himself, when all he ever wanted was to confront him, and he could see Alan standing on the beach."

∽

It was Rebecca who heard the taxi first, putting her book down and going to the window. Izzy had arrived, was emerging legs first from the rear door: heeled shoes, long legs, shoes and legs and hem, and then she was up and out, smoothing her dress, which was halter-necked and silky, a brown and cream polka dot belted tight into her small waist. She was pushing long hair off her face with one hand while she bent at the front window to pay: that same pink-gold cape of hair my mother has in the early photographs. Ottilie has said to me that it isn't easy, seeing herself as a young woman around the house, recognising the loss of all that, the waste. She's said that she has to prevent herself from making grandiose speeches. Izzy came up the steps, an overnight bag in one hand, a red leather bag with beaten gilt corners, the fingers of her other hand trailing in the lichen along the top of the wall. When she got to the terrace she took off her shoes and ran barefoot into the house. Henry's oldest dog, a black and white spaniel waddling stiffly into old age, was in his bed by the study door. Badger had been sleeping, but raised his head and, seeing that it was Izzy, wagged his stumpy tail. Izzy crouched beside him for a few minutes, and then without further ado she went for a bath.

"But where's the entourage?" Mog asked her through the bathroom door.

"Next train. Euan's going. Just one. Terry. The rest are here Saturday."

It annoys Euan that his youngest child doesn't call him Dad.

When Euan got back from the station, Mog and Edith were helping Mrs Welsh with the supper. Izzy appeared, hair wet, smelling of orange blossom and wearing a kimono. She was unruffled when Mrs Welsh told her that smoking was banned in the kitchen. Cigarette planted between her lips, her eyes narrowed against the smoke, Izzy opened one of the sash windows a screeching six inches (the cord was broken, so a paperback book was inserted) and sat along the window sill holding her cigarette so that it was technically outside the building.

"I didn't say anything about ventilation," Mrs Welsh told her. "I said no smoking. Get yourself outside."

Izzy was blithely unconcerned, picking stray tobacco off her bottom lip; Mrs Welsh's withering glances didn't wither her in the least. Terry came into the room and was introduced. He'd met Izzy on the modelling circuit and was a perfect specimen, unnervingly perfect, with light brown hair and amber eyes and cheekbones that could cut bread; when he smiled his white smile at Mog she blushed. He stood beside Izzy with one hand resting on her thigh, and leaned in close to her ear.

"Do you know what I'd love right now?" His voice revealed him to be American. Everyone waited, agog. "One of those roll-ups of yours."

"Mrs Welsh, I'd appreciate it if you could go and make up a bed for Terry," Edith said. "We'll finish the tidying-up." Mrs Welsh had been to the salon in readiness for the party and looked disconcertingly like Margaret Thatcher in her prime, other than for the housecoat and sheepskin zip slippers.

~

When they gathered at seven o'clock, people had done as instructed by Joan and dressed up in evening clothes, despite the deepening chill and threat of rain. They arrived on the terrace in cocktail dresses and dinner jackets (all except for Euan, in his usual linen suit), and shivered as they downed their tepid white wine. When Mog arrived, Rebecca was helping Vita with the positioning of a purple tam o'shanter, angling the hat slightly over one eye at Vita's instruction, her hand grasped in gratitude. Mog heard Michael's name mentioned. She put her hand around Rebecca's elbow. "No Michael talk," she said into her ear. "Ottilie's arrived."

Euan was to have catered: he'd planned a three-course meal and had been about to embark on a day of cooking when he was intercepted. Joan waited until he was readying himself in the old kitchen, cookery books wedged open on Victorian tables, ingredients amassed in thematic order, before announcing that, having courted the opinion of the group, nobody much fancied a complicated dinner. They ate their ham and salad in the formal dining room, and though the occasion hadn't been quite distinguished enough to bother cleaning the silver, the table was polished and smelled freshly beeswaxy. It was discovered too late that the radiator wasn't functioning, and so Joan sent Mog up to collect woollen garments and rugs from various rooms, scribbling her a list of where and what. Vita ate her supper wearing a fine lacy shawl wrapped closely around her throat, and, over the top of it, a dog-hairy tartan blanket that hadn't been authorised.

While Mog was off gathering woollens, Alastair stood beside Ursula, awaiting seating instructions and holding his drink.

"I do like your green dress," he said, gesturing with his glass.

"It isn't green," Ursula told him.

"It isn't? I'm sorry, I thought it was."

"It's blue."

"A greenish blue."

"It's blue."

"Turquoise."

"Shall we sit down?" Edith asked them all.

"On the floor; the floor, that would be fun," Ursula suggested.

"At the table, I meant."

"Then you should be clear about it. And less orthodox. Let's take our socks off and compare our feet."

"I should be clear; you're quite right," Edith agreed. "Shall we sit at the table and eat food? Will that do?"

"No need for that. That's redundant."

"It's an old dress by the look of it," Alastair said to her as they sat down together. "Vintage. That's the word, isn't it? Or is it?"

"Don't patronise me," Ursula warned him. "I really dislike it."

"I'm sorry, I wasn't aware –"

"You were aware. 'I wasn't aware' is something liars say. Like 'I can only apologise', which isn't an apology at all."

"Sorry," Edith mouthed.

"That's quite alright, Edith," Alastair said. "In business I'm accustomed to the cut and thrust. I think Ursula and I could be great friends. I like plain speaking."

"No you don't – nobody does," Ursula said.

"No, it's true; he really does," Rebecca told her.

Ursula shifted her weight, turning in her chair to poke her leg out and into Alastair's view.

"What do you think of my shoes?"

"I think they're quite outstandingly ugly."

She smiled a broad crooked smile. "It's true. Even though you're just indulging me."

"Not at all. They really are hideous."

"They were your mother's. Before she got married."

"Gosh. My mother liked ugly shoes. That's quite disillusioning."

"You're nice. But I know why you're doing it."

"Why am I doing it?"

"Because you've been briefed."

"Briefed?"

"Warned about me. About my being odd."

Alastair leaned towards her, his thick eyebrows knitted together. "And are you?"

"Yes. But only by choice."

"I see."

"I could be ordinary if I wanted."

"Who'd want to be?"

"It would be more interesting if people said what they were thinking, all the time."

"You don't mean that; I bet *you* don't. Chaos would ensue. Chaos and war."

"The only reason I don't is because other people don't, so the truth looks like rudeness."

"Yes."

"Mostly I just think the rude thing."

Meanwhile, Vita was quizzing Terry, who'd been seated opposite her.

"I hear that you, young man, are living quite openly with my great-granddaughter as man and wife."

"Er – no, not really."

"That is all very well. Your immorality is your own affair.

Personally I've always been rather a fan of immorality. But I can tell you now that you would be much happier if you were married. Have children early. Get them off to school and your life is ahead of you at last. In my day –"

"Granny Top, don't bully Terry," Izzy chided. "You'll frighten him off and then where will I be?"

"Izzy. Dear one."

"You've all got the wrong idea about Terry and me. We share an apartment, that's all."

"You share."

"Terry's a homosexual."

Vita was unfazed. "Tell me. Have you tried sexual relations with women and been disappointed, or is it something you've never pursued, believing yourself to be a bugger from the off?"

"Mother, really," Edith said mildly, trying not to laugh.

"But I'm interested, Edith," Vita told her. "It was quite the thing to be a lesbian when I was young. Sapphic love: terribly spiritual, the union of souls and so on. Men were thought to be war-mongering, corrupted, material creatures and the penis a sort of weapon."

"Oh lord," Edith said, her hand going to her brow.

"But I could never get on with it, you know," Vita continued. "My great friend Georgina and I had a go after a party but our hearts weren't really in it."

"That was when you came out to your family? I thought Izzy told me you came out." Terry looked towards Izzy. "She said you came out when you were 18."

"Came out in Society, Terry," Joan explained. "Something rather different. To do with parties and being available for dating."

"Your uncle Robert is a homosexual, you know," Vita said to nobody in particular.

After supper Mog was sent up to check that Mrs Welsh had done Terry's room, up in the garrets in what were servants' quarters. To get there she had to go downstairs to the old kitchen corridor and up again, as that's the only access to the top floor, a design that enforced segregation of family from staff after hours. No drunken male guest, in the old days, could "accidentally" go up the wrong stairs from the drawing-room landing at night, dressing-gown clad, clutching an incidental bottle of wine: not without going down to the ground floor first, past the butler and housekeeper stations.

Joan had an inkling that Mrs Welsh might have piled the linens folded on the bed for Terry to see to himself, and her inkling was good. Getting the room ready, Mog was aware that in being set this task and in other various small ways she was being punished by her mother, and knew why. It was because she'd raised the possibility of giving up her job and coming home. Joan considers that anything put to her is being put to her for arbitration and is likely to pronounce. She had launched into her own critique, concluding, in short, that Mog should grow up and stay put and try harder.

My room is the only one belonging to the dead that isn't used for guests, but as my mother sleeps in there sometimes, Joan had asked Mrs Welsh to change the sheets. It wasn't worth doing Jet's. Jet doesn't use his room overnight, though he's been seen to come and go in daylight hours. They knew that he wouldn't turn up to any of the pre-party gatherings and that even attendance at the party was moot, though Joan had laid down the law, suggesting possible interruptions to his top-up funding. Jet was no doubt safe in his cottage, within his black-painted walls, his curtains closed. He emerges seldom, except for weekly visits to the post office, dispatching rare LPs that he trades in second-hand, records with mint sleeves and a provenance.

Rebecca was waiting for Mog when she got back.

"Dad's gone up. Tired. He apologises. I think I'll go and sit with him if that's okay."

"Of course it's okay. You don't have to ask. Go and sit with him." She paused, then said, "I heard from Edith about his illness. I'm sorry. Isn't there anything they can do?"

"I'm afraid there isn't. He says that at least this way he doesn't lose his hair." Her smile was brave.

"I'm really sorry."

"Thank you. I'd better go and sit with him."

"Yes. Go, go. I'll see you later."

"We do this. He gets tired and anxious. I sit with him and we read."

"That's lovely. Off you go then. I'll see you later."

Sometimes it distresses me, that words are so inadequate as this, that human contact can be so profoundly inadequate, but at other times it's inexpressibly moving.

Mog found Izzy rapping on her bedroom radiator, which gurgled and rapped back.

"Needs bleeding," she said. "Though I have no idea what that entails, actually. We'll have to get in."

They got under the bedspread and lay facing one another. Izzy had a broad white scarf wrapped around her head and neck. "Ridiculous weather for June."

"I was out with Rebecca at the loch earlier and it felt like it might snow." Mog smoothed back and forth with her palm against the bedspread as she spoke.

The bedspread was one of Tilly's, made the year before she died. I can see her now, her bobbed hair snow white, painstakingly piecing triangles of fabric together, looking over the top of her glasses at the paper plan. When she cupped my chin in her hand, there was calloused skin on the sides of her sewing fingers.

Izzy had washed the quilt in tea to age it further, blunting and softening its colours. Her room is the most interesting of any, full of the stuff she's brought back from London and from her travels. Indian silk's been hung over the four-poster frame (all the principal rooms have these carved-oak beds), African faces are lined up grimacing, and there are framed photographs everywhere: family shots rubbing shoulders with famous friends. She doesn't ever talk about them, these friends, just puts their photos on the wall. They chart ordinary-looking days, snapshots taken in a crowd, laughing in a restaurant or larking in a garden, and it's only later that it twigs that it's Jack Nicholson doing the barbecue.

One wall is dedicated to the great aunts. Dresses that were theirs hang from the picture rail on scented hangers: tea dresses in floral silks, thinning under the arms, the lace trims coming adrift. Shoes that were theirs are lined up along a bookshelf: shell-pink satin dance shoes, cream leather day shoes and tan-coloured buttoned boots that are creased with wear across the front. Fashion magazines are piled beneath the bed, a casual and dusty archive, all of them featuring Izzy on their covers: her wide-spaced grey cat's eyes, wide cheekbones tapering into a small chin, her waterfall of hair and extravagant mouth.

"Rebecca asked me something interesting earlier." Izzy was curling one of Mog's frizzy locks round her finger.

"Do tell," Mog said, mimicking Vita.

"She wanted to know if I thought Michael was dead in the loch."

"Christ. What did you say?"

"I said that I was one of the ones content to leave it as a mystery."

"This wasn't in Ottilie's earshot, I trust."

"I didn't know what she knew."

"Nothing. Village version. I was supposed to tell you that."

"And then, she wanted to know what he was like. She'd heard from Edith that he liked to cook, that he liked to knit.

She's been going around with a questionnaire or something, I swear. Perhaps she's about to write his biography."

"I mentioned the knitting, too."

"I told her, we all have his long scarves. Long scarves every Christmas. I told her that Ursula taught him. And then I stopped myself, but only just in time, from adding *and that's probably how it started*."

Chapter 12

Edith went into town to see her friend Thomas Osborne, under the guise of finding something to wear to the party. Henry didn't approve of the friendship and so her meetings with Thomas, while not exactly secret, were always described thus: as going out to do some shopping. Thomas, the previous minister of St Ninian's, had been a confidant of Edith's for over 40 years, albeit a confidant who didn't know certain key facts. Despite this, he's good at asking the right questions, and continues uncredited for preventing Edith's suicide after Sebastian died.

Thomas said he'd be mother, and poured the tea. "So how's Henry?"

"Why do you always ask first about Henry?" Edith's irritation was something she could indulge in here, but only here, in the safety of his dismal second-floor flat. Thomas, too, enjoyed what he called their banter. "We fight like an old married couple," he'd said.

"You I know about," he said to her now. "I can see how the land lies with you in two seconds, just by the look on your face. Henry, however, is a continuing mystery. I confess myself fascinated by Henry."

"Henry's just the same."

"How's the plan going to get him off the estate, to do other things and see people?"

"I get the children to make suggestions." She shrugged. "But everything he wants is inside the wall."

Everything he wants and everything he dreads.

"Is he talking?" Thomas had found in a cupboard and now put in place a great knitted chicken that served as a tea cosy. Ursula had made it for him to mark the occasion of his retirement.

"Not really. And I'm resigned to that. I don't expect it to get better. If he talks, it's dogs he talks to."

"He's a man in pain."

"I can't explain to you why it is, but there's something about that remark that wounds me."

"I'm sorry, Edith. I didn't intend to imply that his pain is worse."

"I do sometimes feel that it's a competition and that he disdains my efforts to be cheerful as if they're vulgar. A failure of heart, really."

"The two of you have kept the unsaid thing between you for so long."

"That's it exactly. It's almost as if he's been waiting, and so have I, for the thing to be said, but it never will be, and in the meantime this solemn sort of waiting is all that's been – what's the word – honourable."

"He's come round to Saturday's event, though, I take it. He's going to be there, at least."

"He's going to be there. I trust you are."

"I wouldn't miss it for anything."

"Henry's not happy but he wouldn't not come."

"Did you have an argument about it?"

"Good god, no." She winced. "Sorry."

"Don't be. 'Good god' has never offended me."

"Joan has no idea what she's doing, blundering on, bless her, and I know she means well, but the idea of a party, of music and dancing: it's too hard. Henry's miserable about it, and I'm nervous that he'll be antisocial, perhaps even frank – saying that we shouldn't be doing it, that it dishonours Sebastian. But you know, I think it's time. We've had so very many sad Christmases."

When she pulled out of the apartment car park, slowly in the old Rover and onto the main road home, she said, "I'm so sorry Michael; I'm so very sorry." She looked into the car mirror as she was speaking and my nerves prickled. I was in the back seat, there with her.

❧

Joan was hanging photographs at Peattie in the hall. Today, it was the turn of some of the annual staff line-ups from the old days. A picture was taken late every summer, up until the First World War, of the staff standing grouped on the terrace: showing the maids in their black dresses and stout boots; the butler, cook and housekeeper, their finer clothes marking them out; the garden and ground staff standing at the sides of the group, leather-skinned in caps and kilts, not sure how to behave and caught by the camera in the act of wondering. Joan took the 1912 photograph out of a card-backed envelope and slotted it back in its frame. The local newspaper had borrowed the print to scan in for a feature and had returned it that morning by courier. The 1912 line-up is special as there are two versions: the official and the rehearsal shots. The lent photograph was the rehearsal, taken a minute or two before the stiff composure of the official photo, and by far the most compelling, showing the cook squinting down at her apron as if assessing its whiteness; showing one of the maids cradling a Labrador pup and being told to put him on the grass by the cook, her brows beetling; showing the main group of housemaids, their faces lit up by laughter they're attempting not to give rein to, as if one of them's just told a joke. The butler's talking to the gardeners, his creased and open hands gesturing towards the hothouses. His hands and their creases have survived everything.

The local paper did a photo story every summer to coincide with the beginning of Peattie gardens' seasonal run of open days, in aid of one of Edith's charities, though the fact was that by now most visitors came only to see how much worse things had grown, in the borders and lawns and in general estate upkeep, since the summer before. The voyeuristic crowds had grown larger of late. This year, for the first time, the newspaper had run a special pull-out feature on the house itself. They'd taken pictures of Edith and Henry surrounded by dogs, on a sofa with a backdrop of antique tapestry and a silver tea set laid out on the table. Edith had loved it until the minister's wife had been snide and then she saw that it was all wrong, and wished desperately that she hadn't had her hair done and dug out that old frock and jewels as the photographer had urged her, thinking it all a lark, a thing done with half a nod at least to irony. No irony was evident on the page. Though many of the shots were lovely: the main photograph showed the fine old stone of the house bathed pink in afternoon light, the dark hill rising behind. *Glen of Peattie: an outstanding relic from a vanished social order, a vanished world,* the caption read. There was a picture of the coach house in the yard, showing the horse stalls, the faded names on the whitewashed brick, Belle and Bridget, Diana and Harriet, Fern and Emily, the editorial noting that Henry's grandfather would have only mares because he considered gelding a cruelty. Joan had supplied many such anecdotes. There were photos of the folly encircled by dead daffodils; of the ice house, a cross between a cave and a dungeon with a fine vaulted ceiling; of the dairy, its marble benches, the handle-driven ice-cream-makers; of the original kitchen with its enormous old range, the wall-mounted copper pots, the jelly moulds, the fish kettles. There was a picture of the game larder, and another of the glasshouses, describing the figs and grapes and pineapples that were grown in the house's heyday. Henry loved it all. He bought several copies, cutting the photographs out in careful sections and pasting them into an album.

Edith slowed as she drove into the village; there was no traffic behind her and she could dawdle through. Past the cul-de-sac turned in on itself, busy with children on bikes and with long skipping ropes. Past the 1930s houses, on plots that look huge to modern eyes, each quarter-acre domain with its own high hedge and long cinder path. The verges had been trimmed and the air was full of cut-grass smells. Past the large brown sign, put there by the council, directing visitors down the road that leads to *Peattie Heritage Village*. The bus shelter had been decked out with hanging baskets, garish with red and yellow annuals and proud claims about Scotland in Bloom. Next, the low stone-built bungalows, estate-built, that run along the main road. The garden wall runs along the opposite side, a dry-stone dyke built of horizontal storeys of blue-green granite topped with thinner vertical slices stacked spine-up like books, the mosses and alpines creeping between them. There is a post box, a startling tomato red, set into the wall, and a tomato-red phone box beside what was once the tradesman's entrance to the house, now identified officially as a public right of way. *Peattie Loch: Private Property: Strictly No Vehicles,* Henry's own secondary labelling states. Edith slowed the car, straining her eyes towards the cottages. Someone was coming down the lane towards the road, someone in a pale mackintosh, outlined against a backdrop of lavish wild greenery. A wet summer had made the vegetation soar, high and vigorous, turning the verges into rank and atmospheric jungle that was dominated by saucer-sized heads of Queen Anne's lace. They nodded as if sagely in the breeze, a parliament of weeds. Edith slowed the car hummingly to a pause and rolled down her window. Her friend Susan Marriott was already striding towards her.

"You're just the person I want to talk to," Edith called out. Susan joined her in the car and it trundled on further, turning in through the main gate, slowly along the drive and past the gatehouse, the gravel crunching like glass in the absolute quiet, passing between high rhododendron hedges, dark and glossy, their purple flower trumpets just coming into bloom.

Gordon and Susan, the Marriotts, are a reclusive pair, around 60 in age, I'd guess, who live in the village but are assumed by many to be holiday-house owners, so seldom are they seen around the place. They'd been invited to the party, but Edith didn't know this. The guest list was one of the token mysteries left surrounding the event and Edith had been incurious, though if she'd seen it in advance she might have noticed that some of the men were coming quite some distance, names familiar from the deep past; she might quite reasonably have asked if Ottilie had approved these additions. Ottilie hadn't had the chance. Joan had taken control of things and people had let her. She was aware that Susan was "Edith's new friend", in fact, had referred to her in just these terms, a peculiar tone in her voice that was also in evidence when she described her as "God Squad", using paired fingers as quotation marks. It had been Susan's habitual wearing of an almost ostentatiously large crucifix that had prompted her and Edith's first conversation, a few weeks before, standing outside the village shop, each of them holding a carton of milk.

"I hope you don't think me rude, but I'm interested," Edith told her over their first cup of coffee. "I've always wanted to attend a service at St Stephen's. Would that be allowed, despite being a member of the Protestant communion?"

"Allowed or not, I'd love it," Susan had said. Thus had their friendship begun.

Back at Peattie, Ursula and Rebecca had been making short-bread under Joan's tutelage. Edith took a small plateful into the drawing room, where she'd planted Susan while she made a pot of coffee; she liked to keep Susan separate from the family and pre-empt their interactions. Ursula wanted to sit with them, attempting to follow them into the room and admitting quite frankly that she wanted to hear what they talked about, and Edith had to be firm. She barred her way in with an arm placed like a No Entry rope. "The dogs need brushing," she said to her. "Please, Ursula. Just a half-hour. Thirty minutes. Is that going to be possible?"

"It's perfectly possible," Ursula said, turning away as the door was closed between them. As Edith returned to sit with Susan in the relative warmth of the window space, she could hear Ursula singing in the corridor.

"You know, I suppose, that both Gordon and I have been married before," Susan said, biting into an over-browned Christmas tree-shaped biscuit, one made with Ursula's favourite cutter, and dampening it in her cup. Edith shook her head, trying not to look too eager.

"He has two grown-up sons in England. I had a daughter but she died in a car accident."

"Oh no. I'm so sorry."

"It was a long time ago."

"We lost a child," Edith said. She put her coffee down hurriedly as it began to slop. "I'm sorry. It was an even longer time ago, I'm sure, than … I'm sorry." She blew her nose on the handkerchief from her sleeve, one with Tilly's initials embroidered on it. "But I'm sure you know. You will have been told all about it."

"I was told."

"About Michael also, I imagine. His leaving us."

"About Michael also. You don't need to say anything more. Really."

"No, no, I want to talk about it. But everyone avoids the subject. They think I want to avoid the names being spoken. I have to honour that observance. The time hasn't ever come, to downgrade the level of observance."

"It's because you don't talk about it."

"Sebastian's name hasn't been mentioned between Henry and me in private for more than 35 years."

"That's a long time."

"Neither of us is ever going to go first."

"Sometimes it's easier to be frank with strangers. I can recommend a group. In the town."

"Not possible, alas. Everybody knows us. Everybody knows about it."

"Even so."

"I'm still so angry with Henry," Edith interrupted her. "I'm so angry with him."

"It's normal to blame," Susan said.

"He wanted me to get pregnant again, you see. He wanted to have another child as quickly as possible. After Sebastian. He wouldn't talk to me about Sebastian. All he was prepared to say to me, well, it was a question, over and over. Was I prepared to get pregnant again, hope to achieve it quickly, immediately, hoping for another boy? I didn't, I wouldn't, and once I'd convinced him that I wouldn't he had nothing else to say to me. We didn't have intercourse again after that."

They were interrupted by Ursula, who opened the door and put her head around it. "Is it time?"

"No. You know it isn't. Go and cut some flowers for in here, would you? The roses have died in their vase."

Ursula's head withdrew and the door was closed decisively.

Susan said, "Listen, if we're going to be frank with one another, there's something I've been wanting to tell you."

"Oh?"

"I don't know if you know. This is awkward."

"Best just to be straight, then."

"Gossip. In the village, that Michael is ..."

"I can save you the awkwardness. That he's dead. Dead in the loch."

"You did know. I'm glad that you know. I'm relieved."

"The minister has already been round with the news. Could barely hide his excitement."

"You know, then, that someone in the village has been to the police, in the town."

"I know, yes. One reason I'm at such a low ebb."

"Henry knows?"

"About the police? No. It was me the policeman found at home. When he telephoned. I said Henry was away and promised to discuss it with him. Then I went to the police station and said that I had discussed it with him – which was true, but not in the way they assumed. Then, today, I went to see Thomas – Thomas Osborne, you know him, I'm sure."

"I know him a little. Nice man."

"But when I got there I didn't say anything about it. I don't know why."

"What will happen?"

"I went into the police station and showed them his letter. Michael's letter. When he left us there was a letter."

"I'd heard that."

"And then I told them something that might be a lie."

"What did you say?"

"I said that he phoned us, two years ago."

"But he didn't."

"Somebody called and didn't speak, but I could hear them breathing on the other end."

"They didn't speak?"

"No. But I was sure it was Michael."

"Perhaps it was."

Edith didn't respond but looked anxiously towards the door.

"Will you tell Henry? You'll have to tell him." Susan looked very certain.

"Can we talk about Sebastian? It's Sebastian that's on my mind today. I want to talk to Henry about him, but I can't."

"What is it that's stopping you?"

"Thinking. Thoughts I'm thinking. They prevent me."

"What kind of thinking?"

"Thinking that his quietness is something bottled up that I don't want to unbottle. There's a sort of restfulness in not talking. We don't have to face it. We don't have to get so stirred up, or have to recover again from that."

"It's the opposite with us. Gordon thinks I oughtn't to bottle and tries to discuss it, but you see words are the last thing I want to apply. It's really only prayer that comes anywhere close to resolving something that otherwise is never ceasing, that doesn't stop, round and round; how I might have prevented it, how it was really all my fault, how I'll never get over it. Because you don't, do you? Not really. The loss of Julia is just as fresh today in many ways as ever."

"Prayer doesn't help me."

"No?"

"I persist, but more out of superstition about stopping praying than anything."

"We all go through these phases," Susan said blandly, patting Edith's knee. "Do you have enough things that fill the days? I'm sure you must; Peattie's such a big house and your family are all around. I find that a strict timetable works best. Mine is strict from 6am to the half-hour. If I have too much thinking time, I'm floored. I descend."

When Susan smiled she looked rather like a nun, an escaped 60-year-old nun who was unused to wearing ordinary clothes. Her pleated blue skirt and pale blue shirt might have been borrowed just for this occasion. Her scooped-back hair, pepper and salt, looked as if freshly released from the wimple, her cheeks pink from convent scrubbing.

"Working at home helps," Susan said. "I can do that all day and all evening if I have to. And cleaning. I love house-work. It's important not to brood."

"I didn't know that you worked. What is it that you do?"

"We all work, Edith, out in the world, you know," Susan said, gently satirical. "We have an online marketing busi-ness. Marketing people's holiday homes."

I can't imagine that Edith knew what "online" means – there were no computers at Peattie – and I imagine her notion of "marketing" had to do with shopping and fruit stalls. But still. She was nodding intelligently. Then she said, "Do you know who it was?"

"Who it was?"

"Who went to the police."

"No, I'm afraid not."

"That's a pity," Edith said.

Susan stood up. "I must press on, but it was good to see you."

Edith said, "Susan, there's something I want to tell you. I want to tell you something. Something important. Do you have the time?"

"Of course, Edith," Susan said, sitting down again. "What is it?"

When Susan had left, Edith walked down the drive and into the village. She'd meant to go and sit in the church for a while, but when she got through the door into its heavy, stone and polish-scented quietness, she felt repelled by the act of confession that she'd planned: a confession that would have taken place under Protestant rites, whispering her fault in her head, in the Salter family pew. The deity slipped in and out of view. God was there in the stained-glass window, God's son in action, extending his forgiving hand, sweeping it Jedi-like over the heads of the populace, but when she tried to focus on Him she found that He had dissipated into colours. She hurried out again into the churchyard. Tilly she could always talk to. Edith sat on the marble surround of the grave, its little fence marking out Tilly's small territory, and spoke to her in a whisper.

Edith asked me when I was young if I would sit with Great Aunt Tilly sometimes, because she was a lonely old lady. This was during the period in which Vita and Mrs Hammill did all their travelling. I complied, expecting to be itching to get away, expecting it to be a martyrdom, but we became great friends and I sat with her often after that, me with a book and Tilly with her sewing. She was the stillness at the centre of the Peattie world, everybody else rushing and busy around her. She liked to talk as she was making her quilts. In old age she was given to making oracular announcements, though in her youth she had been famously the opposite, someone keen on the facts and scathing about the transcendental. It was the death of her sisters in a car smash that brought about the change; that, and the burden of looking after her mother so diligently, giving up her shop and taking Jo's place; she was Maud's carer until the end of Maud's life. I only ever knew that changed and oracular Tilly. She'd say to me, not looking at me, concentrating on her slow and careful stitching, her thoughts advancing at the same stitched pace, that the life of the house had come to an end, and that it was a natural death and though it was right to grieve, it wasn't healthy to keep grieving. Really, she was talking about Edith and Henry, how they'd been since Sebastian died. She'd seen that I was puzzled by their not talking to one another, the abruptness of their interactions. It was Tilly who was responsible for sowing the seed of the idea in the family that Edith and Henry were united in their suffering. Tilly talked to me often about growing old, also. "You think age is about losing your youth, about loss; people make that mistake. The truth of it is different. It's about constant additions, adding on. The child is still there, intact beneath them all, down at the heart of me; still here." Her sinewy hand would go arched to her breast. "The trick is not to let it be obscured by everything that comes later. All that separates the two of us, Michael, is days."

She'd give me advice on managing the family, on fitting in. Good advice, most of it. She was dismayed by my tendency to argue with Edith about God, in whose non-existence I had a vocal and unshakable faith. "Just let her have her literal heaven," she'd say, chiding softly. "Sebastian lives there, you see."

The years that followed Sebastian's death were years of religious observance for Edith. She talked to God about her troubles. A big part of the estrangement, hers and Henry's, was this continuing, escalating piety of Edith's and the fact that a third party had been admitted to the marriage, albeit a celestial one. I don't think Henry had ever taken it seriously before, Edith's (then) complete and literal faith in God as a person, someone who could advise in a human crisis. Henry made it clear from the first that he didn't want to talk about the accident with anyone and especially not with Him, not even on the therapeutic or Pascalian basis that it couldn't hurt and might even help. Edith annoyed him once by telling us all in his presence that Henry's church was the hillside and his solitude a kind of prayer. His strategy after Sebastian's death was that he kept the world at arm's length. You might imagine that it was difficult, maintaining this detachment over so many years, but in my own experience it isn't. It becomes habitual. You start out owning the thing as a policy, one that you assume can be redrafted, and end up owned in turn. The flayed heart grows a new and tougher coating, and a membrane grows up that proves impermeable. Old ways of thinking and of loving die away. Days lengthen into years and no easy reversal is any longer possible.

Tilly said to me that we are all disappointed but that the chief characteristic of being human is to know that and keep going. Trite, you might think, but I don't think so and didn't then. I was filled with admiration and awe. I must have been quite young; I was only 13 when she died (*after a long last illness, bravely borne*), from the cancer that pared her away. She barely left her chair in the final few weeks, a worn brown velvet one with a long seat that's still in the drawing room; she was helped into it in the morning and out of it again at night. Her sewing became obsessive and continuous towards the end, almost as if so long as she was stitching, death couldn't take her. I can see her now and smell her lily-of-the-valley scent, and also the fabrics – the squares of imported cotton that smelled of dye and brown paper – and the smell of her old clothes. She'd reverted by then to her teenage uniform of wool skirts and thin sweaters, not only in style but in fact, wearing the actual items retrieved from the attic. I overheard her more than once urging Henry to give up Peattie. "It mustn't be the most important thing, Henry. How can you put it first? It's just a house. Let it be flats or a nursing home; it doesn't matter." It mattered to my grandfather, though. In 1900 the estate still owned the whole village, but now there were only four houses left to sell – the terraced cottages on the loch road. Henry would never have parted with those while he still had a marketable kidney.

When she got home from her churchyard visit, Edith went to her bedroom and lay on the bed for an hour and a half, staring at the ceiling. She went to the kitchen to make coffee and found Mog there, sitting at the table with her journal, pen in hand and not moving, looking dreamily towards the window.

Edith sat opposite her and said, "Tell me how you are."

Mog's eyes made their adjustment from internal to external attention. "I'm fine. I'm basically fine."

"Really and truly?"

"It's been hard. I admit that. But nothing worse than hard, than an ordinary sort of hard, and in the scheme of things immensely banal. Everything about my life, in fact, seems to me immensely banal, my successes and my problems equally."

"Hard – you mean to do with this man, this boyfriend?"

"Not Johnnie. It's all about what to do – oh dear, big cliché approaching –with my life."

"Right. Yes. Right." Edith's face was almost unbearably sympathetic. "Go on."

"Why Edinburgh was such a failure and what to do next. What it is, the thing that I should be doing." Mog knocked the heel of her hand against her forehead.

"I wouldn't presume to advise," Edith told her, "but could I just venture the suggestion, and suggestion is the wrong word; I'm not advocating anything. Could I just introduce the idea that perhaps marriage might be a way forward?"

"Marriage to whom?"

"There are lots of suitable men," Edith said. "At least once you get over the idea of falling in love with one of them."

"You sound just like Vita." Mog made a great show of rubbing the back of her neck. "Muscle tension," she explained, before leaning forward onto the table and cupping her face in her hands, the skin over her cheekbones pulled gently back, a tic I know well, one that serves to mask emotion. "You can't force these things," she said.

"No." Edith wouldn't take Joan's usual tack, that effort is required, that clubs must be joined and that one must give off the right signals, show willing. There would be no acid remarks about presentation.

"For now at least it's all about work," Mog said. "And some very basic skills of self-knowledge. Izzy has been a big help. It wasn't a failure, in Edinburgh; it was just a bad fit. It didn't suit me. I need to think about what suits me."

Edith said nothing but her eyes were fixed on Mog's face.

"At what point do people do their thinking?" Mog asked the used coffee cup, tracing her finger around its rim. "That's what I find interesting. I must be slow. It never occurred to me until two weeks ago that I could have a different sort of life."

"Well, you're very welcome to stay here for as long as thinking takes," Edith told her.

Joan came into the room just as Edith was saying this. She didn't look happy.

"Mother, you forget sometimes that my children have a home. They're not orphans. Their home is just down the road at the gatehouse. You remember the gatehouse?"

"Of course, Joan, but we love to have them and they're so helpful with everything."

"I blame you, Mother," Joan said bitterly, standing with her arms crossed. "Mog should be at home. She should eat and sleep there. She should be asking me if it's okay to have this gap year of hers. But no. She'd rather stay here. And who can blame her? Here where nobody challenges her."

"I'm not a child," Mog pointed out.

"Oh, Joan," Edith said.

"Jet doesn't talk to me, you know, nor to his father. He doesn't need to. You gave him a house of his own when he was 17 years old. You give them all this opt-out from me and from their father, always have."

In the evening, Edith went to the Bible group. Not knowing of Edith's antipathy to the new minister, Joan had invited him and his wife to the party. Edith hadn't spoken to anyone about this but she'd developed an almost immediate dislike of the new incumbents of the manse: the pompous red-bearded minister and his sarcastic Australian wife. Kind, bookish, bicycle-riding Thomas Osborne was much more to her taste. He'd call round at the house often, coming in with his cycle clips on and flat cap. He had wispy hair and uneven teeth, beaming at her, keen to chat, completely at home in that bracing priestly way with the raw material of life, frowning and wry over her expressions of failure. He'd come into the kitchen and take a packet of ginger biscuits out of his jacket pocket like a magician, saying "Ta daaaa!" every time as if it were a new joke, which made Edith smile. She found herself smiling, thinking of this flourishing of biscuits inappropriately in the middle of a discussion about St Paul's ideas of love. The urge to talk again to Thomas rose in her and wouldn't be silenced. Again and again it circled her mind, its quiet repetitive imperative. She couldn't tell Susan and not Thomas: the idea was appalling, and carried with it an inarticulate pang of disloyalty. Thomas must know. Thomas must be told everything, not just about Michael, but about the other thing, the thing she hadn't ever dared tell Henry, the thing she referred to as *the lie*. Edith left the group before the end, blaming her early departure on a just-remembered promise made to one of the grand-children to be somewhere else.

Back at Peattie, she returned to her bedroom, lifted the phone receiver and called Thomas.

"I have to see you," she said to him. "There's something I need to tell you."

"Edith – what on earth's the matter? Has something happened?"

"Two things I need to tell you. One of them I told to a friend this afternoon, and now I feel terrible and exposed and I need your advice. The other I didn't tell her; I'll never tell her."

"You must come right over; have you eaten?" Thomas asked. "I'm about to have a lasagne. It's shop-bought but not bad."

So many of our assumptions in life are based on the things people tell each other, but the things people tell each other can all too easily amount only to a line of mythology, misinterpreting itself successively through the generations uncontested. Sometimes people are only too glad to let misunderstandings rest unchallenged. The right kind of misunderstanding could become the foundation stone for a life. Edith and Henry, for instance, were each aware that the consensus in the family about their barely speaking to one another since Sebastian died, continuing apparently happily married – never a word in anger spoken – was evidence of a unity, one that had worked itself through as muteness; muted ways of speaking and thinking, muted sorts of expectations, emerging with a kind of grim beauty out of unspeakable grief. The fact that Sebastian's loss affected them equally profoundly, with a measurable twinned deadening of the eye, was evidence of their being unified and one: two damaged flower bulbs flowering in the same heartbreakingly off-kilter, misshapen way. Despondency and suffering, ungovernable if given free rein, threatened for a time to overwhelm them both, and what could be done about it, what can ever be done other than to push the unspeakable back into the dark and carry on? There were three other children to bring up, and keeping going was all that was possible. It was only much later that Edith spoke to Thomas about her realisation, far too late, that Ursula interpreted her and Henry's reaction, their cooling, their retreat, as a judgment upon her, as a punishment. The three surviving children all felt deeply that their brother's death was their fault, but Ursula more than any of them, Henry said to me once. Ottilie has spoken of it often: how they were standing only a few feet away from Sebastian when he toppled in; how she still feels she could have prevented it, that she could have been quicker. His drowning under those circumstances, with his sisters right there but unable to save him, his proving impossible to find until it was too late: this is interpreted as sinister in the village, cited as something that could only have been invoked by dark forces.

My mother has said to me that she thinks Edith and Henry's retreat into silence after Seb was gone was at least in part influenced by Ursula's own, for how could Ursula's suffering be the more profound? At the time it seemed essential only that grief cut the old life cleanly at the base of the stem. Tilly concurred with this view. There was a kind of heroism to the relinquishment of the old ordinariness, Tilly said. A kind of nobility in it. The most important thing to recognise was that it *was* mutual. She'd paraphrase Wittgenstein to me: there are things that can't be spoken about, that go too deep, beyond the reach of words, and about those things it is best to say nothing. Except that's not how it was at all. I've seen them, Edith and Henry, the day after Sebastian died, her going onto the moor with him in the early morning, at five in the morning, two figures in long coats silhouetted against a white sky. I've seen her push hard at his shoulder and him pushing her in return; her slipping and falling back onto the grass. I've heard their shouted accusations. It was Henry who hired the au pair on the telephone, from the most rudimentary of phone conversations, saying he didn't have time to interview her. It was Edith who let her take the children to the loch unsupervised. It was Henry who told Sebastian he was too busy to come and sail the boat that Andrew had made, threatened by Andrew's bond with the boy. It was Edith who had the hair appointment.

"I'm on my way," Edith told Thomas. She realised that she was calmly in tears, surprise tears that itched wet on her cheeks and cooled ticklish at the corners of her mouth. "One of the things is – one of them is that I know where Michael is, I know Michael is dead. The other thing ... I feel sick just thinking about telling you."

"Edith, stop, you're making yourself ill. Don't drive; I'll come to you. Shall I come now?"

"It's something that Ursula told me, something not even Henry knows, that would break Henry's heart."

"Stay there. I'll get a taxi and I'll be there in half an hour."

"No, not today. I can't do this today. Tomorrow. I'll call you tomorrow."

Chapter 13

On the tenth day after I disappeared, Edith made her afternoon visit to Ottilie determined to be open about the past. As soon as Ottilie answered the door she could see it, something new in her mother's face.

"What is it? Has something happened?"

"I need you to come with me, to come home with me, right now."

"I can't do that. You know that I can't."

"Please. This thing won't close itself. I need to – we need to – say everything to one another about it, so we can say everything and feel everything and it will close."

"What are you talking about?"

"We can empty ourselves, say everything to one another, and then it will close."

"No. We can't and it won't."

"I can't do this again. I need it to end."

"What are you talking about? What do you mean *again*?"

"You know what I mean. You must know what I mean. We've never talked about it, but Ursula told me. She told me, you see. About the lie."

"About the lie," Ottilie echoed.

"Yes. Ursula told me. I haven't breathed a word to anyone, all this time. Not even you girls. Not even Henry. We can't talk about it now."

"Something about Michael?"

"Not about Michael. We can't talk about it now. But I've been coming out here and out here, every day, away from your father, so I could tell you that I knew. I wanted you to know that she told me."

"What did Ursula tell you?"

"You were there. You were a child. You know what I mean."

"I was a *child*?" Ottilie's puzzlement was obvious, but now light began to dawn. "Ursula told you. She told you when?"

"After Joan's wedding."

"Why haven't you said anything to me? All this time. I can't believe it."

"It was my fault," Edith said, her expression stricken.

"Of course it wasn't your fault. How could it have been your fault?"

"I've begun to think that it was the secret she told Michael, that Ursula told Michael in the boat. That that's what they fought about."

"You're not making any sense. How could that be the secret?"

"I don't know. We'll never know probably."

"Well, you could beat it out of her."

"Ottilie."

"There's too much consideration. I'm sorry but that's how I see it. Way too much."

Edith took hold of her arm. "Please come home with me. Please."

"I can't."

"If you would only speak to her."

"Listen to me. This is never going to change. I am never going to speak to her. I am never going to Peattie again."

216

Edith didn't seem to have been prepared for the finality of this. She went home shocked to Henry and threw her arms around his neck, Henry patting her back in response. It was the first intended physical contact for very many years.

Henry left things as they were a few days, knowing about Ottilie and her cooling periods. Left to her own devices, it was possible she'd talk herself out of it, out even of what might appear to be an entrenched position. Eventually he rang her.

"I meant what I said. I won't come to Peattie again," Ottilie told him on the phone.

"You must think of your mother," he persisted. "She's distraught and not sleeping and on blood pressure medication."

Silence. Henry waited.

Finally Ottilie spoke. "I will come. But only if you can promise that I won't see Ursula. I won't talk to her, I won't be in the same room as her, I don't want to catch sight of her. Do you understand?"

"I promise."

"If I find myself accidentally in a room with her I won't be back."

"I understand."

"I mean it."

"I know you do." He paused, then added, "Ottilie – about Michael."

"I don't want to talk about it any more" Ottilie said. "I don't want to hear his name mentioned." Reporting this conversation to Edith, Henry said that he wasn't entirely sure what she meant by that last remark. Edith had to agree. People have always struggled to understand what Ottilie means.

～

At the heart of our relationship, the one between my mother and me, there lay a profound misunderstanding: this is the conclusion I've come to. I don't know how different life would have been if she'd taken me to one side, at any point in our 19 years together, and said, "Look: here's what you have to know: it isn't you; it's not about, never was about not wanting you." She said these words and more to me in my imagination, in my sleep; I'd conjure her up when I felt most transient in her life. "You were wanted from the first moment," she'd say to me, or so I imagined, late at night, stroking the side of my face. "From the moment I felt you kicking under my hand. And I love you more than my life. There wouldn't be a moment's hesitation, Michael."

She doesn't say anything quite this explicit, even now. Instead she talks to me about the work.

"If I didn't put the work first, I'd be afraid of life, every day. How to put this to you. It's difficult to explain. After Sebastian died the world seemed different. It wasn't even about ambition. It was more like just getting through it. A technique. It's almost like I managed to start to live each day as if it might be my last, as my father had said, but that proved to be an absolute curse. The day had to be about making." She made a dissatisfied noise. "Put it this way: today, this moment – this might be the best drawing day I've ever had. This might be the day when the drawing starts to mean something, and begins to mean something to others, and life changes and the world's remade." She sat with her hand on my stone as if it were the conduit, the contact point between worlds. "I'm not always sure I really believe that any more, but it's the only hope and I have to hang onto it."

She spent 19 years living in a paradox. Loving me more than her life; needing to spend a life alone. I know this about her, now. I know that she's afraid every day of dying, that she's been afraid every day since Sebastian fell into the loch, and I know from things that she's told me that she's frightened of ageing further from here, from the point she's now reached, tracking the first subtle failures of skin and bone, recognising that organs are beginning to signal their age. They do that eventually; they turn on you, flaunting their finiteness as a gift and whispering the possibility that they're about to become the enemy. People, sociability, anchor her too far, too evidently in her own mortality. Alone in the studio there is no death, only birth. Only creation, over and over.

When I was 11, I didn't understand the way we lived, the way my mother seemed to want to live. It baffled and angered me.

"Why don't we have houses that are like everyone else's? Why don't we have television?" I'd ask her, tediously often.

"Because ordinary houses are a sign of ordinary souls," she'd say. "And television makes people ordinary."

"It doesn't have to. Why should it have to? That's ridiculous."

"Life is so short, Michael," she'd say to me. "So short. Don't waste a minute on things that don't add something to your experience of it."

"Television *would* add something to my experience of it," I told her, not unreasonably. But in this as in other things she was intransigent.

I found the transition from Peattie to the cottage very hard, perceiving it as an eviction, or at least as a demotion, and I was profoundly ashamed. I made myself unpopular at school by bragging about Peattie and how that was my real home. My mother had bought this other place to serve as a studio, I said, and we stayed over when she worked late. I managed to shut them all up for a while, but my triumph was short-lived. It came to a sorry end at 13 when the news got out that Michael Salter lived in the village all the time and it was a lie about living at Peattie, news that led to a fist-fight just outside the school gate and my tormentor punched accidentally unconscious. There was a permanent mark on my school record after that. Intelligent

219

but volatile: that was me. Intelligent, volatile, a boy with a short fuse, a loner: that was their judgment. I didn't make friends. But then another outcast (small, and late to puberty) started hanging out with me at break time, and after his mother had visited mine, there were many invitations to go and eat with them. Lawrie. I can't remember his surname. We had nothing in common other than unpopularity and a talent for chess. He lived in the new development at the edge of the village. I liked it there. Plush beige carpets covered the whole floor, up and down and the stairs between, and it was always warm, and there were bright cheery paint colours, lime and lilac, the walls flat and perfect as coloured card. It was airy and very orderly, with modern furniture that looked as if it had all been delivered from one shop in a big truck. Lawrie's mother was similarly a vision of bright cleanliness, smiling and chatty and available.

The cottage was a very different order of beast. It had been sold as in need of modernisation, but Ottilie didn't modernise. The plumbing and wiring needed renewing. There wasn't a shower. We didn't have central heating: all the warmth and the hot water were provided by an ungainly black stove. The cottage retains, even now, its original papers and tiles and flooring, its same ugly original light fittings. It's crowded and dusty, piled high with things that Ottilie deemed essential: bits of old furniture she liked, things gifted from Peattie alongside random beach-combings, an absurdly large grandfather clock, towering stalagmites of books. Framed drawings and pastels are stacked against the skirting boards, and all available wall space is taken up with an ever-changing domestic exhibition, much of it work in progress that comes and goes. The kitchen is small and dark, its window looking out past the studio to the sea. There's a butler sink with Victorian taps, open shelving instead of cupboards and flowered curtains serving as doors.

Ottilie agreed to go to Lawrie's house for coffee with his mother. She sat in their modern sitting room, embarrassing me with her freakish 19th-century look, dispensing with questions briskly and dismissively and going on to make stilted, misfiring remarks that puzzled Lawrie's mother, who wasn't the kind of woman who talks very much to people about the poignancy of old hands, or why it is that we think the sea mysterious. Lawrie, picking up on my discomfort, invited me to his room and taught me backgammon, but we left before the game was finished. When we got home Ottilie went into her bedroom, closing the door and putting the radio on at high volume. I went to the door and listened. There was another noise, one secondary to the Elgar and its violins swooping, another noise that played hard and staccato against the melody. We'd gone to visit right after the school day and so I stood outside her room in my uniform, already lanky, my wrists clear of my shirt cuffs, my trousers and blazer a little short. I tapped on the door and asked if everything was alright, and the secondary noise came to a halt. Nothing was said about it when she emerged.

By 14 I'd taken on the housework, not because I was asked to but because I began to crave order. I preferred to live in undusty rooms, preferred newspapers piled and binned and coffee cups washed before they were needed. I took on the laundry – putting a load on before school and levering it up close to the ceiling on the pulley in the scullery when I got home. Ottilie never ironed clothes so I began to do my own; it was good to have a pressed shirt for school. People assumed that my mother had turned over a new leaf and were open in their approval. Inspired by this, I began to cook, teaching myself from library books. My first presentation was a roast chicken with baked potatoes and a bowl of coleslaw; Ottilie was so surprised and so delighted with it that I began to cook most nights and to wash up after, insisting that I didn't mind. I'd stand at the kitchen sink working through the dishes, wearing yellow gloves, my eyes fixed on the studio window, where I could see the back of my mother's head – her chair faced its other window, looking out to sea – watching her moving silently around, already locked in concentration and oblivious to my watching. Don't get the impression that I felt put upon. It was all immensely gratifying – to provide for her and make her happy, to be her support staff, to be referred to as her support staff. I'd go out onto the beach while dinner was cooking and look for treasure: aesthetically wonky shells, stones with holes worn through them, things that had been washed up, bringing these objects home and arranging them in the middle of the table. She'd handle them, passing them gently from hand to hand as if each were a baby bird, and admire my taste, and sometimes things would reappear as art.

Ottilie began to give me money for helping with the chores. I'd always had generous ad hoc donations, and squirrelled most of these away in an emptied biscuit tin labelled "adventures". But now I had direct monthly payments made from my mother's account.

"For all your extraordinary help, for which I'll always be so grateful," she said, presenting the bank book, and I can see her now, saying it as if she were speaking right now, her grey-green eyes so beautiful. "Now that you have all this money, why don't you go out at the weekends? Go to the cinema, up to town, do stuff with your friends."

"I'd rather stay here."

"You are almost 15, Michael. You ought to be out there socialising, meeting girls."

I blushed deeply.

"Why don't you go today? You've got plenty for Saturday trips; I know you're jealous about guarding your travel money but there's easily enough for the bus, the cinema, something to eat. I've put a clothes allowance in there. Your shirts are getting too small again."

"Thank you."

Was it okay, that "thank you"? I'm not sure, even now, whether it trod the line successfully between gratitude and a sickening disappointment. I began finding sleeping difficult, already too tall in my single bed, big feet hanging out of the end and my heart beating fast and hard.

After the first of my Saturdays out – I ran out of things to do early, and sat in a coffee shop with a book until the teatime bus was due – Ottilie was unusually relaxed and attentive, coming to me as I took my shoes off in the hall, beaming and glad, with a coffee pot in her hand and paint crusted on her knuckles. She was just beginning to do the seascapes that would be used as cover illustrations for a poetry series.

"Have you had a lovely time? I've had the best day's painting in an age: the light was spectacular. What did you see? Have you eaten? I'm just about to have a sandwich."

My being away had made her happy, it was an incontrovertible fact, and so there was nothing for it but to make Saturdays in town a habit. The trouble was that other village boys started tagging along, hanging about in teenage clouds by the bus stop, and shadowed me, and that was worse than loneliness. So I started going to Peattie instead, though I had to catch two buses to get there. It was Joan who told my mother. When Ottilie rang, Edith said that not only was I welcome, but I was an enormous help. Michael could come to Peattie on however many Saturdays he felt like it, she said. I was standing beside my grandmother as she spoke, trying to gauge reaction from the other end of the line, hoping for a hint of regret, of jealousy. Edith winked at me, talking to my mother on the phone and attempting to tousle my hair, which was difficult as I was already a good four inches taller than her. What would be lovely, she added as if it had just occurred to her (it hadn't; we'd discussed it), was if he could come and stay the entire weekend sometimes. Could he be spared?

The truth is there wasn't that much in the way of helping with the house and even less so as I got older. The women wouldn't let me do much. Gratefully I realised that I could do at Peattie what I did at home, cocooned away with books and writing. I filled dozens of these notebooks, blue exercise books that Ottilie has filed away in suitcases and brings out at night when Edith's asleep. Some of it was diary, some of it first attempts at journalism, and there were short stories later, in the year before I left. I liked the routine of a Peattie weekend. After the four o'clock tea I'd head to the kitchen; this was the part of the day I enjoyed most. It became a new tradition that I'd make dinner on a Saturday night and that all those in residence would sit around the kitchen table together and eat. If I'd hoped for a reaction to that, to my mother's exclusion from family dinner and family conversations, I wasn't to be granted one. It wouldn't have occurred to her to mind.

Being back at Peattie was such a relief. Peattie was never going to change: it was Peattie that was the living organism, the entity, and succeeding generations of Salters lived its life in all the ways that Peattie demanded; there was security in that. Things at the cottage felt very different. Ever since I could remember I'd felt about my mother that she could make a decision for a different life, any minute and seemingly on a whim. It might be one that didn't suit me. It might even be one that didn't include me. She might come into the room on any day, at any moment, with a new look on her face, one that I'd recognise because I'd anticipated it for years. She'd explain to me that she had to go, that she was moving to Tokyo or to Patagonia. Braced against this probability, at 15 I hugged the idea of Peattie to myself. Mog and I started going to town together on Saturdays and so I began to go to Peattie on Friday nights, straight after school. Ottilie took it in her stride. Now that my weekends there were habitual, she adopted habits of her own and began to make trips away. I was boarded with

Edith for a month every autumn while my mother went travelling.

Euan had done most of the weekend cooking at Peattie up to this point, and for a while he was enthusiastic about our doing it together. I hated this: he couldn't help taking over and being dictatorial about technique. It doesn't really matter how a carrot is cut but Euan is a man for there being only one way; he and Joan have this mindset in common. We argued and Edith intervened and the sessions were abandoned, in favour of taking turns. Even then, he'd come and sit in the kitchen with papers to mark while I was making dinner and try to strike up conversation, though his dislike for my mother was at the heart of most of it. He'd criticise her openly when Edith was around, if always on the basis of fighting my corner.

"Ottilie goes on holiday every year without her child; she never thinks to take her child," he said to my grandmother in my presence once, Edith looking towards me in alarm.

"It's not a holiday; it's work," I told him. "I'm invited to go too. I'm always invited. But it's at a bad time for missing school. And I'd rather be here."

I wished immediately that I hadn't said that final thing.

It wasn't true that I'd been invited, though it shut Euan up. And it occurred to me every October that perhaps this time she wouldn't come back, or that she'd come back with a man in tow and present him to me as a stepfather and move him in. Perhaps he'd be somebody she couldn't see through, someone who'd become determined to oust me. She'd be oblivious, unaware that her new and charming husband had, in her absence, eyes that glittered like a predator's. It wasn't a coincidence that I'd recommended that Mog read *David Copperfield*.

I understand more now about Ottilie's positioning, the way she positions herself in relation to others. I was always convinced that it would have suited her better to be alone in the world, but the truth is that she values attachments, as long as they're long, fine silver threads, very long, very fine, that look fragile, that might even appear invisible, but in truth are immutable and permanent, that provide her with a necessary distance. Her idea of happiness is to be alone but with people at hand. Her happiest days as a mother were days when I wasn't there. I think that's true and it's said without self-pity: the crucial point is that they were also days in which I was coming back, I was expected; I'd frame her solitude and make it work. Her happiest times at Peattie, she's said, have been spent working in the studio, knowing the family is only just outside her concentration, that she can emerge blue-overalled and preoccupied into the drawing room at teatime and will barely be called upon to speak. She takes it with her, she says, this time spent in physical proximity, back to the cottage and back into the work.

So this is how it went. Two weeks after I'd gone, Ottilie laid down to her father the conditions of her return to Peattie, and they were abided by. She'd come at set times so that care could be taken to keep Ursula out of the way, visiting once a week on average, except for those periods in which she wasn't speaking to her parents – because although the agreement about not encountering Ursula held, it didn't result in untroubled years of visiting. For years, Ottilie vacillated. She'd come to the house and seem almost normal, but beneath the surface of calm, its crust, there were tectonic stirrings and shiftings; the heat was garnering itself and rising. Generally there was precious little in the way of a warning. On the day precipitating her longest absence, Edith had been asking blamelessly about the weather at the coast, which was brighter, generally, than the hill-country micro-climate of Peattie. In answer,

Ottilie stared. Then she got to her feet, setting her cup and cake plate carefully down.

"I'm sorry, I have to go."

"But you've just got here," Edith protested.

"Sometimes – I'm sorry – increasingly, I find I can't bear to be in the same room as the two of you."

"Oh, Ottilie." Edith began to cry. Tears sprang from her eyes and rolled down each cheek.

"I can't do this any more," Ottilie said. "I'll be back when I feel differently. Please, please don't come to the cottage."

She was away from Peattie for almost four years and nobody saw her or heard from her, other than in a weekly letter written only to Edith and which Edith answered, sometimes taking days over her responses, writing draft after draft and discarding them. Then one Saturday Edith could be heard squawking excitedly in the hall that there was tremendous news: Ottilie was coming to tea tomorrow. Nobody spoke to her unless to ask about the work, which was the main condition laid down; nor were Ursula's or Michael's names to be mentioned. Sometimes queries about the work carried evident metaphorical weight, though superficially that was all that was discussed.

Gradually, the time Ottilie spent at Peattie began to lengthen again into hours. She brought art materials in her car and began to use her studio at the house before tea, though if something inadvertently tactless was said to her she'd excuse herself and return to seclusion. It was assumed that a loch visit was out of the question and it was never mentioned, but in fact it was at this time that her visits to me began. She didn't announce them to anyone, but she was spotted and the news got out. Ottilie had been seen sitting by my memorial stone, talking aloud as if to me. Nothing was said to her about it, or by her about it, and things achieved a kind of stability, the stable weekend pattern that was in place at the time of Edith's party.

Only Pip has dared mention the long absence. The morning after the winter drama in Ursa's room, Ottilie said at breakfast that she wanted to go to the hospital alone for the morning visiting: not because she had anything particular to say to Edith, but because she wanted to sit quietly with her. Pip followed her out onto the snowy, slushy terrace, on the pretext of having a smoke, and watched her looking for something to clear her windscreen. He went to help, was thanked for his kindness, and then, emboldened, said, "I've always wanted to know something."

"Yes."

"Can I ask you – just one small thing?"

"You can try."

"What made you come back? So suddenly. After so many years away. Was it something that Edith wrote to you?"

"No. It wasn't something Edith wrote. It was just time."

"It can't have been that simple."

"Pip."

"Sorry. I overstepped."

"It was just that I was tired," Ottilie said, getting into the car. "Tired of minding that they put Ursula first. I could live my life without them, but it was exhausting me. In the end it was a decision about myself: it was better for me to end it, to appear to be recovered from it."

"But you're not."

Ottilie closed her door, started her engine and pulled slowly through the whitened gravel, waving briefly out of the open window, Pip acknowledging her with a sort of salute.

Chapter 14

Feeling that she couldn't bear any more cups of coffee and any more confidential chats, chats that could stretch into desperate hours, Mog took Rebecca for a walk around the estate. It was a chilly morning, misty, but the sun was there beyond the milkiness, burning stoically through its tissue paper layers. Nothing could be seen at the other side of the loch through the fog, and Peattie's borders to other worlds could only be guessed at. They went first into the walled gardens, Mog walking slightly ahead so as to limit the conversational flow, then into the courtyard and round to the glasshouses, admiring the neat rows of salad crops, the tangle of greenery that rose ceiling-high, the pleasant warm stink of tomato plants. They followed the lane to where it divides, left to the loch, right to the village, and chose the right-hand fork. Approaching the cottages they saw Alan in his front garden, standing behind a trestle table, potting up seedlings from plastic trays. Alan stopped what he was doing.

"Ladies," he said solicitously. "Nice day for it."

The cottages are miniaturised toytown-sized houses, sitting together joined in a row. Each gate and window frame has been painted and repainted its pre-war black; each of the windows is shaped faux-medievally as an arch, with finely crafted curved and angled stone-cutting supporting them; each porch trimmed in fretwork that's still painted in its same pre-war green. Small, densely planted gardens at the front are divided one from the other by waist-height hedges, and of these little plots only Jet's was untended-looking, bearing the ruins of a sweetpea wigwam gifted by his mother, its former lawn knee-deep in bindweed. George's own plot was dedicated almost entirely to roses, white and dark purple and apricot. George kept up the holiday let, a square of grass edged in herbs and blue geranium, though Alan said he shouldn't bother. It was one of the things they disagreed about. Alan wouldn't let his father do Jet's garden, which was cut by Ursula when she remembered. Ursula's own patch is a tiny meadow dominated by Michaelmas daisies (she doesn't much approve of lawns), and it was as Rebecca was admiring the wild-flowers in Ursula's patch that their owner came rushing out of her cottage and past them at a hurried walk, holding a spade almost as big as she was. Then she came jogging back without it.

"Rebecca, you said you'd like to see inside my house. Come now. I'm here and you're here."

Mog and Rebecca followed Ursula inside.

The cottages are dark and prone to damp; the gothic-revival pointed windows are not so charming from within. Woodlice patrol the carpet edges and in terms of decorative efforts only limewashes survive the clamminess of the old stone. All wallpaper attempts have had to be abandoned, though little shreds remain by skirtings and light switches of old doomed campaigns.

"There are four rooms, two up and two down," Ursula told Rebecca.

Downstairs there's a kitchen and sitting room and, up a narrow wooden staircase, a bedroom and bathroom, squeezed in under the eaves and heavily coombed.

230

Originally these were two bedrooms, when the cottages shared a communal bathhouse at the rear, but only its foundations remain, marked by a grassy hump and rim of stone. The family that lived in what's now Ursula's house in the 1880s had seven children, and Ursula told Rebecca what's known about them. Three slept in a double bed, top to tail, one in a camp bed squeezed in by the wall, the youngest in the cot in the parents' room and two downstairs in a curtained-off recess. She showed Rebecca the recess. "Look how small it is, but I bet it was the warmest, so close to the stove."

Ursula moved into the cottage on the understanding that she would never go beyond the wall alone and that she would continue to come into Peattie House for meals. All this time later she continued to eat with her parents at least once a day, unless Ottilie was at the house, in which case someone was delegated to deliver, trotting down the lane with a covered dish on a tray, soup in a thermos, a bread roll on a plate. Before the companion arrived and the gas stove, Ursula lived out of a fridge and a microwave. She had a toaster and little non-combustible bags designed for making toasted sandwiches.

Ursula's kitchen, unchanged in half a century, retains its sky-blue cupboards and formica surfaces, its poured blue-black flooring flecked with dots and dashes and its elderly rag-rugs; the rest of the cottage is bare boards. "Joan wants to do it but I won't let her," Ursula said. "That would ruin it but Joan doesn't see that. She doesn't see things." She looked to Mog for a response but none came. "It was the same with Granny Vita, yesterday."

Joan had come into Vita's private sitting room, a small, scruffy room, the wallpaper tatty, the carpet going to holes, the only heating from a wood fire, to find Vita and Mrs Hammill having a late breakfast of papadums and mango chutney. Mrs Hammill makes frequent visits late at night to the Indian restaurant in the village. Vita was enrobed in thick satin, a dressing gown that was almost 80 years old, that had been bought for a young bride, a faded sea blue embroidered with kingfishers and pagodas, and was holding, shakily, a tiny china cup with mud-thick espresso in it. She drinks a lot of coffee, joking that it's all that's keeping her heart beating. Joan had been bursting with the news that she'd planned a refurbishment, and was surprised when Vita declined.

"I'm sorry about your moodboard and I'm grateful to you, but it's not for me. I'm old now. Wait till I'm gone."

Joan protested that it was no trouble.

"That isn't it, my dear," Vita explained. "I like to be among things from my life, you see, and it's comforting to outlive some of them."

Ursula's eyes were bright. "And now, come and see." She took Rebecca's hand and led her into the sitting room. "The sofa is new," she said. "Well, not new but new to me." It's a firmly upholstered mustard-coloured affair, all flat planes, with buttoned seats and angled metal legs. She has utility cupboards, a mirror in the shape of a star and shelves heavy with old crockery, things mined at Peattie and at sales Joan takes her to. Generally that's as far afield as Ursula gets. She's never been off the estate unaccompanied. She's never been to the cinema or into a supermarket or on a motorway, but she's intimately acquainted with every church hall, junk emporium and bookshop in the county.

"I like three sorts of things," Ursula said. "Well, four if you count plants. Well, five if you count animals, but we could just keep going, adding and adding. What do you like?"

"Oh, well, I don't know, I suppose the usual things, nice food and films and travel; I like plants and animals too," Rebecca said.

"You have to learn to be more whimsical," Ursula told her. "You're very serious all the time. It makes you boring. What I should have said is the three favourite things for collecting. It's important to be specific, isn't it? Two of them are here, and another one is up the stairs and you'll see in a minute."

One sitting-room wall is composed entirely of old books, a vivid mosaic of purchases chosen for their bindings and illustrations, children's books most of them. The shelving opposite has crowded line-ups of china, all of it oddments, spotted and floral: not only cups and jugs and plates but also kitsch souvenir pieces and what Joan calls granny china – porcelain dogs and shepherdesses. Ursula groups them into tableaux and tells stories about their encounters.

"You mustn't touch, though, so please don't touch," she said to Rebecca as Rebecca's arm was outstretched. "If someone breaks something of mine I break something of theirs. It's only fair."

Together they clomped up the steep wooden staircase in the gloom, through the stair door and into the bedroom. A cumbersome knitting machine sat at the centre of a small clearing, threatened at all sides by tightly packed racks of second-hand clothing, every cut and colour and type of thing, but with an evident favouritism for ball gowns, cocktail dresses and elaborate underwear.

Izzy pops in sometimes to say hello and takes pieces of clothing on loan. In general Ursula doesn't lend, so it's remarkable that she lets Izzy borrow from the collection, though Pip thinks that it's because she enjoys denying Izzy ownership of things. There may be an element of guilty conscience at play. Ursula disgraced herself at Izzy's christening by remarking to a fellow guest and audibly to others that the ravishingly pretty baby swaddled in Great-Grandmother's lace, blinking and cooing in her mother's arms, would be unlucky and die young. Afterwards, in the drawing room at Peattie, Edith had at first tried the play-fulness defence: Ursula hadn't meant it; it was joke, though perhaps – she'd concede this – in poor taste for the occasion. That hadn't convinced anyone, so then Edith said that Ursula hadn't meant for Joan to overhear, and at least she'd had the good grace to look regretful about it.

"You can try some of the things on, if you like, if you're careful," Ursula offered.

"I don't think we have time, but thank you," Rebecca said.

"Oh I see," Ursula said flatly. "You should go, then. No point staying."

So much younger than her twin sisters, so much older than their children, Ursula has always seemed to me to be stuck between generations like a lift that's got stuck between floors. In the old days Edith was assertive, should the subject arise, about her youngest daughter having been a normal happy girl, developing at the usual rate, until the witnessing of Sebastian's death derailed her. Whatever the truth of that, it's agreed that after his death she was an isolated child with pronounced aversions. Various other children came to play at intervals when she was young, attracted by the loch and the pony and the tennis court, but it never worked out. She and I found that we had this much in common. It's one of the things we used to talk about. About that and about my mother. Looking back, it's hard not to admire Ursula's silence on the key question, throughout these conversations. It never occurred to me that Ursula would know who my father was, and so I didn't press her on the topic. But she's good at keeping quiet.

It's hard to know whether Ursula's silence, which lasted for four years after Sebastian died, was a decision arrived at, made to step into line with her quiet parents, or whether it was, as Edith has always insisted, a physical manifestation of shock. What's certain is that whether voluntary or not, Ursula outdid everyone in the quality and reach of her silence. If you spoke she'd just stare at you, her rosebud mouth pursed up with dislike. It was clear she was bright. It wasn't that she didn't know the answers. She'd respond in class by speaking through an interpreter, her desk-partner Sheena, a girl of bovine placidity who was happy to read out Ursula's written responses. In any case, only three years of conventional schooling were managed and Ursula was taken out to be home-educated aged eight, when it was agreed by everybody concerned that she wasn't coping, so she has never sat an exam, though Edith taught her the basics and reading taught her the rest. It's reading tracked along the many dusty bookcases at Peattie – reading that has left her with what some might consider a lopsided knowledge of the world. Plants and butterflies, local geography, John Milton, the history of the English Civil War and of Malaysia: these are some of the things she knows a lot about. Later on it was Edith who bought her the knitting machine. It turned out to be an inspired gift. Ursula enjoys its laborious processes, its slowness and method, its steady productivity. She makes beautiful knitwear with complicated knots and patterns, sweaters and cardigan jackets made with feather-light wools spun finely, from chocolate-brown and buttermilk-coloured sheep, and sells them in the crafts shop in the town, the arts and crafts co-op that was once Tilly's dress shop. Some of the items are left in their natural colours, but others she rinses in plant dyes; part of the garden at Peattie is planted with traditional dye-giving flowers, yellow and green, brick red and violet blue. She's always found her knitwear-proceeds to be bountiful, despite the modesty of her income, because she spends almost nothing. She's supplied with the day-to-day essentials and even some of these are rejected as unnecessary, a situation that has always made Edith happy, speaking deeply to her frugality.

"And now I have to leave," Ursula said, going to the stair door. "Come on, I need to go and so do you." She was already down the stairs. "What did I do with my spade?"

"You left it in the road," Mog called down after her.

Back on the lane, Mog lifted a hand in a wordless greeting to Alan, and she and Rebecca walked on. They were passing Jet's cottage – noting the pizza boxes and the plastic bags spilling empty beer tins that were sitting by his bin, noting the faint thudding of bass – when George came out onto his doorstep holding a tea towel and called out his hello. There wasn't any choice but to turn back, to be polite and make introductions.

"You must be one of Henry's sister's family; you must be Ursa's daughter." George, beaming, thrust his warm pouchy hand into Rebecca's.

"She was my grandmother."

"Of course. I forget that I'm old. Come in, come in, won't you, and have tea with us. I've just made a pot."

Alan had been staring at Rebecca's heavy breasts throughout this exchange. "Alan," his father said sharply. "Open the gate for the girls."

Henry always referred to Alan as the Dixon boy, though at this point the Dixon boy looked anything but boyish. Quite aside from the family's doubts, the family's entrenched disgust about his fathering of me, the family's sometime belief that Alan had lied about my death and their simultaneous deep embarrassment about relying on his secrecy, the village was itself independently suspicious of the Dixon boy. Alan wasn't liked or trusted, and concern about his continuing to live on the estate (sharing a bedroom still with his father, which wasn't thought normal) had been mentioned more than once to Edith at the Bible group. Alan had been visited by the police earlier in the summer for an informal chat about socialising with minors, a visit viewed by a sizable local contingent as damning in itself. It was noted that the police came knocking at Edith's door too. They had stood in her kitchen, looming tall and black-coated like angels of death while she fussed extraneously and mortal with kettle and teabags; they wanted to know if there was any truth in information they'd received that Alan had shown inappropriate interest in her daughters when they were under age, and that he'd fathered a child with one of them. It was a relief that it was only this: it was only to do with Alan and Ottilie, and Edith's relief was obvious, at least to me. She assured the visitors, their dark presence in her light kitchen near-supernatural, that this was idle and unfounded gossip and that the village view wasn't to be taken seriously. Here, there's always a village view, one that's achieved without apparent effort, and once this latest fuss had died down the view was that the allegations that had sparked it were probably bogus. One of the girls involved – described by Betty at the post office as a "well-known slut" – retracted her story pretty smartly. The second wasn't even an allegation. A 14-year-old staying at the holiday cottage had written a diary entry that her mother had read, that'd had her mother straight on the phone. Betty pointed out unprompted that the 14-year-old holiday visitor and the 13-year-old slut had been seen smoking together at the village playground, the Salter Memorial Playing Field.

"Well now, there's nowhere much to sit in here," George said, passing through the kitchen, past the boxed-in staircase, beckoning the visitors to follow. "We'll adjourn to the parlour and hope it's fit to be seen."

George Dixon, local tennis champion in his youth and star turn at the long-defunct town dance hall, still wore the clothes of his prime, the same ancient brown suits. He wore this uniform even in the garden: a checked shirt and green tie could be glimpsed often under his overalls. He has a kind old face, weathered and tanned and bulbous-nosed, and deep-set eyes, still that same sea blue. When I was a child I was fascinated by his bulky hands, their ingrained dirt, and by that scent he carried with him, like warm green apples in a paper bag. Green apple, mower fuel and hothouse smells seemed imprinted not only in George's clothes but also in his skin.

The parlour smelled of bacon and laundry. Remnants of sandwich remained on a plate. A clothes horse in the corner, freshly laden, emitted its laundry soap fug. There were magazines and newpapers in piles by the sofa, a black leather one too big for the room, an outsized television positioned opposite.

"You're here for the do, then," George said. "Sit down, sit down."

"That's right," Rebecca told him. "I've never been up here before."

"Here with your dad."

"That's right."

"Well now, that's nice. That's very good. I'll get the tea."

Alan looked as unkempt as ever. His formal black trousers had a dusty look about them, and were torn at the lower corners of the pockets, showing their white lining. Today he was wearing a grey sweatshirt with *Basketball 1959* printed on it in yellow. His slippers were flattened at the back where his feet crushed them, his sock heels twisted over his feet. His comb-over had gone awry and was hanging longer at one side. Despite all this he retained his old attractive smile, his eyes identical to his father's. The man that might have been looked out of them sometimes.

Mog and Rebecca sat down together; the sofa was a soft enveloping thing and yielded to their weight, in fact kept yielding, tipping them back, something that gave Alan evident pleasure. He watched Mog's face as she looked at the furnishings and personal effects in the room: it was a first visit and she was openly curious, or affected to be so, taking this opportunity for curiosity as a way of avoiding immediate conversation, hoping to wait for George to be intermediary before having to talk, and in the meantime adopting a sort of waiting-room demeanour. But it was Alan who was waiting, and his patience was rewarded. He saw her catch sight of the painting hanging on the wall opposite, above the TV. He saw her expression change. He heard the sharp intake of breath. He saw her fingers tauten on the sofa cushion. When she met his eyes, he was smiling.

The drawing was done in charcoal and fleshed out in paint, its thin and sketchy watercolour skilful in suggesting light on the water and leaf patterns in the trees. The tomb was rendered in several expertly judged blocks, white and cream and grey, a darker grey lending shadow and substance; David's effigy was implied but not stated. It was done from a viewpoint on the loch, showing the shore-line in the foreground, the willows grouped and weeping. Henry told me when I was still a child that I could have the picture when I was older. When I was very young I'd go and sit on his bed while he was dressing, and we'd talk about it and about the great uncle and his sacrifice. Henry said the sketches had been done from a photograph taken from the boat and that he had the original somewhere, that he'd look it out for me, although he never did.

"I want something from them, son," Alan said to me, during our conversation in the garden at night the evening before I disappeared, standing together in the soft hot dusk. We'd talked about his being my father, a stilted, disap-pointing exchange that humiliated us both. Then we'd moved onto safer territory, arranging for him to bring the money to the beach the following afternoon on the basis of a promised fee. "A small thing, a token thing; some-thing symbolic to me," Alan said, glowing with his fake sentimental piety. Perhaps he was thinking specifically of the painting then, as an additional symbol to the £200 I'd promised, though it's unlikely he'd seen it before. More likely it was an opportunistic theft.

George put his head round the door. "It's got a bit stewed so I'm making a fresh one." Then he was gone again, whistling. Alan picked up a fruit knife from a tea plate on the lamp table, cleaned it on the hem of his sweatshirt, then picked out an apple from a raffia bowl, a dark-red and shiny apple, slicing off a piece and eating it. A second slice was offered to Rebecca and declined. A small table was pushed against the wall, its extending leaf lowered and a chair at each side, and now Alan pulled out one of the chairs and sat on it, his chubby legs wide apart. They were old chairs, the kind that have vinyl seats dropped loose inside a wooden frame. Alan corrected his hair, smoothing it into position.

"That picture," he said, half turning and gesturing with the fruit knife, "has hung there for 13 years. You realise where it came from."

"It's the one," Mog told Rebecca discreetly.

"She knows about it then," Alan said, cutting himself another slice.

"She knows about Michael leaving home, going missing, yes."

Would Rebecca pick up on this rather obvious warning? Apparently not. But Alan, in his sharp-eyed way, had received the hint and acknowledged it.

"Does she now," he said.

"She knows Michael took the picture," Mog clarified, with a look that pleaded with him for corroboration. "We thought he took it with him, when he left. But evidently not."

"I said to myself that we'd wait and see how long it would be," Alan said, sorrowful and moral. "How long until somebody came to visit, to see how Dad was doing, to talk to Dad about the garden. It's been too much for him for years and years. And nobody has come. Nobody."

He got up and opened the window, the knife still in his hand. The room was stale and airless. Mog's hands were

240

sweaty on the sofa cushion and she wiped them on the sides of her jeans.

"My boy gave it to me. That and some of the money." Alan returned to his chair. "There. I've surprised you, haven't I? Bet you don't know what I know."

"Alan, please."

"The money. You think Michael stole it. Not true. Henry offered it to him, paid him off, to get him to go away from Peattie."

"What do you mean, paid him off?"

"Michael had found out that I'm his dad."

Rebecca's eyes were like saucers.

"Wait," Mog said, putting her hands palm down on the coffee table and splaying her fingers. "You're saying Michael was bribed to leave Peattie because he was going to tell people that you are his father."

"Course."

"That's what you're saying. That Henry'd do that."

"There's lots about Henry you don't know," Alan said, shaking his head. Mog stood up. "Please sit," Alan said to her. "At least do me the courtesy of hearing me out." Mog sat down again. "My dad is ill, has been ill these 20 years. Heart, hips, and now his waterworks. But he keeps on doing the garden for your grandad, for the estate; the estate's more important than he is! Nobody asks him to, you say. Supposed to be retired, isn't he?"

"Henry doesn't realise," Mog told him emphatically. "Honestly. Has no idea. He thinks he does it for the love of it."

"There's no pension, you know. What do you get for a lifetime of service? Poverty, that's what."

George was standing in the doorway with a tray.

"This house in his lifetime and money at Christmas," Alan said. "That's right, isn't it, Dad?"

"Take the tray, would you, Miss Salter," George said. "I'm going back for biscuits. And when I come in again I want to hear there's been a change of subject. That's all I'm saying about it. I'll talk to you about it later, Alan."

"Nobody comes to see him," Alan continued, lowering his voice. "When Dad was so poorly last year, who came? We got a card at the hospital and that was it. Fruit and a card."

Mog didn't respond as she could have done, that Alan's presence at his father's side might have been a deterrent.

George was back, with Rich Tea fingers fanned out on a plate. "Right then. Cup of tea, Miss Salter?"

"George, I wish you'd call me Mog," Mog said.

"He prefers Miss Salter," Alan told her. "That being the case, where do you get off calling my father George?"

"Alan," George said. A warning shot.

"I didn't think. I'm sorry," Mog exclaimed, flushing.

"Oh, pet, doesn't matter a bit," George said. "We're all modern now. How do you take it?"

Small talk was made with George over tea about the party, and Rebecca supplied some well-intentioned Somerset colour, going into detail about her father's illness, his treatments, his diagnosis. Alan didn't say anything, but crunched on biscuits, one after another, running his eyes over various individual body parts of the visitors, his eyes lingering and returning. Then, cups drained and a second cup drunk down quickly, Mog rose from her seat, extending her hand towards George. "Lovely to see you, but we have to be going."

"Will you not stay?" George was disappointed.

"We'd love to," Mog said, "but we're supposed to be helping. They'll be wondering where we've got to."

"Dad's invited but I'm not, of course," Alan said bitterly.

❧

While Mog and Rebecca were sitting talking to the Dixons, Ursula was talking to Susan Marriott in the flower garden.

242

Edith had taken Susan there in order to have a private conversation, one she'd been rehearsing in her head, backtracking on their last talk and blaming her nerves, blaming a vivid imagination put under stress, but this conversation was rendered impossible by Ursula's arrival. Nor could she monitor what it was that Susan and Ursula were talking about, watching their body language, their facial expressions, their mouths, from her position at the hedge: Edith's mobile had rung out just as Ursula arrived and it was Ottilie on the phone, wanting to talk about Saturday. Susan and Ursula were left standing together at the arched gateway, which frames a view of pasture land rising gently into low hills. At a loss for something to say, Susan commented blandly on the beauty of the scene, the loveliness of the cypresses in the middle of the field, the cows gathered beneath the lateral spread of branches, swishing their tails against the flies.

"You think that it's beauty, but actually it's incredibly brutal," Ursula told her, beginning to dig out a nettle patch.

"Well, that's a pity," Susan replied, an artificial brightness obvious in her voice.

Ursula, alert to the tone, stared hard at her. "All these animals, in all these fields, they're all being fattened to be killed," she said. "It's Hansel and Gretel, really."

"That's a rather dark point of view for such a beautiful day." Again, that same dangerously hearty tone.

Ursula, dressed in a Victorian shirt, baggy bloomers and black wellingtons, leaned on her spade, her long hair falling forward.

"Baby lambs taken from their mothers and killed for eating. Have you seen them, the lambs, when the lorry comes to get them? Trying to get back to their mothers, bleating in panic?"

Edith had appeared now, propelling Susan gently away, a guiding hand at her lower back.

"It isn't beauty, it's obscenity!" Ursula called after them, bending and ripping out a clump of achillea and holding it up like a sword.

※

Later, fixing up strings of coloured lights along the passage that connects the hall with the rear stairs, having talked and talked about Alan the father and Michael the son, Rebecca's supportive stance became a little bruised.

"You don't see it from Alan's point of view, though, do you?" she said suddenly. The change of tone took Mog by surprise. "It must have been terrible for Alan, keeping quiet about it for all these years. Poor Alan."

"Poor Alan?" Mog said, dismayed. "I don't think so. Why do you think Ottilie wouldn't ever talk about it?"

"What – you don't mean rape?"

"It's possible. Or something in a much greyer area, in between."

"Is there an in between?"

"Of course. Acres of grey."

"What? What are you saying? Of course there aren't."

"Calm down. And pass me the hammer and another hook. In fact, can you take the steps for a bit? They're making me dizzy."

They changed positions and worked on in silence a while. Then Mog said, "But it was hardly a secret. We didn't tell Michael; nobody told him, but it wasn't a secret. It wasn't like that. It was something we protected him from. Hardly the same thing, is it?"

"Of course it is."

"No, it isn't."

"I can't believe you." Rebecca got down off the step-ladder. "I can't believe any of you would do that. I'm not often lost for words, but ... Jesus, Mog."

"What?"

"'Protected' is the wrong word. That's all."

"It didn't feel that way."

"Are you really telling me that all of you knew about Alan, even then, 13 years ago?"

"What's clear is that Michael knew. That's what Ursula told him. Now we know for sure."

"Ursula told him?"

"Yes. Just before he disappeared. She hasn't ever told us directly that that's what it was. She said that she told him a secret, one she couldn't tell the rest of us. But that's what I was saying. It wasn't some great secret. She knew that we knew. It doesn't make sense. And the timings – the timings make no sense at all."

"I'm still not clear. When did you find out about Alan?"

"My mother told me. When I was 16. More than half gleeful. Horrible. Swore me to secrecy."

"And you *abided by that*?"

"Course not. Calm down. Not because I promised, but because it would have made everything worse."

"I don't understand you. Really. How could it have been worse?"

"Michael would have been a lot more unhappy, knowing it was Alan Dixon. That was our decision, mine and Pip's. It wasn't right but it felt right. Easy for you to judge, but it felt like the right thing, to us."

"And so what you're saying is that you spent hours and hours with Michael, listening to him obsessing about his dad, who his dad was, and you didn't tell him?"

"I didn't tell him."

"Well, I'm sorry, but that's just despicable."

"I know! I know that, Rebecca. Do you think I don't know that?"

"Now you're shouting."

"Ursula told him that we all knew, that we'd known all along. That was the secret. Our lying to him. That must've been it."

"No wonder he never came back."

"Just shut up! Shut up! You don't know anything about this. It's way more complicated than you think."

"Tell me."

Mog excused herself, saying they'd finish later, and went to find her sister. Izzy was in her room on the phone, but cut her call short, seeing the look on Mog's face, and together they went to the linen room to talk, somewhere that Rebecca probably wouldn't think to look.

"I seem to have spent the day talking about Michael," Mog said.

"And?"

"As I was talking I began to believe Ursula. That it was suicide."

"It's possible, I suppose."

"It's hard to imagine what it was that could have been so final. How on earth could a person give up on life at 19?"

"Brain chemistry probably. A serious depression. A failure of imagination. Not being able to imagine the future as anything good."

"How could Michael's imagination fail him? This is Michael we're talking about. I don't get it. I don't. Even if life is boring and crap, even if it persists for ever in being boring and crap, the point is that even then, notwithstanding general crapness, I know that close to the moment of death I'll be pleading for one more day. Another swim in the loch in summer."

"A last swim with Michael."

"What would you choose?"

"I'm hoping the day hasn't happened yet. I don't have one I'd want to repeat, not yet."

"Really? That surprises me. You and your glamorous life."

"You don't really buy into all that, I hope. Smoke and mirrors, my love. Hype and blisters. And fundamentally just cold, hard and merciless commerce." She looked intently into her sister's face.

"You were in love with him, Mog."

"We were friends," Mog told her. "But those are the days. Not just because of him. Because of childhood and summer. You know."

"I know. I think about it a lot."

Mog got up and rearranged the blanket on the shelf, and said, "I struggle, Izzy; I'm struggling."

"I know."

"How do you not? How do you – what's the word? – I don't know what the word is."

"We all struggle, you know. In our own way."

"You don't seem to."

"With me it's different. It's like this: don't trip me up, don't turn my head, I have to keep going forward."

"Like Pip."

"Like Pip, I suppose. He says we're like sharks. Got to keep moving or else we – or else we die."

"Drown, you were going to say."

"It happened when Pip and I talked about it too. It hits sometimes. It still has the power to hit."

I can see them, the two of them on their imaginary last day. A last fish and chip supper eaten out of the paper, salty and greasy, and beer drunk out of paper cups. The two of them sitting on the end of the jetty, water running down their hair and beading on their brown arms: Michael and Mog, their wet backs and shins, their same olive skin turning gold, their same teeth white in the pinkish dark in the evening of the hottest day of the year. Not saying much. Mog kicking her legs out in a slow and happy way. This was the plan for that last evening, the thing that should have happened, the thing that didn't. Sometimes a thing that has been imagined this many times becomes a memory and is indivisible.

Chapter 15

I must have died on the way to wherever I was going. I froze to death in a ditch on a warm summer's night. I blundered off a cliff in a deserted part of the coast and lie in the under-growth, undiscovered. I was run over by a car in some other part of the country and proved unidentifiable. I was abducted and murdered while hitch-hiking and lie in a shallow grave in some other woods. Over the years more and greater doubt established itself about the circumstances surrounding my death in the loch, the circumstances or just the plain fact of it. Something must have happened to me, it was decided, some ironical second death, and the circumstances of this have been a ripe source of imagining over the years, of speculation and counter-speculation. I survived to establish a life only to perish in an accident or of disease, and they never heard back. I contracted a rapid cancer and, denying having any surviving family, died before I could forgive, my rage proving tenacious, my rage having mutated, and was cremated friendless in some southern memory garden.

Pip was the first to express the opinion in the group that I was still alive, and others followed, though nobody ever said so in front of Ottilie. Perhaps Michael's alive, he said, and perhaps we need to forgive him for that. Perhaps

Michael's still living this new life, cut off from the past. He imagined it sometimes, Pip said. Alan and Henry imagined it better, over the weeks and months and years. Alan initiated. Once Alan had recanted, and produced – for Henry's ears only – his alternative version of the day I'd drowned, supposedly drowned, he seemed to relish the dreaming-up of the possible details of my life. Michael achieved his ambitions, Alan said; he was sure of that, he felt it and was sure. He'd become the woodcutter – the forester, he meant – woodcutter was such an out-of-date word.

"Living in the woods, making a small and perfect living – that's how he described it to me once," Henry said. "He wanted to see how little money he could live on, he said. He wanted to try and make a life that was about other things than things. That's what he said to me."

"You've told me this already."

"It made me angry with him."

Perhaps there were children, Alan said, born to the woodcutter and the woodcutter's wife. Yes, Henry said, children who ran wild and barefoot in the woods. The wife would be beautiful, Alan said; she was bound to be beautiful. It was Henry who came up with the name Elspeth, and Alan who added that she was green-eyed and auburn-haired. She wouldn't be especially tall, Alan said, but with legs long for her height, and creamy skin. Henry said that they didn't need to go into so much detail as that. He added that there would be two children, twin girls, who loved the woods like their father did. He named them Isla and Catriona, so Isla and Catriona they were. When Henry described our house, our little brick house with blue shutters, and the woods around our house, and the girls running down to the lake with the dog, it was as if he had been there with me. Alan and Henry gave me the seeds for the life of my survival, and I'll always be grateful.

The first of their conversations, the important conversation, took place four weeks after I disappeared. We're not talking about something that took place recently, not remotely recently, but 13 years before Henry admitted to it.

It began like an ordinary day: as ordinary as days could be expected to be, barely a month after I'd gone. Henry had engaged in a mammoth tidying of paperwork, filing and settling accounts, and so when Alan knocked at the office door he found Henry sitting behind his desk, papers and receipts spread around him, the unpaid bills on their customary spike. Ordinary summer weather conditions had reasserted themselves and it was a cool grey day; the woodburner gave off a low and flickering orange glow and the faint aroma of chestnut. Henry was wearing a black fleece zip sweater (he wore some item of mourning every day), a pen tucked behind his ear. Alan was enrobed in blue overalls, grass smears spread across the chest, and brought with him an acrid whiff of lawnmower repairs. Henry had no way of knowing how important the conversation was going to be and greeted Alan vaguely, distractedly, his finger placed on a line of typed figures, before looking up.

Alan launched straight in.

"I need to tell you something, Mr Salter. I have the painting. At the cottage. I have it."

Anybody but Henry would have said immediately, wouldn't have been able to stop themselves asking the reflex question, "And the money?" But Henry didn't. Alan felt the thing not said vacating its expected place, and felt he must fill it. "I don't have the money," he added.

"You have the painting."

"Michael took the money with him. I didn't know what to do about the picture. He gave it to me, you see. And it didn't seem right to bring all that up at the time, if you see my meaning."

Henry's face softened into sympathy. "You hang on to it then, Alan, if Michael gave it to you."

"That's very kind."

"It doesn't matter so much to me, having it I mean. Not

as much as the idea that Michael might have wanted you to have it."

Alan began to look agitated.

"Do you want to talk to me about Michael?" Henry asked him.

Alan couldn't keep his hands still. One foot began to judder off the floor. He jumped up from the chair and went to the door.

"I told a lie," he said. He had his back to Henry.

"A lie?"

"About Michael."

"What?"

Alan half turned towards him and spoke to the wall.

"About that day. Ursula was wrong. I don't understand it. Why she thought Michael had died. I agreed with her because. Because."

"What do you mean? I don't understand you."

"Michael – he didn't die that day. He left. He left Peattie. Michael isn't dead."

Henry didn't speak. He stared at Alan, eyes bulging. Alan turned fully now and leaned back hard against the door, his hands tucked behind his back, his head dipped onto his chest. He didn't meet Henry's eyes.

"I'm so embarrassed," he said.

"Michael isn't dead," Henry repeated.

"I heard what Ursula said and I couldn't stop myself. I wanted to punish her, you see. It hurt so bad. Nobody understands how bad."

"Punish Ursula?"

"Punish Ottilie."

"I don't understand you, Alan. You're going to have to start again. Tell me again. You're saying that Michael survived and – and – what you're saying is that he came out of the loch and he left Peattie, and then you came back here and told us he was dead."

"It wasn't me."

251

"But how could you do this? This terrible thing?"

"All I had to do was agree with her. With Ursula. I just agreed with her. I'm used to agreeing; I do what I'm told. It was only afterwards that it hit me. Afterwards I was ill. You remember I was ill."

"You wanted to punish us. By telling us he was dead."

"I didn't tell you he was dead. Ursula did. You're not listening."

"I don't understand how you could do this to us. How could you do this to us?"

"I'm telling you now, aren't I? I'm telling you now. It can all be put right."

"Tell me. Tell me what happened at the loch."

Alan began to tell him. Alan was in the wood from the beginning, and saw and heard everything. Some of what he said was even true.

$\approx$

Ursula and I were out in the boat.

It was a perfect summer day, cloudless and windless. The far end of the loch had dissolved into haze, migrainous and twitching, its greens and blues fluid and dancing. The hills had a parched and wheaty look, the greens subdued into grey, all colour bleached and faded. The heat was strong on my hands and head. I don't burn but Ursula's arms had a lobster-pink tinge, an indistinct pink stripe along the contour of the bone.

Ursula and I were rowing towards the deeps. I was rowing and Ursula was fidgeting. She was rubbing her hands together, fingers poised over her knees. Her lower legs were drawn under the apron of the dress. She looked down into the floor of the boat, avoiding seeing the water, her head tilted away from me, barely visible beneath the hat.

"Henry knows that I'm going," I said to her. "But only Henry." I knew this would get back to Edith. I seemed to be intent on upsetting her, too. Getting Henry into trouble, certainly.

"He gave me some money," I said. Now all I could do was make things worse.

Ursula's studied calm was aggravating. "When did he give it?"

"He didn't physically give it. But he offered it to me, knowing I was leaving."

She didn't ask how much. That's not the sort of thing that interests her. She was quiet, chewing at her lower lip, picking at its dry skin with her teeth. The rhythm of the oars in the water was all I could hear. The turn and the sigh of air, the faint squeaking of oar in oarlock. The breaking-in; the idea of deep, deep water's uppermost membrane being disturbed, its plastic meniscus, though all that lies beneath lay untroubled, and then the flick of the oar as it emerged, the brief contingent scattering, its brief wet gasp; the spray and then the reunion. This was the soothing background music to our conversation.

"You and I belong together," Ursula said. This couldn't but irritate me.

"You're wrong," I told her. "This has just been ... it's a passionate friendship." The truth is, not even that.

He was appallingly arrogant, that boy, but tactful enough to desist from putting her right on one or two things, technical things about adult human relations. I wonder whether she will ever understand what sex really means, whether she'll move on from her belief that it's the insertion of tongues into mouths when kissing. On this basis, kissing me was the first sex she'd ever had. Ursula has a sheltered child's idea of things, having never been given the information by anyone. I'm not sure why that is. Was it Edith's belief that Ursula was certain never to have sexual relationships, thinking it unlikely (or worse inappropriate) in someone she's always considered, secretly, to be profoundly disabled? Or was it the fear that Ursula would take sexual pleasure whenever and wherever she could, uninhibitedly, applying her logical disdain to objections?

I know: there's no excuse. Kissing your aunt is bad enough. Does it help to know that it was Ursula who initiated kissing? All I can tell you in my own defence is that I was very drunk, and so was she. It wasn't anything premeditated, when I brought a bottle of Henry's cognac to the linen room that evening; I'd drunk there in secret for a while. Ursula was determined to join in and it didn't occur to me to stop her. Having had little luck with girls (I sneered at them, entirely self-protectively), Ursula's advance was an opportunity that I couldn't quite talk myself out of taking up. There was no contact other than of lips.

The boat itself was growing hot. Its fine metal rim, one that runs through its top edge, a thin metal-skinned frame indented into the wood, burned under the fingertips and caught searing at my forearms when they glanced against it. I had to change the subject, and so, in the casual manner that's often the hallmark of the momentous, I did something that would change the trajectory of all of our lives for ever after. I said, "I owe it to you, Ursula, to tell you the real reason I'm going."

The truth is that I was peeved that she hadn't been more curious. She accepts facts as facts, that's how she is. And now she was quiet. But she was looking at me from under the hat, and she'd stopped the nervous hand-rubbing.

"It's because I know about Alan," I said.

She was surprised. "What's Alan done?"

She submerged her lower lip beneath her upper, her little nostrils flared, and she was frowning.

"Alan Dixon's my father," I told her.

Henry interrupted Alan's story. "So he knew."

"He knew."

"But she told him, I thought. We all thought. She told him. That was the secret, surely. What was the secret, if it wasn't that?"

"He'd found out from somewhere else, but it was Ursula who told him that the rest of the family had known all the time, that his cousins knew and pretended not to."

"That was the secret?"

"That was it."

Henry closed his eyes before continuing. "And then?"

"Michael was screaming at her."

She opened her mouth and out it came, the information, in her usual deadpan way. Instantly I was on my feet, looming over her and making a lot of noise; I leapt to my feet accusing Ursula of lying. This was the worst possible idea. Her integrity is herself – her truth her integrity her self – all one and inseparable, and the loss of one is the loss of all irrevocably: something like that. To accuse Ursula of lying was to say the most hurtful thing imaginable. So Ursula was pretty aggrieved about my calling her a liar. I found that I had hold of her: I'd let the oars fall slack and had her tightly by the upper arms, her bones frail under my hands. Aware of their frailty, I let go of her abruptly, and she moved as far as was possible away from me.

"Take it back and tell me it's not true," I said.

"It is the truth, the truth," she insisted, her little face thrust forward like a ship's figurehead.

"And you were told this, you but not me; my mother would never tell me but she told you? That's fucking the fucking last straw."

"Nobody told me," Ursula said, calmly. "Nobody told me; I saw them."

This pulled me up short.

"I saw them," she said again.

I was aware that I was not breathing. The world had stopped. It was full of deceit and could no longer function. The world had become something that disproved its own existence, a schoolboy conundrum: the substance that burns through all surfaces and can't be contained.

"You saw them?"

"I saw them talking about it. I heard him saying to her that she must get rid of it. I heard her say she might, but only by getting rid of herself at the same time."

Henry interrupted the account again.

"Alan, you told Ottilie she must get rid of the baby?"

"I'm sorry. It seemed like the best thing at the time. It was never going to work out between us, and she was so young."

"She was considering suicide? I'm so shocked by this, by all of this, I don't know if I want to hear any more."

"You want to know what happened."

"Go on."

≈

At first I was disdainful.

"You saw them, you say. You were, what, nine years old and away with the fairies most of the time. You dreamed this, Ursula, you dreamed it."

I took one of the oars out of its housing, adjusting its weight in my hands.

"What are you doing?" Ursula said, trying to move away a little further and finding she couldn't.

Attempting to shove her into the loch: this I admit to, though with saturating embarrassment. I am in no position to judge her. I, too, know the impulse that is dared by the self to the self, that comes from a dark cave in the mind unchallenged: the impulse acted upon and regretted even as it's being done. The first prod was a warning, but then I prodded her a second time and harder. The look on her face as she lost her footing, as she grabbed onto the oar's end only just in time to save herself – that's a look I will never forget. Horror, and terror, but worse, much worse, a terrible disillusionment: seeing that I, knowing her aquaphobia, having known it all of my life and its cause, could threaten to tip her into the loch, here out in the deeps, Ursula who fears nothing like deep water and drowning, Ursula who cannot swim a stroke. It must have been fear that empowered the answering shove that she gave to the oar, the full weight of her body and something borrowed beyond it. The end I was holding slipped out of my grasp and pushed deep into my ribs, and I went over the side of the boat.

I swam around her three or four times. I could see Alan on the shore, his outline shifting and reforming in the haze, light spangling bright on his pale head, a figure in black and white in a coloured landscape, waiting patiently to hand over the money, one hand poised rigid across his brow so as to see us better through the glare. I put my hands over the edge of the boat and pulled myself up a little. I reached in and got hold of Ursula's leg, and she went at me with the oar and missed. I swam round to the other side and pulled myself up again, intending to board. And that's when she hit me.

"The oar was swung at him," Alan said, "and at the very last possible second, seeing it coming, he ducked. He moved his head to one side and put a protective hand across it. It was the other hand that she hit, the one that was holding on. And that was how his wrist got broken. That was why he left without the car."

I went down as if pulled from beneath. I saw the light, its dusty brown slick on the surface of the water, from the wrong side, as if from a place through the looking glass, and the wavering silhouette of the boat, the mathematical beauty of its base, its perfect lines and symmetry, its corners and its roundedness. I saw Ursula bent over the side, the hat, her long hair, her girl-shape looking down at me, the outline rippling. I went down and down in slow motion, falling through brown and then into black, swallowing water, my eyes wide.

I feel it as well as see it, when Alan tells his tale. I grow tired of sinking. Adrenaline kicks in and I twist off the vertical descent, invoking all the strength in my hips and in my legs. I turn out of the vertical with a merman's shoulders and tail-kick, still grasping the wrist, arms withheld and feet together, with strong and sinuous kicks that flow taut through my body like a wave, away from Ursula and towards the shore. I am ready now for anything. I am reborn. I will go south on a train and find my life; I'll disembark in an ugly town and go deeper into the forest. The ancient woodland is a thing of staggering beauty: every kind of tree shoulder to shoulder, deep planted and spread, a nation of trees of every colour and language. I take these into myself, imprint their imagery on the back of my eyelids, my idea of my eyelids, and am alive again. I see the spring sun through the branches and thick falls of orange leaves. I have been there, to a village among wooded hills, to a little brick house in the clearing. I go south to the life I might have had. I meet Elspeth one day in the village shop, and we meet again at the library and walk together for hours, and seem to know one another well, which is an odd thing and bewitching. She tells me her own sad tale of family proving to be the enemy. Each bitterness goes on to sustain and feed the other, but then, when the twins are born, it begins finally to soften and fade. Their wavy auburn hair, the mischief in their green eyes, their big gap-toothed smiles, their sturdy girl feet: how I miss them. I imagine their growing up into sad-eyed beauties, now that I'm gone, now that I've come back to Peattie. I don't know what happened, but it came to an end. I went to bed with Elspeth one summer night, the thin sheet cast aside, our four brown limbs criss-crossing, and I didn't wake there again.

The truth is that Alan is owed a great debt. Which is an odd way to think of Alan, but life is peculiar and death more so. It is Alan who brings me out of the loch, injured and angry but alive. I can feel my wrist aching, each time he tells it. Each time he tells it I hear him, even here in another country. I feel my wrist aching, the pain radiating through my shoulder and into my neck: I have lived it, and more than once. So I can tell you that it's when I arrived, stumbling and ungainly onto my knees and awkwardly onto my feet, no-handed in the shallows, holding onto the throbbing wrist, and came up onto the beach that it began properly to hurt.

Alan had the money in a bag, a brown-paper sack like a sandwich bag that had been folded down at the top many times, much used and wrinkled from previous excursions, the old folds shiny in the buff of the paper. His expression as he approached was all fatherly concern. "Son, has she hurt you? Let me look at it." He stretched out his arm. I was cradling the damaged wrist in the palm of the other hand, my eyes half shut and my breathing slowed. I was aware that he was talking to me but the pain was still intense, though it had peaked and was beginning to ebb. I was breathing it out, as Tilly taught me when the migraines struck; she was a fellow sufferer. I felt him take hold of the forearm, his first touch gentle, seeking permission to proceed. I felt him take it and bind it tight in one of his big handkerchiefs, knotting the ends. The tenderness of his ministrations was all too much. I was aware that he stepped back and was saying something about needing an x-ray. He used the word *son* again. I opened my eyes. That's when I brought back my good arm and hit him. He wasn't expecting the blow, and so his face betrayed an immense and unguarded surprise, hit hard across the cheekbone by a misplaced punch, falling back on the grit on his arse. Falling, astonished, then looking up at me and bellowing, "What *for*?"

I stood over Alan, blood pumping hard in my ears. "You're getting off very lightly," I told him. "You complete and utter ..." The words failed to match the gravity of the thing. Instead there was a feast of emphasis. "*You* are not my father, Alan. You are *not* my father, Alan. You are not my *father,* Alan."

Every time I come here, I have him. I have him at last. After all these impotent years.

"You are the king of the losers, Alan," I tell him. "You are the king of the fucking losers."

These words never feature in Alan's story, unsurprisingly. Not least because they're my own elaboration.

"So that's how your cheek got bruised," Henry said. "Not by the boat. By Michael on the shore."

"Michael on the shore," Alan agreed.

"But why?"

"Angry with me for not telling him, for not speaking up. Angry that I'd agreed to do that."

"Agreed with whom?"

"With Ottilie. Agreed with Ottilie."

Alan was knocked to the ground, and got to his feet, he said, doing it in such a way that he managed to keep one eye on me, afraid that I would hit him again. He stood rubbing at his cheekbone, which was red and purpling already. A little blood was trickling out of his nose and he searched his trouser pockets for the handkerchief, before having to resort to patting at his nostrils with his sleeve.

"To hell with it," I said, more to myself than anyone. I extended my good hand towards him, the better hand, though it was aching hard in the knuckles. At first he thought I wanted to shake, extending his own hand, embarrassed by my not reciprocating. "Give me the money," I said to him.

"He gave me £200 of the cash," Alan said to Henry. "Do you want it back? I feel I ought to give it back."

"No, no," Henry said. "You keep it, Alan."

Alan said that he was touched to discover that I'd only taken the painting so that I could present it to him. "Once he'd calmed down," Alan said, "he gave it to me, symbolically, he said, and with regret that he was leaving, with the hopes that we would meet again."

"Odd," Henry said.

"He wasn't an ordinary boy; he felt everything deeply. He had a strong sense of justice. Of injustice." There were, Alan added, many expressions of regret about the way the family had behaved over the last 20 years to the father of the heir. Henry didn't want to dwell on these sentiments and asked him to get on with the story.

Michael lost a shoe in the loch, Alan said, in his struggle to live. I shrugged off the remaining shoe, prising it off with the other foot, and lobbed it as far as I could get it. This, Alan said, was the shoe that he came up with; he knew where to look. Now I was barefoot and I was dripping and my bare feet were pricked by the grit, and I needed to get away from there. Alan said he must go and rescue Ursula; Ursula who remained utterly still, a painting of a girl in a blue dress and a white hat, sitting forlornly in a rowing boat, dwarfed by loch and hill scenery, the outlines of the picture pulsing and jagged.

He removed his shirt, a white shirt that had seen better, whiter days, its cuffs dotted with scarlet blood, and draped it over a rock, and I watched him, saying nothing. His stomach and chest were pale and soft, his flesh puckering around the navel where the belt of the trousers dug in. He removed his trainers, putting them neatly paired beside the shirt, by the rock, by the black day-sack. He slipped his trousers off and stood uncomfortably in old-fashioned Y-fronts, and went up onto the jetty and dived into the water.

"You didn't wear your shoes in the loch, you didn't lose them there?"

"No. Michael took them."

Once Alan was in the loch, I picked up his trainers and I took them to the car. I didn't have spare shoes in the bag I'd packed. I left my wet clothes in a pile on the gravel.

Henry interrupted again. "What happened to the clothes?"

"I disposed of them. Stowed them in my wardrobe. Then took them in a bag to the dump."

"Why would you do that?"

"I was going to give them to you. But then Ursula said what she said, and I agreed with her."

"She didn't see him. Why didn't she see him on the beach with you?"

"She was in a sort of trance. You know how she gets."

"Go on."

"I didn't mean to, you know. I want you to understand that. It came out of my mouth and surprised even me."

"I don't understand."

"You've treated me like shit. The heir's father. All of you. Like shit."

"Even so. Even so. It's unforgivable."

"No, Mr Salter. I'd say we're about even."

"How can you say that? You can't possibly believe it."

"I've said I'm sorry. There's not a lot else I can do."

"But why, why did you do it, such a wicked thing?"

"I've told you, it was Ursula. Once I'd let Ursula tell it the way she thought it happened, without contradicting her, it was impossible to put a stop to it. It had a life of its own."

❧

I put on the newest things from the top of the bag, clothes Ottilie hadn't registered as mine and wouldn't miss: this wasn't an intentional aspect but it's how it turned out. She hadn't noticed my newest purchases: new jeans, a new shirt, a brown leather jacket. The wrist made dressing very slow; every little contact and pressure hurt like an abscess bitten down in a mouth. Alan was looking back towards me, and if he noticed that it was his shoes I slipped my feet into (tight, but they'd serve) he didn't show that he'd noticed. This, he said to Henry, is when he got the chest pains: they'd begun just as he was climbing into the boat. He had to sit for a while. He sat with Ursula until the pain subsided and until I was long gone.

Thanks to Alan and his lie, I had the things I needed to make the journey. Everything else I was leaving behind. I didn't want any of it, any of them, none of it, and I said this aloud like a mantra, into the heat of the open car boot, the stifling plastic aroma. I took a carrier bag from the car that had a newspaper in it and a packet of cigarettes, and I emptied them out onto the back seat. I stuffed the wet clothes into it, the jeans, the t-shirt, the underwear, and left it by a tree. The family could think what they liked. Let them puzzle. Let them decide. Let them ponder. Let them debate. And let them wonder why the car was still here, the boot up, doors open, abandoned and inexplicable. Let them wonder why it was all still here, the carefully packed bag, the capsule life, the clothes, the books, the notebooks with their infantile musings – things written yesterday and on previous days, when the world and I had a different relationship to one another. All I needed for the afterlife, I had: Alan's wretched shoes, the leather jacket I couldn't bear to leave, the clothes I stood in, and crucially, most crucial of all, £1800 in a brown-paper bag. Briefly I entertained and then dismissed the idea that this was something else I should leave behind. It was Henry's money, after all. My lip curled in disgust at the memory of Henry and his dossier of likely fathers.

I could see Alan talking to Ursula. The negotiation appeared lopsided: she didn't appear to be responding. That's the last I saw of Peattie as I turned away: Alan crouching to talk to the still immobile Ursula, the sunlight brilliant off his white torso. I turned and walked away, not even pausing for a final regretful glance towards the chimney pots that decorate the treeline.

There he goes, the boy, the tall boy that's almost a man, loping away through the woods, binding the money tight in the brown- paper bag and trying to insert it entire into an inner jacket pocket one-handedly before finding the thing too bulky and discarding the bag on the ground. He has eaten painkillers taken from the car, too preoccupied to register their bitterness, and has disappeared from view, away overland towards the town, joining the road a few miles out of the village and getting a lift to the train station from a truck driver. A few hours after this, not realising what it was that she had, a walker would pick up the bag in the wood and bin it, thinking it picnickers' litter.

Alan rowed Ursula back to the shore, Ursula staring at her feet beneath her hem, knees pulled up beneath her chin, and Alan seated opposite her, his wet fish body dried matt white.

"He's gone," Ursula said. "He's gone, isn't he?"

"Yes."

"He's dead. He's dead, isn't he?"

Alan didn't answer. He was concentrating on rowing, on the rhythm. The sun was beginning to burn his shoulders and the back of his neck.

Henry interrupted again. "But why didn't you say no? Why didn't you just say no, no, he isn't? I don't understand. I'm never going to understand."

"I didn't say he was dead. I was thinking. That's all I can tell you. I was thinking. I admit to that. Seeing what might happen."

"I know that I killed him," Ursula said. "But it wasn't meant, I promise you."

"How could you do that to her?" Henry interrupted again.

"I didn't mean it," Ursula said. "The thing I did and the thing that happened are not the same thing. They're not always the same thing. That's what Mummy said, when I told her. That's the thing to hold on to, no matter what."

Alan paused in the action with the oars. He looked unwell, grey beneath the eyes, lilac in his fingernails. He paused again to rub at his chest with one hand. He was making very slow progress.

"What do you mean you told her? How could you tell her?" he asked.

"She asked me and I told her."

"She was confused; she was so confused," Henry said, interrupting the account again.

"I could see she was confused," Alan admitted. "I was going to put her right and then I didn't."

"We should have realised before this. We should have thought."

"Shall I go on?"

"Yes. Go on." Henry steadied himself against the wall.

"Are you alright, Mr Salter?"

"I feel strange, light-headed. Shock. Anger. Gratitude. And so bizarre."

"I know it's a shock. I'm truly sorry."

What is the boy thinking about, now that he's dismissed the idea of family from his mind? Where to go, where not to, who to be when he gets there, how to make his future unspool constructively out of his rage. At first only about the day ahead, the journey, and then, with a discipline that's magnificent in its way, on the long train-borne hours, only about tomorrow and about how things might begin. The past he has already disinherited. It has seemed not to take a huge effort of mind. There are no constructions necessary, it turns out. The past has been allowed merely to fall, to drop out of consciousness, in a way that feels – for now at any rate – entirely like relief, like freedom. He sloughs all little nascent itches of responsibility off like a scab. It's easy. His heart has evacuated itself and it has felt like a new beginning. It is a new beginning. This is what he tells himself, in the long train-borne hours.

Chapter 16

"People are always trying to make this complicated, but actually it's very simple."

Izzy was painting her toenails, pushing the curtain of hair around her neck and onto the other shoulder. Her feet were misshapen, big toes pushed sharply inward, small toes curled and angled into the same unnatural, shoe-moulded point. "It's very simple. Ursula killed Michael, in self-defence if we're charitable, and Alan stole the picture and the money, pinning the burglary on him."

"He said Michael gave him the picture as a token," Mog told her. "To do with his mistreatment by all of us. Made me feel terrible."

"I don't believe it," Izzy said. "Alan's delusional."

"About what?"

"About being Michael's father. Ottilie and Alan? Come on. What for? Sorry but I'm just not convinced."

Mog was rattled. "But why would he lie?"

Izzy had that look she gets when people are being dense. "Because he's delusional."

"What are you saying, then, that it was some random at a house party?"

"Not some random. One of the friends. I think we're all set up for a whodunnit, only it's a paternity case and not a doing-in. Most of the possible fathers will be here for the thing. Christian Grant for one."

"You're not serious."

Izzy paused, caramel polish lengthening on the brush.

"What you haven't considered, any of you, and what Michael never considered either, I bet you, is that she isn't being obstructive. It isn't about that. What if there isn't a name to tell? It's possible she doesn't know." Mog's scepticism was obvious. "It's perfectly possible," Izzy insisted. "She doesn't know who Michael's father is and is too embarrassed to admit it. Couldn't admit it to Michael. Hence all the stuff about him not being a good man, all that. She doesn't know who it was. She was young, got shit-faced drunk, woke up pregnant. It happens. Have you been to one of those things?"

Mog considered, as if considering were needed, then shook her head.

"Well, I have."

"I know. I remember the fuss."

"General moral turpitude and buckets of booze. Drugs too, these days. Mrs Hostess comes round in her dressing gown at 2am to make sure everyone's in the right beds and lights are out, and goes off thinking what a doddle it all is."

"And?"

"It's then that the fun starts."

They were interrupted by Izzy's mobile. Mog signalled that she'd go and fetch coffee.

When Mog went into the kitchen she found her mother reading a slim volume entitled Surviving Divorce. Just a little too late, Joan slotted it hurriedly in with the cookery books, books yellowed with age and spattered and torn. It sat there in company with the boeuf bourgignon and cauliflower soup, saying nothing but emitting a low and steady throb. Nobody looked at it directly.

Mog had been via the study and brought the newspaper with her. She opened it on the table.

Joan pounced. "What are you doing with that? You know the rules."

"I'll hide it if she comes in."

"You'll be unpopular."

"It'll be fine."

"You'll be unpopular."

"What, you think Ursula's going to grab it from me, read about a ferry disaster, run screaming down the corridor and throw herself off the roof?"

"Alastair's already had his confiscated. That's all I'm saying."

Joan took it from her and put it in her briefcase. "I really must get on. I'm going to ring Robert, see if he'll fly up tomorrow. Family reunion."

"Robert who doesn't speak to Alastair?"

"Perfect opportunity to mend fences."

"Please don't."

"I met him once when I was a girl. He's been here, you know. Came here after his mother was killed. Went to the place where they died. Fought with your grandfather and went home in a rage."

"I know."

"Didn't stay for the funeral."

"I know."

"He said she'd been specific about not wanting ever to be laid to rest at Peattie. Interesting, isn't it, because the way Henry paints it the three girls had this perfect idyllic childhood. You wonder what really went on, don't you?"

"Why did something have to really go on?" Mog's voice was purposefully flat.

"To not want to be buried here. Strikes me it must have been something. And Robert's inherited it, whatever it was, as if she passed the allergy to Peattie on to him. He could barely conceal his dislike."

"She died in water, too."

Edith came into the room. "It's not very intelligent, is it, darling, to believe in a curse? Just because it's old doesn't mean it's worth anything. People will keep making that mistake."

"In any case Aunt Jo was killed by the tree," Joan said, distractedly, looking at her phone and leaving the room. This is true. The car hit the tree before it went into the reservoir.

Nobody would mention the lost boy. Mog had already gone too far, almost invoking the name of Sebastian, and knew it, the knowledge of it written on her face. All she could do was go to Edith, apologising into her hair, Edith replying by means of a forgiving hand rubbed briskly over her arm.

I remember vividly a day when I was 11 and about to move from Peattie out to the cottage. I was a sad boy, and my being reserved about my sadness, loyal to my mother's needs for change (her need for a home further from Joan), had impressed the family enough to cause a loosening of reserve, in which things not talked about were unfettered briefly and aired. There was sympathy, and out of sympathy greater openness comes: open and shut in its camera lens way. That's how it happened that Vita and I had a conversation about death by water.

"But why were we cursed?" I asked her.

"Your grandfather says he doesn't know," she told me. "But in the village they say that she wasn't a witch at all."

"She wasn't a real witch?" I was disappointed.

"No."

"But then what was she?"

"A mad person, an angry person. We don't believe in witches and curses, surely."

"Of course we do," I said.

"Ah, Michael." She ruffled my hair. "You are a silly billy and an intense little soul."

I smiled at her, thinking this a compliment.

What do I know about the witch now? Only the truth: that she was Henry's great-grandfather's rejected lover. As to whether one person's despair can curse another's life, I had better reserve judgment.

At 11 years of age I was so thrilled and honoured that Vita was talking to me in this way, in this way that ordinarily only Tilly spoke to me, that I was driven over to the sceptical camp and even beyond its usual borders, determined to out-doubt Vita and impress her further. I told her that Henry's father didn't count. That, after all, was a heart attack.

"You know where he was when he had the heart attack?" she asked, her voice patient but preparing itself to triumph, the inflection rising. "He was salmon fishing, up to his thighs in icy water. He was 66 and had already had two attacks. He was warned not to go into the Spey."

"Still a heart attack. Not death by water."

"He was still alive when the river took him."

"There's no way of knowing that."

"They can tell these things," she said mysteriously.

Between the decision and the move to the coast I'd developed tonsillitis, a condition thought to be psychosomatic. Whatever the cause, I was confined to bed with a high fever. Henry, attentive and evidently also a little anxious, brought me a hot chocolate and a Jack Russell, the cup in one hand and the terrier under his arm. "A doggy hot-water bottle for you," he said. "I'm told you have cold feet." Vita having just left the bedroom after our chat, and wild themes coursing about in my head, I was bursting to ask him about his father and about the first Henry Salter and the curse, but too nervous of Henry, the way his brow would knit and his face darken when disappointed.

Between the ages of 12 and 19 I was to hear frequently that I'd disappointed him. But never, in all that time, did I work up the nerve to ask him about Sebastian, the query that would have disappointed him the most. When you're a child you love to hear about all the disasters in lurid detail. They have nothing to do with you and your own perfection, your own immutability, your life rolled up tight inside you like a new leaf. Vita seems to illustrate that this appetite for disaster returns in old age. It's a kind of defiance, I suppose. A kind of courage, defiantly disrespectful, egging the grim reaper on.

Mog was thoughtful at the dinner table, sitting apart from Rebecca as they ate their soup and salad, the quiet threads of conversation picking their way around her. The rest of them were talking about the now inevitable land sale, Henry having told Alastair about it. Henry judged that Alastair had a right to know. Edith was doing her sad-but-necessary speech: "We've done our grieving and now we're resigned." Talk of the land sale takes us to the last night that Mog spent with Johnnie.

The evening before Mog broke up with Johnnie, they went to a Scottish dance in Edinburgh, a so-called ball in a hotel function room. Johnnie's brother, his partner and another four of their circle made up the eight. The other girlfriends were part of that tribe of child-women, their twiggy brown legs finished with oil, long hair straightened and lip gloss like jam. Pip and Angelica were also there, that night, Angelica's white-blonde bob newly angled to the chin. Tall Angelica and her tall friends were in tight sheaths of dresses, not intending to participate much other than in a minimalist way, walking through occasional dances. A pity. Reeling should have an abandoned pagan quality about it.

From Angelica Mog received a high, finger-waggling wave, dutiful and indifferent, delivered even as she was turning away and scanning the other tables. Pip kept his distance until the men in Mog's party had gone off to the bar, a swagger of tuxedos, men with rugby club manners. Then he came and sat by Mog.

"About last night: Angelica didn't mean it that way," he said. "You upset her. Don't punish her by being chilly with her, Mog."

"That's so perfect," Mog told him. "That's how it is exactly. Angelica's rude but somehow it's a worse rudeness to be offended by her. How does that work? It's quite a trick, isn't it?"

"You're drunk."

"I've had enough to say what I think. Get a grip, Pip. She's the one who was insulting."

"It was a joke. Half joking. She is offended, actually. She says she thought she was getting somewhere with you and that you were getting into a sisterly thing, one that allows for banter. But apparently not."

"I am again found wanting."

Pip sighed, smiling. "I love you and this is said in a loving way: lighten up. You need to lighten up."

"Oh thanks. Bingo."

"Sense of humour. A sense of humour's important."

"What's funny about life?"

"She meant well. She was trying to warn you."

"Because normally Johnnie goes for beauties so what could he want with me other than money. Or rather in this case, property. Imaginary money. Imaginary aristocracy."

"That's the gist of what his brother's saying, yes. Angelica was just reporting."

"Considerate of her." Mog stood up. "I need some air."

Pip went after her, saying that he wanted a smoke. They went out onto the steps of the hotel. It was chilly and Mog wrapped her shawl closer around her dress, an old-fashioned-looking affair with Grecian drapes and folds. Pip lit his cigarette and smoked it in silence, looking out over the grounds, the uplit statuary, a dark line of parked cars.

Mog said, "I think it's all come to an end."

"Johnnie?"

"All of it. This constant *striving*. Pretending everything's fine. Doing the happy face that leads to happiness."

"Mother's full of shit."

"I'm so – I'm just so tired."

Pip put his arms around her, one hand at her nape, his cheek against hers: the highest compliment of understanding. He seemed taller than usual, and down at the trouser hem there were unmistakably stacked heels.

"We need whisky," he said.

"No. No more, thanks." She sat down heavily onto the step.

He sat beside her. "I need to talk to you about Christian. He has a new partner."

"Anyone we know?" Mog's face betrayed a stab of disappointment. Even though she knew she would never want to see Christian naked, he'd had a special place in her mind lately as an ideal candidate for a passionless marriage, passionless but chummy, with not-unpleasant procurement of heirs.

"Business partner. Don't know him. But it means he has the money."

"So, all the rest of it. The pasture."

"Necessary."

"Makes sense. Still seems mad."

Each of them contemplated this possibility.

"You're out of touch," Pip said. "Peattie's heavily in demand. Prices are going through the roof."

"Henry won't agree to a housing estate, not there, right opposite the house."

"Ah, but that's where Christian's clever. You should see the plans."

274

"You've seen the plans?"

"It's to be traditionally built, faced in stone, replicating the village style, but bigger houses, and then extra bits, big glassed-out kitchens hidden round the back. It's got a pretty good chance in planning."

"Sounds a bit Prince Charlesish."

He made a face. "And what's wrong with Prince Charles?"

"But we wouldn't."

"Wouldn't we? What would you rather have? Christian's Brigadoon, or Peattie sold to a hotel group? Because it will come to that."

"I suppose."

Pip took out another cigarette, from a tooled silver case that belonged to Henry's father, and produced Henry's old cigarette lighter. He lit the cigarette, clicked the lighter shut, pocketing it, and drew deeply before letting out a slow drift of smoke. "Course, Henry's got ten years, at least ten; another 20 wouldn't surprise me. But he says he thinks he'll be ready earlier. And I think it might be coming soon."

"Ready?"

"To move out."

"Move out? You're joking. Henry? I don't think so."

"I would have said the same. But that was before I spoke to Edith."

"She wants to leave?"

"She wants a few years at least of another life."

"Another life?"

"She wouldn't elaborate."

"She wouldn't elaborate." Mog repeated the words dully. "Do you think ..."

"To live apart from Henry? Maybe. Hard to say."

"Oh ... Oh god."

"What is it?"

Mog's head was in her hands. "It's just the thought of it. No Henry and Edith at Peattie. I need them to be there."

"Henry's had enough."

"Where do you get this from?"

"I think he might realise, once he's out, what a relief it is."

"I'm not convinced."

"He's stuck. Stuck in a moment, can't get out of it. As the philosopher Bono has written."

"But Peattie …"

"Decades, literally decades, half a lifetime of mourning. Half a lifetime."

"Where does all this … I mean, how have you – "

"We've been talking. Henry and I. On the phone," Pip said. "But I promised I wouldn't say. So you don't know that."

"Christ."

Mog took an offered cigarette.

"So what happens, what happens to Peattie?"

"They'll move out."

"And then what?"

"Angelica and I are happy to take it on. Do the hotel thing, in a small way. On an 'eat with the aristocracy' basis, all round one table together. Americans are very into it. More shoots probably. All that mallarkey. Angelica's the marketing guru."

Words of Izzy's came to her lips. "And once you have her in captivity I imagine there'll be breeding."

"I'm counting on it."

"Aren't you forgetting one crucial thing?"

"What's that?"

"Co-ownership, Pippin. Co-inheritance."

"We'd have to clear it with the rest of you, obviously. Getting ahead of myself."

"Very slightly."

"It's just that it seems like a fact now because it's what I promised Henry, to reassure him."

"You promised Henry."

"Anybody who wants to can move into the main house. We can remodel bits into flats, that is if we can get the funding. Christian's offer makes it possible."

That's my house he's talking about. My should-have-been house. Eldest child of the eldest child.

Henry told me when I turned 18. There were two gifts: an old car, and disinheritance. He announced that he would name all five of us, the grandchildren, as joint heirs upon his death.

"Henry," I said – and it was the only time I called him Henry, and I was very calm – "are you telling me that you are breaking with four generations of Peattie tradition, and instead of it going to me you are going to split it five ways, just to keep the bastard out of the direct line?"

"This step is bloody cold." Mog got to her feet and Pip followed. "I must stop smoking," she said. "Makes me nauseous." She stamped out her cigarette. "So where will they go?"

"We haven't got that far. Henry's only at the very early stages of thinking. Let's be clear about that. Thinking the unthinkable, it takes time."

"Seems all such a shame."

"Look. The land isn't optional. Things are serious. The windows are already desperate. Pointing well overdue, stone crumbling off the side wall. Dry rot everywhere."

"Is there?"

"And the damp. Have you been down to the old kitchen lately? Along the corridor? Powdery, the paint is, flaking off like diseased skin. Something has to be done about the heating. It's all money."

"Yes."

"And if we're to live there …"

"Of course."

"Angelica will want a budget. There'll be replastering. New floors. Wiring. We need Christian's money."

"How much is it?"

"Henry's asked me not to say for the moment. They're still haggling. But enough."

"It's almost like once he's allowed Peattie to be spoiled, the new houses next door, it's all over and that's really why he's going." Mog looked at her brother searchingly.

"It's not that," Pip said in a quiet voice. "It's Sebastian."

"Well, of course that's what it really is. I do know that."

"He's lived in the same place as this – this *stain* – for, what, 37 years. This watermark stain. This boy that would have been 41 now, and the heir. The golden boy."

"This is how he talks about him."

"I'm afraid it is. The golden boy who should be 41 but is forever four years old."

There's a picture of Sebastian on Henry's desk. The boy in the photograph has a fishing net, a red zip sweater with snowflakes knitted into it, a sandy-blond pudding-bowl haircut and a sharply cut little pink mouth. I commented once to Vita how angelic he looked.

"Angelic? Don't you believe it for a second," Vita said. "Absolute rascal. Played on his beauty. Always got his own way, or expected to, and wasn't checked nearly enough. But so adored. So very, very wanted; a boy at last. Poor Ursula was quite overshadowed."

Mog told me about a conversation she'd had with Edith when she was a child. Edith was, at that time, quite certain about heaven, and talked about it as if it were just at the end of the garden: something actual and close at hand.

"But will Uncle Sebastian still be little when I meet him there?" Mog had asked. "Smaller than me? Still four?" It seemed all wrong for an uncle.

"I don't know." Edith sounded as if she had given it thought and really didn't. "I hope sometimes that he'll be older, that he's done some growing up in heaven, has had a kind of life. Imagine that, growing up in heaven."

"Sitting on a cloud and eating marshmallows," the ten-year-old Mog had said. Edith had managed to smile.

Mog drew her wrap tighter around herself.

"We should go back in; we'll be missed," Pip said.

They went into the porch of the hotel, but didn't go further, not immediately.

"Easy to idealise Sebastian, when you think of him like that," Mog said. "Forever four years old, the golden boy. He never got the chance to disappoint anyone."

"Henry," Pip began. He began again. "Henry's tormented. Unable to walk away. Someone should have done something sooner."

"Like what?"

"No idea at all."

"And Michael too," Mog said. "Another stain. Another watermark."

"Michael? No. He's angry with Michael. Still angry."

"Angry?"

Pip looked at her as if appraisingly. "He doesn't think Michael is dead."

"Still?"

"Something else I'm not supposed to talk about. Convinced of it. Michael's alive. Hard-hearted, living his life somewhere without giving us all another thought. He thinks Michael doesn't understand good manners – no, I'm serious, this is what he said – because he didn't see that the money was a promise."

"What kind of promise?"

"To keep in touch, I suppose. To feel an obligation."

"But that's nuts. Really. It's just Henry's way of dealing with it."

"He said that he realised it a few weeks after. He had a revelation. And then he waited. Giving him time to get in touch. Giving him the chance to be alive. That's how he put it. But then the year turned and he knew Michael wanted to be dead. So he let him be dead."

"Henry's way of not having two deaths on his conscience."

"Why on his conscience?"

"I don't know. I don't know why I said that. I've had too much wine."

"It's good to tell somebody about the phone calls."

"I'm glad you told me."

"Something else," he said, putting his hand softly to her wrist. "Alan. Henry's admitted that Alan is the father. That he's always known it. Despite everything he said to Michael, casting doubts. That the time is coming to acknowledge him. Despite everything. Despite Alan's fondness for little girls."

"Is Alan, is he …"

"A paedophile? I don't think so. Henry doesn't think so. But like so many things it comes down to line-drawing. How would you classify what seems to be a compulsion to entertain young girls in your bedroom, listening to music and playing cards, and encouraging them to strip to their underwear?"

"Alan's been … what?"

"Henry told me. Apparently it was in the diary, the one written by that girl staying in the cottage. But look. I need to talk to you. About the money. The plan. You and Izzy. Jet, if we can get him. We need to know that we're in agreement. I'll arrange for Christian to come and talk to you when you're home for the party."

Mog looked downhearted and my bet is that it wasn't the money at the root of it, but clear indications that Pip was taking charge of Peattie's future, and that despite this being a benign enough dictatorship, nobody was going to be able to resist his vision. That and the prospect, now apparently confirmed, of some permanence to Angelica. What had Mog thought, that the four of them, the surviving heirs, would live here together in unmarried sibling eccentricity, like the great aunts once planned? Their scheme hadn't gone far, after all. Henry had made a belated arrival in the world and Henry had asserted his rights.

Pip was talking about school fees. "They couldn't go to the local."

"What's wrong with it? We managed fine."

"Ask Angelica. There's no way."

"I see."

"And about the development. Christian's calling it Salter's Field."

"Well, that's … descriptive of him."

The sale had been on Henry's mind at dinner, because the day in question had come, the day Christian Grant was coming to set things officially in train. Christian was waiting, even now, to deliver his pitch to the grandchildren, and so when Mog went into the drawing room she found him there already, looking through folded drawings and paperwork in a sugar-paper file. He rose to greet her, bushy-bearded, lantern-jawed, his mousy hair close-cropped around large ears. There was noticeable grey in the beard now, and at the sideburns, as he leapt to his feet to shake Mog's hand, to kiss her cheek. Something puppyish remains in Christian, and Mog was experiencing the familiar cycle: prefixing their meeting sure that he'd make a good husband, but faced with the man himself, feeling her resolve to give him more of a chance withering away. Edith came in on Mog's heels, bringing tea, and small talk was exchanged until Izzy arrived. Jet was supposed to be there too but had excused himself, which surprised Christian but nobody else. An hour was spent listening to the laying-out of reasonable plans, entirely reasonable and sound but delivered with tactless enthusiasm, such that after an hour, glancing at her watch, Edith brought things almost rudely to a halt, saying they had a lot to think about and thank you. She'd talk again to Henry, she said; she believed that Christian was going to the study now, to meet with him. Christian confirmed that he was.

Once he'd left, loping out with his folder under his arm, unaware of having given or received offence, Edith and Izzy followed him out, leaving Mog in the drawing room alone. She saw that Vita had left one of her photograph albums sitting on the table – one that was unmistakably Vita's, that was cobalt blue with gold ribboning (she has a whole shelf full of them, all identical). Mog moved close to the fire – it was late by now and the chill had deepened – and began to leaf through the pages, the old photos lifting stiffly out of their glued corners. She hadn't got very far when Vita came into the room.

"Ah, there it is," she said. "I was wondering where I'd left it."

Mog lifted the album up, directing it towards Vita using both hands to present two open pages, and tapped at one of the prints with her finger. "Who's this? I don't recognise him."

"That's Sebastian Lilley."

"Sebastian. Another Sebastian. Did Edith name our Sebastian for him?"

"Well now. Your mother hasn't told you about that." Vita came unsteadily towards her and sat in the closest chair.

"Never. Why?"

Vita looked at her. "Did it ever occur to you to wonder why I had only one child?"

"I've heard the family story."

"Which is ... oh come, come. I've heard it too."

"You got the certificate from the doctor. The letter to say that having any more would be dangerous."

"I was married at 19, you know," Vita told her. "It's a family tradition, marrying early. Your mother is keen on tradition. Sometimes it works out and sometimes it really doesn't. Well now. Your grandmother Edith turned up only after seven years. I thought I'd have five children by then. Every month after the honeymoon had a disappointment in it."

She paused and Mog said, "I see."

"We had a different attitude, in my set. Different from today. Which was this: get children born while you're very young yourself, get them off to school, have your 30s without pregnancies, semi at liberty at least, and your 40s to yourself. Live your life a little."

Mog waited.

"Andrew and I had problems with conceiving. He blamed himself. A childhood illness. Some reproductive deficiency. He said that a specialist had confirmed this. I don't know if he even saw a specialist. I have to say I rather doubt it." She ran her fingers through the wig, correcting the line of the bob. "So. At 26 I had Edith. And then I organised a letter from the doctor to say we should stop trying for another child. But you see it was for Andrew, the letter. People do insist on misinterpreting things. I'm perfectly well aware of how it has been painted. My waving a doctor's letter under the nose of my mother-in-law, under my husband's nose, because I was too vain to be pregnant again. And then people found out the real reason and that didn't help matters."

"How did people find out?"

"Andrew. Was so very open, always. He didn't really see that other people weren't as open. He thought everyone … well, he hadn't encountered any real *malice*, you see."

"No."

"He was 11 when the First World War ended, 32 when the second one started. He had the heart condition by then. So he carried on being a country solicitor."

Mog could see that they were beginning to stray from the point.

"So. Sebastian."

"Sebastian Lilley. He was a friend of mine. A good friend. And you see, it was Andrew's fault in a way. He had been so very open about his being at fault."

Mog began to see.

"Andrew had said he was infertile. But then we had a child. And there had been gossip, unfortunate gossip, started by Mary."

"Mary?"

"Andrew's sister."

"I'm named for her. Am I?"

"You're a Catto Mary, I think."

"So Mary was a gossip."

"Mary started the rumours. I believe so at least. I had been seeing a lot of Sebastian. He loved to play tennis and ride and hill-walk, you see. Things poor Andrew couldn't do."

"They thought he was Edith's father."

"They did."

"What happened to him?"

"He died in the war."

Both knew what Mog wanted to ask, and they smiled at each other in recognition of this.

"So," Mog said. "Edith named Sebastian in honour of your ... friend."

"No, dear. Well, yes. But it wasn't quite like that."

"Why not?"

"Isn't it obvious?"

"What?"

"Edith named him because she was convinced that Sebastian Lilley was her father."

"No!"

"She still is."

"No!"

"Yes."

"But why?"

"Because Andrew was also sure, and felt that Edith should know."

Chapter 17

It was Vita who told me that Alan was my father. It was Vita who let me know, without intending to, that everyone around us had known all along, and that I was the only one in the dark. She wasn't prepared to comment on the ethics.

If I had mentioned Alan in the letter, told them what Vita had said, told them that I'd spoken to Alan the night before, they would have known right at the beginning that it wasn't news broken to me by Ursula in the boat. The letter was more concerned with the failings of mothers and grandparents, and with the inadequacy, the treachery, of noble silence. Intoxicated by this credo, by the dogma of confession and disclosure that Ursula had spoken up for, and then informed of the facts of life – of my life – by Vita, I felt quite suddenly depleted by Peattie and by what I began to think of as a clinging on tight to tragedy, a fidelity to tragedy, the whole architecture of the family built upon it.

Vita's news, that my father had been so close for so many years; someone we'd seen in the gardens, someone rarely spoken to, rarely spoken of, other than to disdain ... it was almost overwhelming. It was hard to act upon it. It was hard to think how. I explained away the family's unanimous contempt for Alan as fear, fear of him and his information, though this was no more than an adopted view and couldn't really survive any kind of thinking about what Alan was and is. For the moment, though, I wasn't doing that thinking. I was beyond rage; I entered a calm white zone of hatred. Its credo was rejection, spontaneous and absolute. Love died. It had died: that's what I told myself. Something took its place, the ripening of a decision to which, loyally, the heart consented. I told myself that hatred was the wrong word; it had to be because it was too emotive an idea, and the truth had done a much more neutral and effective job, a slim knife expertly placed, and that I felt nothing. Ideas about punishment began to suggest themselves, ideas forming spontaneously out of this mud of rage.

Where did it start, the train of events that brings us here? Further back than I'd imagined. We follow it upstream as far as we can and find ourselves in the summer school holidays the year the twins were 14. In fact it goes back further, to the Easter of that year. When the summer holidays arrived, Ottilie and Joan were still talking about Easter and Easter's momentous events.

Let me take you, as I have been taken, to that cool grey summer day of long ago. It seems sometimes that the past is still there, lurking under the painted surfaces of the present, and that it would take only the scratch of a thumbnail to reveal it all still going on. Perhaps we're back at the frontiers only of science here, and there's nothing supernatural about it – just the emergence, through a thinning divide, of physical space shared with all that's thought dead and lost.

We are walking along the track towards the loch, you and I, in veiled summer sunlight, the sky luminously pearly and the wind gusting cold. Neither of us makes a sound on the grit surface of the path. We have taken our places in a procession, following my mother and her siblings as children, and have been overtaken by a fifth person as we walk: Petra, the children's German au pair, who came for two months and lasted less than a week.

They were dressed the same, the teenage Joan and Ottilie, in yellow shorts (because it was summer) and Aran sweaters that Tilly knitted (because it didn't feel like it), though at 14 twinning must have been growing tedious. They looked almost identical from the back, their similar-length hair reaching to the shoulder blade – Ottilie's was of a pinker sort of blonde and wavier – but when they turned to see if Ursula and Petra were following it was clear immediately that one was pretty and one not. The pretty one had a green batik scarf across the top of her fringe, disappearing under her hairline at the ears, and beautiful skin. The other was wearing hoop earrings and pale lipstick, and had applied a thick coat of beige-coloured make-up in an effort to conceal an angry-looking acne. Sometimes the genetic fairy is merciless in the distribution of gifts.

What must it have been like to be Joan, I wonder, growing up like this, having people compare you day to day and moment to moment, consciously and unconsciously, with the pretty twin, seeing the differential register on people's faces when introduced? A twin, after all, a better-looking twin, presents a might-have-been to the world, a cruelly perfect template from which you are the deviation. It's a bold claim but you could make a case for everything that followed as explicable in just one of those differential-registering looks.

They'd been sent to the loch, as they were sent every day in all weathers. If it was raining they took shelter in the wood: fresh air and exercise were paramount. Today was dry at least. They spread the picnic rug just inside the treeline for shelter from the wind.

Joan lay down on her back, crossing her legs at the ankle. Small flies hovered in clusters, doing their airborne square dance. She clasped her hands behind her head.

"This time next week Euan will be here" she said.

Ottilie, sitting next to her and smoothing a page in her sketchbook, looked up towards the heavens, crossing and uncrossing her eyes. She said "God give me strength."

There was a pause and then Joan said, "You're quite superficial about men, aren't you?"

Ottilie snorted. "No. Just discriminating."

The Catto family had stayed in the holiday cottage over the Easter weekend and were set to return for a fortnight. They were science teachers, Joyce and Richard Catto, and their son Euan, then 19 and studying English, hoped to be a university academic. He was given to explaining, as a corollary to this, that really he was a poet who had to make a living somehow. He'd been published twice in the small presses and all were agreed that this was a very sound start. His parents talked of inevitable fame, of bestsellers and a house in France: all the riches that were bound to follow from being good with words. Joan was very taken with Euan's tallness. He wasn't handsome but his face was serious and clever; he said serious, clever things. Aside from his height, he took after his mother; only his tall lanky boniness, his long-fingered hands, are his father's, only his skeletal self. It's a pity he didn't inherit his father's kindliness, a quality that shines out of Richard Catto's eyes, an eagerness to please and to be pleased in return; I've never seen anything shine out of Euan's other than victory. He has his mother's straight brown hair, and even now wears it as he did then, in the same schoolboy way. He's one of those men who age well, a Peter Pan type who – until you get close up – might be taken for 35.

The first time that Euan held Joan's hand was after a tennis game at Easter, their first doubles match, the two of them versus Ottilie and Alan. Joan was vile to Alan throughout and petitioned Ottilie to find a more suitable partner, not always caring if Alan heard. At 20 he wasn't bad-looking, though this impression was more

288

about musculature than beauty. He had a sporty, strong body, good legs, discreet blocks of muscle showing above the knees. He had a soldier's square-faced kind of handsomeness; genetically there was something of his mother's family who had come from Poland during the war. His was a recent arrival at Peattie, though technically a re-arrival, having lived here as a baby. He'd come from his mother's house in Glasgow; she left George when their son was barely two years old, citing lack of ambition, and had taken Alan with her and had remarried. Alan had come to help, to live at the cottage with his father for an indefinite period, to gain some informal gardening experience. George had developed a dodgy back and needed help with the heavier work.

The sisters, who were enemies on most days of the year, had brief and absolute intimacies, periods of ceasefire that were as intense as their usual loathing. The air wasn't just cleared, in these occasional reversals, but thick with confidentiality. All was told and shared, in bouts of friendship that began quite suddenly and ended just as bluntly, without apology or post-mortem. They began with one of the twins telling the other a secret. The other must respond in kind: those were the rules, though rules had never been discussed. The intimacy came to an end with one twin failing to speak to the other when spoken to: that was the signal that the period of friendship was over. Nothing was ever said about why it should end; it just ended. Easter, the events of Easter, the arrival of temporary Euan and (theoretically at least) permanent Alan, the surprising transformation of routine school holidays by an unforeseen double romance: these had been the triggers to the sisters' most intense closeness.

Ottilie told Joan, at Easter, that when she and Alan were fetching the racquets from the summerhouse, Alan had kissed her. She said that he was rough and bristly and that he put his tongue in her mouth; a fat tongue, probing and wet with saliva. Joan protested that it sounded disgusting, looking over Ottilie's shoulder in wonder at the blameless-looking Alan, who was warming up with Euan, his serving growing more and more competitive. Euan and Joan were easily defeated, 6-2, 6-1. Alan's backhand shots were usually winners and he patted Ottilie on the behind when he won a point, something which had become ritualised, Alan insisting on his "good luck pat" and Ottilie protesting good-humouredly. After Ottilie told her about the kiss, Joan confided to a school friend that she needed a boyfriend of her own and that this Euan Catto would do, despite having knock knees and patting at the ball like a girl.

Euan was living at home while he was a college student in order to save money. He'd given Joan his parents' address and had said he would write to her first, but he hadn't yet. Perhaps she should write to him, Joan said. By now, in early August, all of her and Ottilie's Easter intimacy had long since ceased. Joan was using the echo of that intimacy as an irritant, and Ottilie's body language signalled that she was succeeding. Aware of this and relishing it, rolling over and stretching on the rug like a cat, Joan wondered aloud if she should write to tell Euan that she was excited about seeing him again. "Although. Not excited. That's too keen. Looking forward. Still too keen. To say that he should remember to bring his better racquet. Maybe I should phone."

"Phone then, but stop going on about it," Ottilie told her, getting up and going to the beach, to Petra and Sebastian down on the shore. After a few moments Joan went after her, and, catching up, began to talk about Euan again. She couldn't help rubbing Ottilie's nose in it, in the fact that she had a boyfriend and Ottilie didn't. Of the two romances, only Joan's had survived into the summer. Ottilie had been banned from seeing Alan, a ban dating from an afternoon in April when she didn't come straight home from school and was tracked down at the Dixons' cottage, found in the bedroom with him, though Edith told Henry that it was all perfectly innocent: all they were doing was listening to records. Privately, Edith didn't think it was innocent at all. She'd been aware that she'd interrupted something, and if Joan hadn't tipped her off ... When they got back to the house Edith had a frank discussion with Ottilie about men and their intentions. Girls of 14 shouldn't get involved with boys of 20, young men of 20, she'd said. That was the point, that 20-year-old boys were young men, and had different ideas about love. Ottilie had been banned from seeing Alan or even talking to him, and had been warned that if she flouted this ban Edith was sure to hear of it. The consequences would be serious, not for Ottilie perhaps, but certainly for Alan, who would be sent away for good and what would poor George do then?

Alan had come to the wood, was standing behind the great uncle's tomb, smoking a cigarette and watching the girls on the beach. Petra, noticing him there, went up to say hello. He'd been kind to her, introducing her to his friends at the hotel, taking her to the bar on her first evening here. Alan offered her a cigarette and Petra said she mustn't leave Sebastian alone. Alan pointed out that Sebastian wasn't remotely alone and hoisted Petra up to sit on the tomb, facing the loch so that she could keep an eye on things. He came round to be on the same side, and leaned back, his elbows resting on its lid, close to a shining marble shin. Petra wasn't a beauty by any means – her hairline was very high, her forehead curving like a planet, and she had a noticeable overbite – but she had a lovely body, shown to best advantage in today's tight white trousers and low-cut white sweater. She shone white in the gloom of the wood. She made it obvious, in contrasting, how grey the marble of the tomb really was.

The two of them began talking about education. Petra had done badly in her university exams that summer. Her view was that the process was entirely memory-oriented, was really only regurgitation, and that as she had a poor memory it was harder for her than for others. Alan made the point that education was class-based, resting its value on those who'd been initiated into the language of examinations.

Joan interrupted them in full flow, striding forward into view. "Petra" she said, "Sebastian is asking for you."

Petra handed her cigarette to Alan, and jumped down and went to the shore.

Now that Petra was gone Alan began beckoning to Ottilie. Joan told her very firmly that she absolutely mustn't on any account have anything to do with him ever again, mustn't even speak to him. This advice was instrumental. Ottilie went to the tomb and Alan lifted her up by the waist, into Petra's place, setting her down where the bowl of the submerged chest and stomach of the great uncle makes a comfortable enough seat. He came and stood in front of her, stepping up onto the plinth. He placed his big hands on her small knees, opening them and smiling into her face. He placed her lower legs at either side of his waist and moved in closer. He took her arms and hooked them one after the other around his neck. He put his hands gently, lightly down the back of her shorts. All this she tolerated, while protesting in a jokey fashion. But his attempts to kiss her on the mouth were foiled as she ducked him, laughing an uncertain laugh.

Petra saw what was happening and began to come back up the beach, going as fast as the shingle allowed, the stones shifting and resettling. She was calling Alan's name in a way designed to get his immediate attention, sharp calls that put the emphasis on the first syllable. Joan had come forward and was pointing at him, jabbing at the air.

"Alan Dixon, leave her alone. I'll tell."

Alan clasped Ottilie closer. Ottilie strained her neck to one side, laughing and awkward, and was kissed on it twice.

"I'll tell," Joan said again. And Joan did tell. But not straight away, because of what was to happen next.

❧

It's been easy to blame the au pair all these years, for what happened. Petra and Alan were off in the wood arguing, out of sight and out of auditory range of the loch. Petra was absent a vital few minutes; she was responsible and she had failed. Alan they couldn't blame – he'd gone off out of the back of the wood, angrily, just as the crisis unfolded: they couldn't blame him for that. He didn't know what was about to happen, and hadn't in any case any supervisory role; his being there at all was accidental. Even bad people can be heroic: when Alan was alerted, it was Alan who found Sebastian, who brought Sebastian up from under the jetty, and knew what to do to try to revive him. But if only, if only. *If only*, my mother has said to me, a hundred times. If only Alan had been watching from the tomb at the crucial moment, and had seen. Edith especially has been haunted by this alternative outcome.

Edith was at the hairdresser's in the town. Vita called the number, found on the board in the kitchen, and spoke to the receptionist, saying it was urgent that she speak to her daughter, that it was an emergency, but the receptionist mustn't say so, please, or give any indication that something was wrong when she called Edith to the phone. Vita said to Edith only that she must come straight home: Edith standing with her hair half cut, a towel around her shoulders, in the cramped office of the salon, pleading with Vita to tell her what it was. It couldn't be just that she had missed tea, surely: they were supposed to be going out to dinner, and Henry knew this was the only appointment she'd been able to get.

Aware that Edith would be driving herself home, aware that Edith's driving was often erratic, Vita found herself reassuring her that it wasn't anything terrible.

"It isn't anything terrible, but you must come straight home. We need you."

"What do you mean, what on earth's going on? Tell me. Tell me now."

"Just come home, Edith. Come now."

Poor Edith. Driving home with her hair half cut, imagining the worst and getting to Peattie to find that indeed the worst had happened. She didn't cry when they told her: it wasn't like upset, Ottilie has said to me. It was more like she'd been killed, like her killing had been set in progress and was inevitable, like she had begun on the road of a slow death. All that had made her herself began at once efficiently to dim. Not even when she'd viewed him laid out on the bed, his hair already dried, did the tears come. His hair had mis-dried rumpled into another shape, as if already he wasn't her child but had become something other, something shared and public and other.

The crying was left to others.

"We'd been in the wood," Ottilie told her, weeping. She didn't add that they'd been watching Petra and Alan.

"Sebastian and Ursula went onto the jetty," Joan said, her voice breaking. "We were away two minutes and they went straight on there. Even though we'd made them promise they wouldn't."

"We got back to the beach and they were throwing stones," Ottilie said, her voice unrecognisable.

"And you went straight up there," Edith prompted. "Straight up there" would have been the correct response.

"We didn't, we didn't, we didn't, we didn't." Ottilie's words grew progressively more distorted. "We stood on the beach by the steps and demanded they come down."

"Ursula was taunting him. I'm sorry but it's true." Joan's voice grew authoritative, anticipating Edith's dissent. "She told him she was the queen of the loch and he would never be able to beat her. He threw his pebble so hard, threw his arm back so hard, threw his body forward so hard that he went in as well."

"He went in as well," Ottilie repeated.

"He wouldn't come until he'd thrown one last pebble," Joan said. "One more, one more pebble, one last pebble, and he ran at it and he lobbed and he was too close to the edge and in he went."

"In and gone, in and lost," Ottilie wailed. "He couldn't find him, Alan couldn't find him."

"I was in there first," Joan said. "Before Alan arrived. I was straight in. But it was like Seb wasn't there, I couldn't find him. Ottilie went off to find you, to find someone, and came back with Grandpa Andrew. By that time Alan was there. Alan dived and dived, under and under, but Sebastian wasn't where he'd fallen. He was under the jetty; he was under the jetty."

Edith's fingernails were driven productively into her own palms.

Four years after this, Joan married Euan. At the time of the wedding Alan had been back at Peattie five months. His return had been by special dispensation, because George had been ill in the spring with bronchitis, too ill to look after himself. Henry gave his permission, and Alan needed that special consent. Theoretically he was in exile. I'm not sure if Edith knows, even now, the real reason why Alan left after Sebastian died; I suspect that she thought it entirely to do with the shock of Sebastian's loss. When Joan gave her account of Alan and Ottilie "canoodling" at the loch, an account that portrayed her sister as enthusiastic in kissing him back, it wasn't Edith that she told. Instead, the day after Sebastian's funeral, Joan went to her father and Henry saw to things. I don't know how it was managed or whether George was informed about reasons.

I suspect not. I suspect that he too thought Alan's departure to do with the shock of events.

Alan wasn't invited to Joan and Euan's wedding. Alan, the problem of Alan, was much discussed at the reception, conversations initiated by Joan: Alan seemed to have taken root, and how were they to dislodge him? The plain fact was that George could have whomsoever he liked living with him at the cottage. George was invited and wrote a formal RSVP to Joan, putting himself in the third person and saying that Mr George Dixon was delighted to accept. He was splendid in his father's dinner suit, broadcasting its gentle scent of cedar-lined box. Everyone looked splendid, out in their finery, without need of warm layers to protect them from the cold; the weather conditions were close to ideal. It was one of those violet evenings; things could barely be seen when looked at squarely, and only a sideways approach brought them into focus. Guests drifted from house to marquee and back again, camouflaged by dusk.

It was Ursula who saw Ottilie slipping out of the gardens, the greyish cream of Ottilie's bridesmaid dress and the satin matching shoes glowing. The clothing appeared almost to be autonomous, the body that was attached to it rendered near invisible, the satin dress and shoes looking as if they were picking their way independently across the grass, through the orchard and onto the lane. Ursula followed at a distance. Ottilie knew she was there, notwithstanding Ursula's fleetness of foot, her fox-like trotting and darting. She had taken the trouble of chatting to Ursula just before leaving, walking along with Ursula towards the side garden door, saying that she had something to do but she wouldn't be long. Despite this Ottilie didn't give any impression of knowing that she was followed. She went purposefully to the wood, to the tomb where Alan was waiting, and Ursula saw her kiss him. A nearly full moon painted the loch in broad strokes. I don't think it has ever occurred to Ursula that she was meant to see. It had been Ottilie's intention to bring Alan back to the garden, to lead him back there hand in hand and dance with him in front of them all, but this turned out not to be necessary. Instead, having seen Ursula watching from the trees, having seen Ursula run off full pelt back towards the house impatiently bearing her news, she returned alone to face them.

Alone among the Salters, Joan was unsurprised by the news of the kiss. The truth was that Ottilie had barely spoken to Alan since his return, but this hadn't been Joan's take on things. Joan's happiness at being engaged at 17 and set to marry on her 18th birthday had taken an unfortunate shape. It made her recklessly and giddily insulting. She'd grown, as her mother told her, too big for her boots, even before the engagement was official. She'd teased Ottilie for five straight months about Alan's return, had imagined trysts where there were none, had raised her eyebrows at every instance of Ottilie's going for a walk or using the telephone. Joan had referred to Alan at dinner as the handsome under-gardener, as Alan the Bold, as the Princely Alan. And when she had the opportunity, seeing Alan cutting the grass, she'd marched right up to him and told him that he was out of his league.

Joan was slightly out of control, but the truth was that she was genuinely, deeply rattled. In kissing Alan on the night of the wedding, Ottilie had done something she knew would bother her sister on honeymoon and nag at her – this sister who'd ruined their long-laid 18th-birthday plans apparently maliciously, debooking the band, discarding the menus, dismissing the planned guest list in favour of one over which she had sole charge; Joan who had revelled in it all.

"I'll need the birthday list and I'll be inviting many of the same people, but not so many of Ottilie's," she'd said.

In giving the impression that there really was a danger of her falling for Alan, Ottilie had come up with the perfect revenge. What could follow? Marriage?

"She won't. Please tell me she won't. I can't bear to think about it. I can't bear it." Joan said this and variants on this over and over in Florence to her new husband.

"Of course she won't; she's only doing it to spite you," Euan told her, as they walked around the Uffizi, barely registering the rooms full of pictures, the chattering school parties, the swooning English ladies fanning themselves with gallery floorplans. "Please, please stop going on about it. Please, Joan, try, at least try to put it out of your mind."

"That's the thing you don't understand," Joan said. "Ottilie would marry someone just to spite me."

"Don't be ridiculous."

"I'm not being ridiculous. I asked her what she thought she was doing."

"You told me. You've told me this already."

"And all she would say was that life is mysterious. But I know that smile. That bloody Mona Lisa smile."

"It's a passing thing. It's bound to be. Ottilie isn't going to end up with someone like Alan. There's no way. You're taking this far too seriously."

"You don't know my sister like I do. She's a very odd person. She blames me for Sebastian's death for instance. No, I'm serious. In Ottilie's mind it was all my fault."

"How could it have been your fault?"

"She was running all over the estate looking for Alan to come and rescue him. Meanwhile I was left alone to try and find Sebastian under the water. And yet in her mind it was all my fault."

"Can we stop talking about Ottilie now? This has been the fourth day of talking about Ottilie and Alan and it's getting really boring."

"I'm sorry. But I can't stop thinking about it. Alan and Ottilie. I can't bear it."

Months later, the news that Ottilie was pregnant, that she'd been "knocked up" (Joan's phrase) at the Grants' party, came as an undisguised relief to Joan. Now Ottilie was pregnant, Alan would no longer want her. Why would it matter so much? It mattered because Ottilie was the elder twin, older than Joan by seven minutes. This had become significant since Sebastian was lost. At that time Henry's mind was fixed, apparently immovably, on the importance of their being one clear and individual heir to Peattie: one name, one heir, one line. Ottilie was being groomed for inheritance. She'd been plucked out of the high school and sent to the fee-paying establishment, one set in many green and manicured acres outside town, leaving Joan behind. She learned her art skills there, in their better facilities, in the perfect light of their purpose-built studios, with their one-to-one coaching in technique. The reason given was that Ottilie was to be an artist and would benefit, but in due course it began to be obvious that the move had been made for social reasons: Henry was concerned about Ottilie making the right choice of husband, a man happy to become a Salter in name as well as in spirit, with Salter children making their appearance later on. So here it was: the shocking thought, the shocking prospect. If Ottilie married Alan and they had children, Alan would be the inheritor of Peattie. Alan's descendants would be the heirs of Peattie. To Joan, who cherished ideas of aristocracy as meaning something biological, who believes still in material nobility of blood, that was just about the worst prospect imaginable. And of course that was me, that worst prospect in Joan's mind when the rumours began, rumours that it was Alan who was the father, rumours that the house party story was a convenient smokescreen.

Vita had hinted to me for months before she told me, but I wasn't listening properly and didn't understand what she was trying to say when she talked about Alan and his taste for girls, Alan's being sent away for four years when Ottilie and Joan were young. Finally, though, the hints solidified into an account. I heard about the tennis at Easter. I heard more about Seb's death. She told me the story of the wedding party, the kiss: all of this was news to me. Finally I asked her straight out. Was Alan my father? Yes, she believed so, she said. What was I to do with this information? What would my mother's reaction have been had I burst into the studio, hackles up and ready to fight? Even the thought of that encounter made me nauseous. She'd have been disastrously calm and elusive. It wasn't the thought of that great and engulfing calm that made me ill, but the fear of my own reaction to it. There was a risk that I'd hit her, that I'd hurt her, that even if I managed to prevent myself from violence to Ottilie I'd go like a madman around the studio smashing it up and defacing the work. And what if her reaction to that, to my smashing up the studio, had itself been disastrously calm and elusive? There'd be no coming back from that.

The fundamental point was that I didn't believe, even now when presented with Vita's certainty, with my own certainty, that my mother would confirm or deny. She'd be like a prisoner of war tortured by the enemy and holding stubbornly to silence. She'd said already, a hundred times, that she wasn't going to discuss it. She resented the whole idea that I would find the father and form a relationship with him.

"He showed no interest in you at all, in fact he counselled abortion. He's a man who wanted you dead. What would you have to say to each other?"

I didn't have a ready answer. My mouth opened and closed.

"Tell me the rest," I'd implored her. "Just tell me. Tell me more about what he isn't. You don't have to give me a name."

"Michael, I'm never going to talk to you in any greater detail than this, about this," she'd said, provokingly composed as ever. "Never. You have to understand that. But this much I will say. He's not somebody I would want you to know. Nothing that makes you yourself has come down from him. He's coarse and stupid and cruel, shallow and self-regarding. He'd make you unhappy. He'd make me unhappy. I'm not prepared to risk that. I'm sorry."

Instead of going to my mother, I went to Alan, the night before I disappeared. Alan agreed that he was my father but didn't seem to feel that it was anything huge in our lives; not personally, not as humans, not on an emotional basis. No hidden impact, quietly accruing greater breadth and depth like interest in a secret bank account, was there waiting to be unleashed. His focus was political and sentimental. He was much more interested in telling me how he'd been abused by the Salters.

"The family know, they all know, they've known all this time," he said, spit gathering at the corners of his mouth. "And what do you think they did about it? I'll tell you, Michael. They threatened us with eviction. Said they'd throw us out on our arses if I spoke up. Paid me off with a lifetime's free rent of this crap little house. What could I do? My dad's got nowhere to go, no money. I couldn't do that to him. He's lived here 55 years."

"That's terrible," I said, looking in disbelief at this man who was my father.

I told him that I was going away the following day, a plan I could see he approved, and we made arrangements about meeting in the afternoon and about the money.

After this I went and found Henry on the hill. Henry was in his usual spot, dogs panting around him. He was sitting under one of the birches that grow by the stream, pink-faced under his khaki fisherman's hat.

"I went to see Alan," I told him, sitting down beside him and getting straight to the point. "I know from what he said that he's – he's him. My father."

Henry didn't speak. He looked at the worked silver head of his walking stick, one Joan gave him for his 60th birthday, as if noticing its interlocking patterns for the first time.

"Say something."

"There's no evidence of that," he said at once. "Speaking for myself I wouldn't take Alan Dixon's word for anything."

"I don't know what else to think."

Henry worked at dividing and then flattening a patch of weed just below his feet, using the end of the stick. Then he said, "I think it might be time to contact the boys on the list."

The list. The list that I'd had for months. Henry had taken me into his study one afternoon, saying he had something for me. The second drawer of the Chinese cabinet was unlocked and a buff-paper file closed with an elastic band was handed to me.

"What's this?"

"That is the dossier."

"The dossier. Really? You still have it."

"I did but now you do."

Here they are in my mind's eye, the boys in the house party photographs. Nigel Wallis, Graham Barker-Howden, Hamish Masterton and the others, names I've learned and spoken and conversations I've rehearsed. The smoothie with the tan and the teeth and a copious Brylcreemed quiff, a photograph labelled William Bingham. Miles Martineau, the blond one, my height, and something about him around the eyes. Names marked on the back in pencil. Christian Grant, his horse face and tombstone smile. Some boys in shadow. Others in flash, with red metallic eyes, beers in their hands and hair dishevelled.

I'd taken it home, the dossier, and hidden it under the bed in a suitcase that had a lock, and over the weeks that followed I'd worn it out with handling. I made notes. I looked people up in address books. I intended to act but then on the point of taking action I seemed to lose the will. Sitting in bed, wakeful in the dark, leaning on the window sill and watching my mother's silhouette in her studio, her black shape against the yellow light, I began to see Henry's gift quite differently. How perfect this dossier was as a false trail, a self-perpetuating and bottomless mystery, tantalising and ineffable. In this dossier was my father – that was the family position: the implication that I should be reassured by this. All of them were well-bred, well-mannered young men, well born and at a safe distance. One collective daddy who'd never be distilled into an individual identity.

If I'd been surprised to be handed the dossier I'd been even more stunned to be offered the money. What was I to make of the offer of £2000 in cash, the information that Henry had put it aside for me in the bureau in the secret drawer? It was no secret, the drawer. Henry had shown it to us all when we were young. It looked like a piece of moulding separating the desktop from the drawer beneath, but at a push was released on its spring, revealing itself blue velvet lined.

Henry took his hat off and waved it ineffectively towards his face. "I've never known heat like this," he said.

"Why did you offer me the money, why really?" I asked him.

"To get you started," Henry said.

"Started on what?"

"On whatever you do when you get there."

"How do you – what makes you think I'm going anywhere?"

"Well you are, aren't you? Leaving us."

That was the last time I spoke to Henry.

Chapter 18

Thomas said he would be there by 11am but his taxi was delayed by a jack-knifed fuel lorry that had blocked the road, so by the time he arrived at Peattie it was lunchtime and Edith had been through a lengthy journey of her own, one that had its physical counterpart in walking the corridors of the house.

I could tell by her face, as she went down the steps to the drive, that the words and the tears were backed up in her, that a kind word could prove the enemy of self-control. It wasn't clear, as Thomas paid his fare, emerged onto the gravel, closed the car door, whether she could risk even eye contact in full view of so many windows, so much accidental evidence at hand; even the rear-view mirror had the potential for betrayal, and so as Thomas's arm was raised to her shoulder she stepped decisively away, her eyes lowered to his shoes – serious shoes, as architectural and coal black as a policeman's – and said tersely to him that they must wait until they were inside. They went to the kitchen, Edith not talking, not looking at him, standing with the kettle beside the sink.

"Are you sure it's coffee you want?" Thomas asked her.

"You're right, it isn't," she said, setting the kettle back on its stand and leaving the room.

They went to the study – Edith going first, seeing the door left ajar – and took a bottle of whisky and two stubby glasses from Henry's drinks cupboard, and then she led the way down to Ottilie's studio on the ground floor, a big space lit by two tall windows, its interior all hard surfaces. Two wooden chairs (as it happens, bought from the church during a refit) had been positioned next to the heater. It was a two-bar electric fire that Ottilie used when she was working, and it buzzed and hummed into life as Thomas poured the Scotch. A faint aroma of burning dust emanated.

They sat down together. "So. Tell me everything." Thomas laid his glass by his feet and Edith did the same.

Still she didn't look at him. She had mastered her impulse and so she began just as she had with Susan on the phone. She'd telephoned Susan while Thomas was en route. "I'm sorry, I've been an idiot," she'd said. He inched his chair closer and reached out to her and she reciprocated warmly, firmly, to his grasp of her two hands, a gesture perfected at the church door. It was a gesture that was granted to parishioners in times of trouble, transmitting through its brief skin contact all the power of collective and authoritative empathy. She withdrew again after a moment because kindness continued to threaten her resolve.

Susan had affected as much careful sympathy for Edith's explanatory bumbling – nerves were cited, nerves and stress – as she had for the initial confession, which Edith knew was a bad sign. Possibly Susan thought that both equally were evidence of a burgeoning madness and that a calm acceptance of each was for the best. Edith was beginning to see that Susan's authenticity as a soul-mate was at least partly performance, and that what lay behind it could just as easily be condemnation as approval. So many people she knew at the church were similar. The carapace of acceptance was like the frozen surface of a pond. Beneath it, there were unseen energies; the real life teemed obscurely underneath. Thomas was a different fish entirely. To Thomas she could say anything, no matter how dreadful. His understanding was a deep well, apparently bottomless: she could throw any size or variety of stone into it, her faithless sin, and he would take it into himself like a communion wafer and become only ever more hers: a knack, perhaps, or a genetic trick, or something that had been trained and learned.

"You can tell me, you know," he said. He'd watched her and he'd read her thoughts.

"The trouble is ..." She looked into his face now, as if beginning to compose the announcement. The trouble is, Thomas, that you are Jesus, you are the god of the black shoes, the double handclasp at the door. She looked steadily into his eyes with an odd expression, and even if he couldn't read that language, it was obvious to me that she knew that though his forgiveness would be as little a fabricated thing as possible, it would also mean the end of their friendship.

"I wouldn't normally do this," Thomas said, lifting the glass and swigging from it – and Edith smiled at first, thinking he was talking about the whisky, "because my policy is always that people say what they're ready to say and I don't push it."

"No."

"I've heard the rumours you know," he said. "There are many informants hereabouts, all of them possessed of telephones, and I don't have to tell you that bad news about the Salters isn't bad news for everyone. Salter schadenfreude is a whole sub-category of its own."

"Yes."

"So let me help you out a bit. Michael. You said that it's about Michael. One of your burdens at least. You said there were two and I have no idea about the other. I just wanted to point that out. If there were other whispers and hints on the bush telegraph, I'd tell you."

Edith stared at her lap.

Eventually Thomas spoke. "I've just had a trivial revelation. I don't like whisky. I'm not going to drink it any more." He got up and went to the sink and poured his drink down it. "And this is a terrible room for talking in. Let's go outside and walk. I've always found walking good for secret-sharing. Let's go out on the hill, shall we?"

"Henry," Edith said. "Henry's probably there."

"Somewhere else then. We'll go off the other way, across the road and onto the bridletrack."

"We'll be seen."

"Does that matter? Seems it does. Better stay here then." He went across to one of Ottilie's painted screens, done in her teenage years in Bloomsbury style in chalky colours, a three-part screen, five feet high and decorated with a trio of muscular angels. Thomas half pulled and half carried it across the floor, before opening it into a false wall, cupping the two of them into their corner. Now, they inhabited an antechamber sealed off from the rest of the room, from easels and boards and mess, one that protected them from observers pausing at the door, the upper part of which was a glass panel.

"Let me get this thing started with a robust opening statement," Thomas said. "There's gossip, that Michael died. The gossip says that Michael died here, that he never left, that he killed himself by drowning in the loch and that the whole family knows as much, that you've known it all along, because he left a note saying that's what he was going to do."

"We don't know what happened to him, not for sure," Edith said immediately. "They might be right. We think that might have been it but we don't know for sure. The note you're wrong about – it didn't mention suicide; it was about leaving and that's all."

"I see."

"I was idiotic. To phone you in such a state. I'm sorry. I have days when possible things seem as if they must be true. I have days when I'm sure Michael is dead and that it was my fault."

"How could it have been your fault?"

"Because I neglected him. Kept clear of him, put off by his teenage sulking. He spent a lot of time here and we left him alone. He was lonely. He read and he wrote and we barely spoke to him. He read and wrote constantly and was on his own most of the time; these are things children do when they're lonely. I didn't take his unhappiness seriously. None of us did."

"So. That's one thing. One down, and one to go. Moving on, now. What's the other secret?"

"What?"

"Tell me the other thing, and then we can go and have lunch. I'm hungry."

"Why are you talking in that strange way?"

"Because, Edith, it's obvious you're not telling the truth."

"I'm not ready. Not yet."

"That's fine. I'm here when you are. Or rather, I'm *there*." He got up and put his jacket on.

"Thomas."

"You've got to trust me, Edith. I'm offended by lack of trust."

"Sit down, please; I'm sorry. Would you pour me another drink, first? I'll have to drink alone. There's water in the tap over there for you."

He smiled at her and half filled her glass, and moved his chair so it was directly opposite hers.

"This is the bare bones of it," she said to him, tipping and angling the whisky so the light caught it, amber and gold. She concentrated on its patterns. "We know that Michael killed himself. Ursula told us; she was there. She'd been talking to him. He was very unhappy, in despair. He went down into the loch and he didn't come up again. She came running to us and we rushed down there and of course it was too late. He wasn't anywhere to be found, though we looked and looked, for hours and hours."

"You didn't alert anyone, the police?" Thomas couldn't quite hide his disapproval.

"No. He couldn't be found. And then we began to have doubts about what Ursula had told us. Her account was so like what she'd told us after Joan's wedding."

"About Sebastian, you mean."

"Yes. We looked for Michael, but it was obvious he wouldn't be found easily. And then we decided against telling."

"I see."

"That's our family secret. I know you said to me that nothing I told you would ever go further, but you need to confirm that with me now, because I've frightened myself, telling you all this."

"Nothing you say to me will ever go further. I'm very sorry to hear this news, and to imagine how it's burdened you for all of these years."

Edith drank and Thomas watched her. She realised she had sipped at the whisky too quickly. Its darkness pressed at the back of her head and she put her hand to the place and said she must stop, but then finished it anyway, a quarter-glass in a long gulp.

"You're taking this very well," she said. "Michael, the news about him."

"You're not even sure of the facts."

"The truth is I am sure. I'm sure."

Thomas crossed his legs and leaned towards her. He had surprisingly small hands. "I like to have time to consider things. I'll think about it and then I might have observations. I learned in my old trade not to give in to immediate reactions."

"The second thing is about Ursula," Edith said immediately.

Thomas waited.

"She did something. A long time ago, something very wrong. I'm not going to go into details, not today. I need to work up to it. I may have to write to you about it first."

Thomas's face was attentive and neutral. "Go on."

"She came to me and told me, afterwards, after the event, what it was that she'd done, about this wrong thing. It doesn't matter what it was, does it. It doesn't matter. The point is that I didn't get a chance to think. It's interesting what you say about that. I was upset. She was hysterical. She was so sorry, you see. So sorry. I said to her things I shouldn't have."

"You mean you were censorious, cruel?"

"No."

"I don't understand."

"It was the opposite. I told her it was alright. She was hysterical and I needed her to be calm. I've always needed her to be calm and happy. If she'd stayed so upset ..."

"Yes?"

"I didn't know what would happen next. I could see things spiralling. A really and truly horrendous spiralling. It could have broken the whole family. We all had our own versions, you see, of what had happened. It was vital we kept all having our own versions. I told her that it's what you intend that matters. If things go badly, it isn't always your fault. It might seem an obvious point, to you and me, but it wasn't to Ursula. Not then. Not at that time. She was very clear about cause and effect. She was very clear that she was to blame, she wanted to take it all on, she wanted to be punished. And I found myself convincing her that there was nothing to be punished for, that it was a sort of accident. When she did the bad thing, she didn't intend to happen what happened next, you see. If things get out of hand sometimes, that's just bad luck. This was radical. This was absolutely new thinking for her."

"It all sounds perfectly reasonable."

"You wouldn't say that if you knew."

"Tell me then."

"She's literal. Ursula's literal about things. They're black and white. They're A and B, or rather they're A *or* B" – Edith sliced at her knee with the side of her hand three times in saying so – "and so Ursula went from one extreme to another, one dogma to another."

"So you're saying she stopped thinking it was her fault."

"She stopped thinking that anything was her fault. As long as she was sorry, genuinely truly sorry, all fault was expunged."

"It's a viewpoint I have some sympathy with."

"It's Roman Catholic though, isn't it, as a doctrine? I've been looking into it. It interests me, this whole question of forgiveness. It's begun to preoccupy me very much."

"Well, they don't have to be wrong about everything," Thomas said wryly. "And you know, it isn't quite that simple."

Edith was chewing her fingernails.

"For what it's worth, and from what I've heard, I don't think you have anything to reproach yourself for," Thomas told her.

"Thank you, but that wasn't really it."

"What was it then, Edith?" He leaned forward further in his chair.

"The reason I was so reassuring to Ursula, so overly reassuring, was that I couldn't bear for Henry to know. I told her that Henry didn't have to be told. I told her he wouldn't understand, that it would be a bad thing to make him so unhappy. There were so many lies about it, about the day, you see. I knew that Ottilie and Joan had lied and I knew why. Ursula told me about their lying: she doesn't have any inhibitions about informing on people; she's always been my faithful little reporter. I've known all this time that the girls lied to me. But I couldn't tell them that I knew; I *still* haven't told them that I know. The lie and my believing the lie were imperative to us carrying on, to our surviving. That's how it seemed but it was wrong. Henry doesn't know but I have got to tell him."

"Why have you got to tell him?"

"The truth's important. It has to become important. I think that's the only way we'll be saved. We need to say everything to one another about it, so that it will close."

"We'll talk about that again. Promise me you won't say anything to anyone else until we talk again. I'll phone you in the morning. You should come to the flat and have lunch with me."

"Everything I did was for Henry."

"Here, have my handkerchief. Don't talk any more. You're making yourself ill. You're shaking. Your hands are icy cold. Come, come with me and we'll get you into a soft chair and find a blanket. You should rest now, Edith."

Edith went to her bedroom, having said a perfunctory goodbye in the hall to Thomas, leaving him to go out onto the terrace and wait for his taxi home. She got into her bed fully clothed, forgetting even to remove her shoes, and slept for a while. When she woke she had a pressure headache, as if the whisky had collected at the base of her skull, and so she went down to the kitchen to find aspirin and make a pot of tea, praying she wouldn't encounter anyone. Mog was there, eating cheese on toast, and so Edith found herself discussing the party and what she might wear as if the conversation with Thomas had never happened, though she was dog-tired and the careless words had to be dug deeply out of her, out of some emergency neurological fund.

Then Ursula arrived with news. She burst in, coming into the new kitchen at a rush, and went immediately to Edith for a private conference. They used to bother me, these conversations, but actually, having eavesdropped, I've realised that usually they concern quotidian things: meals, health, washing, work, money; remarks delivered, all of them, whatever their gravity, in the same urgent confiding way. Ursula was wearing a green pinafore dress in sprigged cotton, low-waisted and faded, with sagging pockets. It stretched almost to the ankle and would have been girlish were it not for the fact that she wasn't wearing anything underneath. The dress was generously cut but the outer curves of small white breasts showed at the sides of the bib.

"There's someone to see you, Mog," she said, and when she turned on her heel to go, her narrow back was strikingly smooth and pale, the pinafore straps criss-crossing it.

"Someone? Who is it?" Mog called after her, pursuing.

"Johnnie," Ursula said over her shoulder.

Pip told Izzy that Mog had dumped Johnnie by text message but that wasn't true. She'd written him a letter and put it through his door very early in the morning, just as it was getting light. It was only then that she'd sent him the text message. Luckily security at the paper is tight these days, and Johnnie was rebuffed at the front desk, first by girlish receptionists, superficially friendly but hard as nails, and then by security guards with a hundred pounds apiece of metabolic advantage. Fortunately Pip's flat was also good for repelling boarders: it was on the second floor, with a clear view of the street through wall-high windows. The buzzer was at the main door downstairs, and an indomitable wheezy old fossil, resident of ground floor 1/a, acted as a kind of organic repellent, shuffling out imperiously to demand to know what callers wanted. Johnnie wasn't to find Mog at home again, but there wasn't really any way of preventing his leaving messages on the answerphone.

"Please do get back to me today, Mog; this is the fifth time I've had to do this, and I have to tell you that my patience is being severely tested."

He'd come at breakfast and in the early evening, and hang about looking at his watch, standing on the cobbles, the high black railings and evergreen foliage of the residents' garden behind him; staring up expressionless, hands in pockets, jawline shifting as if chewing on imaginary gum, bulky in his banker's overcoat.

When Mog brought Johnnie to the house back in the spring, she chose a day when she knew Edith would be out. Edith and also Joan: they'd gone to Inverness to look at curtains. Henry was easy to avoid, and if he couldn't be avoided would greet friends of the grandchildren in friendly terms and think no more about them and never mention them again. It was best, though, not to run into Edith, and vital not to run into Joan. Vita and Mrs Hammill, if left to themselves, rose only shortly before lunch, so a morning visit was likely to be safe. They went to Peattie early and unannounced, she and Johnnie, having stayed in a B&B in the town the night before, capitalising on a run of fine cold weather, to see the snowdrops, thousands of them in thickets; to see the sun rise over the loch; to see the first rays hit David's tomb in the way that his brother planned. Mog told Johnnie what Henry had said about the wolf, that malign fate is a wolf at the door just waiting for its chance to enter, pressing on though Johnnie had begun to be sceptical and finally grew openly disparaging.

"Not Michael again, please, for god's sake," he had said.

"He went out to the wolf," she told him. "I think he chose the wolf. Everybody was always angry with him, for being bolshy about the father, the trouble at school, for his sarcasm, for being work-shy, for not wanting to go to university, for not appreciating his opportunities: that's how Henry put it, *not appreciating his opportunities*. Henry's never spoken to any of the rest of us like that. As if Michael were a foundling child who needed to keep being grateful."

"You don't get it, do you? I don't want to hear any more of this garbage."

They'd had an argument, she and Johnnie, and had cut their visit short, returning to Edinburgh in the hire car in silence.

~

Johnnie was standing at the end of the corridor, a big man, not unusually tall but heavy-set, a player of weekend sport. He was ordinary-looking, his brown hair sharply receded, leaving a pointed hairline; ordinary-looking aside from around the eyes. His eyes were hard to look into: everybody found this. They looked at you as if they knew you, as if deciding what to do about you. Even if you were meeting for the first time, his eyes suggested that you shared something, as if great intimacy had been experienced and might be offered again; an intimacy that might, should you misstep, be taken as abruptly away. You might be about to be admitted to the club, the club of Johnnie: but at what cost? It was hard to explain this to people, though Mog had tried: what it was that Johnnie offered, what turned out to be the cost, the need to sign up for the cult of Johnnie and live in it, but all her explanations foundered.

"You're just going to have to take it from me," she'd said to Joan, having been called upon to explain herself. "He's not trustworthy, he's not truthful." Her mother had raised one eyebrow and said nothing; it was clear to her that this was Mog's depression talking and a policy of not engaging with it had proven best.

Evidently Johnnie hadn't only dropped by: a new overnight bag was sitting at his feet. He was wearing an expensive-looking suit in fine wool, tan with subtle green and gold stripes, new clothes bought for the occasion, and this, the cunningly plotted curve of this special effort, was what made it impossible to banish him outright and unheard. His understanding of her weaknesses: that had been information he'd accepted with particular gratitude.

Johnnie stepped back into the shadow that falls at the side of the stairway, and she joined him there and they looked at each other.

Finally he said, "It's good to see you."

His eyes didn't say that, though. His eyes said "so what's your next move?"

"You're not thinking you'll stay," Mog warned him, trying not to be lobby-briefed by the newness of the tweed, and the luggage.

"But you invited me," he said. Like all scoundrels, Johnnie Brandt believes in the truth. He half removed the invitation from his pocket, the one that Joan argued with the printers about because the typeface was wrong, lifting it illustratively into view and letting it drop back.

It's funny how people behave in a crisis, how often they opt for good manners when something more instinctive would be justified, more limbic-propelled, dialled in from a red phone in the prehistoric nub of the brain. This is how people are killed by psychopaths, I imagine, in the gap that falls between trying to think the best of people and shrinking from the embarrassment of misidentifying danger; jumping to conclusions can be a humiliating business. Not that this was that kind of emergency, nothing like, but it had crossed her mind that Johnnie might do this. Mog said merely and redundantly, "You let the taxi go." She could hear it crunching out of gravel onto tarmac, accelerating from one surface to the other as it turned onto the road and made its way back towards the town. "I'll call you another."

But Johnnie was looking over her shoulder and smiling. Edith had followed Mog from the kitchen. Johnnie's hand was thrust towards her, Edith's responding with impeccably polite limpness.

"I've heard so much about you, Edith," he said. Mog winced at the informality. "And you've heard so much about me." Edith's expression was unchanged. "Mog invited me for the weekend." He and Edith looked down at the bag.

"If there's no room here I can stay at the inn, of course," he said.

"There's no room here, I'm afraid," Edith answered levelly.

They followed him out onto the terrace. Ursula was standing at the gate to the tennis court. Johnnie left his bag and went down the steps and over to her and Mog followed him, though keeping her distance. Anticipating and disapproving this, Edith caught hold of her shirt at the hem, before having to let go again, the shirt straining and threatening to rip.

Johnnie went over and spoke to Ursula, keeping his back to them. Mog stood at the foot of the steps, her hands clenched in her pockets. Now she went forward, arms folded across her midriff.

"To the inn, then," Johnnie said, turning on his heel. "Ursula here says she'll show me the way."

"I can take you as far as the main gate," Ursula said.

Johnnie smiled at Edith. "Hang on. I almost forgot."

Running past Mog at an elegant trot, Johnnie ascended the stairs, two at a time on surprisingly light feet. As he came towards her Edith took a step back, placing her right hand diagonally across her chest and onto her left shoulder. Johnnie bent and unzipped the overnight bag, saying, "I'd better give you this now."

A lavishly wrapped gift came out of the bag, a necklace-sized box in embossed silver paper, trailing great curls of silver ribbon. "Birthday present."

"Many thanks," Edith murmured, not opening it, standing with the gift in her hand. "I'll save it for the day."

Johnnie turned away and trotted back down the stairs. On Monday Edith would return the gift to him unopened.

Over on the tennis court Izzy was playing Terry, with shrieking and twirling and playful brandishing of racquets. The ball was flying upward, mostly, though Izzy can play well if she tries. Today she had elected not to. She's good at the net but today she was standing on the baseline, smoking.

"Hey Izzy!" Johnnie shouted. Izzy offered a careless wave, not looking, pretending to focus on the next shot, her cigarette in her mouth so she could use both hands. She was wearing a short halter-neck tennis dress, hair piled on her head. Now Johnnie turned to Mog.

"Any chance of a cup of tea before I go?"

"Absolutely not." She walked away, bent forward a little over her folded arms and looking at the ground, up the steps to the terrace, looking like someone who wanted to run but wasn't going to. Briefly she linked hands with Edith, who'd been standing watching, worrying at her beads with one hand. After a moment's consultation, Mog disappeared into the house. The vast floor-standing mirror on the end of the corridor wall, framed in gilded and inter-twining ivy, revealed an anxious-looking woman in city clothes, remnants of a uniform, black and white.

Mog went into the drawing room, crouching as she closed in on the window, peeping above the sill. She could see the entrance to the tennis court and movement showing in flashes from within: momentary views of Terry, who was standing at the near end, just glimpsed through the wire enclosure and through the greenery that had grown up around it. Mog moved across to the far left pane, rolling her forehead across the glass, trying to angle the sightline, just in time to catch sight of Ursula and Johnnie as they passed round the side of the house. It was possible she was bringing him in via the back stairs.

Howls of protest rose from the tennis court. Izzy's voice.

"Terry, if you keep serving like Federer I'm not going to play with you again."

"If I served like him you wouldn't even see it coming."

"Do you understand what serve means? *Serve* it to me."

Mog went out into the corridor, listening, holding her breath. There was no hint of an approach across the hard-tiled surfaces of the entrances, no human murmuring, no noise. She went forward at a jog on tiptoe, pausing in the picture gallery, steadying herself against a Japanese cabinet, one too damaged to be worth selling on. Nothing to be heard, not a peep. She turned the corner into the hall, her heart surging with adrenaline and, although there was nobody there, ran up the stairs as fast as she could and into her room, and dragged her dressing table in front of the door.

Then she lay on the bed, very still and very quiet.

Then she got up and walked around.

Then she sat on her bed, chewing her lip, picking at her cuticles, and took her socks off and attended to the dry skin around her toes.

When Izzy came, still in her tennis whites and holding her racquet, Mog was in the bathroom, the only room which had a lock. She had the water running, though it would be a shallow kind of soak, dispiritingly shallow, limbs protruding and chilly, because there's never enough hot water. Peattie baths are big enough to sleep in and have been slept in on occasion, padded out with cushions, notably at parties Henry and Edith gave when they were newly married. Izzy tapped on the door and a rapid conversation was held through it. Johnnie had gone to the village with Ursula, Izzy assured her, Mog calling out her thanks in a protracted sing-song way, faking unconcern over the noise of water rushing.

An hour or so later there was a knock at Mog's door. She'd heard someone approaching and was standing right behind it.

"Izzy?"

"It's only me."

Mog emerged, wearing different clothes. Pink and orange. Izzy was still in the tennis dress.

"So he's gone, definitely gone," Mog said.

"Definitely. Saw them go." A skinny arm was looped around Mog's shoulder.

"He's going to come to the party."

"Would he be that thick-skinned? What for?"

"To punish me."

"That looks good on you, by the way," Izzy told her.

Mog looked down at herself. "It's a bit like the monkeys and the typewriters. Eventually something works, but it's always an accident."

"Well. It isn't quite Shakespeare. But that skirt shape really works for you. It skims over the lumps. And just below the knee is your length. Your calves are curvy. Wrap tops are great for people with a tummy, cutting across the bulge." She was rearranging it. "But you need to stand up straighter. When you slouch along you look even heavier."

Sometimes it's a disheartening business when Izzy Salter pays a compliment.

Afternoon tea featured things left over from lunch, preserved under foil: sandwiches laid out on a tray, apples in a bowl and packets of crisps arranged on a platter. Only Henry and Vita and Mog were in attendance. Izzy and Terry were off in the hills, Ottilie was at home, Alastair and Rebecca had gone with Joan to tea at the Grants' house and Mrs Hammill was resting. Euan had declared himself too busy in the kitchen to attend. He was making preparations for the party.

"Where's Gran?" Mog poured herself tea through a silver strainer provided by her mother. Light penetrated the walls of the thin floral china. Joan had hidden the mugs somewhere.

"Gone to town. Optician." Henry was reading a magazine that had arrived in the post, that emitted its pungent solvent aroma.

Edith had lied about the optician. She wanted to see Thomas and talk to him again. They sat in his sitting room eating fruit cake and reprised their conversation, the second part of it, almost word for word. Edith made the same partial and inaccurate confession and received the same unsatisfying provisional forgiveness. Once that was done, Edith realised she wanted urgently to be at the church in the village. She excused herself, pleading arrangements that were out of her hands, drove at 25 miles an hour back down the country roads home – taking corners at 15 – and stopped at the florist's on the way. Tilly had loved roses: ordinarily Edith brought her flowers from the garden but she didn't want to go back to the house yet, so these perfect and soulless, aroma-less blooms would have to do. She took them to Tilly in the churchyard and sat with her a while, having stood first for a few minutes in the porch, by the open door, apparently unable to enter.

Tilly was the only Salter buried outside of the estate wall. After Sebastian's death the mausoleum in the grounds had been closed a final time. It's presumed sometimes that this was an act with emotional significance but the truth is that there was no room for more residents, so Tilly went to the churchyard alone. Henry kept the mausoleum locked and was the gatekeeper, its big iron key hanging on the wall in his study. After Tilly's death he took us into the mausoleum, the cousins and me, through the arched and decorated metal door, the key noisy in the lock. He lit the candles that had remained unlit since Seb's funeral, each silver candlestick bearing long wax drips, their solidified wax tears. This gesture of his, relighting them, made it seem as if we had come in at the end of the ceremony and as if time had been collapsed. There they were, the family dead, encased and rotted away, or perhaps just dried up, shrunken and papery (if you thought about it like that, and at 13 you did): the remains of Henry's father, of Ursa and Jo, and Sebastian himself, stacked together in limestone magnificence, along with the remoter, more anonymous Salter dead, in undisturbed dimness and silence.

Henry, eating a sandwich, looked at Mog over the top of his glasses.

"I hear you have a visitor."

"Had. He's gone now."

"No. He's here. Ursula's bringing him to tea."

No sooner had he said this than Mog could hear them: two sets of footsteps, a pair of squeaky plimsolls and a pair of brogues coming through the picture gallery. Mog reached for a magazine and sat beside Henry, pulling Tilly's chair adjacent to his.

Ursula's hair had been brushed and she'd changed into a swirly-patterned dress with billowing sleeves, a frock that was once Edith's. Johnnie followed her into the room, undaunted at the sight of Mog and ignoring her, introducing himself to the others, his suit gleaming with cashmere and his tie bearing the coat of arms of a school: its design had been printed in gold, denoting charitable generosity to the Old Boys' League. He wasn't ever a pupil there, but no matter. When Johnnie introduced himself to Vita she lifted her wrist; Johnnie kissed the back of it and she murmured her approval.

"Johnnie Brandt. Delighted to meet you at last."

"Mr Brandt." She smiled up at him; perhaps she hadn't realised that this was Mog's ex-boyfriend. Or perhaps she had. You never know. "Is that of German origin, your name? Won't you have tea with us? A drink? Henry, can we get some sherry? We're dull and spiritless left to ourselves so much."

"My father was Austrian," Johnnie said, sitting in the chair closest to her and bending forward sociably. He rested his elbows on his knees, linking his fingers lightly together as if he were to be interviewed on a television show: that same practised readiness. "He came over in the war, fleeing Hitler, and was interned in England. Our estates were sequestered in his absence and we lost everything we had."

"How fascinating."

Ursula handed Johnnie a teacup. Mog kept her eyes on the magazine but made a dismissive noise.

"You are a friend of my granddaughter." Vita glanced at Ursula.

"Mog's friend, until recently. Her boyfriend. But she decided –"

He was interrupted by Vita. "Mog's boyfriend you say. But aren't you a good deal older than her?"

"Yes, I'm pushing 50, alas."

"Do get something to eat. Railway food today, I'm afraid, though the ham is rather delicious."

Mog sank diagonally into the long chair, hoisting one leg over its arm and closing her eyes.

"We should go," Henry's voice said. "We need to go and look at the new saplings, take the dogs out. Come on."

"After another cup," she told him, getting up to go to the tea table. A cool sun was streaming into the drawing room and Vita and Johnnie and the attendant, silent Ursula were seen through a fog of sunshine, in velvet chairs by the windows, gathered around a card table.

"I work in finance," Johnnie was telling Vita. "In Edinburgh."

"How splendid. And so you must be friends with our Peter: Pip Salter-Catto."

"I know Pip, yes, of course. Pip's a tremendous fellow."

Ursula was staring at Mog and unblinking. She was resting her head into a wing of the chair, her legs tucked up into the seat. When Mog met her eyes, Ursula smiled at her. One hand stroked her thigh idly, and with the other she twiddled a strand of hair around one finger.

"I'm ready now," Mog said.

Chapter 19

Ursa's room has a lovely view, in one direction looking across the vegetable gardens and over the topiary hedges that have been cut abstractly into swooping curves by Ursula, and in the other direction across the pasture fields where cattle – another family's cattle, now – stand under broadly spread trees, under crabbed and lateral branches, looking as if they've been painted in oils. Henry found the arrival of other people's livestock difficult: if the land was put to crops that wasn't so hard – there had been hired tractors in the fields for decades, but livestock was a different matter. The world was advancing and encroaching; it had them surrounded. Recently a bull had leaned against the wall and bowed it and parts of it had fallen. Mog was watching the stonemason at work, making his complicated jigsaw, picking up and discarding, picking up and fitting. She was sitting on the window seat, along its length with her feet up, leaning back against the shutter. Gazing out of the window had proved successful in slowing down the rate of questioning, but she was beginning to feel bad about this failure of hospitality, so she turned her attention back into the room. Rebecca had lifted and was admiring a picture of her grandmother from the chest of drawers, one of Ursa on her bike, hitching a ride down the drive, holding onto an umbrella hooked onto the back of her father's antique car, her face delighted, showing her small teeth and a pink rim of gum. She rode her bike everywhere, even into town 12 miles away, and sometimes there was a dog in the front basket.

"Do you think the laws of physics were different then, that kept dogs in bicycle baskets?" Mog asked, earning a quizzical look from Rebecca. The world *was* different then, I said to Mog once, when we were looking at the photograph together, and people seemed happy in a way they just don't any more. I used to say that kind of thing, but now I see that nostalgia is just a kind of cowardice.

Rebecca came and leaned over Mog and looked down into the garden, where George was standing with a hoe and mopping his brow.

"You look so disapproving," Mog said.

"Do I? I'm sorry. But it's obvious he's struggling."

"As far as George is concerned this is his garden. Don't listen to Alan. George refuses to retire, point blank. He said to me once that he wants to die on the lawn in high summer, just after mowing it into stripes. He doesn't do it all on his own, you know. Alan does most of the heavy work and my father helps with the grass. He says it's good for inexpressible rage."

Rebecca was straight onto this. "Why would he be in a rage?"

"He doesn't need a reason," Mog told her. "It's innate. Plus, Ursula helps with the borders. George says she has a gift for pruning. She even gets to do his roses."

"But it's obvious he's struggling. Can't anything be done?"

They heard a car coming down the drive; Pip had arrived. Rebecca said she had things she needed to do, so Mog went out alone to meet him. Pip was sorting through things in the boot.

"The painting's turned up," Mog said to his back. "And also Johnnie."

Pip lifted out the bags, slammed the lid shut, and walked away from her and up the steps.

"Beastly journey, thanks," Angelica said, following him. She appeared to be wearing jodhpurs. "Caravans nose to nose on the A9. Accident at Drumnadrochit."

"Nose to tail you mean."

"No, these were nose to nose, which is worse."

They followed Pip into the hall. He'd come straight from the office and was still in the chalk pinstripe, the pink shirt. His shoulders and upper arms were bulky in the jacket, but infant blond curls whisped onto his jacket collar at the back. He put the bags down.

"Johnnie's here," Mog said.

He paused, mid-hang of jacket on hook. "Johnnie?"

"My ears are burning," Johnnie's voice said, and then he was there, emerging from the picture gallery hand in hand with Ursula. Both of them had a bright-eyed unfocussed look. Now that she had come to a halt, Ursula seemed to be having trouble keeping upright, adjusting her feet as if she were sailing in a gale. She'd changed out of the dress into a white shirt, black tux trousers with a satin cuff and Johnnie's old school tie.

"You've met my brother, I see," Pip said, straight-faced. "And how is he?"

"He's fine but his stuff's too expensive," Johnnie told him, equally deadpan.

"Will we be seeing Jet this weekend?" Pip took Angelica's coat.

"Why are you asking me?" Johnnie said sourly. "I'm just a customer."

The two of them eyed each other up like dogs kept apart only by leashes, their hackles up.

"So you'll be leaving now," Pip told him. "You must know you're not welcome."

"Oh, but I am. I'm installed at the inn and I'm Ursula's invited guest. Her date" – he paused, enjoying the foreign-ness of the word – "Her *date* at the party." Ursula was nodding.

"Have you given her something?"

"What do you mean?"

"One of Jet's special cigarettes."

"No, I haven't. I suspect she's always like this." Ursula did a little twirl and curtsied low to the ground. "Actually I think she did have a small one."

Ursula was laughing. She went out onto the terrace and Johnnie followed her out, saying, "Pleasure, as always."

"Ursula high," Angelica said. "Doesn't sound good to me."

Mog was looking at Pip. "What will happen?"

"Happen?"

"Will she be alright? Isn't she likely to ..." Her eyes flickered towards Angelica. "Never mind."

"I'll talk to you about it later," Pip said.

Angelica sighed noisily, half-sigh and half-growl. "You two. School playground mode again. Secrets, secrets. It does get tedious."

"Somebody has to go after her," Pip said. "Sorry, Mog."

"That's fine, I'm used to it," Mog said, only mildly resentfully. She went out onto the terrace and spoke out towards the garden – the two of them had gone off in the direction of the folly together – her voice projecting: "Ursula, you need to come in, your mother's looking for you, she needs your help." These words were always effec-tive and Ursula returned.

"Stay away from her," Mog instructed Johnnie, who continued standing as if awaiting his own orders. "As you wish," he said. "I'll be at the inn, but I'm coming for supper as Ursula's guest. She asked your mother. Sorry." He didn't sound remotely sorry.

Mog had been asked by Angelica if she could leave them to unpack and to rest, so Mog retreated to my room, something she does at moments of anxiety. She was reading poetry that I'd left there in the bookcase, reading my own margin notes first, speaking some of them aloud, lying on her side with the book propped up. She fell asleep, and when she woke jumped straight up, leaving the Elizabeth Bishop crushed spine-flat on the bed – *the art of losing isn't hard to master* – and went along to Pip's room, but there was no answer to her knock. Pip's phone went straight to message. Nor were they in Angelica's room up in the garrets; ordinarily Angelica would be housed in a bedroom on the family floor, but she'd been asked by Joan if she would mind, just this once, giving way to elderly guests who'd been offered a billet for after the party, and had been gracious in agreeing; she wasn't intending to sleep there anyway. Her official room was empty, empty even of her belongings, and the bed still crisply made. Mog returned down the kitchen stairs – spooky stairs, they've always seemed to me, haunted by a particular hopelessness – along the corridor, up to the main hall and up again to Pip's room. The door opened onto bags and belongings deserted half-handled: Angelica's suitcase was open on the bed. Mog went to the door and peered out, then returned to the case and rifled through it, lifting out hold-up stockings with lace tops and tiny, translucent slivers of underwear, balanced weightless in her fingers. She looked in the wardrobe and found two dresses, and tried them against herself in the mirror: one of them a dark silky green and the other sheer and black with deep bands of velvet sewn into it. She examined the pills on the night table and read the backs of the books stacked beside them before leaving the room.

When the dinner bell rang Mog had been back and forth to the mirror on the landing a dozen times. Izzy came to her aid, providing a stretchy red dress and scarlet lipstick and heavily outlining her eyes. "We'll show him," Izzy said, pushing up her kimono sleeves and pulling a vast trunk of clothes out from under her bed. "This was meant to be worn loose but it's going to look good on you, I think." Mog's sandals were vetoed. "What did you do," Izzy asked, casting them aside, "buy these out of the back pages of a colour supplement?"

⚋⚋

In the drawing room everyone else was assembled and drinks were being dispensed. As Mog opened the door she heard Joan saying, "Don't fuss, Euan, we can easily set an extra place." Euan muttered something inaudible and there came a crisp reply: "On the other hand it might teach her a useful lesson about life."

Ursula was there and also Ottilie. Ursula was there and also in the *same room* there was Ottilie. This was a first, the first time they'd coincided purposely in 13 years, though Ottilie was sitting with her back to her sister. Perhaps the concession was made on the basis that the situation was too tricky to explain to visitors. Johnnie was there, too, in one of the threadbare velvet chairs, looking meditatively out with a glass of sherry in his hand. Joan had demanded formality and he, Pip and Henry were wearing dinner jackets. Euan, a tuxedo refusenik, was dressed in his usual putty-coloured suit, the usual brown shoes, his neck rough and pink from hurried shaving. Vita, widowish in black and weighed down by many long ropes of fake pearls, was told by Rebecca that she looked like Coco Chanel and was unamused. Once Vita had observed that it was good to dress for dinner as they used to always, and Mrs Hammill had chipped in with her usual remark about slipping stand-ards at home being emblematic; once these rituals had been observed, a silence descended – one of those mutually disempowered silences that feel as if they might obliterate the occasion. It settled and deepened as they drank their drinks. Vita saved the situation by speaking to Johnnie. "I see you have been admiring that picture."

"It's very fine. And I think it might be of you, done when you were young. Am I right?"

"Quite right, quite right." Vita was delighted. "The artist was a family friend. I sat for him on Saturdays. It was terribly dull. He kept coming over to reorganise me and had the most dreadfully bad breath. And wandering hands. Tell me, because I've never understood about tits; what *is* it exactly about them –"

Edith fired a warning shot. "Mother."

"He also did the sketch above the fireplace," Johnnie said. He'd been in here earlier with Ursula asking questions, and was well informed.

"You have quite the eye. Ruskin, you know, said drawing was as important to the development of the soul of a child as writing. Imagine if that were true. What a shameful negligence in the schools."

"I don't like that one much" Johnnie said, gesturing with his glass towards a landscape on the opposing wall. "It's almost photographic, and what's the point in that? Take the photograph."

"I do so agree," Vita said, showing all of her remaining teeth.

"When I look at a painting" – Johnnie leaned forward, his expression earnest – "what I'm looking for is proof of life. Do you know what I mean? Of individual life, an individual soul."

"Unbelievable." Mog had spoken and all eyes turned to her but she was looking at the carpet. "First internment and now this."

Johnnie continued unabashed. "Proof that people were once that alive, were passionate with colour, had doubts, were in love, feared death. People long dead. They're still alive in the picture. The brushstrokes are just done and drying. I like to think of them and their painting day, the arrangements, the travel, the easel. It's ..." He looked for the word.

"Completely thrilling," Vita offered. "A kind of time travel."

Johnnie offered her something in return, one of his special and exclusive smiles.

"Mog and I were in the National often, in Edinburgh," he said. "Many, many happy hours." He took a handful of peanuts and tossed them into his mouth one at a time.

Henry handed Mog another drink. Gin and tonic. No bubbles remained in the tonic. Henry kept it in the bookcase.

"He'd pin postcards up on a board, ones I chose, and get me to talk him through them," Mog said, continuing to talk to the carpet.

"But that reflects well on both of you," Euan said. "Surely."

"You sound so unhappy," Johnnie told her, his voice without emotion. "I'm sorry if I'm the cause of that."

"Don't flatter yourself."

"As I recall they were happy times, mutually enthusiastic. But forgive me if I haven't given the tutorial aspects better credit."

Mog looked at him. "What are you *doing* here?"

"I came to see you," Johnnie said. "But you refuse to hear me out."

"I'm not interested in anything you have to say," Mog told him.

Johnnie smiled towards Euan and Joan. "Do you know that I proposed marriage? I proposed and I was refused by text message. By *text message*. Mog's refused to talk to me since."

"I'm so very sorry to hear that," Euan said.

"Oh no," Joan said, putting her hand to her forehead.

Mrs Welsh came in and said that the supper was laid out ready and that they should come through. They seated themselves in the dining room. Joan had provided name cards, and Ottilie found that she had been placed at the other end of the table to Ursula. They'd been seated on the same side so that they didn't have to see or hear each other: an arrangement that Joan described as *enemy positions*.

Mrs Hammill, glorious in a vast blue taffeta tent, had a hip flask secreted away in her evening bag. She wasn't always discreet about dipping into it.

"Well, this is terribly nice," she said.

"Yes, isn't it; no Jet, though." Pip was helping himself to soup. He looked around. "And no Izzy either."

Euan had made the gazpacho with too much garlic, and not chopped up enough for Vita, who chewed each spoonful gamely. Henry confined himself to toast, which he tore off a mouthful at a time, spreading each slice thickly with cold butter.

"I called in on Jet earlier," Edith said. "But he wasn't feeling at all well. He's terribly pale. I worry about him, keeping so much to himself."

It was a sombre sort of table. Mrs Hammill slurping her soup, adding more sherry to it. Vita lost in her own thoughts. Edith talking to Pip about the bank.

"Pip and I have been decorating," Angelica said to Joan. "You must come down and see."

"I can't imagine that," Edith said. "Pip with a wallpaper brush."

"You misunderstand, Mother," Joan said, sharing a half-smile with Angelica. "They got the decorators in."

Vita was looking flustered. "At my flat, she means," Pip said to her, leaning into her ear. "At my apartment in Edinburgh."

"But when are you to marry, Peter?" If it was "Peter" it must be serious.

"It's our apartment, it's to be ours when we do, so I've been helping choose the furnishings," Angelica explained. Vita was protected from the scandalous fact of their having lived together for over a year. Her libertarianism was largely theoretical, set aside for the past.

"Well, hurry up and choose a date. I want a great-great-grandchild before I go."

"You'll outlive all of us," Pip soothed.

"It's awful, not knowing when," she said to him. "Every morning has a question mark in it. I'm not afraid of death itself, because that's nothingness, like the time before birth, but pain, yes. I'm afraid very much of pain. I don't want to be frightened. I'm frightened of being frightened."

"Oh, Mother, you don't give it a moment's thought," Edith said. "Please don't drink any more wine."

"So this is where you're all hiding." Izzy came into the room, Terry trailing a little shyly. "Hello everyone, hello, hello. Oh, we're seated formally, lovely. I won't have to exchange any more stiff pleasantries with Terry: what a relief."

Terry cuffed her gently around the head.

"I'm not kidding, that time it really hurt," she said, rubbing the place. She cast her eye around the company as she took her seat. "Goodness. Did anybody else die? No? Good. I hate to miss things."

She turned to Henry. "Sorry about being late. Traffic. Masses of traffic. Terry shook his fist at it but it didn't seem to help."

"You're forgiven," Henry said.

"So tell me, somebody, do. What've I missed? Scandals? News? No? That's very boring of you all. Does anyone know a really filthy joke?"

"Izzy," Euan said in his admonitory voice.

"Euan," she returned in the same tone. She scanned the table again. "We're all looking very overdressed and uncomfortable, that's good, that's very good, bodes well. And Johnnie's still here, I see. We haven't set the dogs on him yet."

"He's Ursula's guest," Edith told her quietly.

Johnnie succeeded in catching Euan's eye. "I bought a copy of Membrane."

Euan was surprised. "Where on earth did you find it?"

"I ordered it from your publisher online. I liked the poem 'Meniscus' very much. *The unseen line, the unseen door, the happy blindness of the day; processing sightless the imagined road.*"

Euan tried and failed to prevent himself from looking pleased. "I've just finished the new collection. Auto-Didact."

"Ursula's been reciting bits of Paradise Lost to me," Johnnie said. "It's staggeringly beautiful."

An uncertainty crossed Euan's face. "You are staying at the inn, though?"

"I'm staying at the inn. Three nights. I've booked a table at L'Assiette for Sunday. I'm hoping Mog will consent to dinner. Dinner at the least."

"I'm not going to have dinner with you," Mog said.

"That's stupid," Joan piped up.

"At least hear him out," Euan said.

"Look, I brought the ring with me," Johnnie said, producing a black velvet box from his pocket.

"He's lying to you, he didn't propose," Mog said. "He just likes to play games with people."

"Oh honestly, Mog," Joan said.

"He didn't propose; I challenged him about something and he hit me with a chair."

"Hit you with a chair?" Joan couldn't help giggling.

"For crying out loud," Euan said.

"It was an accident," Johnnie said. "Of course, though technically she's absolutely right. We'd been to a dance and went back to mine, and I was trying to pass a chair over the kitchen table, avoiding the candles, and it hit the light fitting and broke it, and cack-handedly I dropped the chair and it hit Mog on the head. I've said sorry a hundred times. The thing she challenged me about, by the way, was that I was only after her money."

Joan clapped her hand to her mouth. "Oh no. That's the funniest thing."

"We had a row. About my being a gold-digger." He rotated his expensive watch on his wrist. "Well, I don't have to tell all of you, it's not exactly the likeliest scenario. She's been unwell. We won't dwell on that now: you know about her unwellness. I was just trying to move a kitchen chair across the table, and broke the light fitting, and got a jolt, and the chair flew out of my hand and knocked her flying. I've apologised and apologised and I don't know what else I can do."

"Well, quite," Euan said. "It's hard to know."

"The thing is, that I love her, heart and soul," Johnnie said. "I love her and I want to spend the rest of my life with her." He looked imploringly towards Mog. "My proposal still stands. I think that it will always stand, whatever happens."

"Oh that's lovely, isn't that lovely?" Joan said.

Johnnie opened the box and a vast shiny ring sparkled out of the dark plush interior. There were general gasps of appreciation.

"Do I have to go down on one knee?" Johnnie said. "I've come all this way to do this. I want to get it right." He slid off his chair and into position.

Mog looked at the open box, at the vast and sparkling rock. "I recognise it: it's his brother's girlfriend's ring" she said.

"It may be similar," Johnnie said, looking at it more closely. He closed the box. "Well, that's put me in my place." He got up onto his feet again. "Goodness. This is embarrassing."

"Oh, Mog; *Mog*," Joan said, sounding ashamed.

Euan put his cutlery down with a clatter.

Johnnie stood up. "I'm sorry, I think I should leave."

"Please don't," Euan urged him. "I'm so sorry about this scene. It's very unfortunate."

"Yes, isn't it," Izzy said.

Now Ottilie was on her feet, and was pointing with her wine glass at Euan. "Why would you do that, why? Side with someone so dubious against your own child? You're such an irredeemable arsehole."

Johnnie excused himself and swept out. Pip followed him, saying he was no longer hungry. He went down the back stairs to the yard and found Johnnie waiting for him there.

"Come to challenge me to a duel?"

Pip took his cigarettes out. "Come to smoke," he said.

"Pistols or swords?"

Pip looked closely at the packet. "Filter-tipped, I think."

"Wanker," Johnnie said, curling his lip and turning away, then turning back again. "It was true, by the way, about the chair. I don't know what story she told you. But that's how it was. Sorry to disillusion."

"Mog's not a liar."

"Depressed, though. And attention seeking. Good story I'm sure. Unstable boyfriend with a violent streak."

"Your words, not mine. Why did you come here?"

"I was invited."

"Oh, come off it."

"Mog wrote a letter and I wanted right of reply. But she won't hear me out. I'm going away to write it instead. It will be long and forlorn."

"But you're already hooked up with someone else, aren't you. That's the truth of the matter. You're already sleeping with someone else. Why play these weird games?"

"A person has to find his entertainment where he can," Johnnie said, as if sincerely.

"I think you're the one who's a trifle unwell, mate," Pip responded.

Johnnie looked disgusted. "Oh, fuck off. You're so arse-numbingly *boring*."

"Okay then," Pip said, turning away, then swivelling back to say, "Mog tells me you spent your childhood in foster homes and I'm sorry for you."

Johnnie was shaking his head. "Just part of her myth of me, I'm afraid to say. My mother's still alive and she's a doctor. Sorry."

"I particularly liked the term spent being unimpressed by Harvard, and the charity walk in Nepal."

"The charity walk's for real. Don't diss that. Don't you dare. Those children in the hospice. Wanker." Johnnie was already walking away, his middle finger raised above his head.

Izzy found Mog in the linen room after dinner.

"Everybody's worried about you down there," she said.

"Are they? That's nice."

"What now?"

"Now, nothing. Now, hiding. Tomorrow, keeping a low profile. The day after, skulking about the house. The day after that, forced jollity. That's the usual pattern, isn't it? I wouldn't want to let anybody down."

"It wasn't that bad."

"Huh."

"You shout, they shout back. It's how it goes."

"I always feel like I'm in the wrong. Especially when I'm right."

"It's because you get emotional. That gives them ammunition." She got up. "Come on."

"Where are we going?"

"To see Ursula. She insisted on going back to the cottage, had the screaming abdabs. Dad was all for locking her in, or rather locking out He Who Shall Not Be Named, but Gran wasn't having it. She called the inn about an hour ago and spoke to Johnnie, apologising for the ruckus. Really, it was her way of checking he'd gone back to the village."

"So why are we going to see her?"

"Just checking. Said I'd check."

The grass was saturated and cold, their feet damp and the world tranquil. The stable block, greenhouses and garden walls: all looked foreign in the dusk, the grey sky streaked with flashes of gold. They ran through the orchard, where fallen early apples like small round rocks were bruising under their soles, and where they disturbed an owl that in its haste flew right at them, almost colliding with Izzy, before emerging onto the lane. One of the cottages was brightly lit but it wasn't Ursula's. The Dixons' house, too, was all in darkness. It was the holidaymakers who were up and uncurtained, their harshly lit sitting room revealing a man in an armchair reading a book, and a woman standing talking to him holding a map. Jet's curtains were closed but illuminated by the unsteady blue light of a bedroom television. All was quiet at Ursula's cottage. The shadows at the side of the sitting-room curtains were uneven, and then the unevenness was revealed as a person, and the person was revealed as Johnnie. Mog hung back and let Izzy go forward. Mog went and crouched behind the hedge, listening.

The door opened before Izzy could knock.

"Hello there; want a drink?" Johnnie's voice.

"No," Izzy said. "What I want, what all of us want is for you to go back to the inn right now. You shouldn't be here. Go back to the inn and go home in the morning. You're not welcome here."

"This is disappointingly dreary."

"Where's Ursula?" Izzy pushed past him into the kitchen. "Ursula?"

"What?" a bad-tempered voice responded from upstairs.

"Are you alright?"

"That's a stupid question. What do you want? Go away."

"I'm taking Johnnie with me," Izzy shouted back.

Silence.

"It's all about not making a fuss," Izzy told Johnnie, speaking more quietly. She could hear Ursula coming down the stairs, a step at a time. "You're the latest thing not to make a fuss about. But everyone will be relieved when Sunday comes and you're gone. You are going on Sunday, aren't you?"

"Yes."

"You haven't booked a table at L'Assiette, then."

"I haven't," he conceded.

There was a noise from within, a human noise, a small explosion of dissent, and Ursula appeared, striding past Johnnie and ignoring Izzy and making off towards the house.

"Though that may be an unpopular decision," Johnnie said, and then brightly, "Can I interest you in a nightcap?"

Izzy produced a key from her pocket. "I'm going to close the door now and lock it, so if you have anything of yours here you had better get it now."

"Fine, fine," Johnnie said, putting up his hands and stepping out into the garden, onto the lane and towards the village.

❧

Izzy went to play cards with Ursula in the kitchen and make bacon sandwiches, and Mog went to the drawing room, hearing Rebecca's voice coming from that direction. She stopped outside the half-open door, listening. Pip was talking now.

"They never got along. Ottilie disapproved of him as a husband for Mum, and Mum thought she was jealous. It was much worse when Michael went."

"How's that?"

"He won't ever be forgiven, for things he said to Ottilie on the day."

"What things?"

"That it was Ottilie's fault that he'd gone," Pip said. "That she wasn't a good enough mother, not attentive enough."

Mog went into the room. She told Pip that she needed to talk to him, and Rebecca absented herself immediately.

"About Johnnie," Pip began, but Mog cut him off.

"It's not about Johnnie. I want to talk to you some more about the picture, and about Alan." As she was speaking she was closing the door, returning to sit by him at the fireside.

"What do you want to do?"

"I think we should tell Henry."

"I could tell him on the phone. In person he'll be shocked and will probably shut down. Might be better on the phone."

"On the phone? For heaven's sake."

"That's how it is. There are things that Henry can say to me, in the early hours."

"How early?"

"This insomnia of his is a real problem. Sometimes it's five in the morning when he rings and often he hasn't yet slept. I tell him that I'm awake then, in the summer when it's light, that I like getting to the office early. It's worth it. I don't mind."

"I didn't know he had trouble sleeping."

"He hides it well, even from Edith."

"In the same room."

"It's been a problem for a long time. He barely sleeps at night."

"I didn't know."

"You know where Henry is, the afternoons we think he's out on the hill? Asleep, usually. Can only sleep in the daylight. Curls up on the sofa in the study, locks the door."

"I thought the locked door meant he was out."

"Everybody does. But that's the point. When he comes in at teatime looking so tired with stories from the hill, sometimes they're true but generally they're invented. Henry, I've discovered, can tell a story. He's tired because he's just waking up. Sets his phone alarm for a quarter to four."

"And Edith doesn't know this? How could she not know?"

"He doesn't think she does, but let's be real, what are the odds?"

Joan came into the room holding a glass of red wine. "I need to speak to you, to the two of you." She shut the door behind her.

"What is it?" Pip asked wearily.

"Your father went to the pub, after the scene at dinner. He was upset." Her eyes rested momentarily on Mog. "He's just phoned me. Alan was there. Alan said he'd met Johnnie at the loch this afternoon. Johnnie and Ursula together."

"What about it?"

"Alan was thrilled to pass on the news to your father that Johnnie was asking Ursula about Michael. Mog, did you confide in Johnnie? I need honesty and a straight answer."

"No, of course not."

"Not even a hint?"

"No."

"That's odd, because Johnnie said to Ursula that you thought he was dead."

"I brought him here. I brought Johnnie here in the spring. We talked a bit about Michael going missing, possible solutions to the mystery. We all talk that like to people."

"I don't."

"No, Mother," Pip interjected. "We know."

"You brought Johnnie here? Why didn't you say? Why didn't I get to meet him?"

"You weren't here," Mog told her. "You were off shopping. And all I said to him was that we thought Michael had gone out to the wolf."

"For god's sake, not that again."

"It's the kind of thing we say all the time to people," Pip said, raising his voice. "That we suspect it may have been suicide. It would be odder not to talk about it, in my opinion."

Joan said, "But you see, my darlings, Johnnie asked Ursula what *she* thought."

"What did she say?"

"She said she wasn't able to talk about it, that she'd promised not to. Which is tantamount to a confession."

"What are you going to do?"

"We need to keep them apart. Johnnie and Ursula. There'll be a rota for tomorrow and for tomorrow evening, and she'll sleep here until he's gone."

Chapter 20

The first person to be up and about on Saturday morning was Edith. She'd been into the village and back by the time the others emerged in pyjamas and bathrobes, foraging for breakfast. She'd gone to church early to be there alone, walking like a ghost through the village before anyone else was around, creaking the door of St Ninian's open, its small usual noises amplified by the silence of the street so early in the day.

"I don't know what I'm hoping for," she told the altar. "It's hard even to know what the question is."

St Ninian's was built and endowed by the first Henry Salter, and the family has always held a proprietorial key. Ninian was the first missionary to come to Scotland, well before the publicity-grabbing Columba, and Henry One, as he's known, went down to Whithorn to the site of the saint's first church, joining the pilgrims at Ninian's cave, a journey that he made after the visit to Peattie of the so-called witch. Edith had always enjoyed the family association with the church, its walls full of plaques and markers, but of late she'd begun to feel nervous about being there for services: so much anti-Salter feeling seemed to be erupting out of nowhere, and her continuing attendance, sitting alone in the family pew like some kind of representative of all that was wrong with the past, like some unfortunate and freakish survival, was becoming a matter of dread at Sunday breakfast. It wasn't only that. Recent events, conversations that had turned into events, were making it impossible to conjure up that old Edith, that old Edith/church relationship that had been the basis of her life, the rock on which she'd built an achieved state almost of contentment, putting herself dizzyingly into the perspective of centuries, leading through paragraphs of other lives in other generations to her own. Edith was beginning to see that a period of grieving was upon her – she recognised its heaviness in her stomach. It didn't any longer seem obvious that she and St Ninian's, even if stripped back of its politics, its political spin, would always love and understand one another.

She walked back to Peattie with a troubled heart, made more troubled by the fact that it was her birthday, that there was to be a party, that she was to be the centre of attention and subject to close scrutiny. The day required an adoption of false jollity: there was no choice. She came into the kitchen exclaiming her good mornings to all and was greeted by a chorus of happy birthday wishes. She carried the scent of church with her into the room, its spray polish and damp stone and the foetid sweetness of holiness. She'd been exchanging the flower arrangements for blooms cut fresh from Peattie's garden.

Once presents had been given and opened, Mog said that she'd go into the village and get the shopping. She put the rucksack on her back – a tattered old thing, dark green and worn and frayed, that was in use for this purpose even when I was a child – and took Edith's list and went off on the bike. Her father turned up at the shop just after her, buying groceries for the gatehouse. "You left before I could give you my list," he complained. He put his basket on the freezer counter and stood to face her. "Mary. We need to have a talk."

"What is it? Is something wrong?"

"Your mother has just told me that you've resigned, that you're moving in with Edith and Henry and having some kind of a career break."

"She's only just told you?"

"I think you'll find that's not the point. But since you bring it up, you should have told me. You know how your mother is. You should have realised she'd tell me only when she was ready to."

"I'm sorry; I didn't think."

She could see it now: the news kept aside, kept in the quiver with all the other arrows, until the perfect moment announced itself. *Mog didn't mention it? I've known for over a week.*

"No, well, thinking's not something you're known for, is it?" her father said, his face betraying its secret hurt but his mouth continuing sarcastically.

"Sorry."

"Thinking. Not something you've ever really gone in for much."

"It's all very new – the decision, I mean. I wasn't even really sure."

Her announcement of the plan to her mother had also taken place in the shop. The timing had been less than ideal. Pip says she's like one of those pheasants that sit in the verge and wait for a car to come by before they rush across the road just in front of it. The confession wasn't planned but the village store, crowded with a coach party and noisy and ordinary, had seemed quite suddenly like the ideal venue. The explosion came, but within those four walls and between chattering Japanese people buying bottles of water and postcards it was controlled, smothered, *whoomph*.

Her mother had gone quiet. That was her way. Quietness first, a quiet metabolising, before coming up with her response. When it was delivered, finally, it came in whole and prepared paragraphs, its rebuttals built in, already anticipating others' responses.

Euan's reaction, however, was immediate. "You're a fool."

"Oh – thanks, Dad. Thanks for all the support."

"You are. Work in the hotel, are you mad? Really, Mary. What on earth is going on with you? I barely recognise you in these decisions."

"I'm not intending it to be permanent. I need a change of pace for a bit. I have other things I want to do."

"Writing, you mean. Bloody stupid idea." He opened the chill cabinet with unnecessary force. "No money in it. And precious little point."

The chill cabinet was slammed shut again, *whap*. Mog followed him down the aisle and he talked to her over his shoulder. "It's all rejection and heartache, Mary. Thousands, hundreds of thousands of you chasing the same little slots. Rejection, self-doubt and unpaid bills."

"Some people have to succeed. There's no reason that it shouldn't be me."

"No reason? I could give you a hundred reasons."

"Go on then. A hundred reasons."

"Don't be cheeky."

"Don't be cheeky? I'm almost 30."

"I can give you the reason that matters most. You don't have the talent for it. Harsh words, but there you are. Better to know the truth now than to struggle."

"How would you know? Really, how? Have you read anything I've written in the last ten years?"

"And the other thing is, it's all nepotism. This is what you don't understand. People who get published – they're people with contacts, with family in there, friends giving them a leg-up."

"They can't all be."

Euan selected a newspaper and folded it under his arm. "You need a profession. You need structure. I'm all for having a break, but the hotel! That's a waste of your time. A waste of a good brain. I can't bear it. I can't." He rifled through the bags of bread, looking for the palest rolls. Joan would send them back if they were too brown. "Promise me you'll consider the college. I'll get a prospectus sent on to you. And don't talk about writing, for pity's sake. Please. Just drop it."

"I need to try or I'm always going to wonder. I have enough money saved."

"You need to have a good long think about what it is that interests you, really interests you, and start working towards that." He put his packet of butter, the carton of milk, the newspaper and bag of morning rolls decisively onto the counter. It was the newspaper she worked for. Used to work for. Both of them stared at it.

"I knew that job was a mistake. I told you. I told you, didn't I? But you wouldn't have it. You're so bloody stubborn. Never wrong, you're never bloody wrong." And then, without a pause, "Yes, morning Mrs Pym; fine, thanks; yes, really peculiar weather."

That was when Mog walked away, turning and giving him her most wounded look. She left the shop and kept walking, forgetting all about the bicycle.

"Oh yes, there she goes, typical," he called after her, coming to the door.

Edith and Pip were on the terrace. Edith was working her way along the urns, dead-heading flowers and evicting sprouting weeds. Pip was using his phone to reply to email.

"I've been thinking about Michael a good deal this week," Edith said, unearthing a dandelion by the root and discarding it.

"Me too," Pip replied absent-mindedly.

"It's because we have visitors, I suppose."

"And his name has been mentioned a lot," Pip added.

Edith stopped what she was doing and turned to him, her hands in floral garden gloves. "Has it?"

"Don't worry," Pip said blandly, frowning at his screen. "All fine. Nothing to worry about."

Edith dropped her secateurs and went into the house at a rush, fumbling with the door handle. Pip stared after her, then followed. He heard the ballroom door opening and closing, its particular whoosh and metallic definitive click. He found Edith in there, already on her way out, opening the French windows that lead back onto the terrace.

"It occurred to me to air the room for the party," she said. "I don't know if your Joan had it on there – your mother, I mean – on the list for today."

"You're upset."

"It was the way you said that. I felt suddenly like ... like a conspirator."

"Well, that can't be helped," Pip said reasonably. "And look. The conspiracy, such as it is, is protective of someone and not damaging to another. So it was the right decision. On one side, protective, and on the other, unable to make anything worse. It didn't make Michael any more dead."

"Oh, Pip. *Pip.*"

"I'm sorry – that was rather crudely put. But please, please, let's try not to romanticise it. Let's hold onto the facts. Those facts."

"Yes."

They returned outside. Edith leaned against the balustrade and Pip stood beside her.

"I've been having the most vivid dreams," Edith told him. "Exhausting dreams. Things from the past, the deep past, some of them. Things I feel as if I'm witnessing, that feel true."

"Like?"

"Even though I wasn't there. Ursa and Jo for instance, the accident." She shivered. "As if I was in the car with them. The lorry on the wrong side of the road. Ursa swerving away and then –"

"Don't."

"It's so real, it feels so real. I've been through a long period of things not seeming as real as that. It feels new; the sharpness of it."

"It's because Alastair's here."

"I know. I know; you're right."

"It will all settle down again on Monday when everyone's gone."

"I'm dreading Monday."

"Please don't cry. Please don't. It's your birthday."

"I was fine earlier. I was happy. I walked home from church feeling anxious, but then I saw you all in the kitchen and decided everything was going to be fine."

"It will be."

"I feel as if something has started that can't be stopped."

"What on earth, why would you feel that?"

"I should be happy. But I feel this … this terrible dread."

"I can stay on for a couple of days if you like. And Mog will be here. Mog will be here with you for probably a whole year – think of that. You're going to love it."

She dried her eyes. "I know. You're right."

Pip squeezed her hand. "What on earth is it? I wish you'd tell me."

"I'm stirred up, that's all."

"I think we all are."

She turned to look at him. "Really? Are we? Are we together in this?"

"Of course. And it will settle. Things will go back to their lovely quiet ploddy state very soon."

"But I keep seeing this image, Pip. You will think me very foolish. I think I'm very foolish. I'd be the first to say so. It's a glider, gliding behind the plane, and when the string or whatever is cut, when the line is released, the glider swoops down and crashes and breaks and bounces along and it's all silent, no sound at all."

"You're feeling the strain."

"I keep seeing this. It comes into my head. It's not even a dream. I can't wake up from it, Pip."

"It will pass. These things always pass."

"It's how I feel about Monday. I won't be able to ... I don't think I can carry on."

"Mog will be here though."

Fresh tears fell.

"What on earth is it? Is there anything I can do?"

"There's something I need to tell you."

"Okay."

"I told someone."

"You told someone what?"

"I told Susan Marriott. About Michael."

"About Michael what?"

"About Michael. About the loch."

"About the loch."

"Yes. The loch, Ursula, the day. The accident."

"Oh god."

"I know, I'm sorry."

"Oh no. You didn't. Tell me you didn't. About Ursula?"

"Yes. Everything."

"I can't believe it. After all this time. What on earth made you do that?" His voice was heroically unexcited. "I can't believe it. Why would you?"

"I don't know. I had to. I'm sorry. I tried to take it back. I rang her and said I'd been idiotic. I'm not sure what she thinks of me now, and what she believes. Our friendship has come to an end. But I trust her. I do trust her."

"Right."

"You're angry with me."

"I think it was a mistake."

"Also, I'm becoming a Catholic."

"What? Where did that come from?"

"I have no one to talk to, Pip."

"And that has anything to do with anything because?"

"I'm so sorry about Susan. You're angry. We'll talk about it another time."

"Another time?" He laughed mirthlessly, and leaned down, hands on the balustrade. "Oh shit."

"Susan's a Catholic," Edith explained. "No – that's not the reason. But I needed to know from her what would happen if I told the priest."

"About Ursula killing Michael."

"Please lower your voice."

"You needed to know that it would stay in the confessional."

"Yes."

"And?"

"She didn't know. About – about something like this."

"What if Susan decides it's her duty to tell someone? Or can't help herself confiding in a friend, and then they feel they have to report it? What about Ursula? I thought Ursula came first."

"I think I wanted to be punished. I think I wanted Susan to ring the police. At the moment I told her, I mean. But she surprised me completely. I told her what happened and she said that she would have done exactly the same."

"Well, that's something."

"It started in hospital," Edith said. "Wanting someone to tell. Lying there on my own a lot. Don't look like that. I don't blame Henry for not coming. Henry's Henry and that's that. It wasn't that. Lying in hospital, knowing I might die, all I could think about was Michael and how we handled things."

"We all think about it, all the time, believe me. I don't think I've ever had a conversation with Mog that hasn't come back to it in some way. Seriously."

351

"It was wrong, Pip."

"There wasn't any choice," Pip said. "You didn't feel like you had any choice. We all get that. We understand it."

"Will you tell? Tell the others, what I've done?"

"I won't tell the others anything. Sometimes keeping quiet is the best policy. If we keep quiet it may all blow over and be nothing."

By six o'clock that evening, Joan's plans had all reached fruition. Out in the flower garden, a trestle table spread with a red gingham cloth was laden with the kind of food that a television cook thinks children like, and plastic jugs heavy with ice had been filled with fresh juices, a pastel-fruit array of them, jugs topped by fly-nets weighted by polished pebbles. The weedy profusion of the flower garden was at its most successful point of the growing year, its most convincingly apparently designed, the weeds forming a soft green backdrop to flowers in drifts. The white lilac was out, late flowering after a cold spring, and the backs of the borders glowed shell pink with plate-sized black-hearted poppies. Waterproof-backed rugs had been spread around, and books, toys and musical instruments had been left sitting in strategic piles. A nanny hired for the occasion had prepared the cut-potato printing, a pass-the-parcel package, the paddling pool for hook-a-duck. She was wearing jeans and cowboy boots and a man's pale blue shirt knotted at the front, sunglasses ready on the top of her head, and seemed the most relaxed of anyone: relaxed and voluble and patently used to being in charge.

Over the stile, beside the most photogenic of Peattie's threatened meadows, cushions had been positioned encircling the fire pit. I dug out this fire pit, lined it with stones and created the stone slab seating around the edge, for my

352

19th-birthday party. Henry wasn't impressed, or so I heard via Vita, who reported that the word *vandalism* had been mentioned. We disagreed, Henry and I, about heritage and fun – the two seemed often to be at odds with one another. Henry had argued that he was merely the custodian. "You're not just a custodian," I'd told him. "This is your life. This is your house. You can do what you like with it. What would you like to do with it? Do some of it." (Henry looking appropriately blank.)

Inside the great hall, Gail the coat attendant was reading a magazine, seated at a table upon which stood rows of glasses of steadily warming and flattening champagne. Joan had already been in, irritably, to complain that she had pre-poured, instead of keeping the bottles in the ice beneath the table until needed, as instructed. White fairy lights led the way along the passage towards the picture gallery, and the ropes of heavier coloured globes Mog and Rebecca had fixed up marked the children's route, through the gothic studded door (wedged open tonight with a warming iron) and down the stairs into the flower garden. Gail was supposed to telephone the nanny in the garden on her mobile – Joan had provided the phones – to come and fetch those who were known to be or appeared to be under the age of 13. Some of these children, refusing to comply, had decamped en masse to the ballroom. Joan's decision not to use it for the evening proved the right one; there's something persistently cheerless about its great size and grandeur, its murals and gilt. A gang of small girls, clad every one as fairies or princesses in slightly too-large-dressing-up clothes, was running and sliding in white ankle socks and making the most of the echo.

Joan was in the hall, her smile looking fixed. A number of guests had failed to be funnelled along the passage and had clotted there, ignoring Joan's brightly bossy invocations, urging them to move further on, further in, and carried on regardless, chatting and clogging. When Joan turned defeated to leave, her muttered "for god's own sake" wasn't quite as discreet as she'd hoped.

Izzy and friends had lit a fire. They had been supplied with skewers and marshmallows by her mother, and potatoes for baking ready-wrapped in foil. There were tupperware boxes of potato fillings and salad, and butter wrapped up with a freezer block, and a basket with paper plates and napkins and cutlery. Shrink-wrapped tubes of interlocking plastic waited to be assembled into wine glasses, and instructions had been penned on a pink file card, detailing which of the fridges they were to go to for the allotted white wine and beer. A music system had been rigged up to work from a battery pack, and in the broad-leaf trees surrounding, Ottilie and Mog had installed many little glass jars bearing tea-light candles, wired into the branches. The summeriness of all this was somewhat at odds with the poor light levels and chill. There was worry about the weather. A persistent lead-grey hat of cloud, ragged already in the distance with its delivery of rain, had settled over the valley in the late afternoon.

By eight o'clock the rain began to fall, first with a wet sudden spotting like paint flicked from a brush, and then in a sky-opening, sheeting bucketing roar, a slow roll of thunder accompanying it. Children fled the garden in groups under picnic rugs held up by their corners, a system put in place under the nanny's orders. Izzy and friends retreated under the trees, impromptu cocktails in hand. The bottles of white wine and beer, lying post-it-note-adorned on their shelves, languished unopened, thanks to friends from the surrounding villages who had turned up in numbers with off-licence bags of spirits and mixers.

Sandy the fiddler had embarked on a programme of dance tunes in the main part of the picture gallery, which had been cleared of its bigger furnishings; they'd been pushed and dragged into the narrower section towards the hall, and the smaller pieces of furniture had been removed altogether. Now, with its rugs rolled up, this broad space with its springy wood floor was as good a place to have a ceilidh as any in the world. The dancing had begun, and four sets of eight weaved around each other in practised serpentine tracks, turning and turning again.

Joan came to stand beside Edith. "Your friend called. Susan. To say she isn't coming because she doesn't feel very well."

"Thanks for letting me know."

In the drawing room two uniformed waiters, elegant in black and white with red cummerbunds and rosebud buttonholes that had been provided by Joan, were restocking the drinks tables and circulating with trays of finger food, portions of delicious things in miniature and tiny filo-pastry parcels. The tables were laid with blue plaid cloths, and garlands of the same fabric had been strung festively across the ceiling and along the cornices, bunched and clasped with bouquets of gilded leaves. The plaid was the same fabric that had been used for Edith's going-away outfit after her wedding, 52 years ago on this day. Credit must be given to Joan for Edith's being moved, genuinely so, by this, her heart touched by the scale of the effort and its kindness. The tapers in the great silver candelabra had been lit, and twinkle lights delineated the edges of windows and doors. Everything glowed more diffusely in the watery grey light the rainstorm had brought.

Edith saw that Thomas had arrived, looking very slight in his old suit. He raised a hand to her across the room, his expression indeterminate.

The drawing room looked very different that night: not only in styling but in shape. Its size had been doubled by opening up the false wall, one made up of quadruple wallpapered doors that folded back into an adjoining, secondary drawing room that was used only rarely because it was draughty and its fireplace smoked. Joan had papered its dowdy walls, which had been oil-painted a pale yellow at some point in the past and had acquired a hospital look. The paper revealed itself as the same blue plaid, which had been stretched tight and fixed with studs. It was decorated with many old mirrors from other rooms, their glass panels draped with more fairy lights and garlands of dried white hydrangea. The food had been laid out there on a row of white-clothed tables. Big pans of kedgeree (being cooked up even now by Mrs Welsh, under Euan's instruction) were to be served there at midnight – hours earlier than the dawn breakfasts of old – as a soaker-up of alcohol and a signal that the party was over.

The new arrivals, having circled and admired the double drawing room, having tasted the miniature tarts laid out appetisingly on their platters, the prawn toast triangles, the quail eggs, the buttery mouthfuls of shortbread (that Joan had stayed up till the early hours making, having ditched Ursula's singed, Christmassy efforts), now made their way, drinks in hand, back to the picture gallery. The dance had been lit by a succession of warmly tinted bulbs, which made the faces of the participants glow as rosy as a pink dusk.

Thomas came across, extricating himself from ex-parishioners, to wish Edith a happy birthday. He produced a box about six inches square, wrapped in newsprint and tied up with string. He and Edith went into the hall together, away from the noise, and Edith opened the box. Inside there was a snow globe, a very old-looking one of heavy glass. The house inside the dome might almost have been Peattie, surrounded by idealised hills. When she upended and then returned the globe to the upright, the snow drifted down around the house in slow, twirling flakes. Edith found she had tears in her eyes. She said that she was feeling overheated, and went out onto the terrace, saying to Thomas that she'd come and find him in a little while. The rain had turned into a sort of tepid wet mist. Out on the terrace, she mimed her overheatedness, flapping at the top hem of her dress to allow the air to pass in. Her dress, she said to Euan, who was looking at her doing this, was a lovely thing but rather too warm; it was a thick velvet, and a lovely sea green, and it had been Henry's favourite, a long time ago. She'd worn it hoping it would take them back to an old day, reuniting them for a moment in remembering a happy evening they'd spent once: she'd worn the dress, and Sebastian had been safely tucked up in bed at home. But Henry had seemed to be put out by her wearing it. He'd seemed annoyed.

The terrace was lined with ashtrays tonight along its balustrade, and wine tables had been placed along it at intervals, bearing drinks and snacks for those who, as Joan knew from experience, would come out here for a smoke earlyish in the proceedings, find congenial company among other exiles and fail to return indoors. Enamel buckets dressed with ivy and filled with crushed ice bore bottles of fizzy wine and water; whisky bottles and tumblers had been placed alongside. Among the likely members of the smoking sub-group were some of Henry's oldest friends, and he was keen to provide for them. Some of these people he hadn't seen since Sebastian died. They, the longest-lost, adjourned to the study with him when the rain came, promising themselves a private catch-up out of the fray, but finding, once installed there, that conversation proved elusive. When the past presents so much that's forbidden, that's non-traversable, the present becomes just as intangible. So little could be talked about that stayed clear of Sebastian and the years of social withdrawal that had followed. Which is how it came to pass that half a dozen septuagenarians who hadn't come together for over 35 years were discussing land prices and local politics with slightly too much heartiness.

Once the rain shower had slowed to a drizzle, Izzy and some of the friends (the ones Joan had invited) emerged damply from tree shelter and came into the house, Izzy turning heads in a white column of a dress that draped from a halter-neck to her bare brown feet, her hair coiled in plaits around her head. She and her party brought an unforced jollity, brought the scent of outdoors and summer rain into the drawing room with them. They took bottles of wine from the trough beneath the table and, producing one of the plastic columns of glasses, went and occupied the window seat. Mog and Rebecca, each dressed in black, joined them there. Ottilie, wearing a grey silk patterned darker with leaves, could be seen moving among the older generation of guests who'd seated themselves in the newly renovated side of the drawing room, away from the worst of the crush and the noise. She had part-closed the folding doors to ensure greater quiet, ignoring Joan's demand that she put them back as they were.

"This isn't about the photograph," Ottilie told her.

"What photograph? What are you talking about?"

"The one in your head. The one House and Garden would take."

Joan stepped forward as if she'd push one of the doors back anyway, but Ottilie was there first and with a steely look took hold of the partition firmly in two hands. Joan wasn't about to engage in a physical struggle. Once her sister had retreated Ottilie went to sit for a while beside Christian's parents, chatting to them and fetching drinks for their neighbours.

Edith had been persuaded by Thomas to dance, albeit in a highly self-conscious way, moving stiffly and watching the door for sightings of Henry. Vita watched them, banging her stick to the rhythm, Sandy's fiddle singing its mellifluous up-and-down song. His son Angus, arriving late from Inverness thanks to a delayed train, joined in mid-reel on his accordion. Mrs Hammill was circulating, in her gracious-hostess way, welcoming people to Peattie and looking even now a little the worse for wear. Joan was now hovering close by the waiters' table, supervising and looking very thin in a silvery knee-length dress, one that looked as if made out of fish scales. Jet had appeared for five minutes to gather up other sons and loners and had borne them off with the promise of better music, though one of them had already returned with one of Jet's t-shirts, opening it out on the food table and stacking its central area efficiently, before gathering it up and bearing it carefully away again.

When Pip and Angelica went into the kitchen for glasses of water, they found Ursula there. They made a striking-looking couple, standing together at the kitchen door: Pip immaculate in probable Armani, Angelica serene and trim in the dark green dress and heavy jet jewellery that had been Henry's mother's. Ursula had wedged herself into the corner between the stove and the door. She would say only that she hated Johnnie, that she'd sent Johnnie away.

"How did they end up anywhere together alone?" Pip asked rhetorically. "What about Mother's blasted rota?"

"She's been with Edith for most of the time," Angelica said, "having refused to hold your mother's hand, or sit with Vita. But then the minister came –"

"Thomas Osborne? He's the ex-minister."

"Yes – Thomas Osborne came and she went off with him, and so I took charge of Ursula. Then Edith came back and took her from me. But the next thing I saw, Edith was dancing. I assumed Ursula had been handed over to someone else. And we all thought Johnnie had gone."

"Where is he now? Where's Johnnie now?"

Ursula didn't respond, but looked ill and clammy, her eyes pink. She looked cold.

Angelica put her hand on Pip's shoulder. "Gently, gently. Drugs, do you think?"

"Dunno. Possibly. Get her something warmer to wear." Ursula was clad in an ill-fitting black lace dress – too long, too broad on the shoulder – that came from Tilly's wardrobe, that Tilly had worn to Ursa and Jo's funeral. It swamped Ursula's little frame and she'd hitched it up at the waist with a man's white dinner scarf, a heavily fringed scarf that she'd knotted into a belt. Angelica offered her shawl, folding it around Ursula's shoulders. Ursula gathered it tight in her small hands and dipped her chin into its folds.

"Something up, that's for sure," Pip said, taking her pulse and not meeting resistance. "I don't know what to do for the best."

Ursula had fixed her eyes on Angelica, and Pip, cottoning on, asked Ursula if she would like to talk to her privately. Ursula nodded and Pip went out of the room, saying that if things got worse he wouldn't be far away, and winking as he said so. He went out and closed the door five-sixths shut, and stood behind it, listening.

He heard Angelica saying, "Come and sit down."

Ursula slid into a chair and Angelica pulled another closer to it.

"Tell me," Angelica said.

"I'm sorry," Ursula said. "I've said sorry to God. I didn't mean to."

"What have you done to be sorry for?"

"He tried –" Ursula faltered. Angelica waited. "He touched me."

"Touched you …"

"Johnnie."

Angelica lowered her head the better to hear. "Johnnie what?"

"We had sex together."

"You had sex together."

"And after that ..."

"What happened?"

"He put ... he tried to put his hands ... inside."

"Inside?"

"Inside my clothes."

Angelica was flummoxed but, to her credit, tactful, merely asking what she could do to help, although she looked physically thwarted, her body language ripe with misfirings, going to hug Ursula and then desisting, and all at sixes and sevens. Ursula said that she'd like some hot chocolate and Angelica leapt up, glad to be directed.

Pip, outside the door, was having trouble deciding what to do next. It was going to be difficult to hunt down Johnnie and accuse him of anything. Ursula couldn't be protected, not at 42, from such misunderstandings, after all, arising from her misconstruing the kind of relationship men wanted with her and being offended by them. An attempted skin contact, leading on from intimacy that might have appeared introductory – that attempt didn't in itself amount to an assault. Not in Pip's mind, at least. His thoughtfulness, poised between rage and bafflement as he leaned against the door jamb, was manifesting itself physically, in the loosening of limbs previously stiffened for retribution, and now, as Angelica heated the milk, in the attention paid to chewing down his thumbnail.

The telephone rang, and Pip went back into the kitchen to answer it. He lifted the receiver and said, "Peattie House." A voice on the other end said, "Taxi for Brand."

"Brand?"

"Mr John Brand, it says here. Been waiting ten minutes already – can you tell Brand to come down, mate?"

Pip went to the window and saw the cab, its lights bright and refractive in the downpour – the rain had returned – and its windscreen wipers swishing. He saw Johnnie hurrying down the steps with his overnight bag, one hand pushed inside and up into the chest of his coat.

Edith came into the room, pushing the door open with her hip and half-turned away, talking to other people, invisible people who presented only as disembodied voices. She continued talking to them, half in and half out of the door.

"Ursula's feeling unwell," Pip told her.

"I'll just be a moment," Edith said to the corridor. "Sorry. Just a moment."

She went to Ursula. "I told you not to drink it. It isn't lemonade. Best go and have a lie-down next door in Granny's room."

"Could you?" Pip asked of Angelica, and Angelica shepherded Ursula out, settling her under a blanket on Vita's chaise longue.

"What's going on?" Edith asked Pip, as soon as the kitchen door had closed behind the two of them.

"Johnnie trouble, we think."

"Johnnie's just been and said goodbye to me. You won't have heard the hoo-hah. Johnnie and one of the dogs. You've missed all the commotion, if you've been in here long."

"Johnnie and one of the dogs?"

"Johnnie got bitten by one of the dogs; he's gone off to the hospital to get it stitched, and then he's going to stay in town overnight, he said, and go straight home from there. So he's gone. Henry's mortified. He and Mog are rounding the dogs up and shutting them in the study."

Not all of them were happy to comply. They'd spent a pleasant evening, wandering and petted and vacuuming up crumbs, fed by solicitous children on filo-pastry parcels.

"He got bitten by a dog?"

Angelica came into the room. "Who got bitten?"

"Johnnie," Edith told her. "All he would say about it was that it was one of the bitches."

Pip said nothing but directed a wide-eyed look at Angelica. Angelica looked back, her hand over her mouth.

"He wouldn't hear of having it cleaned up," Edith's said. "Wouldn't even let me look at it. Poor Henry's completely mortified."

Pip went and found Mog and then, because the rain had stopped, they went into the garden, over sodden grass and around puddles to stand together at the fountain, which hasn't worked for well over a decade and has become almost a garden. Even when it was functioning, I always thought there was something actively unpleasant about it, about its giant concrete fish centrepiece, twisting its body like a leaping salmon, its mouth and conduit gaping.

Mog didn't think events as significant as Pip did. Pip was sure. "I'm telling you: Ursula's a virgin. There's no doubt about it."

"But she doesn't lie."

"No you're wrong." Pip threw his hands up. "She does, you see. She's always getting things wrong. I'm not in any doubt about this. She feels about sex like she feels about water."

"Well, maybe that's the point – that they've *become* linked because of Michael, but only since Michael."

"We never talk about this," Pip said, sitting on the fountain's damp edge. "It's the one thing, all these years, that we've never said. It's the last taboo."

"What are you talking about?"

"Michael and Ursula. How disgusted we all were. How secretly disgusted, despising him, thinking he was guilty of a kind of abuse. Gran saw it that way, certainly. It helped excuse Ursula's hitting out, this idea that he'd been sexually abusing her."

"What? That's ridiculous."

"It isn't."

"Sexual abuse? Hardly that."

"That's what they thought."

"Well, I never did. I didn't. It didn't even occur to me. Never has, to see it that way."

"But it didn't happen, you see. She thinks she's had sex with Johnnie."

"Well, maybe they did."

"No. I'm absolutely positive they didn't."

"So?"

"Michael. Leaving him down there, in the loch unretrieved. The fact has to be faced and admitted to. In part it was a kind of punishment."

Izzy and friends were oblivious to the crisis, having decamped to the ballroom with the CD player. They'd established a disco there and had thrown open the doors to the terrace, despite Euan's protests that this was a quiet zone and they didn't want to hear that godawful racket, thanks very much. Izzy, having replied with her tongue stuck out, a brief dismissive raspberry, went into the drawing room to gather support and get more wine. Beauty has natural authority. She walked into the room and she had their attention.

"Everyone. Hello, by the way, if we haven't hello'd already. Lovely to see you. I'm here to say that there's boogying in the ballroom. Anyone who wants to shake their thing, and I can tell just by looking that that's most of you, please follow me."

A steady trickle of the younger generation of guests followed, most of the children and most of the remaining single men, including Christian Grant. Soon he was dancing with elbows cocked, partnering Izzy and looking absurdly hopeful.

Chapter 21

The impromptu bar in the drawing room had been worked over pretty thoroughly, and its trays had acquired a dishevelled look. Tops had detached from bottles and bottles had emptied and spilled: a lake of a sticky whisky-and-cream liqueur had slopped across the cloth. It had got to the stage of the evening in which it was important to hold onto your glass; the table presented no fresh goblets or tumblers, just other people's empties. So when Alan arrived the first that most guests saw of him was a view of a man's back, a man standing at the table working his way through the glasses, angling one after another patiently and equivalently into the light, trying to spot tell-tale signs of a residue or signs of a mouth having left its greasy print on a rim.

Alan was wearing his father's old dress shoes, which were creased decisively at the point where the foot bends at the toe, marking their original owner's many hours of ceilidh dancing. His trousers were of their customary waiterly black, their customary slight shortness. His white shirt was big-collared, his black tie tied into a fat knot. His jacket, pale grey with a darker raised stitch, was way too large, falling well below his hip, stretching wider than the shoulder, its sleeves rolled up to the elbow.

Behind him, a small group had gathered: Edith, Joan, Mrs Hammill, Mog. Alan seemed oblivious to their presence, as well he might be; the music and its accompanying stamp of feet masked all the talk going on around him. He continued working his way through the glasses and, finding none of them clean, took one and refreshed it on a handkerchief, one he brought from his trouser pocket, producing and unfolding it with a flick of the wrist.

"There won't be a fuss," Joan said. "One of us will simply – will take him by the arm and steer him out."

Mog said, "What, like a bouncer?"

"Don't be glib," Mrs Hammill cut in sharply. "What do you suggest?"

"What I'd suggest is leaving him alone: he's already pretty drunk."

Mog was right. All the signs were there. Alan's posture, the self-control evident in the definiteness of his gestures, his steadying himself on the table edge: all of these were giveaways.

"I'm not having him here. He's not invited and he's not staying," Joan said, her voice petulant.

Without waiting for a response from the group, she stepped forward to stand alongside Alan at the table, pretending to join him in searching through the glasses. It was clear from Alan's turning to look at her, turning 45 degrees, the suddenness of it and his look of surprise, that she was saying something unexpectedly direct. Alan didn't answer. He poured himself a glass of wine, emptying the dregs of three abandoned bottles before adding brandy to the mixture and downing his cocktail in one swallow. Then he put the glass back among the others and walked away, threading his way around people, out of the drawing room and into the picture gallery, ploughing through the middle of the dancers.

Joan returned to the others. "I'll see to it; you stay here. We don't want a scene."

Alan went through the lower part of the gallery, down the double step, running his hand over table tops and chair backs and lightly over the topmost surfaces of chipped porcelain and tarnished bronze. Joan saw him go into the hall and out of the main door, onto the terrace and down onto the drive. She returned to the drawing room and told the waiting group that Alan had gone home and that it was best, at least for now, to leave things as they were. As she was saying this, Alan was going back into the house. There was nobody in the hall or at the reception table. Nobody was there to see him making his way up the stairs to the family bedrooms, silently and with moderate haste in his father's old shoes.

The corridors going off in both directions were badly and dimly lit, and the many dusty orange bulb-shades cast a sickly light. Alan paused, looking in each direction before deciding on left. He was about to move when he saw Rebecca come out of her room, pulling the door carefully shut and smoothing the back of her dress. She turned towards the stairs and saw Alan standing there. Her reaction was immediate: she opened her door and went back inside.

Alan went to the door and spoke to her through it.

"What was that? You're going to hide in there until I've gone?"

No answer. But at the other side Rebecca was leaning as heavily as she could, her back firm against its panelling and her legs angled so as to provide further buttressing. Her phone was in her hand.

Alan turned the handle. "Are you leaning against the door? I know there's no lock. There's no lock on any of them."

"How do you know that?" a muffled voice asked.

"What have they told you?" Alan asked the door. "It's all lies, you know. Lies and then more lies to cover up the first lot of lies. Covering themselves. They'll say anything."

Rebecca's voice said, "I forgot something. I'll be out in a moment."

The door made a subtle noise, sighing as the weight was removed from it. Alan went to lean on the wall opposite.

After a while, Rebecca having failed to emerge, he went forward again and opened the door, putting his head around it. "Knock knock!"

Rebecca was sitting on the edge of her bed, texting someone. She jumped to her feet.

"Alan – what do you want?"

"I just want to talk."

"Wait. I'll be out in a minute. I told you."

"Righto."

"Alan. I'll be out in a minute. I'm not going to talk to you in here."

"Sorry." He backed away and closed the door behind him.

When she came out, saying, "What is it Alan? I have a headache", the attempt at casualness commendable but her unease obvious, he directed her – "Please, just for a few minutes" – to the chairs that were grouped on the landing. They came from Sri Lanka when it was Ceylon and when Salters were interested in Ceylon tea. They are made of a fine gauge of cane, tightly woven and padded out with dense horsehair cushions. Alan sat and Rebecca seated herself opposite.

"I have something to tell you," he said. "A story, a true story; the truth about the Salters. When I've finished, all I ask is that you tell them that you know, you tell them what you know. We'll see what happens after that."

❧

When Alan came down the stairs again, alone, he had the misfortune to see Joan, catching sight of her just at the same moment that she saw him. She was standing in the hall saying goodbye to a group of people about to leave, handing out coats and umbrellas and complaining about hired help, about help being entirely the wrong word.

"Alan, stop," she said as he strode past. "Can you wait, please, I need to speak to you."

Ignoring her challenge, Alan went out of the door and down the steps and kept walking. Joan pursued him, standing on the terrace and shouting at him to come back, warning him that he would have to leave the estate, calling after him that things had gone too far, that they'd reached the end of the road. She couldn't pursue him further than the terrace. There had to be a feigned appearance of a fall-ing-away of concern, a putting back into proportion, while she assured the guests who'd followed her out that it was nothing, it was only trouble with the staff, and apologised for losing her temper. Once they'd left she went back into the house and up the stairs two at a time, saying aloud to herself, "I bet he's been rifling. What has he been looking for? What has he taken?" and "Well this is it, this really is it, he has to go."

She was surprised to find Rebecca on the landing, sitting in one of the colonial chairs with her eyes closed.

"Rebecca – are you alright? Has something happened?"

"Migraine," Rebecca said. "Could you get pills out of my bag? It's on my bed. Front pocket. Sorry, but it affects my vision and if I try to focus I start to feel sick."

Joan went and got the tablets, then went downstairs to the reception table and fetched a half-glass of abandoned champagne for Rebecca to wash them down with.

"Did you see Alan?" Joan asked her. "A few minutes ago? I saw him coming downstairs."

"Yes, he was here."

"Did you see where he came from?"

"He came to see me, that's all."

"Oh – I – to see you?"

Rebecca half opened one eye and closed it again. "Yes."

"Sorry – does it hurt to talk?"

"Bit."

"We'll talk later if that's better."

"It's fine," Rebecca said softly. "It's not really pain. Just weirdness and flashing zigzags. Black and white. And nausea."

"That sounds unpleasant."

"I can deal with it as long as I keep my eyes closed."

"He didn't go in the rooms?"

"I don't think so."

"What did he want?"

"He's a strange man, isn't he? Very strange. He said he wanted to tell me the truth about Michael, and then I was to tell you that I know."

"About Michael? What did he say?"

Rebecca didn't tell the story the way that anybody who lived at Peattie would have done. When Alan said, "Michael isn't really dead", she failed to be astonished, just gave him that look that had been growing on her face since he put his head around her bedroom door, part alarm and part pity, an amalgam that swam in her eyes visibly and embarrassed him. "Michael survived it," he said. "The day he vanished. He walked away. He left Peattie. I saw him walk away."

"Well, yes," she said. And then, "I know."

Alan looked confused.

"What do you mean, *survived it*?" Rebecca added.

"What do you mean, what do I mean?"

"I know that he left Peattie, if that's what you mean. Everyone knows that. What do you mean, survived it?"

"They told you?"

"I don't understand what you're saying. I think we must be talking at cross purposes." She flinched, raising her shoulders and tipping her skull gently back. "I don't understand what you're saying."

Alan moved his chair closer towards her, his breath sour and warm.

"You know that they think Michael is dead in the loch; that most of them think that. That's the starting point. You do know that."

"I didn't know that. That's surprising." She didn't sound surprised, though the concise speaking style the migraine necessitated was partly to blame.

"Yes! Yes! They thought Ursula killed him."

"They did not."

"They did. They thought Ursula killed him."

"Okay."

"I'm going to tell them that he's alive."

"Okay."

"I already have. I told one of them at the time. But they preferred not to share the information. The only conclusion possible is that they prefer him to be dead." He looked at her intently. "You don't believe me."

"Of course I do. But if I were you I'd go home now."

"You Salter women are all the same."

"Thanks. Charming. Now go home, Alan."

So you see, Joan and Rebecca's subsequent conversation, seated in those same cane chairs, was not the sensation it might have been. Joan got the measure of the situation quickly and is an able firefighter.

"What did he say to you exactly?"

"That Michael isn't dead, but that you all think he is."

"Some of us do, certainly, but not all of us, by any means. And over the years, we've all gone through phases of thinking it, and not thinking it."

"No – it wasn't like that. It wasn't about what happened when he left here. It was about him never leaving here."

"What do you mean?"

Rebecca opened her eyes. "Dead in the loch. Murdered."

"Oh, *that*; is that all?" Joan said, deadpan.

Even Rebecca laughed, although economically because it hurt. "He said that most of you think that's what happened, but one of you knows he's alive."

"What?"

"He said that one of you knows he's alive."

"One of us *knows*? How come? I don't follow."

"I can't remember exactly how it went. And that Ursula killed him. Or you thought she did, but she didn't."

"He said *what*?"

"I didn't realise," Rebecca continued. "That he's – you know. Ill or whatever."

"We try not to make too much of it," Joan said, her voice full of self-approving tolerance. "In fact we down-play it, his mental disadvantage, but it's obvious actually, isn't it – you just have to look at him; you just have to listen to the way he talks. And why else does a 57-year-old man share a bedroom with his father?"

"Such a shame."

"Excuse me, there's something that I need to ..." Joan said, not finishing the thought but getting up and going down the stairs.

"I'm going to go and lie down," Rebecca told her.

It took Joan a little while to locate Euan. He was in the study, a room that had become cluttered with dogs, standing talking with friends of Henry's, though Henry was absent. They were drinking whisky in a serious and critical way, Euan drawing out new and fresher examples from the bookcase of older and rarer malts: bottlings that Henry had put some energy into collecting and which he continued to receive as presents. There was no longer any need to find things to talk about. The tasting provided its own content: the whiskies themselves had become the conversation and there was exuberant relief in participation in the game. When Joan came into the study she found Euan playing the host to a throng of half-recognised semi-strangers, faces that swam in and out of old memories. All of them were men, interrupting their chat only momentarily to greet her and ask after her health, with purposeful chivalry, before continuing on and paying her no heed.

Joan tugged at Euan's sleeve. "I need to speak to you. Outside."

"Really, Joan, can't you just –"

"Urgently."

When Euan got to George's cottage he found Alan sitting in the porch. He was sitting on a vegetable box that had been made into a seat with a derelict chintz cushion that dated from his mother's era.

"Got locked out," Alan explained.

He looked tired. His head lolled back against the old plaster of the porch wall. Above it, flesh-pink geraniums leaned down from a shelf on long stems. "I'm sorry about earlier," he said, "if that's why you're here. I only went upstairs because I needed the bathroom."

"It's not about that," Euan told him. "That's not why I'm here. You know why I'm here. We need to talk about Michael. Why did you say that thing you said to Rebecca?"

"Because it's true."

The conversation proceeded with unlikely calm. Euan stood with his hands in his pockets, and Alan sat on the chintz cushion, each in deadly earnest. Stand-off. Stalemate.

"You say anything like this again to anyone and you're out, you're out of here. It's that simple," Euan told him. "In fact, Joan thinks it's too late and she's probably right. We're at the end of the road now."

Alan looked Euan in the eye. "I have a question for you."

"Fire away," Euan said blandly.

"Why did you marry Joan when it was Ottilie that you wanted?"

The two men stared at each other.

"You've got it all wrong," Euan said eventually. "And what makes you – what makes you say –"

"It wasn't just Michael that she told."

"That who told?"

"Ursula. You know who and you know what. Don't play the innocent with me."

"Ursula. How would Ursula know this and why would she confide in you?"

"That'd be telling."

"I thought we'd already established that Ursula's really a liar."

"I'm just interested."

"Well, seeing as we're asking intimate questions, I've one for you. Why'd you pretend to be the father, all these years? All these years, Alan."

"I never pretended. I never claimed. I didn't say anything about it, since you ask. Other people decided."

"The truth doesn't lie in what people don't tell each other."

"What?"

"You've let them think it."

Alan got up and moved forward. "Which suited you very well! Hypocrite. Total bloody hypocrite."

Euan took several steps hurriedly back, out of the porch, and stood holding onto the top of the door frame, hands placed above his head.

"She could have put a stop to it in 30 seconds flat," Alan said. "You could have put a stop to it in 30 seconds flat. Nobody did though, did they? Suited you. Suited her. The least I could do was agree."

"What was it for you, Alan?" Euan asked him. "Was it a sort of *prestige*?"

Alan was shaking his head. "I might ask you the same question. What was it for you? You had sex with her the night before your wedding. The night before your wedding! And then you went ahead and married her sister."

"You're completely barking."

"Barking and up the wrong tree? I don't think so."

"Ursula is easily misled. Tell her something and she believes it."

"Ah, but you see it wasn't Ursula who told me. It was Michael, before he left here."

"You're a piece of work, aren't you?"

"He came to me before he left, and he told me it was you. Before he left here for good. That's what happened."

"Enough. Enough."

"It's time to own up," Alan said. "You tell them or I will."

"Own up?"

"Tell Joan or I will."

It was obvious, the bubbling-up and then the collapse of Euan's indignation. "She wouldn't have me, Alan," he said.

"She wouldn't have me either, and that makes us brothers."

"That doesn't make us anything," Euan said flatly.

"I think it's time the truth was told, don't you?" Alan's suggestion was unmistakably a threat.

"What truth is that? Yours or someone else's?"

"There is only one."

"Course there isn't." Euan turned away, went to the gate, and stood with it half open.

Alan came after him. "Think what you like," he said. "I'm not here to try and convince you of anything." He seemed to be having trouble catching his breath, and began to fidget, putting his hands to his ears and to his waist and to his ears once more. Now he was flattening his hand at his throat. Now he was looking at his wrist, putting his fingers to his pulse.

"What's the matter with you?" Euan asked him.

"I get – everything goes fast sometimes. It comes on suddenly. Heart racing. And racing thoughts." Alan began circling the small garden in the drizzly rain, breathing with great concentration, in through the nose and out through the mouth. "I'll be alright. In a little while. I over-breathe when I'm upset."

Euan waited and then he said, "You've got to give up on this, Alan. This business about Michael. This lie."

Alan bent forward, clasping his knees, and came up again. "It isn't a lie. Ask Henry. Henry's lied to all of you. He's known all along that Michael survived it."

"What? What do you mean? How could he think that?"

"Because I told him. Right afterwards. A few weeks afterwards. He said he'd get in touch with the police and then he did nothing. Because it was better for him if Michael was dead. Look at your face." Euan's mouth had gaped open. "You don't get it. You're not very bright really, are you? Actually a bit thick. Good at books and talking but actually a bit thick."

Euan went out of the gate and stood at the other side of the hedge. "I don't think you've thought this through, Alan. When they find out you're not Michael's father: what will they do then?"

"They'll know that it's you and that you lied and you'll be out of here, pal."

"Don't you 'pal' me," Euan said hotly. "It's the lie you told Henry that's the unforgivable lie. The other thing was Ottilie's choice and my behaviour was gentlemanly."

"Gentlemanly, my arse."

"Let's get out of La La Land a minute and face facts. Michael didn't tell you anything. He didn't know about me until he got into the boat with Ursula. That's what she told him in the boat; that's the secret. I know that. I've known that all along: it's something I've had to live with. But spare me this sanctimonious cant. Michael didn't tell you. Ursula did, afterwards, didn't she, in the boat, rowing back? Come on, Alan. Admit it."

"I've known a lot longer than that," Alan said. "You've me to thank for Ursula not telling her mother. Back when Ottilie was pregnant."

"That's rubbish."

"Not rubbish. Ursula knew then, and Ursula came to me. She needed to talk to somebody who wasn't family. She tried my father first but he stopped her before she could tell, saying he didn't want to know, he was sorry but she wasn't to tell him any more of it. Ignorance is bliss, that's Dad's motto. So she came to me. She overheard you, the two of you. She was watching, at the loch, when you went to have your private chat and you demanded Ottilie get an abortion. Ursula was only a little girl. She didn't know what it meant. It was me that persuaded her not to tell. I've carried this for you all of these years, Euan Catto."

"So Ursula does what you tell her. That's interesting. That's a different perspective on things. I've just had a big question answered. I've wondered why it was that Ursula told him the secret, that particular day. What made her decide, suddenly, to do it. And now I know. You told her to, didn't you?"

"I might have. I thought it was time."

When Euan left Alan, knowing he'd have to own up to my paternity: that walk home was a journey of five minutes and a decade, ageing him by ten years at the least. By the time he walked into the house, hearing – in the porch as he hung up his jacket and wearily eased off his shoes – Joan's imperious call of his name, her from-upstairs called-out demand for news, fresh worry-lines had etched themselves on his forehead, had worried at the skin around his eyes, had provoked a more insistent dusting of grey at his temples. His mouth had taken a distinctive downturn, as if it had taken its imprint from the practice of years. White hair was springing victoriously through the brown, skin had furrowed on the backs of his hands and his upper spine had embarked on its rounding. The man who opened the door from the porch into the house, who stood among its glowing Scandinavian furniture, the man who cleared his throat and said, not as loudly as he'd anticipated, towards the stairs, "Yes, there's news": he was a different man.

Joan trotted down towards him, still unaware for these few moments, still assuming she was dealing with the old Euan. As she came she was complaining that she'd been kept waiting, and why hadn't he texted, why hadn't he phoned. Still not looking at him directly, she went to correct a vase of peonies on the hall table that had drooped their blooms over to one side, and as she did this she was asking why everything he did had to take so long, for heaven's sake, why it was that he had to make every transaction into an epic, talking and talking. Finally she turned to look at him and gasped. The man Joan saw was so changed from the man of earlier that she was stopped in her tracks, mid-sentence.

"Euan, my god, what's happened?"

"I need a drink."

She followed him into the kitchen, watched him remove the pedal bin from its corner position and bend to rummage among the bottles hidden behind the cereal boxes, emerging with a bottle that had three inches of Scotch remaining. He took the top off and swigged.

"Euan!"

"Don't. Just don't."

"This thing about Michael ..."

"Rubbish. All rubbish. Forget it. Rubbish and lies. What goes on in Alan's head – I can't fathom it. It's unfathomable. How he could do that to Henry."

Joan was silenced, watching with growing alarm as he swigged and swigged again. Finally, having shaken the last dribble into his throat, he put the bottle on the worktop and said, "We have to talk."

She followed him into the sitting room.

"You're frightening me. What is it? Tell me now. I have to get back to the party."

He sank down heavily onto the sofa and positioned himself three-quarters turned away, looking towards the window. She went and sat on the window seat, still in the fish-scale dress, intercepting the direction of his gaze, her hands laced tightly together on her knees, her posture tipped forward. He turned his attention to the fireplace, where the woodburner glowed orange.

"First, I've a question for you," he said. It was a weary voice that asked this question apparently of the woodburner.

"Yes?"

"Why weren't you surprised?"

"About what? Surprised about what?"

"When you told me that Alan was saying Michael is alive. You weren't surprised. Why was that?"

"I need a cigarette," Joan said, and then, raising her hand, "Just don't. I know where your stash is." She left the room and was back almost immediately, lighting up two and handing one to Euan, who waved it away. "Dad told me."

"Henry."

"He told me Alan had recanted. Alan confessed he'd lied about Michael, that Michael was alive."

"Henry told you when?"

"Recently. He's known for years. Almost the whole time. He told me and he told Pip and he swore us to secrecy."

"You should have told me."

"Why would I?"

They looked at each other: Joan defiant and Euan unaffected by her defiance.

His gaze returned to the woodburner. "Ottilie doesn't know?"

"No."

"Why doesn't Ottilie know?"

"He decided that it would be worse for her."

His fists drummed briefly into the sofa linen. "Bullshit! Bullshit! Just listen to yourself!"

"Calm down."

"You just want to believe it because it twists the knife a little bit more into Ottilie."

"That's a terrible thing to say." Joan got up and went out of the room, and came back a few minutes later with a tall drink. Euan had moved to the window seat.

"I don't know what's happened to you," he said. "It's like you've made it unreal, this death. You've made it a game."

"I've never thought Michael's dead. And I think he chose. He chose to cut us off without another thought, to cut his mother off, and that's too hard. That's harder for her than his dying."

"Nice rationalising. He'll retract it, even if I have to hold a gun to his head."

"That's big talk, big man." The sarcasm was penetrating.

Euan looked her steadily in the eye. "Joan, I have something to tell you." She waited. "But first you have to promise not to tell. You can do this. You've done it before."

Joan looked shocked. "You know about Sebastian?"

"What? No. What about Sebastian?"

"I misunderstood you."

Euan got to his feet. "But first I have stuff I need to do." He left the room.

"I'll make coffee," she shouted after him, hearing him going up the stairs.

She went into the kitchen and boiled the kettle and cleaned the cafetiere, then reboiled the kettle, and heaped in the coffee and filled it. She put bread and cheese and some of the home-made apple pickle onto a platter, and carried it through on a tray. When she'd waited ten minutes, she went into the hall and called his name. Without answering her he came down the stairs with two suitcases.

"Euan! What are you doing?"

"I'm leaving, Joan. I'm moving out." He put the cases by the door and went up again. "I'll come back at the weekend and get some more stuff then."

"Euan. Euan." Joan's voice shook. "What do you mean?" It shook further as she followed him out to the car, repeating the words and variants on them. It was only once he'd got the engine running and had lowered the driver's window that Euan looked at her.

"I'm Michael's father," he said, and she didn't hear him so he had to repeat it, had at last to shout it, and then he pulled out and went slowly down the drive to the gate, seeing Joan on the road behind him, her face utterly vacant, staring after him, her arms held out at an angle from her body and her fingers stiff and splayed.

Chapter 22

The day after the party, the light dawned grey and soft over Peattie House. Henry was up by then; he had spoken to Rebecca before going to bed, and sleep had been fitful. Later he would try to explain that the coming of morning felt to him like a return to twilight, rather than the progression of hours; like time had become something rocking gently to a halt, back and forth: not marked by the pendulum but become the pendulum itself. Twilight had gone and was back. Later, in the afternoon, it would be four o'clock again and Michael would die: when the night returned it was only as a tormenting introduction to the next afternoon. The days would keep coming, and Michael would keep dying. Henry went out into the wood with the dogs, and onto the beach, throwing sticks from the shore. Dogs made things seem normal and as if life could be just about feeding and exercise and rest. That's what he needed, he thought, a dog life, the peaceful eating up of time, blind to all of its meanings. A dog in the water made death feel normal, life properly temporary. It was what followed on from feeding and exercise and rest. It didn't matter.

He walked up and down the edge of the loch, his breath white in the damp morning, round-shouldered in his old wax coat, as various of the pack ran along the treeline, nosing rabbit trails around the tomb, or swam in the cold morning water, the spaniels sodden and dripping, the water extending their long belly hairs, the Labradors shaking themselves with impressive corkscrew winding and unwinding on the gravel, their close-knit fur tufting wet into carpets. Henry decided that it couldn't wait another day: he had to go and talk to Ursula.

All looked quiet at the gatehouse at 5.30am, but inside, wearing white pyjamas and a pale overcoat, Joan was sitting cross-legged on the sitting-room floor, smoking a cigarette and tapping its ash into the fireplace. Her mobile phone lay black and inert on the rug, a miniature plastic monolith that had failed, in an intolerable and stubborn way, minute after minute, either to ring or to beep its receipt of a message. She'd barely slept, dozing for scant half-hours before waking freshly to the shock of what had happened, her stomach heaving, her heart thumping and racing. At least the children wouldn't be too badly affected. As she said to herself, over and over, a mantra newly adopted, it was a good thing the children weren't here, that they were grown up; a good thing they were so independent. She could be proud at least of the independence she had nurtured in them. She was alone in the house and nobody had been disturbed, in either sense, by her making of peppermint tea at three and by her drinking of vodka at five. No detailed attempt at justification was made, other than for a single uttered word at the mouth of the cupboard. "Emergency."

Many impassioned, angry, conciliatory, flippant, pleading, contemptuous messages had been left on Euan's phone, Joan working through her own night-aided process from rage to acceptance and back to rage, and the tone of the messages tracking this circle. She had been talking aloud to the empty house for hours, to the empty rooms as if each of them were him. "So if that's how it seems to you, forget it. I shed you with an equal indifference." But the truth was that she was shaken. Their relationship had been turbulent always, but that was an emotional engagement; turbulence was never less than alive and engaged. This quiet cutting-off, this silence: was this where they'd been headed all along, was this where they had stood teetering? Had this been the view ahead, this cliff, this imminent nothingness? This was how she'd speak to Mog about it later on, leaving Mog floundering, ill-equipped to answer.

Eventually, cold and stiff from sitting on the carpet, Joan got up, placed the cigarettes on the coffee table in full view, patting the box as she did so, and went and dressed. She put her phone in her pocket – taking it out and turning it off before returning it there – and went up to Peattie. Henry was standing looking vague, at the top of the drive with the dogs.

"Euan's gone," she told him bluntly as she approached. "For good, I think. We argued. It's over. Don't look like that."

"I imagine I look as if I'm sorry. There's little I can do about being sorry, Joan."

"You're not just sorry. You're not surprised. You're wondering how it took this long."

"That's ungenerous of you."

"I know that will be the first thought of everybody who hears about it."

"We must go and wake your mother."

"I don't want to. Not yet. Please. I'm going back to the gatehouse. I'm cold."

"Let me put the dogs in and come to you."

"Alright. But no sneaking up to whisper in Mother's ear. I couldn't take it, not the two of you looking wounded."

"As you wish."

"I'm glad he's gone. I don't want him back. I'm going to have a new life and I don't want to talk about it. Not till later."

Her father nodded absently, the dogs milling around him, prompting him with noses pushed into his hands, wanting to be off.

"What I need is to talk to you about Alan," Joan said.

"I know about it. I know what Alan said to Rebecca, if that's what you mean. After you left the party, Rebecca went to Edith, and Edith brought her to me."

It was from the gatehouse that Henry telephoned Pip on his mobile, just before 7am. When Henry called, Pip was in a deep sleep, having got to bed very late, and the ring-tone prompted sincere groans from Angelica, who said he should tell the office to stuff it, whatever it was; it was too early and they were on holiday. When he got out of bed, saying that he needed to go and talk to his mother and she should go back to sleep, she put her head under the pillow.

Pip got to the gatehouse to find Joan looking washed out and Henry's expression unclassifiable. Henry had warned Pip on the phone that there had been a fight and that his father had gone to the flat and that it was better not to unleash his mother on the subject just yet, unless she brought it up herself. She didn't. She didn't mention Euan once. She explained the crisis to Pip even before he was properly through the door: that this was about Alan's behaviour and that Henry needed advice. They went over the facts of the night before, Henry insisting that Ottilie mustn't be upset.

"You have to tell her some time," Joan said.

"Why?"

"Because she has a right to know what Alan is telling people. She needs to hear it from us before she hears it from someone else."

"But it's a lie," Henry said, as if that were obvious.

Joan looked flummoxed. "But when you told us, when you told Pip and me – you believed it then."

"I've always known that it's a lie. For a start, I know he has the money. All of the money."

"How do you know?" Pip and Joan asked simultaneously.

"Alan was over-careful about explaining to me how he could afford a van – that white one that's been parked in the yard. Told me twice that he'd inherited the money. Some guff about a legacy from an uncle."

"Maybe there was a legacy," Pip said.

"Not according to George. There isn't an uncle. But you see, Alan and I had an agreement. I was very clear. I told Alan that if he kept it to himself he could stay at the cottage, have lifetime use of it after George has gone. He said Michael had given him £200 and I told him he could keep the money. And I told him that if I heard a peep of it from anywhere, he and George would both be evicted and out."

"So now what?" Joan said. "You're not proposing to throw George out of his house?"

"Of course not."

"I'm going to see Alan," Pip said, pushing his kitchen chair back scrapingly against the tiles. Henry followed him out. Joan said she wouldn't come if they didn't mind; she needed to shower. "And Pip – I just need to speak to Dad about something else, for a moment: can he catch you up?" Once Pip had left the house, Joan asked Henry if he had his mobile phone, and he told her that of course he did: he'd phoned Pip with it from her sitting room.

"Look," she said. "I can't face Alan. Can't face him. But I need you to phone me if anything is said about Euan."

"What kind of thing?"

"Just anything. Anything surprising."

❧

The van was parked outside the Dixons' cottage with its back doors open. Alan was loading it with his few possessions, boxed up, and was still wearing the clothes from the night before. George was standing beside the rear doors in clean blue overalls and looked acutely uncomfortable as

386

he saw Pip and Henry walking towards them.

"Alan," they heard him say, in what might have been a warning voice. "Mr Salter."

Alan climbed out of the van, sending it bobbing as he came down, a short and ungainly jump onto the tarmac. He walked quickly towards them.

"I'm going; time to go," he said, forestalling every rehearsed dismissal that had been in Henry's mind and the speech that Pip had been formulating in walking here. "I'm not going to argue with you" – as he spoke he was walking past them – "but would you follow me please, I don't want my dad overhearing this."

Henry and Pip did as he asked and George was content to watch the three of them, heads close together. He stood by the van doors and watched and crinkled up his eyes the better to focus.

"You have disappointed me so deeply, Alan," Henry said, his face and his voice composed.

"Whatever. Well, I'm off. I'll send for Dad when I'm settled."

Henry took the loss of George Dixon in his stride. Perhaps he'd anticipated this. He didn't flinch. "Whatever George wants to do is of course fine with us," he said.

Alan lowered his head and spoke to the old road. "It's up to you, but I haven't said anything to Dad about Michael, and nothing about Euan either. Do me this one favour and keep Dad out of it."

Then Alan strode back towards his father, grinning at him, George's face relaxing a little, reassured.

"What do you mean, 'about Euan'?" Pip called after him.

❧

At lunchtime, before Alan left for France, he went to Ursula's cottage and knocked on the door. He'd left the van ready to go, packed with his few boxes of things. He'd left his father sitting on the leather couch with his head in his hands. There wasn't any reply at Ursula's house, so Alan went down to the loch thinking she might be there, and she was. Ursula was sitting on the beach, in a long white petticoat, ribbon-trimmed, and a big khaki sweater with patched elbows. It had been raining again and the shingle was wet, but Ursula didn't seem to notice, sitting upright with her legs folded neatly in front. She didn't acknowledge Alan or look at him when he sat beside her.

"I'm leaving today," he said to her.

"Yes." They sat together, Alan looking at the loch, following Ursula's gaze, his attention returning from time to time to her face. Eventually he said, "Well, that's that then, I just wanted to say goodbye" and got to his feet, brushing damp stones from the seat of his trousers.

"Why did you lie?" Ursula asked him.

"About what?"

"My father telephoned me this morning. He told me what you'd said to him, in private, after Michael died. That Michael hadn't died, that it was a mistake. I don't understand. Can you explain it to me?"

"I wanted him to be alive for your sake. And for your father's sake."

"Did I hit him on the wrist, Alan? Was it his wrist that I hit?"

"No."

"Why did you tell me afterwards, on that day afterwards, that it was his wrist and that he chose? Why do you lie to people in private, Alan?"

"We needed to make it better. First we gave them the wrist. Then we said he'd survived it."

"I didn't. You did."

"I did."

"Why did you lie? Lying causes suffering to God."

"I wanted you to be happy, to have a happy life. I wanted Henry to have a happier life, knowing Michael was alive. So it was a kindness, you see. And I wanted to protect you."

"You should have protected me at the beginning, then. Why did you lie to Rebecca?"

"I was afraid you were about to be arrested."

"It's a sin to lie."

"No. You're wrong about that. People lie all the time."

"That doesn't mean it's not a sin."

"They lie all day, sometimes in unusual ways. Just by doing things they lie, sometimes. Life depends on lies. It runs on them. Your father lies."

"He doesn't. He doesn't."

"He does: he's adjusting what he says, what he says he believes, all the time, depending on who he's talking to."

"Why did you think I'd be arrested?"

"The police have been here, talking to your mother."

"A policeman."

"Yes. Somebody told them Michael was dead in the loch. I don't know what your mother told them but she wouldn't lie to a policeman, would she?"

"She's lied for me all along."

"They all have. They've all pretended Michael left Peattie."

"I'm not talking about Michael. You wouldn't understand. Mummy did, though. The policeman would understand if she explained it to him properly."

"I wouldn't count on it."

"They'll see how it happened. They'll tell me it's alright."

"Talk to your mother about it first," Alan told her.

"I'm going to see my father; I'm going to talk it over with my father. He's coming here now, to talk to me." She looked towards the path. There was no sign of Henry yet.

Alan began walking across the beach. "Goodbye then," he said, turning his head and raising his hand. "I don't think we're going to meet again."

"Alan!"

He stopped and turned properly to face her. "Yes?" He began walking back.

"Joan was here. She told me that Euan has gone to live at the flat, that he won't be doing the garden with me today. Usually we meet at two o'clock on Sundays."

"I know. I know you do."

"Was it because of you? Did you tell Joan? I shouldn't have told you."

"Euan told her himself."

"I think you were wrong when you said that I should keep Euan and Ottilie's baby a secret. I should have told Mummy."

"At the time it was the right thing. It was the kind thing. It wasn't your secret; it was theirs."

"But does Joan know, now?"

"Yes. Joan knows. It's not a secret any more. I think it would be best if you told everyone about their baby now. That would be best."

Henry's depression arrived the day after this. It was there when he woke, like a delivery, like new weather, having settled over him in the night. While he slept it had taken shape in him and taken root, and he woke to find its reflection in the mirror already embedded there, waiting. There wasn't any point in carrying on: he said this to himself without self-pity. It was merely a fact. He got up and went to the bathroom and then, too exhausted to wash, he returned to bed. Edith found him there later in the morning. He wouldn't leave the bedroom, or dress, and wouldn't at first give reasons. This was a source of some exasperation to Edith. She wasn't able to do as Joan urged and leave him alone. The days turned into a week and Edith began to feel desperate. She went and tapped on the bedroom door several times a day, asking if she could do anything for him, if she could fetch a doctor, if he wouldn't perhaps feel better if he got some air and exercise. He ignored her questions. She'd sit on his bed, looking at him lying on his side, one side or the other, the quilt grasped tight in his hand and lifted to rest at his mouth, his eyes open and his expression unreadable. She'd open curtains that became closed again during her absences. She'd fuss over undrunk pots of tea and eggs left to go cold.

Finally Edith rang Pip at the office.

"I wish you'd told me before," he said to her. "I'm sorry I haven't telephoned. It's been mad here and the hours run away with me."

"I didn't want to worry you," Edith told him. "I'm confused by what's happening. I thought that it would lift on its own, but things aren't improving. I thought he'd be happy that Michael's alive. That he might be alive."

Pip decided against taking on this statement. Surely even Edith would have to let go of this absurdity now.

"Have you heard any more from Alan?" he asked her instead.

"No. George says he rings every evening. He's setting up a gardening business. For British people, George says, and not for the French; he despises the French. British people with holiday houses out there."

"How are you bearing up?"

"I'm worried about everybody. About Henry. About whether your parents are alright."

"My parents are fine. Don't go wasting a minute fretting about them. They're fine at the flat, getting along fine."

"Joan said she's moving out of the gatehouse."

"Best thing that could have happened to them. They're united in outrage."

"I don't understand you."

"Ottilie's the common enemy now. Mum takes Dad's side; thinks him noble for keeping quiet."

"It's Ottilie I worry about most."

"You haven't told her? Nobody's told her?"

"No. Henry's adamant. I don't know what to do."

"I had better talk to him."

∽

When Henry answered the phone it was clear from his voice that he'd been woken by its ringing.

"I'm sorry, you were sleeping; I'll call again later," Pip said.

"It's fine," Henry told him. "It's fine. I'd rather not have to worry about being here later."

"You're going somewhere?"

"No."

"Are you feeling alright? You're speaking a bit oddly."

"Am I? Odd how?"

"Slowly. Very slowly. The words spaced out."

"I'm not aware of slowness."

"I told Gran that I'd call. She's worried about you."

"I wish she'd stop. Her worrying about me is tiring. I'm so tired."

"She can't help it. Maybe if you made an appearance…"

"I can't do anything about it, and that's that."

"What is it? What's going on?"

"It's nothing I can really talk about."

"Tell me what it is. What's it about, specifically?"

"Something Ursula told me."

"Something Ursula told you. About Michael?"

"Not about Michael."

"What then? Please tell me. What did she tell you?"

"Your grandmother has lied to me for a very long time."

"I wish you'd tell me what's going on."

"It wasn't something she said. It was something she didn't."

"Something she didn't."

"This Rebecca business," Henry said, changing the subject. "About Michael, Alan saying Michael is alive. I need to make sure you know it isn't true. Michael's dead. He's dead, Pip. And Ursula killed him. That's the truth. The whole thing opened up suddenly."

"I think you need to see a doctor. You don't sound yourself."

"No doctors."

Pip heard Henry putting the receiver onto the table and blowing his nose.

"I'll come up," he said, when Henry returned. "I can take tomorrow off and make it a long weekend."

"Please don't. I'd rather you didn't. I'd really rather you didn't. I just want to be left alone. For now. I can't do it. I can't do it, Pip."

"What can't you do?"

No answer.

"Gran," Pip said. "Gran, she believes it, that Michael's alive."

"No. No she doesn't. Edith's only saying that she does for my sake. I wish she wouldn't. I'm so sick of deceit." Henry could be heard breathing. Pip waited. "I'll try and explain it to you," Henry said. "It isn't easy. And then please. Please don't talk to anyone else about it. Please."

"I won't until you give me leave to."

"Before Alan talked to Rebecca, Michael being alive was something unlikely but true. It was true in all of our hopes. We could keep it as our own unlikely truth, and say nothing, and it got us through the years and years. Secret belief. A secret belief that Alan lied and that Ursula was mistaken, mixing up the day with another day."

"I see. I sort of see."

"And even though the edifice, the whole edifice of it depended on my being civil to the man who had lied, I was prepared to do that. Alan became somebody I could talk to about Michael as if he were alive."

"You talked to Alan about Michael?"

"Frequently. We'd imagine what he'd done, what life he was living."

"Really?"

"Yes. It was essential to me, Pip. Essential. Like a drug. It kept me going."

"With Alan, though. I can't imagine it."

"We invented this whole other life for him. A woodcutter. It sounds faintly ludicrous, like a fairy tale, doesn't it? A woodcutter. I doubt that woodcutters even exist any longer. Probably not. It's an archaic description, but maybe that was part of the point. It's just men in overalls and protective goggles now, working heavy machinery. But anyway, that was the story. A woodcutter, and a green-eyed auburn-haired wife."

"A green-eyed auburn-haired wife?"

"That was Alan. His idea. I gave Michael the children. Two lively daughters. In a cottage in the woods. We'd go into such detail. So much detail. We'd pretend we'd had letters from him. That's how we'd recommence. *I had a letter from Michael.* We gave him his writing, the way he wanted. He was writing for the newspapers. It started as an article about being a woodcutter and not being able to write. Alan didn't care. He just waved it through. He was kind to me, Pip. That's the thing I don't get. Why be kind to me? And then Michael went on to write a book about living in the woods. I wrote some of it for him, at night when I couldn't sleep. I imagined parts in which he talked about his life at Peattie, missing Peattie; it helped. It was about to be published, in the game I mean, when Alastair and Rebecca arrived. But it's all come to an end now. It's come to a halt in any case. Alan's gone. It's all over."

There was a pause and then Pip said, "Jesus."

"And then I talked to Ursula."

"I wish you'd tell me what Ursula said."

"I can't. I'll write it down. I'll write it all down."

"Do it then, do that. Please."

"Michael being alive: it didn't ever bear much examination, is the truth of it. Not talking among ourselves about it was what kept it true. Like a deep-down faith in God."

"Which you have also."

"Only if I don't allow myself to go into the detail. The way He behaved in the Bible. So morally inferior to humanity."

"This is all very odd."

"We tolerated Alan because he was Michael's father. We knew that for sure. And now he isn't. He isn't, suddenly, and we've had 30 years of being sure that he was. Over 30 years. It's shocking. It's been a real shock."

"Yes."

"His revenge on us doesn't make sense now. It doesn't follow. When he was Michael's father I could make allowances, do you see? I was guilty. About the way we'd treated Alan. I made allowances. But now that Michael's your half-brother ..."

"It's not an idea I'm ever going to get used to."

"I heard about your meeting with your dad in Edinburgh."

"He came down, made speeches. It wasn't a good day. But I don't want to talk about that now. Carry on. You were saying."

"What was I saying?"

"You made allowances."

"I made allowances for Alan when he was Michael's father. But now he isn't ... The only explanation is that he's a bad person. An evil man." Pip could hear that Henry was becoming upset. Henry paused, blowing his nose again,

395

and when his voice returned it was more composed. "It's going to be easy for people to blame Ottilie."

"It is easy. It's what's happening. Everyone's furious with her for letting us think it was Alan. Letting us argue between Alan and the boys."

"Ottilie's the one, all along, the only one who never held the secret hope. She said from the beginning that she could sense him, Michael, his spirit, when she went into the wood. She says that sometimes she can almost see him."

"I thought Ottilie didn't believe in life after death."

"Ah but she saw him you know. David. The day the children saw him. She was shaken up by it."

"You're kidding."

"Pip, I need to go back to sleep. I'll talk to you again soon."

Pip rang Henry again in the early evening.

"It's me again. Sorry to pester you. Did you sleep? Are you feeling better rested?"

"I slept. What do you want to know?"

"This thing about Ursula," Pip said. "What Ursula told you. I haven't been able to stop thinking about it."

"I can't. I'm sorry."

"We need a plan. We need to get you up and about."

"I can't do it any more. Carry on. Out there. Outside the room."

"It'll get better. I think you should get some help. Get Dr Nixon in. She's lovely. Warm. Lovely voice."

"I can't talk to her. I can't see her any more."

"Dr Nixon?"

"Ursula." His voice wavered, speaking the name. "And I mean it. I'm afraid that I mean it. I can't speak to her again. I can't see her. Not even far off, over in the garden. It's not safe to leave the room."

"You can't hide from her for ever."

"Yes. I can do that."

"Look. You're the ones, you and Gran, all these years, who've reassured her, over and over and over, that it was self-defence. That her lashing out wasn't something wicked, but understandable. A reflex. And that's still true."

"I can't speak to her ever again. I can't see her even in the garden."

"I'm going to call Dr Nixon."

"You're wasting your time. I don't want to be medicated out of this – this clarity – and to have it taken away. This is the true world and I need to live in it now. But away from here. We should have left here after Sebastian."

"I know that you –"

Henry interrupted him. "You don't know. You don't know anything. We told the truth to each other before Sebastian. But after Sebastian everything was a lie."

"I don't understand, I'm sorry."

"It wasn't possible to carry on. But we carried on. That was the lie."

"I'm coming up to see you."

"I won't see you. I won't see anyone. Only Edith with the tray. I need to be left alone for now."

"I'll come up on Sunday. It's Thursday today. By Sunday you'll be ready to dress and go out on the hill."

"I can't see her."

"Tell Gran that I'm coming and to keep Ursula away. And I'll see you on Sunday afternoon."

It wasn't unusual for Pip to have to go into the office on a Saturday, not the way things were going at the bank, the papers full of alarmist rumours. That's why he hadn't promised Saturday. But having to give up the whole weekend to 14-hour days: that was unprecedented. Pip had to ring and speak to Edith on Sunday morning and tell her that he couldn't come.

"There's a crisis – a real one," he told her. "I wouldn't cancel if it were something I could get out of. But this is serious. This is survival."

"I heard about it on the radio," Edith said. "I understand. Henry will understand. Don't worry about it. He's better, I think, getting better. He's eating now, and sleep seems to be helping. He's been outside for a little while today. His colour's much better."

Pip was all set to come up the following Friday evening, but on Thursday he got the call from Joan to say that Henry had been found on the hill, looking as if he were sleeping, pale and certain in the moss.

Chapter 23

Why did Euan marry Joan, when it was Ottilie that he wanted? It's a good question, to which there are multiple possible answers. In other words, I don't know. I'm not likely ever to know. Joan's own enthusiasm for marriage may have been a key point. Joan, the second sister, the less pretty one, the one said to be the clever one but overlooked, all eyes on the beauty – Joan was determined, after Sebastian died and Ottilie became the heir of Peattie, that she would marry first. She would marry before Ottilie and on her 18th birthday as their mother had done. Gaining the attention and approval of their mother had become tacitly a competition by then. Everybody talks about Ursula's closing down after Sebastian died, but nobody much discusses Edith doing the same. In the four years that passed between Seb's death and Joan's marriage, Edith suffered seriously from depression, although if necessary – on birthdays, at Christmas, presented by a child with good news – she would up her game, snapping out of her withdrawn, monosyllabic normality, returning to the present with unconvincing words that all was well.

What you have to understand, my mother has said to me since I died, sitting with me in the wood, is that everybody was always trying to make Edith smile. Ottilie and Joan, specifically, were always trying to make their mother smile. The bringing of temporary sorts of lightness into her life: that was a project on the footing of a constant unofficial campaign. So, at 17 Joan came up with what seemed like the ultimate good news: she announced there would be a wedding, a small, white, perfect family wedding. Joan feigned her passion for Euan, her belief in their future together so skilfully that her mother was entranced by it. The house was full of love, of plans, of possibility again; Edith was caught up in the spirit of the thing and seemed almost like her old self, Henry said, his gratitude obvious. For a time Joan was the heroine of the dynasty.

But why did Euan consent? There might have been an element of wanting to be close to the beloved, though that seems particularly wet, even for him. I suppose that it was his only chance to stay in the Peattie circle, but I struggle to make sense even of that. My mother's theory is that Euan cooled off and Joan threatened to tell. What she had to tell was that she'd been under age when they began having sex, only just 15, a situation that was illegal and actionable. Joyce and Richard Catto, unaware of this development in their courtship, brought Euan to Peattie three times a year, not only for the summer holiday but during the Easter and October school breaks. Even so, why would Euan care enough about the threat of scandal to marry someone he didn't much like? Certainly he fooled them all. Everyone regarded the boy Alan, the winking, wandering-eyed, innuendo-making, cheeky and lascivious boy Alan, as the likely source of trouble with daughters, and went to lengths to protect them from him. Meanwhile, the attention of parents and friends successfully diverted, it was studious, lanky, rather saturnine, ambitious and well-mannered Euan who harvested the virginity first of Joan and then of her sister. Not that either was unwilling.

Ottilie was puzzled by the engagement. It had been obvious from the beginning, to Ottilie anyway: Joan's being second choice. Even at 14 she'd been aware of it, during the Easter that Euan first visited. She'd been aware of Euan looking at her, his calm observant absorption of her, his trying repeatedly to meet her eyes with his. It became seriously awkward. He wasn't deterred when Ottilie let it be known that Alan had kissed her. She'd let Alan kiss her, for heaven's sake, better to get the message across, to suggest that there was another pairing, that she was unavailable. It didn't seem to help. Even when he became engaged officially to Joan, Euan had engineered their being alone together. In the outhouses, getting the tennis racquets, backing Ottilie against the wall and placing his hands either side of her, closing in, a look of pathetic sincerity on his face as he bent to kiss, Ottilie ducking under his arms and away. He sought her out repeatedly, in outhouses, over the net, at the loch, in the wood, in the linen room: Euan Catto made his declarations and Euan Catto was rebuffed.

"It wasn't as if he knew me, even. He never got the chance to know me." Ottilie said this to me, recently. "I never gave him anything of myself, no encouragement. It was all in his head. In his eyes. That was all it was. It wasn't about me. I don't think we ever had a proper conversation. Joan kept him on a tight leash, but he'd devise excuses to slip the leash and come looking. When he made his declarations they were always abstract: how he loved and worshipped me, how he was yearning. He didn't know what I liked, what I felt, what I wanted, what I didn't want, what I thought about anything. He wasn't interested. He wanted to screw me – sorry Michael, but there you are. He wanted to screw me: that's all it was, and I don't know even now whether he dressed it up purposely – my eyes like the sea in winter – all that stuff, purely to try and get me to have sex with him ... the cynicism of that! It takes my breath away. Or whether he thought that he meant it, whether he had bought into it himself and meant every word. I felt it later, like a cold wind, Michael, the cost, the implications of looking as I did. You didn't see me then but at 16 I was ridiculously lovely, I say that without vanity; well, without much vanity. I couldn't help it, and I hated it. My body was the enemy. It seemed like it was intent on betraying me, whoring without permission, advertising itself to men, my arse so pert in the bloody shorts, my little waist curving in. I let my hair grow long thinking it was unvain and unworldly to have this long little-girl hair, but looking back, looking at the photographs, it was down to my waist and wavy and did yet more advertising. The irony was that I didn't want it, this power I had over men, over Euan, over Alan, over Christian. I'd go into the village and be stared at and wolf-whistled at and it was just *horrible*. But it seemed to me that it was all about a woman as a receptacle, a cup and a vice, a woman as a commodity. That's an appalling way to look at a person, isn't it? I was so afraid you'd become one of them. I admit it, I was afraid. Because what's the outcome of that world view? It has a hundred devastating outcomes, I promise you. And what happens later, when the bloom of youth has gone? The man who sees a woman that way, as something of use, as a service, he's going to move on. So that's what happened, and that's why I never hooked up with anyone, I suppose. It was the terms of Euan's desire; they were educational. I realised I didn't want to be part of it. I didn't want to be any part of it."

Feeling this way and this strongly, why would Ottilie go to Euan the night before he married Joan? Only because of Joan's mistake, her grave mistake, cancelling the long-planned 18th-birthday party, insisting that the birthday had to be the date of the wedding. When Ottilie protested Joan told her that she didn't care what Ottilie thought, that Ottilie was a spoilt cow who'd had everything her own way too long, that Ottilie was a vain prima donna, that she, Joan, was looking forward more to leaving Ottilie behind than to any other facet of her marriage (the plan, then, being that Euan would work at an English college or else overseas). It was only after this that Ottilie decided to exercise her power. And so it was, having said nothing in response to this outburst, having been accused, in Joan's parting shot, of being an ice queen, a cold fish who cared for nothing and no one but her sketchbooks, that Ottilie contrived to be alone with Euan. She joined him in the bathroom at the end of the corridor, an unsolicited visit timed to coincide with Euan's, preparing for his stag night in the village. Ottilie came into the bathroom uninvited, to find Euan dressed other than for his shirt, and shaving. She shut the door behind her and came to him, dressed only in a silk robe that once was Tilly's.

Sometimes a pact can be achieved without any obvious negotiations taking place, without a single word being spoken, and this was one of those times. The whole house party narrative thread: that was always wishful thinking on Henry's part. He knew, or thought he knew, what the rest of the family imagined: that Alan was the probable father. Nothing could be said to Alan about this, of course. Not at the time. As Henry said, if Alan thought himself the father, Alan would in all likelihood assert his rights. It was vital to keep quiet, to focus on the house party. Meanwhile, Ottilie was subjected to a sequence of inquisitions. She wouldn't tell, but nor would she deny Alan. Vita wrote an account of a conversation she had with Ottilie at the time, and when I went to her she had looked out the old notebook and had found the page, the book shaking in her shrivelled old hands, and handed it to me, pointing at the relevant paragraph.

"Just tell me this one thing," I said to her. "And I promise you that it will never go further. It will never be spoken of outside this room."

She looked at me, her beautiful sad eyes.

"I'll tell you what I think," I said to her. "I feel disinclined to agree with Henry about this dossier of his. Tell me and I won't say a word to him, or to anyone, ever so long as I live. It wasn't at the house party, was it?"

She shook her head and she left the room in tears, and that's when it became clear to me that Alan Dixon was the father of the child.

The rumour that Alan was the father got to the village. Ottilie has always assumed that Euan was the source, the original source way up river of the news, and that seems most likely. Alan, teased and congratulated at the pub, waited for his chance and eventually got his opportunity to speak, stopping to talk to Ottilie as she went by with the dogs one morning, heavily pregnant and lovelier than ever.

"Apparently I'm the father," he said.

"Apparently," she answered, her face giving no clue.

"Why'd you tell them that?"

"I didn't."

"Well, that's what they think."

"I'm aware."

"But you and me, we didn't do it."

"You have a short memory," she said to him. "Don't you remember our night of passion, the night of the wedding, under the white moon in the wood?"

Alan looked as if he was having to reconsider. "But we didn't do it," he said again.

Two days after this a lucky encounter brought some enlightenment. He'd gone down to the loch in his lunch break and as he approached through the field, heard raised voices and realised that it was the twins. It was an easy matter, standing at the edge of the wood and listening; they were too busy arguing to think to look for eavesdroppers. Alan saw what value his being the father had to Ottilie, how deeply the idea angered and disturbed her sister, how passively Ottilie let her sister become more greatly angered and disturbed. How by turns thunderstruck and furious Joan was, and vitally how very impotent. Joan's impotence was crucial. Joan raged and demanded and Ottilie was impervious. By the time he returned to the cottage, Alan had convinced himself that it must be true, that whatever the facts it was going to be true. Mixed in with his apprehension there began to be sparks of euphoria. He envisioned a deal being done with Henry: a quiet marriage, a modest settlement. Later, reflecting more coolly on things, when it was obvious that Ottilie wouldn't agree to the marriage, the settlement still seemed likely. If Ottilie had decided that he was the official father of the baby, there would be rights and responsibilities. And there would be status. Or so he thought.

Pip never got the written explanation that Henry promised him. Instead, Henry wrote to Edith, a letter written during his period of seclusion, a letter that Edith has refused to show anyone else. In it, Henry expressed a wish that he be buried in the family mausoleum alongside Sebastian. My mother, in her many rather one-sided dialogues with me in the wood, has expressed the worry that what Henry wanted, what Henry specified, was that he be buried with Sebastian and that Edith should be interred elsewhere. Whatever the case, the letter had a huge effect on Edith. I've seen it, as a physical object, its seven or eight pale blue sheets twice folded, and have glimpsed Henry's handwriting, characteristically small and perfect across the pages, as even as if typewritten in a handwriting font. I haven't read it but I have seen it. Edith takes it out of its envelope and reads it almost daily. Information trickled out from its contents piecemeal.

"Henry wants to be laid to rest in the mausoleum" was the first thing that was announced, the only thing that was

said about the letter on the day it was opened. The mausoleum, of course, was full, the bodies stacked in a format
rather like a sinister limestone chest of drawers, so one of
the Victorians was removed to the village. The point was
made that perhaps a second 19th-century Salter should be
moved to make way for Edith to lie alongside Henry, but
Edith didn't want to discuss it. This is what made Ottilie
suspicious.

The second of his wishes Edith went directly to Ottilie
about. She arrived unannounced at the cottage the day
after Henry's funeral, wearing black and grey versions of
her usual clothes, the wide trousers, plimsolls, overshirt,
beads. She knocked on the studio door and when Ottilie
answered, paint-spattered in dungarees, Edith told her that
she'd come to talk about Michael, that it was something
important and they had to talk. The studio was in its usual
cluttered state. Ottilie had to clear a pile of sketches and
opened books, musty clothbound books of 19th-century
engravings laid one upon the other, taking them up with
care from the sofa cushions to make room for her mother
to sit. She settled Edith there and opened the cupboard that
proves to be a tiny kitchen of sorts, revealing sink, microwave and kettle. Nothing much was said while Ottilie made
the coffee. Edith looked around her, at the mylar stencils
pegged up on a line to dry, at the shelves of stones and
shells, at the meths-scented jam jars, lids long gone, from
which brushes poked of different gauges and at different
angles, beechwood and oxblood; at the boxes and stacks
of paints and charcoals. Every wall was shelved above the
dado rail, and every shelf was fully laden. Beneath the work
table and pushed hard to one side a large cardboard box
contained folded-up bedclothes, used ones, decrisped and
unsquared in their folding and flopping, a pillow placed on
top and a glimpse of striped cotton pyjama.

"You're living here?"

"Of course."

"No, I mean, you're living in here in the studio, sleeping here?"

"Sometimes I don't like to be in the cottage."

"You sleep here on this sofa?"

"It's fine. The house can feel too ... too housey. It makes housey demands on me. A housey life of things and doings. I don't like it. It's good to be surrounded by the work. Life's here and ongoing. When I am awake in the middle of the night I can get on with it. It's cosy. Like a child's playhouse."

"When did you last sleep in your bedroom?"

"It's been a little while."

"But – "

"Mother. Please don't fuss. It's all as I wish it. What did you want to say to me about Michael?"

"Your father wrote me a letter."

"I know."

"He wants Michael to be found. No matter the consequences for Ursula."

"I know, about Dad wanting Michael retrieved. He told me. When I went to see him."

"He told you. When was this?"

"When he was living in the bedroom. He telephoned me. He wanted to talk and I said I was in the middle of making a print and could I call back, and then I abandoned what I was doing and drove up to Peattie."

"He didn't tell me."

"I told him I was happy for him to get his wish."

They looked at each other.

"Is this all you've been waiting for?" Ottilie asked her mother. "Dad making a move? Someone to break the silence?"

"There's something sacred about last wishes."

Edith sipped repetitively at her coffee, her eyes vague.

"How do you feel about it?" Ottilie asked her.

"I need to get away from her," Edith said, as if it were an answer.

"From Ursula."

"Yes."

"But why, after all these years?"

"I can't talk about it."

Ottilie climbed her mahogany library steps, borrowed one weekend from Peattie and never returned, so as to reach the highest shelf, and brought down a box from among a stack of tupperware. The lid was removed and she offered her mother lemon cake. Edith broke a small piece from one of the sponge fingers and ate it, looking up enquiringly.

"I cook, in the middle of the night," Ottilie explained, "if I'm not in the right frame of mind for working. And there are biscuits. I throw most of them away because I don't really like to eat them. I just enjoy making them." She took a tin down from the bookshelf, adjusting the books that were leaning against it, repropping them so they didn't fall. Within were cherry-topped pale rounds, rendered paler with white icing.

"I'm teaching myself from Michael's books. I'm cooking my way round them." She saw that Edith was staring at her. "What?"

"You're not actually a curious person; not about people, anyway," Edith said. "I've never seen that about you until today."

"How do you mean?"

"You don't seem curious about why it is that I say I can't see Ursula."

"You said you couldn't talk about it. Of course I'm curious. Just hampered by good manners, like all of us."

"I have to tell someone. I almost told Thomas but then I found I couldn't."

"What is it?" Ottilie came to sit beside her mother, the two of them side by side, each holding a mug of coffee in just the same way, left hands threaded through the handles, right hands cradling the cup, their hands identical.

"I told Henry something I shouldn't have," Edith said.

"What do you mean?"

"Something about Ursula."

"When was this?"

"The evening before he took root in the bedroom."

"What about it? Something about Michael?"

"Not about Michael."

"Then what?"

"You know what it was. We never talk about it but we allude to it. I think we should talk about it, Ottilie."

"You mean the lie, don't you? The lie about Sebastian."

Edith gasped. "That's what I call it. The lie."

"I was never going to tell you," Ottilie said. "Never. I don't know about Joan; we've never talked about it, not once. Have you spoken about it with Joan?"

"No. And I'm not going to."

"How long have you known? You said it was after Joan's wedding."

"Ursula came to me. You'd got her talking again."

"I'm sorry. It had all got out of hand. Joan and I – we were near deranged trying to outdo one another. It was a kind of mental illness, I think. She'd never have married Euan if it hadn't been for Sebastian, you know. We have this one thing in common, Joan and I: neither one of us has ever been in love."

"That makes me very sad."

"I'm sorry. I'm sorry. I'm sorry about lying to you. Grandpa Andrew asked us to."

"I know. Ursula told me. Ursula told me everything."

"I don't want to say any more about it. Do you?"

"Your poor father. Such a shock. He was heartbroken, absolutely heartbroken."

"That we'd lied? I'm so sorry."

"Not that you'd *lied*. He understood that much. You were trying to protect us from the truth."

"I don't get what you mean."

"Ursula was upset too, because she couldn't make him understand. She'd waited all these years to tell him, asking me over and over if she should tell him or not tell him. But then she had this fateful conversation with Alan, the day he went off to France: you know about that."

"No. What happened? Fateful how?"

"They had a conversation about the police. She'd suggested they'd see her side. He suggested they wouldn't. He was talking about Michael. In any case, Ursula decided she had to talk to Henry. Henry would understand. When I told Henry, it turned out that Ursula had told him already, earlier that day. I went to see her and she was distraught, burning with the injustice of it. She told me she hated her father; she'd told him she hated him. She couldn't make him see how it had happened. He wasn't interested in her explanation, you see. He told her that it didn't matter what she'd felt and what she'd intended. Which of course was the exact opposite of what I'd been saying to her."

"I think you were right. It must be the intention that matters. Nobody thinks she intended Michael to die. I'm hardest on her – I can't forgive – but not even I think differently."

"About Sebastian ..."

"About lying, I'm so sorry. Grandpa Andrew insisted. We weren't there, we didn't see. We lied to you, saying we'd seen. It was too late when we got there, already too late. Not that it changes anything." Ottilie paused, biting down on her lip. "The thing I've had to live with is that it could have changed everything. If we'd been there. If we'd only been there."

Edith looked carefully into her daughter's face, and it was at this point, I think, that she realised that Ottilie didn't know what she knew; that they'd been talking at cross-purposes. Only Edith had known the truth about Sebastian, all of these years. Edith and then Henry. Edith made a decision: she could have told all; she decided to say nothing.

"Mother. What is it?"

"I'm so cold suddenly. I'm cold, can you pass me the blanket?"

Edith handed Ottilie the coffee cup and curled up against the sofa arm, closing her eyes. "I'm sorry but I need to sleep. It comes on, it comes over me like this."

"You're ill," Ottilie said. "I'll get someone. Your hands are ice cold. I'll go and telephone."

Edith was sleeping when Patricia Nixon called by, curled on her side and sleeping deeply, and had to be woken so that the doctor could reassure herself that vital signs were convincingly vital. Dr Nixon diagnosed nervous exhaustion and spoke of the need for proper rest. Henry's funeral was, after all, less than 24 hours in the past, and these things take their physical toll. She presented Edith with pills, just to get over this little hump, she said, this little blip, and Ottilie said that she'd keep Edith with her for a day or two and keep an eye on her. Edith slept and woke to drink tea, and didn't say much, her eyes unfocussed, and slept again under the blanket, and dozed throughout an evening which Ottilie spent with her, sitting in the chair by the window.

Ottilie passed the time in silence, at first drawing and reading and then, having abandoned both of these, looking out of the window, a woman in outline in the dusk. She took her hair down and put it up again several times, took her jewellery off and put it on again, her earrings, the silver bracelet of intertwining snakes she'd bought in South Africa. She looked at her hands, pressing them against the glass. Edith half opened her eyes from time to time and was aware of these things going on, and had a response to them, but couldn't summon the words. She didn't speak but she produced an account, her own account, a narrative record, letting feelings speak for her, thinking and not speaking her

411

responses. I understand; I have felt the same. Occasionally, I've thought them so emphatically that it seemed almost as if they *were* spoken, as if they had entered the record and must be acknowledged by others; as if I'd be able to appeal to the others, should the subject arise, on the grounds of my own strong inner dialogue having been heard.

On the second day Edith had a walk along the beach. She returned to the studio tired and spent the remainder of the daylight hours on the studio sofa under the blue rug, reading and napping and following the progress of the work. Ottilie was absorbed in preliminary sketches from black-and-white photographs she'd taken in the wood. At dusk they went into the cottage; they should move into the cottage properly, Ottilie said. She made up the bed in my old room and in the early morning, through the half-open door, she saw Edith handling my things, watched her murmuring advance through one item, one drawer, one piece of clothing after another, holding old shirts of mine to her nose and inhaling. The phone had begun to ring, and it was Pip, wanting to speak to Edith, and Edith was called, and emerged holding a pair of my socks.

"Would you like to stay on for a while?" Ottilie asked her mother afterwards. She'd heard Edith on the phone, had picked up on her uncertainty in answering Pip's queries about when she was returning home. Edith's relief at being asked to stay on was absolute, and it was agreed she'd remain at the cottage until she felt stronger. Pip reassured her in his daily telephone calls that this was fine; it wasn't even an issue: Mog and Joan had taken on the running of Peattie and so far it had all been remarkably amicable. Finally he confessed that he'd been calling from the house, having taken a second week's compassionate leave. He didn't care about the demotion that was certain to follow this, he said, as he was about to hand in his notice anyway.

When Pip and Mog came to the cottage to see Edith the following weekend, Edith told them she didn't want to return to Peattie to live.

"What, not ever?" Mog was astonished.

"This feeling will pass, at least it may pass," Pip told her. "You need to give it time before making these big decisions."

"I don't intend even to visit."

"You can't mean for ever," Mog said. "You can't."

"It's too early at any rate," Pip told her soothingly. "What you need is to take some time."

"Not ever, and I don't want to talk about it."

"It's important we do talk about it, though."

"I don't want ever to go back."

"But this is what happens when one's bereaved," Pip pointed out. "It'll take time to readjust."

"I'm not going to; I hope not to," Edith said. "Recovering, going back, adjusting. These would be a failure. Don't wish that for me." The realisation that she was continuing to live in her own unexplained version of life – that this was necessary – crossed her face, crossing her mind like an animal swift across a busy road, dodging traffic.

Pip looked at Ottilie helplessly. "So she's going to stay on with you for now?"

"She's going to live with me."

"Permanently?"

"For as long as she wants. For now she says permanently."

"What will happen to Peattie?"

"There are options that need to be talked about."

"Here's what I've decided," Edith was already saying. "Peattie can be sold – wait, don't look like that, I haven't finished – or you can take it on, you children. I've already spoken to your mother and she and Euan don't want to, though she'd like to manage the gatehouse and the cottages. Redecorate them and manage them."

"George isn't coming back?"

"I spoke to him," Ottilie said, "and he wants to stay at the care home, at least for now. He might go out to France when he feels stronger."

Jet had already moved into a flat in the town, to live with friends. Pip and Mog were itching to mention Ursula, what was going to happen about Ursula, but neither of them did so.

Ottilie said, "While I have the three of you here together, I should say to you that I know about Alan; Dad told me what he said about Michael, about Michael surviving. It is of course nonsense and I don't want to talk about it, actually, so we won't, but I wanted you to know." The others murmured their sympathy. "Please, no pity," she begged. "I can't."

"Oh, darling," Edith said.

"Mother. Please don't. There's really no need and I'd rather be practical. I'll be fine about it. I don't want to talk about it any more. Getting back to Peattie, and what's to be done about Peattie. What do you think?" She turned her attention to Pip exclusively. "God knows where the money will come from. A hotel of some sort is the only paying way, I imagine."

"We've already given it some thought," Pip said. "Angelica's willing. We'll consult with Mog, of course, Mog and the others."

"We'll do as Dad wished," Ottilie said, stacking the coffee cups. "We'll lay Michael properly to rest and we'll deal with whatever the consequences are, and then there will be the memory of Michael but there will no longer be the mystery of Michael, and that's what I need." She scraped cake from the tea plates. "I can't tell you how much I need that."

Mog put her hand over Edith's. "This is really what you want, to live here?"

"Yes." Edith's face was full of melancholy.

"Though we're going to travel as much as we can for the next 12 months," Ottilie added. "As much as we can afford."

"Where will you travel to?"

"I have a few things planned. Morocco. The south of Spain. And then we'll see."

They wouldn't be going to France. Marseille had been planned but was now abandoned. Unsure of Alan's location, the whole country had become saturated in threat. Not that anyone feared running into him: that would have been supernatural among coincidences, but George had been vague about where Alan had settled, saying he couldn't remember the name of the town, and so it was instinctive with Edith and Ottilie to stay clear of France altogether. Alan had told George on the phone that he was in the Perigord.

"People call this area the Dordogne, but really it's the Perigord," he'd said.

This was information that George wouldn't be passing on to anyone. Alan confided in his father just before he left: that secretly he was Michael's father, that Henry had given him the money to buy the van, that the whole family knew the truth. Alan rings weekly from France, telling George a fund of funny stories about his new life as a gardener and handyman, his own boss at last. He omits, though, to describe the nights he spends at the café in the village, installing himself at his usual table in the corner just after six, sweaty from the day's work in holiday house gardens. He's acquired a reputation as a loudmouth, someone few people want to argue with, haunting the café till late, a pudgy, sun-pinked Ancient Mariner who stoppeth one in three, telling his tale over and over of how he fathered a boy out of wedlock, a boy born into a noble family.

"One of the highest-ranking families in Scotland," he says, tapping his nose, the sun blisters crusting on it.

Ursula's paid companion is a woman Susan Marriott recommended to Edith, an ex-foster mother of many difficult children. She comes in from the town every morning and goes home at night, after reporting each evening to Pip at the house. Ursula's first repetitive enquiries about when her mother would come back were answered with the news that Edith was poorly – not seriously ill but too ill to come home. She needed somebody to look after her: Ursula understood this. She asks Edith every Saturday how she is and if she's well enough yet to return, and Edith says not yet, but soon, she hopes it will be soon, feeling unable to do anything but tell a lie. The companion brings Ursula to the cottage, to the studio, once a week for tea at four o'clock. Ottilie is always present, because Edith says she can't do it alone. My mother is lovely to Ursula. They never talk about what's past. Instead, they make art together.

The possibility of Edith's return to Peattie is still spoken of as likely though no one really believes it. It will happen when she is ready, they say to each other. Thus far she hasn't ever been ready and hasn't returned. The things she wants are ferried out to her and the things she doesn't want are ferried back. She has consigned Peattie to the past.

"Don't you want to visit Henry?" Pip asks her on the phone from time to time.

"Henry's here," she tells him. "Henry's with me wherever I go."

Chapter 24

Petra said that she would carry the shrimping net and the bucket, that they weighed nothing. Eager to be seen to be helpful, she went on to load herself up with the rest: the picnic bag, the rug that was rubberised on the back and the badminton set, zipped into its red vinyl cover. Ottilie took the rug and the picnic from her. She had her own canvas bag, her art bag, a purple one with a long handle that hooked across the body and was dotted with slogan-bearing badges. Joan took the sailing boat that Andrew had made for Sebastian, one hand placed at each end of it, presenting it held out slightly in front of her body. This was to be its maiden voyage.

Sebastian insisted on walking at the front, because Henry had told him, perhaps too often, that all this land, all these buildings and trees, were his, would be his. It was Henry's way of talking to him, of getting his attention: it was this big thing they had in common. Sebastian may have been the fourth of Edith and Henry's children, but thanks to long-established precedent he was also sole heir to the estate. People recognised this, outsiders and neighbours recognised it, as well as family friends, as well as family members. Sebastian the little prince was treated with a kind of comprehending awe. Nobody called with congratulations when Ursula was born. Ursula had overheard some friends of Edith's gossiping to this effect, and being inherently quick on the uptake, had asked her sisters why this was.

"It's because you're only a girl," Joan told her.

"It was the same with us," Ottilie added, her tone consoling. "That's how it is with the Salters."

"Only boys count," Joan clarified, somewhat brutally.

"It was the same with Daddy," Ottilie said. "He had three big sisters too."

"Only Daddy got given Peattie," Joan added. "The sisters were thrown out to starve on the street."

"But Tilly lives here," Ursula said, reasonably enough.

"Only because she used to look after Granny. Actually, she's a sort of servant."

"Joan, you go too far," Ottilie reprimanded. "For heaven's sake."

"Well, it's true, isn't it? Why should it be Dad's house and only Dad's just because he's a man?"

"Joan."

"Well I think it was all wrong. They'd made their plans. They were going to live here together, open the hotel. Ursa was – what – 20 when Daddy was born. But that didn't count for anything. Whoosh. Everything was his. Instantly."

"Will you please just shut up."

Sebastian was stamping along at the front, his elbows raised and his knees lifting with every step of the march, raising the dust of the path, looking very small for a soldier in his red sandals, blue shorts, green windcheater. He was an adorable child, his doting mother said, his doting mother was always saying, day in and day out, unable to prevent herself from public and continual adoration. She'd look to his much older sisters for confirmation, for ratification. Her eyes shone with it, infatuated. Her hand kept going to his small blond head, and cupping his bottom, or encompassing the baby fat above his knees, squeezing its wobbly baby softness. He couldn't run past her without Edith reaching and grabbing and making playful carnivorous noises as he struggled to be free. Sebastian Henry Salter was too mollycoddled, Henry said. Too mothered. He was turning into the sort of boy who cried if he got dirty or if you tried to lower him onto a pony. Henry worried that Sebastian was showing signs of effeminacy. Like Ottilie, he liked to draw. He loved books. That was all very well; drawing and reading were to be encouraged. But there had to be balance. Sebastian had asked for a doll for his birthday, and wanted to wear Ursula's swimsuit, one with bows across the bodice, and had attempted to paint his toenails with polish of Joan's. These were facts that Henry was incapable of being phlegmatic about.

At four, Sebastian had babyish curls at his neck, wavy wispy curls that his mother insisted on keeping intact until he was old enough to go to school, when – and she could see Henry's point – they might become a trigger for persecution. Sebastian's name was down for an establishment a hundred miles south of here, where he was to be a weekly boarder because of the travelling. Until he turned seven the plan was that he be taught at home by Edith. The twins were at the local high school and were uncomplaining – quite the reverse: they'd said they'd hate to be sent away – but Ursula was about to start at the village primary and felt the differentiation from Sebastian keenly. Why couldn't she stay at home and be taught by Mummy till she was older? Why not though? Why not really? Edith was asked again and again. Didn't she want Ursula to be at home and learn with Sebastian? Edith's explanations were unconvincing.

Ursula was at the back of the procession, and dragging her feet. She had been instructed to hurry up, to hurry and catch up right now, but she dawdled along nonetheless, a picture of five-year-old non-compliance. Wearing clothes she despised, clothes that Edith had more or less to manhandle her into, red jeans and a striped sweater and strikingly small blue plimsolls, she stared morosely at the ground, scuffing her play shoes into the grit, until her dreaminess was interrupted by something big looming its shadow over her. Joan, her mouth pursed and her face determined, took Ursula's hot little hand and began to pull her along, Ursula leaning back uncooperatively on the diagonal. At five she was already demonstrably highly strung. Battles were fought daily over many things. Her father had told her, in a fit of impatience he brooded over, that she was nothing but a thorn in his side, and Ursula wouldn't forget this. Ursula doesn't believe in people not meaning what they say. She has a phenomenal memory and remembers everything, even now, mentally filing and cataloguing all of it, every casually directed word. People said she was selfish, that she was stubborn, but from Ursula's point of view that wasn't it at all. It was other people, the way other people behaved, that made no sense. The question of fresh air, for instance. Why must she go out for a walk with Sebastian, and try to play badminton with Ottilie in a gale, when she could just as easily get the air from an open window? Grown-ups and sisters said that it wasn't the same but they were not logical, a word that Grandpa Andrew, delighting in her precocious vocabulary, had taught her. She didn't want to go to the loch. She wanted to be in the house, in her room alone with her things and a chair barricading the door. She thought fresh air was stupid. She thought her haircut was stupid. Her wavy hair, which had been pleasingly straggly until last week, uncut since her birth, had been shorn into a bob like her grandmother's with the same long fringe, and after her bath Edith blow-dried it straight. Vita said it was darling but Ursula told her that *she* was stupid as well.

When they arrived at the wood, Ottilie spread the picnic rug at the edge of the beach and put the picnic – a rudimentary one of crisps and warm fruit squash – propped in its bag against a tree root, though Sebastian raided it almost immediately. Ursula went off and sat on the plinth of the tomb, where the day before she had left a line of pink stones in a row. Sebastian took his snack to the water's edge to watch Petra launching the boat. Petra suggested crisps as ideal boat cargo, and Sebastian went back to raid the bag a second time, whining that he needed Ursula's crisps too, for the game. Joan couldn't be bothered to argue. He enjoyed arranging the crisps, with accompanying commentary, arranging and rearranging them in the hold. Grandpa Andrew had made a huge amount of effort with the design of the boat, giving it living quarters whittled out inside the hatch and lots of little carved details.

Joan wasn't aware that she'd gone to sleep until she opened her eyes. When she woke, stiff and chilly on the rug, the breeze blowing her hair across her face, she couldn't hear anything at first. The quiet was ominous. She raised her head from the shoulder, went up on her elbows and was relieved to see the others, shin-deep in water, quietly purposeful in the shallows, their shoes scattered on the beach; Ottilie, Sebastian, Petra. Ursula was standing on tiptoe not far away, scratching at the bark of a tree with a stone and singing one of her made-up songs. Seeing Joan watching, she stopped what she was doing and came across. Joan thought Ursula was going to speak to her but instead she went right past, to the tree root where Ottilie had stowed the picnic bag.

"I'm afraid Sebastian took your crisps," Joan told her. "Your drink's there, though, if you want it."

Ursula ignored her. She pulled something light and pale-coloured, something folded up, out of the bag, and went back through the trees to where she'd come from.

"What's that, what have you got there?" Joan called after her, sitting up properly and paying attention. It was a length of old netting, thick and creamy French netting, the kind that Henry's mother had decided should be installed at all the windows, blocking out the light. Sunlight was the enemy, fading the curtains and furnishings. It was the first thing Henry did when he inherited: he took the netting down. Once at at a safer distance, Ursula began wrapping the curtain netting carefully around herself with nimble hands. She pulled a long string of ivy from a tree, the ivy putting up only token resistance, coming away from the trunk in several small gasps, and wound this around the net costume, tying and tucking it. Joan, knowing better than to remonstrate, said nothing. When Ursula tried to meet her gaze, Joan pretended not to have seen her, pretended to be fascinated by one of the willows around the tomb. That's what people were always advising, when Ursula was odd. "Pretend not to notice; that's best."

Sebastian had eaten the second packet of crisps, taking them out of the hold one at a time and crunching on them. He told Petra she must find him something else, and so she went off obediently, smiling, finding his imperious tone amusing, looking for narrow stones and offering them with amused faux-humility as personnel for the Wind Ranger: that was the name of the boat, painted by Andrew in italic on the side. Once all the stones had been approved and put in place, Sebastian said he was bored. He got up and went and sat beside Ottilie on the jetty steps and began telling her a pirate story.

"Then the girls are tied up and have to walk the plank." He was determined about this.

"That doesn't seem kind," Ottilie said, entertained.

"It's bad luck to have a girl on board, you know."

"I'm sure modern pirates don't think so. They'd quite like to have their eyepatches laundered and eat something different from boiled fish, wouldn't they?"

"They love fish, especially the guts. They hate girls, though."

Now Petra came and stood shyly beside them, and Ottilie began speaking to her in school German. Joan, who hadn't a word of German but who heard the word *Alan* spoken, was suspicious immediately, what it was that Petra and Ottilie could be talking about. She went down to the shore to interrupt them.

Ursula watched as Ottilie put Sebastian on her shoulders, watched as Ottilie jogged with him away along the shore-line, bouncing him gently up and down as if in a rising trot. Everybody was always trying to make Sebastian happy. Nobody suggested games that Ursula might like; Ursula was left to herself whether she felt like it or not. Distorted by the rocking, the up-and-down motion, Sebastian's voice was heard asking if they could make some horse jumps in the wood. Returning to the jetty, and lifting Sebastian gently from her shoulders to set him down, Ottilie asked Petra to give her a hand with the making of them. Petra assented and Joan followed them into the trees.

The boat had been left sitting on the beach, and after some moments of indecision, advancing and retreating, Ursula darted forward and took it. She ran with it, holding it out in front of her with both hands, finding it heavy and stumbling as she went, running along the shingle, up onto the steps, the netting unwinding and trailing and almost tripping her; she had to stop and yank it free, leaving it there in a heap. She placed her first small foot on the jetty, poised there, one small foot forward, looking around her, knowing it was forbidden and dealing with prohibitory internal voices. Her mother's voice. Her father's. The jetty was strictly out of bounds unless they were accompanied by a grown-up or sister, something they'd had drummed into them a thousand times. She paused almost a moment too long. Joan had seen her, and ran towards her now, shouting that she mustn't, that she wouldn't dare, but

Ursula must and would. She ran along the slatted planks, and had almost reached the end when she let the boat fall, and crouching beside it, snapped the slender masts and ripped the rigging and threw the cotton sails aside. Just as Joan reached her, she picked up the boat carcass and threw it into the loch. It disappeared into the tea-brown water and bobbed up again, not far away, though well out of reach. Joan said nothing, just took hold of Ursula and hoisted her into the air. She was a skinny little thing, under-sized, underweight, hardly ate. Joan slotted her under one arm and marched her off the jetty, Ursula unresisting and limp as a doll. Then she put her down on the beach and hit her as hard as she could. Joan smacked her so hard on the behind that she jarred her wrist and had to shake the pain out, wincing and cursing. Ursula didn't run or cower or protest or even flinch. With the other hand Joan slapped her on the thigh and the arm and then, provoked by her lack of reaction, by the stoical blankness of her staring, she hit her hard across the face, and all the time that she was hitting her she was shouting.

"You evil child! What the hell did you do that for? All that effort by Grandpa Andrew! Do you know how upset he'll be? And he's ill, Ursula, he has a bad heart. Look at Sebastian crying. You did that. You! How could you be so bloody wicked?" Ursula stared at Joan. She didn't cry. She didn't speak. The first flush of a red hand-print was blooming on her cheek.

Ottilie took no notice of all this, acting as if she hadn't seen, which seemed to Ursula like a betrayal. Ottilie had always been the sister she could rely on, and if Ottilie had asked Ursula would have told her: she would have explained everything and would have found sympathy. But Ottilie didn't ask. She was gathering up the broken boat pieces on the jetty with one hand and holding tight onto Sebastian's arm with the other. Petra, who had remained in the wood, keeping out of the way, came forward now, shouting up, asking Ottilie if she could help. Meanwhile, Joan stood on the shore, looking out at the water and narrating her dissatisfaction, her self-justification, in a steady monologue loud enough for all to bear witness to.

"I shouldn't have slapped her. I know that. You don't have to tell me that. But honestly. Day after day. It's continual provocation. Day after day the same. I know I shouldn't have lost my temper. I do know that. It was a mistake but sometimes a person has just had enough."

Petra was the first to see Alan. She heard the sound of the cigarette lighter, its click and flare and second click; the first greedy inhalation. There was movement in the wood, around the tomb, a flash of something pale, and her face was alarmed as she turned to look, having heard about the ghost. But it was only Alan. He was leaning against the tomb and lighting up, his other hand raised to Petra in silent greeting. She went to him, complaining in heavily accented English about the children's behaviour.

Ottilie reached as far as she could with the stick, a slim and pliable willow stick that proved next to useless. She got down on all fours and held onto the edge of the jetty as she leaned, trying to get to the boat and redirect it back towards her or at the least towards the shore, but it remained stubbornly six inches out of reach. Sebastian was holding onto the hem of her sweater and whining. She tried again, batting at the water, but she couldn't get the boat to nudge any closer and into reach. What she needed was something with a hook.

"I'm going to have to go in and get it for you," she said eventually. Sebastian was interested enough in her plan for his whining to subside. "I know: shrimping net," she told him. Shrimps were never caught here but Sebastian liked to scoop out assortments of small creatures and tiny fish and keep them in jam jars until they ran out of food and oxygen and floated, inevitably, to the surface. Ursula saved what she could. Many an aquatic life form had met its end on the path to the loch, gasping and broken, splashed out as Sebastian, racing after his sister, tried to wrest the jars and buckets back into his possession.

Joan, aware of Petra and Alan's conversation, pretended to walk off down the shore before doubling back into the trees to watch them unobserved. Petra was looking at Alan and Alan was watching Ottilie, who had returned to the picnic rug and had lifted the shrimping net. She didn't acknowledge Alan and Petra, but, taking the net back onto the beach and standing examining it, she was able to see them in peripheral vision. Alan, aware of this, smiled to himself, a reaction inappropriate to Petra's intense Germanic protests about the failings of educational method. Ottilie, frowning and intent, was examining the point at which the bowl-shaped net was wired tight onto the bamboo stem. Alan smiled again as he saw her pretending to adjust it, tilting her head a little towards the wood so as to have a clearer view of him. Then she went and retrieved the boat, finding she could do so easily from the jetty, guiding the net surging through the brown water and hooking it onto the prow before pushing it back, walking it slowly back to the shore, where Sebastian waited excitedly.

"Let me have them," he said, his little square palms outstretched and flat, and Ottilie sat him down in the shingle, putting her hand into his lap and releasing what looked like small sticks and handkerchiefs, but were bits of the boat, its shaped and whittled masts, the neatly stitched cotton triangles contributed by Tilly.

Ursula had gone off to the other end of the beach and was sitting with her back to a tree, arms around her raised knees. She saw that Sebastian had been set up with a task by Ottilie: the boat had been placed on its side, and he was to try and match the broken pieces and decide where they should go. She saw that her revenge had been counter-productive: it had brought Ottilie and Sebastian closer together.

"I'll go and get my sketchbook," Ottilie said to him, "and we can draw it all out and make a plan."

She went to the rug and picked up her notebook and a pencil, and lingered a few moments, watching Joan watching. When Ottilie returned to her brother, Joan heard him saying, "I don't want you, I want Petra."

When Joan stepped forward, telling Petra that Sebastian was asking for her, the rebuke in her voice was evident to all. Petra jumped down from the tomb, handing her cigarette to Alan, and as she did so, Alan placed his free hand at her lower back. She went and lay down beside Sebastian, propped on her forearms, and Sebastian began to instruct her.

Ottilie had been lifted to sit on the tomb in Petra's place. Seeing Alan standing between the seated Ottilie's legs, seeing him loop Ottilie's arms one after the other limply around his shoulders, seeing Alan kissing Ottilie reverently on the side of the neck, Petra dropped the rigging that she was untangling and came up from the beach. Alan took his hands out from the back of Ottilie's shorts and said, "That's my cue." Ignoring Petra, he strode away through the wood. Petra followed, saying at first quietly and then again, "Alan, Alan can you stop, please. I need to talk to you."

"I told you," Joan said to her sister. "I did tell you but you wouldn't listen." Ottilie didn't answer. She got down from the tomb and went slowly after Petra, and Joan brought up the rear.

Ursula had possession of the crew. They'd been well chosen, a group of similarly sized and weighted pebbles, elongated small ovals that had been washed smooth. She was already on the jetty with them, Sebastian following timidly. She'd suggested a game: they'd make the crew walk the plank. They weren't the real crew, she said; in fact, they weren't the crew at all, they were lady pirates. Sebastian's interest couldn't help but be piqued. They'd

427

throw them into the loch, Ursula said. Sebastian agreed and she put them down next to her feet, tipping them out of her cupped hands with a clatter.

There were eight stones. They threw three each, and then Sebastian wouldn't give the seventh to Ursula, even though it should have been her turn. He said he was going to throw the last two himself. "These are my stones," he said. Ursula told him that they weren't, that stones didn't belong to anybody, but Sebastian insisted. "All the stones are mine and only mine," he said. It was meaningless, this assertion, merely the stubbornness of a four-year-old used to getting his own way, but it was an unfortunate choice of words. He threw the seventh stone and wouldn't give up the last. Ursula tried to get it off him and he resisted with all his little might. He had the stone held tight and had bent over at the waist, his hands pushed tight between his small thighs.

Joan and Ottilie were unaware. They were standing at the other side of Sanctuary Wood, watching Petra and Alan arguing. They were standing where the trees thin out and in plain view of one another, but Alan and Petra didn't acknowledge the girls. They were too busy shouting at each other.

"Don't say you didn't," Petra shouted, "because you did; I saw you; Alan, she's 14 years old."

"You're imagining things, you silly bitch," Alan shouted back.

What did he think he was doing? Petra asked him. Was that the kind of man he was? Apparently so. In which case, she didn't want his friendship and their trip to the cinema was off. Petra was being completely ridiculous, Alan said. They were talking about someone he'd known all his life, someone like a sister to him, a girl he'd grown up with. It was only a joke. Petra was being a nag and a ranter, just like his mother. Petra was middle-aged before her time, he said: a 20-year-old hag and a dried-up old maid. He was walking briskly away as he said these last hurtful words.

Joan was walking back to the loch when she heard the splash. She hurried her pace, already composing the sentences in her mind, I'd bet: how she'd deal with the children, how she'd report them to the parents. Sebastian and Ursula had both behaved appallingly today. She could get Alan sent away; she could get Petra sacked. Petra had proved unreliable. "It's not about what I think of her, but this is a serious matter, Dad," she'd say. "She wasn't watching Sebastian properly." When the jetty came into view, Joan could see Ursula, standing almost at its end and in profile, looking down into the water. *The children have gone onto the jetty; they have thrown something in. Ursula has thrown in the boat again, well that's typical. No, the boat's on the beach, still on the beach. Sebastian must be standing directly behind her. They're going to be in so much trouble.*

She was on the jetty before she realised. Her immediate reaction was that she must find Ottilie. She turned, half jumping down the steps, and as she landed, twisting her foot and crying out, saw Ottilie emerging from the trees.

"Ottilie, Ottilie, quick!" Joan shouted. "Ottilie, he's in the water! He's in the loch! Ottilie, Ottilie, Sebastian."

Ottilie ran after her. "Sebastian! Sebastian!" The word was full of dread.

The two of them thundered along the slatted wooden walkway of the jetty, Joan limping, running towards Ursula, who hadn't moved, who was standing very still looking down into the water. Sebastian was nowhere to be seen.

"Ursula, tell me quick," Joan demanded. "Where's Sebastian? Is he in there? URSULA."

Ursula said nothing. Ursula didn't move.

Joan turned to Ottilie. "Go and get help!" She threw off her Aran sweater and kicked off her tennis shoes. She jumped off the jetty and into the loch, holding her nostrils closed, a pale girl in yellow shorts and a tennis shirt with a button-down collar.

"Find Alan!" she yelled, surfacing again almost at once, her voice distorted by the cold. The t-shirt clung tight and wet to her small buds of breasts. "Find him! Now! Don't stand there! Go and find Alan!"

Joan took charge, though she wasn't the stronger swimmer. What could Ottilie do? Argue? Jump in beside her? She must get help, one of them must. Ottilie was by far the stronger swimmer, but Joan was already in the water and there wasn't anything to do other than obey.

Joan has always blamed Ottilie for not finding Alan. But Alan was out of sight. Alan, unaware of the crisis, seemed to have vanished. It was Petra's shouts that he'd hear, returning to the loch intending to say more to her. He had more he wanted to say. He heard Petra's shouts and Joan's reprimands and knew that something was wrong. It wasn't Ottilie's calls that he heard, her long and echoey calls. Alan wasn't anywhere to be seen but Ottilie found Petra – Petra had paused in the wood to cry, and to mop her eyes – and sent her to the jetty, and then she ran onward, taking a diagonal route back onto the path further up, at the copse.

Petra hurried to the loch, and, summoned and abused by Joan – what the hell had she been doing? – waded at first hurriedly and then tentatively into the water, her white jeans staining tea-coloured with peat. She discovered that the bottom is uneven, full of small craters and bigger rocks, and then she tripped, going down chin-deep into the water, and was shouting out unintelligibly, panicking and forgetting her English, as Joan surfaced and dived again.

"Over here, over here," Joan barked at her. "You're no good there." Joan didn't stay long beneath the surface. She wasn't getting deep enough and was bothered by the wet dark, the brown and suffocating dark, the pond smell and the wafting arms of lake vegetation. Petra waded as far as her waist and seemed unable to go further. The ground was tipping away from her and she took her first step back just as Ursula, peering down from the jetty, vomited her lunch noisily into the scene.

Poor, poor Petra, who'd lied on the agency form that she could swim. Swimming was essential, she'd been told, and it had been easy to tick the box, confident she could come up with good enough reasons to avoid swimming. She was driven to the station in the early evening in the old car: sitting in the back seat alone, Henry driving, his cap pulled tight over his head, his fingers whitened on the grip of the steering wheel. Her eyes so big. Her face so wet. She begged forgiveness all the way there. It was my fault. I'm sorry; forgive me, forgive me. "Es tut mir leid; verzeih mir, bitte verzeih mir." No forgiveness was forthcoming. Nothing was said. He took her bags out of the boot and put them onto the kerb and drove away without uttering a word.

❧

When Ottilie got onto the lane she had to make a decision. Which way? Perhaps Alan had gone home. She sprinted towards the Dixons' cottage, but it turned out there was nobody there. Where the hell had Alan gone? She took off at a run towards the house, still calling his name, increasingly desperately, noting that the green-houses stood empty of human activity and that no one was in the yard. It was going to be too late. Joan and Petra wouldn't save him. The dull certainty of this throbbed dully in her head. When she burst into the study looking for Henry, she found Grandpa Andrew there, sitting looking at a letter from the bank, frowning over the top of his specs. Andrew said at first that he must tell his wife where he was going, not understanding the gravity of the situation, and called out Vita's name in the hall, before Ottilie made him see there wasn't time for that. They ran all the way back to the loch, the two of them; Ottilie running ahead, Andrew alternately jogging and walking, speeding up and jogging for a few paces before having to return to a walk, huffing and puffing, a tall white-haired figure, Roman-nosed, his face turning red. Ottilie was out ahead and so it was Ottilie who saw the scene on the jetty first. Alan was there, giving Sebastian the kiss of life, Seb's little head smeared green with weed, his face streaked brown with silt. Joan turned a grey face to Ottilie, saying, "Where the hell have you *been*?"

Anxious but methodical, Andrew began talking to Alan, making sensible, briefly-worded suggestions. Alan told him, between efforts made to breathe life in, to force water out, that Sebastian tried to swim underwater or was pushed there by the currents, was under the jetty, caught up in great ropes of weed, and if only it hadn't been so bloody dark. He'd blundered into him only by chance. Sebastian's limp little body, one perfect small foot bare, a foot that had barely begun to walk in the world, the other still in its red sandal, was turned over and his back thumped, but Sebastian was dead, irretrievably dead, a bundle of dead flesh like laundry, lying limp and in his small way heavy on the jetty, gravity having triumphed over life. Alan began to pump at his chest while Andrew took over the breathing.

It seemed a long time later that they gave up the effort, but it was only a matter of minutes, ten minutes perhaps of determined activity ending in failure. It was Andrew who recognised first that the situation had passed beyond hope. He didn't say so but he stopped doing everything that up till then he had done with so much conviction and energy. He stopped quite suddenly, sitting down beside the body. Alan, watching him, continued for a few moments before Andrew placed a hand gently on his arm. It was quiet, other than for the breeze ruffling branches in the wood. After a while they heard the teatime bell going, for what must have been a second or third time. It had been brought down to the back door and rung again, sending its message and questioning their absence.

Unanimously and without discussion, no one hurried away. Andrew said he had a pain in his back and should sit a while. It was fine, he said, nothing to fret about; it was just that he wasn't supposed to run. Joan wrapped herself in the blanket that Ottilie brought from the house, one that had been intended for Sebastian, to keep him warm and carry him home. Petra's teeth were chattering: she was sent back to the house by Andrew and instructed not to say anything until they got there. She was to go straight to her room and stay there. Petra had already been blamed, had been assigned blame even as she was dismissed from the scene, and everyone was aware that this was to be her role, including poor Petra herself, powerless to resist. When she set off down the path, turning and shouting out in German, declaring that she was only partially at fault, the silence at the jetty reasserted itself. Ottilie has told me that she was thinking of her parents during those quiet moments, wishing them a few minutes more of believing their world to be safe, of thinking the worst thing about today would be a demand from the bank, a day characterised otherwise by the usual small irritations, the children back late for tea and how they'd chastise them.

It was then that Andrew said to Ottilie and Joan that he wanted to speak to them alone. Apologising to Alan, he asked them to follow him for a private word. He took them back along the jetty, down the steps and to the edge of the wood, and seeing that Alan was watching, turned his back to the shore. He had a very special favour to ask of the girls, Andrew said. He wanted to treat them like grown-ups. What they had to do was be very brave. They'd have to take a grown-up approach.

"Promise me that you'll tell your mother and father that you were here."

"We *were* here," Joan asserted. Her grief was of the irritable kind.

"I mean, tell her that you saw what happened. That you were here nearby when it happened. I know it's not true. I know it was too late by the time you got here; Ottilie told me what happened. But sometimes a lie is necessary, and sometimes a lie is a kindness, and this is one of those times. It's going to be so much worse for Edith if she knows that you weren't watching. And worse for the two of you. And this was an accident after all. So it doesn't matter if we adjust the order of events a little. Do you see? As a kindness. It's important to be kind."

"More important than the truth?" Ottilie's voice.

"Sometimes, yes. It's what we call a white lie."

"There are different colours?" Ottilie's words were broken by hiccupping sobs.

Andrew led the way back to the jetty and to Alan, who was standing beside Sebastian, a small boy lying on his side looking as if he were dreaming. Ursula continued staring into the water. Andrew said, "Who will carry him home?" and his voice fractured and he began to weep noisily, his forearm over his eyes. He picked Sebastian up and enacted an awful, sad, inexpressibly tender squeezing of him against his upper chest and throat, pressing his face into Sebastian's belly. He said through his tears that he would take him. No one could dissuade him from this and they began their slow walk back to the house. All the way back, Ottilie and Joan, having distanced themselves from the procession, talked about what Andrew had asked of them and what they should say, though their conversation was of the shocked kind: bitty and abbreviated, and straight to the point. While they were deciding what to say to their mother, they took turns to ask the same question of each other.

First, Ottilie. "You don't think she did it on purpose?"

"No," Joan said. "Of course not."

It was agreed between the sisters – by the time the house came into view and Andrew had gone in through the back stairs, followed by Alan and Ursula – that they'd seen the children arguing, that they'd seen Sebastian running and hurling his last pebble, that they'd stood only feet away and had seen everything unfold.

"It's what happened, after all," Ottilie said.

"You don't think she did it on purpose?" Joan asked.

"No," Ottilie said. "Of course not."

When they reached the door themselves, they could hear Henry, wailing like a wounded animal, bellowing, the sound echoing down from the hall.

Ottilie barred Joan's way in. "It isn't possible, is it." It wasn't really a question but Joan answered anyway.

"Not possible."

Andrew didn't have the heart attack until three hours afterwards, tucked up in a rug by the fire with a nip of whisky on the table, an untouched mug of soup, some painkillers because it was thought that he'd wrenched his back. Joan and Ottilie were in their rooms, each sprawled on their beds, red-eyed with wet handkerchiefs, and Ursula was with Vita in the kitchen, being fed soft-boiled eggs and toast soldiers. Ursula hadn't spoken and wouldn't speak for years. Nobody could bear to blame her. They shouldn't have been on the jetty, but who was to know whose fault it was? Sebastian lost his balance, and the loch was too dangerous and dark. Edith was insistent that the girls mustn't claim the fault. It was an accident, and as such was sealed off from blame. Blame was an obscenity in such a case.

But I saw her. I saw you, Ursula. The loch's own memory has shown you to me. I saw you shove him and I saw him fall. It could be interpreted in a dozen ways, the shove, the paralysis ensuing in your reaction to his falling, the look partly of horror and partly of surprise. But I think I interpret you correctly. You had changed your mind, I see that, the moment it was done, even before the moment led to it being done, the change manifesting itself in your eyes in the niche of time between the two. You wanted the moment returned to you, the choice, the impulsive thing undone, even before your hand was off his back.

Chapter 25

My mother was here this afternoon. Yesterday. Yesterday, now. It's the early hours of the morning after and getting light again.

"Michael," she said to me, as if I were sitting next to her. "Today's the day. We think today will be the day."

We sat on the beach together, her in her upright, straight-backed manner, in her black dress that stretched almost to the ankle, a black scarf flattening her fringe onto her eyebrows, her hair striped with white. We sat side by side looking out at the hills, at the water, the daylight streaming sodium yellow from gaps in the clouds. She turned her head from time to time to look towards the wood, towards the tomb; when she looked towards the house she looked right through me, her tears falling unannounced and in absolute silence. She wiped them from her cheeks with sudden rapid movements. With her other hand she lifted and then dropped handfuls of small stones. Paint was lodged under her fingernails. The skin of her wrist was puckered around her watch.

Eventually, she rose from the beach and went into the wood. She took some photographs, looking upward, pictures of canopy and sky, a dark figure seen moving unhurriedly, deliberately among the trees. Then she returned to the water's edge. She picked up a stone, a small oval, its surface weathered flat as skin, and turned it over in her hand, smoothing it with her thumb and turning it, smoothing and turning.

"You," she said, looking at it in her palm. "So apparently innocent."

She threw the pebble into the shallows, then brought her camera out of her pocket and took pictures of the beach, of stone groupings, rearranging them before photographing them again. From time to time she pointed her camera towards the other end of the loch and looked through the viewfinder, using the zoom. Finally there was something new to see and she stepped forward. A tiny inverted triangle of red had appeared on the horizon, topped by a white quadrilateral. A boat was coming towards us, a red boat with a white cabin. Ottilie began taking pictures of it, first landscape and then portrait, successively as it made its slow approach.

We saw the fishing boat before we heard it, but then we heard its soft chug. Its outboard motor chugged louder as it moved towards us, and then became exaggerated, its chugging amplified by the bowl of hills. Its red livery glowed orangeish in the stormy light, and so did the red buoy that had been positioned on the loch the day before, the marker. Two men in wetsuits were fussing with equipment at the back. I could smell the diesel, its odour overlaying the aromas of stone and wet and weed and pine and leaf litter.

Joan and Edith were in town together while this was happening. Neither wanted to be present at the loch on this day, though they'd been briefed and had been invited. Edith refused to come to Peattie and Joan refused to go out to the cottage whether Ottilie was in residence or not, so Edith

438

made the journey into town on the bus, having given up the car. They met on neutral ground in a coffee shop. Joan was the one drinking coffee, from one of those glass jugs with the press-down plunge filter. She was having trouble with the mechanism, and the whole thing threatened to tip over when she exerted even light pressure. She'd taken the jug to the counter to complain, leaving Edith stirring inside her teapot with a long-handled spoon. It was chamomile tea, and damp hay smells emanated from the lidless pot as she stirred. The coffee shop was small and straddled its own border between gentility and domestic squalor: it had lace cloths and waitresses in black dresses with crisp white aprons, but a lingering eye on sills and carpet and – worse still – into the kitchen, might have seen things that troubled it a little. No matter. The dozen tables were all occupied. Most of its clients were women of a certain age, good coats hooked over chair backs and carrier bags parked at their feet. Spoons clinked against china. Napkins were put into use. Above this Joan's voice could be heard at the counter saying, "But it's no good if it doesn't work, is it? I'm sure you'll find there isn't a popular demand for that. It will spill hot coffee onto your tablecloth and at some point onto somebody's lap."

"Well, we've had no complaints before," the waitress who might be the owner said. She looked like a once-attractive person does when they've dedicated half a life-time to smoking. The lines closed around her mouth like a string bag.

"Perhaps, then, it's just a question of its being faulty today," Joan's voice said. "Or it could be my incompetence. I'd welcome a lesson. Could you very sweetly press it down for me, so I can see how it's done? My mother's waiting over there. Edith Salter. And I'm Joan."

"I know who you are, Mrs Catto," the waitress said.

Joan took her seat with her decanted coffee, grains floating dismally on its surface.

439

"Now," Edith said. "Joan. I don't want to pussyfoot around this issue. I want to have a frank discussion, all cards on the table. And that will be that. One frank discussion and we need never discuss it again. It doesn't help anyone to keep going over things."

"No."

"Not things to which there are no solution."

"No." Joan cut her meringue in half, shattering it into polystyrene shards.

"I want you to talk to your sister about it."

"Mother. I've told you. I'm not going to."

"So you propose never to speak to her again."

"There may be a time for the conversation but it isn't now. I just don't feel like it. And that's that."

"You've decided it was her fault. Without even talking."

"Of course it was her fault. He was my boyfriend. He was approached." She leaned forward on her elbows and lowered her voice. "In the *bathroom*. The night before the wedding. We can't discuss it here, Mother."

"What I don't understand ..." Edith said, frowning, "... is why he told you at all. Why tell you? It's upset everybody."

"You think he should have kept it to himself? And you think I should have kept it to myself?"

"It's upset everybody," Edith said again.

"It was Ottilie's decision to tell you and not mine," Joan told her. "I've explained this. We've been over it. I wasn't going to tell anyone. When I went to her it was only to tell her that I knew. It wasn't a threat of exposure."

"I think it may have come across that way."

"Can we go for a walk? I'm not comfortable. This place is so second-rate."

"You don't want your coffee?"

"No. Drink up your tea. Come on."

They went to the riverside and sat together on a bench.

440

"It's going to rain," Joan observed, looking up at the lilac-brown clouds. "The sky seems very low today."

"I think you should be wary of taking Euan's word for things," Edith said.

Joan gave her a sharp look. "She's said something to you."

"Not at all, not at all."

"Euan kept quiet for 33 years, Mother. For 19 of those he could have had a relationship with his son."

"I think you should talk to Ottilie, hear her side."

"Hear her *side*?"

"Yes."

"It'll never end, will it?"

"What won't?"

"It doesn't matter. Forget it. This isn't the time."

"Just talk to her. Please."

"I'm not interested, I'm afraid." She paused and then she said, "This is Ottilie's side. She seduced my husband the night before we were married, specifically as a revenge, because she was jealous. She forced himself on him."

"Nobody was forced."

"She offered herself to him when he was nervous and a bit drunk. And then, and then, she led us all a merry dance afterwards, letting us all debate about Alan, letting us choose between Alan and the house party. I'm sorry but that was contemptible. And what interests me specifically is that my husband has been unhappy about it for 33 years and has been unable to speak up."

"Why's that?"

"Because she made it clear that she wanted him to keep quiet. Keeping quiet was his kindness. I'm not sure you see that. It was honourable, the honourable thing to do. So tell me, what other side is there than that?"

Edith didn't respond.

"It's caused so much unhappiness, Mother. So much unhappiness. I only understand now, knowing what I know

now, how it was at the root of everything like a poison. The reason that Euan and I were so miserable."

⟨flourish⟩

Mog came down to the beach and sat beside Ottilie on the shore. They were watching the divers, who'd tied the boat up to the buoy. One of the men was in the water.

Mog and Ottilie were discussing Edith.

"She says she isn't ready," Ottilie said.

"Not even for this? But I'm not surprised."

"I'm confident she'll be along for the service."

"Did you speak to Vita?"

"Yes. Dissuaded her from coming. George had told her he wanted to come too, bless him. I think the two of them were all set to get a taxi down here. You know that they've become close friends, that they play cards together."

"She's settling in well."

"It's more like a country club than a care home. Queen of all she surveys. And I think the shedding of Mrs H has been a big relief."

"I don't know how George affords it."

"Your grandfather pays. It was one of the things in the letter. But keep that between ourselves."

"I'm glad to hear it. That makes me feel better about him."

"About George?"

"About grandfather. And about George."

"I felt bad about putting them off but I didn't want people here today. Church is different. That's Mother's way. That's her day. Everybody will be there and that's fine."

Mog looked at her in profile. "You alright?"

"No."

"Silly question."

"Boring answer. The truth is" – she paused, considering it – "I'm achieving something of what I want. Quietness

442

about it. That's all I want. Quietness. Working my way forwards. I will be so glad – not glad – but – you know."

"Me too. When it's over with finally."

Both men were in the water now with breathing equipment, and one of them had disappeared under the surface.

Ottilie stiffened. She averted her eyes.

"Me too," Mog said. "Come on. Let's go back."

"I thought I wanted to see but now I don't."

"Me neither. Come on." Mog was already up, holding out a steadying hand to her aunt.

They walked away from the beach in silence, back down the path. The cottages came into view, and the end of the house, its fine dressed corner stones, a pair of corner chimneys, the entrance to the walled gardens.

"It's going to be so hard saying goodbye to it," Mog said.

"You have an important lesson to learn," Ottilie told her.

"What's that?"

"To be as sentimental about the future as you are about the past."

They went in at the back door and up the back stairs to the hall, through the gothic arched door and past what's now Pip's office. Henry's dogs were there in the hallway – all but one of the dogs – and they looked to Mog as she came in with a definite canine air of expectancy. Badger wasn't there because Edith had moved Badger and Badger's bed to Ottilie's cottage. Edith has become a keen evangelist of salt-water therapy and joins the old dog often in his swim, going out there together in all weathers. She keeps busy. She's learning to cook. She reads a lot, sitting with Ottilie in the studio in the afternoons, the books piled up beside her. She says she needs to get herself an education, and has been reading about Spanish history, Spanish art. She goes daily to church. She's had no contact with Thomas Osborne or Susan Marriott since she moved away from Peattie. Susan has made no effort to keep in touch, for which Edith's grateful. Thomas left a message on the answerphone that she hasn't yet answered.

"I'd better take the dogs out," Mog said.

"Can't you put them in the walled?"

"Tried that. They dug and trampled. Not a huge success with Angelica."

Ottilie seated herself on the second-to-bottom stair, crouching over a little as if she were cold.

"Don't think about it," Mog told her. "What we need is distraction."

"Toast," Ottilie said. "I've remembered I haven't eaten anything today. Might feel better."

"I'll pop the dogs out first and then I'll make some."

"I'll make it."

"If you like, but I'm happy to. You look tired."

"The truth is, I am. Exhausted. I'll wait for you here. Close my eyes for a bit."

"Go sit in the drawing room."

Mog was gone for what seemed like a long time and Ottilie barely moved, sitting with her head resting on the wall. Then Mog appeared with a tray.

"Shall we?" Mog asked her, inclining her head and turning to go down the corridor.

"Can we do it here?"

"Here?"

"Do you mind?"

"Course not."

"I've always disliked the drawing room. Even before."

Mog took the tray to the stairs and placed it on a tread above where Ottilie was sitting, and the two of them ate toast and drank tea in silence.

When they'd finished, Ottilie said, "I'm going back down there."

"You don't want to be there," Mog said, without looking up.

"I do. And I want to go alone. Do you mind?"

"Of course I don't. If you're sure."

"The stupid thing is, I've been losing sleep over it and it's Ursula I've been worried about."

"I know."

"What if?"

"I know. But we'll deal with it as we go. You know what Pip thinks. It won't go any further."

"Maybe so but it will be all over the papers."

"Unavoidable."

"There's something I need to tell you. We're going away on our trip, immediately it's over with."

"I'm glad for you. And for Gran. It's absolutely what she needs."

"She's always wanted to travel and Henry wouldn't."

"Not because – I mean – you won't stay away, will you?"

"The truth is, we can't afford to be away for long. We need to be careful with money, at least until the sale goes through, and even then ..."

"It won't be a fortune once the debts are paid."

"It won't be a fortune." Ottilie kissed Mog on the cheek, and went back through the gothic door and down the back stairs. A few minutes later the phone began to ring.

Angelica appeared out of nowhere, rushing past and into the office. She answered and was quiet, murmuring her responses. She laid the handset down on the desk and then she came out again, looking solemn.

"We need Pip. Where's Pip? Do you know where Pip is?"

"I'm sorry, I don't," Mog told her.

Pip came in from the terrace. "What is it?"

"It's them," she said. "They've found him and it's starting."

Pip was standing on the end of the jetty, talking to a man in a wetsuit. Both of them had their backs to the boat, which was tied up alongside. Ottilie was in it, sitting in it, talking apparently to the deck. There was something on the floor of the boat, something large, something long, positioned under a big piece of dark green plastic or in a dark green plastic bag. Pip began to speak about arrangements, and used the word *remains*, and the police diver put a hand on his shoulder. I felt as if my neck were held from behind by a strong hand, preventing me from looking away.

What I'd like is to dream new memories and make them true. With proper attention to detail they could be as true as the old ones. The truth is that I have lived the escaped life, on and off, in snatches, for brief spectacular snatches. We've run together through southern woods, my children and I. My wife has beautiful eyes and there was love in them. And what I've discovered is that there's all the time in the world. There's time to read and also to write, and my writing is beginning to find its footing. There's nothing but hopefulness. The days stretch long and warm and the meadows around our house are permanently in flower, aside from a Christmas that I visited, or made or whatever it was, one furnished with log fires and games and time spent in the kitchen together. Fantasy: that's a word I've grown stubborn about, one I won't admit to. I know what I know, and what I have done and where I have been. I think that I lived it. I lived it all.

You're sceptical. But in the end it doesn't matter how much of it was ever really mine. These were still experiences. This was still my life. Memories are all we ever have, after even a day in the world, and who's to make a judgment on what's real and what's not? I know, I know. It's pathetic and it won't do. We all know what's real and what isn't. I concede. But the mind is a potent other world and conjures up realities if you'll allow it to. That much you must now concede. That is how I escaped Ursula, Ursula's oar, escaping with a broken wrist and swimming to the shore. I took the money and went south to a new world, and met the woman I was meant to meet and felt my girls kick under my hand. None of this you could dissuade me from. I'm sad for my mother, that none of this will ever also be hers. That's my sustaining emotion now, that I'm sad for my mother.

~

Pip sent Angelica a text message. She read it and then she said to Mog, "He says that we should come down."

"I don't want to see," Mog told her. "I'll stay. You go, and I'll stay here."

Angelica came forward and put a hand onto Mog's, folding it into her own. "We'll walk down together."

"I don't want to go, really not, I can't," Mog said to her. "You go though. You go."

"We'll go to the wood. Just that far. We'll go across the field and into the wood. We'll go to the tomb and then, if we don't want to go further, we won't. We'll come back across the field again. They'll never know we were there."

"Okay."

"Okay?"

"Let's go, then. I know later that I'll be sorry if I don't."

They came down to the wood, walking across the field in the peculiar light. The lilac cloud cover was turning increasingly brown, and the humidity was building again, building into release, into rainfall. The women went into the back of the wood and made their way slowly to the tomb, Angelica leading. Angelica went first.

"There's nothing to see," she said, turning to Mog. "Nothing disturbing. Just the boat at the jetty. Ottilie's in the boat. Pip's talking to one of the divers."

They seemed, incongruously, to be talking about wine. One of the divers had been on holiday to the vineyards in Chile, was recommending South America for travelling, and Pip was saying that before he and his girlfriend got married, before he and his wife had children, they might take six months off and go there and see for themselves. The estate was up for sale, Pip explained, and the diver said that he knew, he'd heard, and it was such a shame. It will be best for all of us, Pip told him, to make a new start. It was inevitable in any case, unavoidable, the only possible decision. The money they made from the sale of the land was only ever going to be a stop-gap, and as it turned out it had been just enough to get the house into a saleable shape. Bed and breakfast, it's like treading water, he said; there's no real money in it. Break even was never going to be enough. "This way," he said, "everyone gets seed money to start something somewhere else."

His wife had always wanted to go riding in Argentina, Pip said. The diver was encouraging him, beginning to suggest places to stay, and Pip took his phone out of his pocket and began making notes. He wasn't really thinking of how this chatter might appear to onlookers. He was doing it protectively of Ottilie, masking her talking to me, what once was me, producing a sort of white noise that furnished her with privacy. She was sitting beside the green plastic, one hand placed upon it.

She was looking down at me. She was looking right at me, her hand on my forehead as if I were a child ill in bed. I was in the green package. I was there. I was looking back at her, her sad face looking down. Part of me. Part of there. "I'm so glad, I'm so relieved to see you again," she said. "I knew that Alan was lying, that Joan was wrong. I knew it. I knew you wouldn't leave me, say nothing to me ever again, edit me out of your life and carry on. I knew they were wrong. I'm so relieved. I love you so much."

Everything else I can deal with. I can forgive.

And now I must sleep.

An Interview with the Author

What was the gestation of this novel? How long did it take you to write?

The White Lie had a fairly long gestation, though most of that time was actually more of an interruption, while the manuscript lay unread in a drawer. The process started in 2004 with a sketchy first draft in a first person that was Mog's and not Michael's. It was Mog who told the story, though Michael was constantly talked about. Then in 2005 I entered the *Keeper* period, in which I was looking after my mother-in-law and living in a big secluded house in the far, far north of Scotland. It had 22 rooms and an overgrown four-acre garden with a small wood in it, all enclosed inside a high Victorian wall, and a view across the sea to islands, and there's no doubt that living there fed into the imagining of Glen of Peattie estate. We lived there for two years, returning to southern Scotland in 2007, whereupon my diary of life with someone with Alzheimer's disease became *Keeper* – and was published in 2009, also by Short Books. So it wasn't until 2010 that I took *The White Lie* out of the drawer and began to rework it. By that time, odd though this might sound, Michael Salter had begun to talk to me, and the story began to be dictated by him, in his voice and from his perspective.

You say that the house you lived in in northern Scotland when you were looking after your mother-in-law fed into the imagining of the setting for this novel. Where did the original inspiration for the story come from?

In 2004, it started on a bus. We were living in the Eastern Highlands at the time, between Inverness and Aberdeen, and as I can't drive I went everywhere on the local bus service. It was a glorious crisp sunny day. We trundled along very slowly past a beautiful dry-stone wall, the outer wall of an old estate. Through the trees I saw a glimpse of lawns and of a big old house. It looked pretty run down. The wall was enormously long, and for most of its length all that could be seen were trees, thick with ivy, and gardens choked by rhododendron, and tantalising ends of paths leading into the greenery. As we rumbled along on the bus, and the wall came to an end and took a sharp turn to mark the corner of the grounds, and we left the property behind, I found myself thinking about how an old estate like that is a private world, in which things could happen that were never discussed outside, and in which secrets could be kept that were never disclosed. They might do things their own way in a small walled kingdom like that. Things might have their own internal logic.

The Salter family began to be delivered to me: that's how it felt. Suddenly my head was full of them, the Salters and their predicament. It's about Edith and Henry, I said to myself. Edith and Henry, who are in their 70s and have had a series of disasters in their lives, and who are not happily married at all, but who hold it all together for the sake of the family, the children and grandchildren, and who have come to a sort of negotiated settlement with the past. It's coming to an end, though; it's all about to unravel. The truth is about to emerge. The scenario began to suggest itself to me. It wasn't a stretch. By the time I got off the bus in my own small village I had the story of Michael Salter, their grandson, and how they thought he was killed by one of their own, and how they kept the secret for 14 years; how they'd been damaged by the death of their own child many years before, and what the truth was that united both these deaths. I more or less ran up the hill and into the house. I had the scenario and a Salter family tree down on paper within two hours, and they are the same characters and the same plot development that you have encountered in this novel today.

The White Lie *is a novel very much preoccupied with the interplay between memory and truth – themes that you explored in detail in your memoir about Alzheimers,* Keeper ...

Yes, I don't think it's a coincidence that when I returned to the novel in 2010, the narrator had switched from a woman bullied by her mother into a dead man who only survives as a consciousness. I had spent two years living with someone with dementia and had written a book about that experience. In the course of this I had done a lot of research and reading about the brain, the mind and the memory. *The White Lie* isn't, of course, a book "about" any of those things but it's true to say that it was influenced, in its reworking. Michael is a filter for the memories of others; he is changed by the things he sees from others' perspectives. All the characters have developed strategies for survival, or have failed to, in the situation in which they find themselves. Some of them cling to fantasy; they have told themselves lies to survive, and they tell others lies to help preserve the fantasy. I was interested in how subjective recollection is. Memory serves us well, but let's not kid ourselves that it always delivers to us what really happened in the past. Memory is a personal tool, dedicated to our psychological health, rather than an objective record. Often, all we have to go on in The White Lie, as in life, is what people tell us is true. The characters of the novel are constantly telling us what's true and what's not, including Michael, but how do we know? As Edith says, "It's facts that we need. Interpretation isn't going to get us anywhere."

Andrea Gillies has had a diverse career, encompassing theatre publicity work, editorship of an inflight magazine, reference book editing and drinks writing. For a while this meant she had a garage full of booze and free flights to Paris. Her first book, *Keeper*, about looking after someone with dementia, won the Orwell Prize and the Wellcome Trust Book Prize. She lives in Edinburgh with her family. This is her first novel.